Harmony

Book three
(The Crystal Series)

Nia Markos

Cover design by: Cynthia Amato
Model: closeupimages(133833278)/Shutterstock.com
Editor: Jacqueline Snider

For Seb who has inspired the main character in my new upcoming series.

Prologue

Rhea, mother of all gods, defender of the earth, watched, listened and plotted. The serene, somewhat bored expression on her exquisitely ethereal face hid the calculated, surreptitious way with which she looked forward to outsmarting her husband. Cronus, as usual, gave no thought to anyone or anything but his own importance. He presided over the proceedings, lording his position, trying to undermine all she and her daughter, Meredith, were trying to accomplish. Meredith had been barred from attending the assembly.

In fact, Rhea had no idea where Cronus held her daughter. Cronus detained her somewhere, making sure she could not influence the other gods who were present. *He would not dare mistreat my daughter!* Rhea tried to brush aside her worry that he might harm Meredith in any way. She knew too much of his own indiscretions, and the multitude of offspring those had spawned. Harming one of her own children would lead to direct retaliation. Rhea was not above exacting her own pointed vengeance.

Her siblings, gods in their own right, were also, for their own purposes, biding their time. *Cronus expects us all to bow to his whims.* Rhea knew that more than a few of her brothers and sisters were eager to garner as much power as they could for themselves. The heavens were not as secure under his dominion as Cronus imagined.

Aside from those present, Rhea was aware of other gods who were patiently watching and waiting. Long forgotten to time, Zeus, her beloved son, hungered for his own return to power. Born from her union with Cronus, Zeus remembered well his father's attempt to end his life at birth. It was only through the actions of others that Zeus had managed to survive.

Zeus, for the longest time, believed his father remained imprisoned in Tartarus where he had placed him. Having tossed his father into the endless abyss to languish forever in torment, Zeus, unfortunately, had put him out of his mind. *If only we had known.* Rhea would have done everything in her power to stop her husband's return. Cronus escaped his prison having spent less than ten years in the abyss.

Rescued by Poseidon and Hera, two of her other children, Cronus kept himself hidden for centuries before making his presence known. Why their other children had saved him, Rhea never found out. *What had Cronus promised them?* Whatever it was, he must have never made good on it. She knew with certainty that Poseidon and Hera were now aligned with Zeus.

Sitting on her assigned pedestal seat, ignoring Cronus's droning, she pretended to study her nails. Anyone glancing her way would see indifference to her husband's speech. They would be wrong, however. Rhea was paying attention to every word her husband uttered. Every now and then, she casually shifted in her seat, drawing Cronus's eyes her way. She had taken extra care with her appearance before the meeting. Rhea knew Cronus had a particular liking for the gown she had chosen. Blue as the sky, the gossamer material hugged her every curve. The bodice dipped so low it made its necessity obsolete. Her ample bosom, almost fully exposed for his shrewd examination, entranced him.

She hid a smile at how hard he endeavored to concentrate on what he wished to articulate. Leaning forward, seemingly to be attentive, Rhea caught his momentary loss of focus. Resuming his speech, Cronus's gaze fell on Rhea, who ran her hand leisurely through her hair, brushing it out of the way. Waves of golden blond curls ran free, fanning her shoulders, as they cascaded down her back. His eyes raked over her, in much the same way as when she had first entered the meeting arena.

Rhea suppressed a shudder of revulsion before he could see it. *Does he know how much I detest him?* Cronus fancied himself above any and all gods. He could never imagine his near-perfect looks and physique would be matched by anyone. Rhea could name several mortal men she had sampled who had put him to shame.

Mortals were the very reason they had been called into that meeting. Her daughter's actions were regrettable, but Rhea saw an opportunity arise from them. Meredith, born of a passionate and impetuous affair with a Sidhe warrior, caused immeasurable problems with her most recent actions. At the time Rhea met Meredith's father, she believed him to be a mortal man. She should have known, guessed, he was something more. Even a goddess could be fallible.

The Sidhe race, a secretive and mysterious race of faeries, hid their very existence from the outside world, for a reason. Humans were an unpredictable race. Anything unknown would be judged a threat. Her affair with the Sidhe occurred during Cronus's imprisonment.

When Meredith was born, Rhea gave her care over to Zeus. Where he had placed her, who had actually raised her, Rhea had never thought to ask. Only many centuries later had she formed a relationship with her daughter.

Meredith's own involvement with the Sidhe race should not have come as a surprise. Curiosity over her father led her to search for the Sidhe home world. As impetuous as her mother, she set in motion a chain of events presently threatening the continuation of humanity. Cronus was incensed at her actions. He held Meredith accountable for the perils she had unleashed on his precious earth.

When the Sidhe Elsam captured Meredith, torturing her to gain power over his queen Eliana, Meredith did not foresee what she would end up setting in motion. Sidhe power lay in their protective crystal, the Kaemorra. It afforded their island protection, hiding them from the prying eyes of humans. Within their cloak of invincibility, they lived an idyllic life. In one careless move, not thinking of the consequences, Meredith spelled the crystal to disappear. Her need to punish Eliana and her people for Elsam's actions, drove her to make them all pay for her treatment. Not even Eliana's imprisonment of Elsam swayed Meredith from her course.

The crystal vanished, hidden from the Sidhe race for over a thousand years. The queen had no alternative but to force her people to scatter across the far reaches of the earth. As an added hindrance to keeping her race safe, Eliana lost her connection to the Kaemorra. Without its magical properties to guide her, her ability to foresee the future diminished. Nearly powerless in seeing coming dangers, she ordered her people to stay isolated and not affect the natural course of history.

Meredith cast one final obstacle in thwarting Eliana from reclaiming the Kaemorra. If the Kaemorra was brought back to the island to re-establish its invincibility, Eliana's payment would be the loss of one of her sons. Aidan, thought to be the oldest of the queen's children, would perish, if the queen decided to return her people to their island of Eruva.

Through the long years that followed, a quest, a prophesy grew out of the search for the Kaemorra. Meredith unknowingly dragged her own descendant into the melee. *Alexa, that is her name.* Rhea knew the young woman exuded strength and was worthy of her lineage. Meredith had not anticipated what Alexa's birth would set in motion. Alexa, along with Aidan, were destined to work together to retrieve the crystal from where Meredith had hidden it.

At the time she spelled the Kaemorra to vanish, Meredith had no idea that Alexa would become bonded, be the one true soul mate to Aidan. When this became known to her, stopping the prophesy, or what it entailed, made it almost impossible to gauge an outcome. *And it might still be too late.* Rhea saw many differing endings to the saga. It all hinged on Cronus and stopping his interference.

Aidan, over six-feet tall, with hair as black as coal, had Rhea wishing he did not have a bond with her descendant. She would have liked to sample what he had to offer herself. His Herculean physique reminded her of past legends. Blessed with the most incredible emerald eyes, Aidan had been drawn to Alexa without ever having met her. She, in turn, wanted nothing to do with him.

Finding herself bonded to Aidan, she fought the attraction by turning to his brother, Liam. There was nothing wrong with Liam either. Almost as tall as Aidan, his sandy blond hair and sinewy physique were quite pleasing in and of themselves. Having the same emerald eyes, possessed by all Sidhe, his were just as captivating.

Alexa, petite, auburn haired with enchanting gray eyes, enamored both brothers, creating further upheaval to the goal set before them. A descendant of Meredith, with her own mother a witch and her father a Sidhe, Alexa could be nothing less than as powerful as her ancestors. Even before her nineteenth birthday, when her full abilities manifested, the young woman showed signs of heightened senses and powers. Meredith searched for a way to undo what she had set in motion in order to save Alexa. Subtly she changed the spell cast over the Kaemorra. It allowed a way out of the predicament she had created.

As time drew near for the Kaemorra to be discovered, Elsam's imprisonment came to an end. Released after his thousand-year sentence, the angry Sidhe resumed his plans for power. Using the legendary creatures known as the shadows, Elsam forged an alliance with them through subterfuge and cunning. Along with the shadows, Elsam had been working with Manar, the Daimon prince. That alliance was quickly falling apart. Manar had his own plans for the Kaemorra.

Elsam was learning he held little sway with the rest of his followers. Myrick, the warlock in his employ, grew weary of Elsam's motivations. The capture of Bet, Eliana's daughter, and Alexa's parents should have given Elsam the upper hand. Their torture at the hands of

Myrick yielded no results. Elsam did not garner new information as to where the Kaemorra was located. Instead, they somehow managed to escape. Elsam was unaware who had aided them.

It was an added impediment to their quest that Aidan, thinking Alexa had turned to his brother, allowed himself to be captured. *If she knew his condition, Alexa would surely blame herself.* Rhea hoped Alexa would be able to reach him before it was too late. Missing for months, Aidan's plight remained perilous. Alexa had placed her own self in harm's way in order to save him. Hoping to rescue him, she let herself be apprehended by Myrick. That noble, but foolish act, threw her friends and family into disarray.

Everyone believed she had perished aboard the boat, which exploded seconds before they could rescue her. Liam was the most affected by her loss. Everything, all their efforts to find the Kaemorra, were thrown into chaos. Meredith had once again intervened, contacting Eliana directly with the news that Alexa lived. Giving the queen information was the latest act that put her in Cronus's crosshairs. She had been warned after her last visit with Alexa not to interfere again.

Meredith had done the unthinkable. Appearing to Alexa, with Rhea's blessing, she explained why she had acted to hide the Kaemorra, even Rhea was surprised by her daughter's actions. Bestowing all her powers on Alexa, including her immortality, Meredith for all intents and purposes, was now human. *She never ceases to surprise me.* Rhea did all she could to protect Meredith from Cronus's fury. *I must protect Meredith at all costs.*

Rhea convinced Cronus to hold an assembly to discuss her

punishment, but she saw no clear resolution from those in attendance. The other gods were equally in an uproar over Meredith's most recent actions. There were those who wanted Meredith banished, while others were more inclined to see her ended. Alexa, unaware of exactly what Meredith had done, had no idea she was immortal.

Hearing her name spoken, Rhea snapped out of her musings. Luckily, Cronus only mentioned her and required no response. With his back to her, while he continued speaking, Rhea caught the tail end of his statement. The word Tartarus sent a chill through her. *He would not dare, would he?* She was unsure under what context the Titan prison had been mentioned. Still, she paid attention in order to catch up to what he had been saying.

More than one of the gods was now staring at her. Keeping her face neutral, she ignored them all. Cronus wanted them to put an end to the entire race of Sidhe, especially Eliana and Elsam. He saw both of them as responsible for the chaos in the world below. He had yet to mention Meredith and what he wanted to be done with her. Across the room, the one god she could absolutely count on was following Cronus's movements. Rhea eyed her brother Hyperion, trying to catch his attention. Keeping his eyes on Cronus, Hyperion acknowledged her by lifting his forefinger. The message was clear. They would meet as soon as Cronus had ended his tirade.

It was fortunate that some of her other siblings were also not as enamored with Cronus's wishes. The infighting among the gods had been going on for as long as Rhea could remember. They each had their own needs and wants. Most of the time, Cronus managed to keep them in line. This, Rhea could see, would not be one of them. She had sat silently for hours while her husband voiced his concerns and the way to remedy them. When Cronus stopped speaking to take a breath, she saw her opportunity. Rising from her seat, all turned to see what she would do.

"Cronus, darling, we need a rest." She said, as she sashayed towards him.

Putting her arm through his, she leaned into him so he could feel the press of her breast on his arm. The action resulted in the desired outcome. Cronus's eyes dropped to her cleavage. Rhea could have gagged at the hungry way he stared, if not for her need to keep him placated. Giving him her most adoring look, he took the bait.

"Yes, let's adjourn for now. We can meet again in a couple of hours." He absentmindedly spoke, while his gaze lingered on Rhea's breasts.

Her siblings gladly started to leave. Hyperion gave her a pointed look before departing. She knew where to meet him. Cronus wrapped his arms around her, dragging her up against his chest. Behind his back, she rolled her eyes and grimaced. His intent was clear. He wanted to take what she had offered. Rhea knew she would have little choice but to go through with it. Sleeping with him always mellowed him. She just needed a few minutes alone with Hyperion first.

"Darling, why don't you go to my rooms. I will join you there after I get your surprise." She teased him.

Cronus, as always, led by his baser instincts, bought it. Smiling seductively at his wife, he pinched her behind before retiring to her rooms. Rhea craftily hid her frown at having to give herself to him. All the playacting in the world would be needed to pretend she enjoyed his touch. Once he retreated out of sight, Rhea departed for her meeting with Hyperion. Arriving at the location, she found her brother with Helios, his son. The two had been arguing. Rhea made her presence known, giving Hyperion a questioning look.

"Helios has returned with news. I thought it best he reports directly to you." Hyperion let her know.

Where Hyperion was larger than life, tall and blessed with unbelievable strength, Helios was slight, compact and appeared weak. The impression was wrong. Helios had his own strengths, not requiring brawn, but stamina. What he had been up to, Rhea had no idea.

"There is a new entrant in the quest for the Kaemorra." Helios started. "I think time is on our side."

Rhea looked down at the world, finding and understanding what Helios spoke of. She laughed, delighted at what she had discovered. Hyperion joined in, just as pleased as she. *Yes, things might work out better than I had hoped.* Helios excused himself, having nothing more to add. His father and aunt knew everything now.

"You know what you must do," Hyperion told her.

"I will keep him occupied. I loathe every moment I spend with him, but I will do what I must. It is all in Alexa's hands now. I have to go. He is waiting." Rhea left Hyperion, dreading each step.

Stopping in the servants' quarters, she eyed the many young nubile women who were present. Finding one that would be pleasing to Cronus, she beckoned the woman to follow. She chose her because the young woman matched her in shape and height, but had dark features and hair. Cronus would appreciate the contrast.

Entering her rooms, Cronus already lay naked atop her bed. Walking towards him, she slipped her dress off her shoulders to let it drop to the floor. His eyes widened expectantly at seeing her naked. The young woman followed behind Rhea, untying her robe and also letting it fall. She knew exactly what was expected of her.

Rhea brought her along to act as a buffer. She hoped the young woman would take up most of his attention. Stepping up to the bed, she lay down next to him on his right, while the other woman took his left. Cronus greedily turned to the young woman, giving her his full attention. Rhea inwardly smiled that her plan had worked. She would find as many women as it took to keep his mind off of what was going on down below.

Chapter 1 - Aidan

It was deathly quiet, save for the intermittent rasping heard in the chamber that for all intents and purposes gave the impression of being vacant. Carved out in the depths of the tower that rose high above it, the cave-like dungeon was a sea of blackness. That far down, there were no windows for any ray of light to penetrate the stifling environment. The air was musty, stale and oppressive.

One would be hard-pressed to make out anything within the bleak, rock-faced walls, least of all the prisoner in the center of the space. Down on his knees, sitting back on his heels on the damp stone floor, lost within the darkness, he was invisible to the naked eye. The plinking sound of sporadic water drops, which welled and fell from the slate ceiling, accompanied the harsh breathing from the sole occupant. The lone figure did not move, did not give any indication that he was otherwise alive.

Staring off into the distance, only his chest rising, then falling, from his labored breath gave the only sign that he still lived. The single bulb overhead had burned out long before. Replacing it had been deemed unnecessary. The prisoner gave no indication he missed the light, but rather seemed to welcome the loss of it. Anyone who knew him, seeing him in his present condition, would find it difficult to identify him.

If he could speak, he himself would probably be unable to recall his name. It had been months since he had uttered a single word. His descent into oblivion was complete. Aidan was all but forgotten, not just to himself, but also by those who had imprisoned him. No one came to visit or check up on him anymore. Even the guards outside his prison walls had been reassigned elsewhere. There was no need to keep an eye on him. Aidan was not going anywhere.

His jailer's attempts to cajole him into accepting food or water had failed miserably. The offered plates and cups placed within his reach on the floor had languished where they had left them. He took not one bite or sip. Eventually, the futility of their efforts sank in. Since then, the guards had pretty much given up on him, just as he had given up on himself.

Living held no interest for him. Thinking, feeling brought him pain. Only the silence was his constant companion. Time had finally brought the relief he craved. Now, he felt nothing. Aidan had essentially stopped thinking. His mind was empty of everything, especially of the woman who left him wounded beyond a will to live. He obliviously stared, unseeing, at the far wall of his cell. His mind registered none of his surroundings.

Around his wrists and ankles, iron manacles were attached to a heavy linked chain that ran down from the ceiling. Iron was the one metal that could hold the Sidhe. His race could not combat the effects the ore had on their species. It ate away at their strength and diminished their powers. It also caused excruciating pain from the blistering burns that developed wherever iron touched skin.

Before the wounds had gotten too unbearable, he had been able to stand, although his movements were hindered by the length of the chain. The three feet it allowed him, gave him enough latitude to walk in circles around the space. His legs had eventually collapsed from under him, however. The iron had dug into his ankles and wrists, exposing muscle tissue and even bone in some places. Luckily, he no longer felt the pain from the raw open wounds. That too had been blocked. In his mind, there was no sound, no image or sense of self. He was a shell, nothing more.

Before blocking everything out, his wounds only added to the already intense suffering from a heart that lay broken. Facing his memories, plus his blistering skin, he did not know which caused him more torture. Haunted by unending thoughts of her, the image of Alexa's face had been burned into his psyche. Her fresh-faced beauty remained fixed in his mind's eye. At first, it had been impossible to banish her floral scent. It clung to his clothes, to his hands. Their bond had from the first affected him more profoundly than her.

Without being fully linked to him, Alexa had no idea what being near her, being held at bay put him through. She never grasped the full meaning of being joined. That she had not completed the bonding with him gave her an out, a choice of who to love. She had made her choice. He could not understand why his heart had not stopped beating on that devastating day. That it still drummed on after what she had done to him, continued to surprise him. *How can I go on without her? Why would I want to?*

He remembered for a time he had been happy. Alexa finally stopped thinking of Liam. Her thoughts were free of any romantic intentions towards his brother. They were to leave together, search for the Kaemorra. The Kaemorra was the magical, all powerful crystal that had protected their land. It went missing long ago. His race had been forced to abandon their homeland when their island's invisibility fell. Without the Kaemorra they were exposed to the humans.

The queen, his mother, ordered her people to find refuge, away from the prying eyes of the inhabitants of that world. Aidan had been tasked to find the crystal, to save his people. Alexa was to accompany him. She left him for one final task before they were to depart. He continued on his own preparations unaware of where she had gone. Finding her with Liam, crying over him, dealt him a physical blow. Listening to her begging his brother to come back to her had undone Aidan. Her expression, a mix of guilt and remorse, cut him to the quick.

What reason was there to remain? He could not bear to stay and watch them be together. His options were limited. Her freedom was the only thing he could offer. It killed him to admit that she would never be his. In a daze, he watched her rise from his brother's bedside, while he remained frozen in the doorway. He saw her coming towards him, her hands outstretched, her face pained. *What could she mean to say to undo the damage already done?* There was nothing she could say to minimize the sudden loss he felt.

His world was torn apart by the devastation he experienced. He never gave her a chance to utter a word. His mind was consumed by endless questions. *How did she trick me?* Her mind had been free of his brother. *Why did I not see the deception? She loved Liam, wanted Liam.* His mind refused to function coherently. All he saw was her in Liam's arms, both of them laughing at him. Anger was slow in coming, but when it did, he lost all control. If he had stayed any longer, he would have harmed her. Blinded by rage, he did the only thing he could. He left.

He left with no plans on where to go. Appearing on the cliff near Meredith's home was instinctual. It was close to his homeland. The island, far off in the distance, was visible from the cliffs of the mainland. Memories of her continued to assail him wherever he looked. He pictured her everywhere. In the house, where her face lit up over her accomplishment of transforming the living space, he could still envision her child-like enthusiasm. The bedrooms were still as she had designed them.

In her room, he sat on her bed for hours. He finally left its confines when hunger called him away. The kitchen was well stocked from their last visit. He pulled cheeses and bread out of the cupboard, placing them on a plate that lay next to the sink. Sitting down to eat, he fought to banish the image of her. In that room, her eyes had glowed at conjuring food for all of them. His hand stilled from biting into the hard cheese he held. His appetite had left him. Pushing away his plate, he stood to go outside.

Night had fallen while he had been lost in his memories. Outside, the calm did nothing to ease his misery. His feet took him dangerously close to the cliff. Sitting down, his legs dangling down the long slope, he leaned back to watch the stars. Clear of clouds, the sky was lit up with diamond-studded brilliance. Falling on his back, he tried to clear his thoughts. With his heart hammering in his chest, closing his eyes only brought her face more into focus. *How can I survive this?*

She was everywhere. In the open field behind him, she took to her training apprehensively, not sure of what she was doing. He watched her grow, marveled at how easily she accepted coming into her powers. He had unconsciously come to that location to get away from her. He saw it was a mistake. It was the last place he should have come. The pain became unbearable. Reliving it all did nothing to ease his anguish. Less than a day and he knew he had to leave. He could not take anymore.

Life without her was not worth living. He knew that their link could only be broken one way. Doing it himself would leave her still bound to him. He needed to find another way. The joining could only be severed if someone else took his life. He gave no thought to what it would do to his family or friends. There had to be some way to end the suffering. His vision blurred as tears welled. He must do it for her, for himself. He could not go on like that. It would only get worse as time went by. Their joining would draw him to her endlessly. There was no other way.

Without hesitation, he transported to Greenwich. Standing outside Elsam's tower, he waited to be discovered. He had no more wish to go on living. He hoped to be captured and have his life ended. Sinking down to his knees, he did not have long to wait. Elsam's guards were out patrolling the area. He did not put up a fight when they surrounded him. *What would be the point? I have nothing to fight for.* Everything he cared about was gone. Dragged into the tower's lower levels, they tossed him into his cell. How long ago that was, he did not care. Why they kept him alive was a mystery.

The guards had manacled his wrists and ankles in iron before leaving him. Welts and burns formed on contact. He had been agonized over her absence and the excruciating burns for what seemed like days. The link between Aidan and Alexa kept expanding. It pulled on him to return to her. He fought against the urge, knowing how hopeless it was. She would never care about him. His desire for her though continued to grow with each moment that passed. His need nearly overpowered him. He had to find a way to end his suffering. His heart bled, his whole being became consumed by her. *There was no escaping her, or was there?*

His decision on his final course of action was interrupted by the arrival of the guards. What he meant to do was postponed by their presence. They released the chain, but did not remove the manacles. Pushing him forward, they led him up the stairs into the audience room. Each step he took brought fresh blood-stained marks on his ankles. He tried to keep his hands as still as possible. Even with the effort, the iron around his wrists tore through his skin.

Propelled into the throne room, Aidan stumbled, falling to his knees in front of the ornate, bejeweled throne. Facing Elsam, who exulted at having him in his possession, Aidan could not have cared less. He gave no responses or acknowledgments to the man's questions.

Elsam grew more and more incensed at Aidan's refusal to answer him. The man showed every sign of having lost all his faculties. He jerkily paced in front of Aidan. The twitching of his left eye grew more pronounced with each second that Aidan knelt silently on the floor. Elsam's voice rose thunderously, bouncing off the walls of the chamber.

His descent into madness should have caused Aidan to worry for his safety. Instead, he lowered his head and waited for death to claim him.

Elsam did not give Aidan what he craved. He screamed at his guards to remove Aidan from his presence. Aidan watched Elsam's retreat, as he strode angrily from the room. As the guards manhandled Aidan from the chamber, returning him down, deep into the dungeons, Aidan started to withdraw into himself. With each step, he cut himself off from the world around him. The first thing he lost was the image of her face. Then slowly any feeling was driven away. Nearing the cell they pushed him into, Aidan blocked out all sounds. By the time they reattached the iron manacles to the overhead chain, he had lost himself in an abyss of darkness.

Days passed, then a month, maybe more. He had no sense of time, no sense of who he was or where he was. His hair grew out, reaching past his shoulders. Unkempt, bearded, he looked nothing like his former self. The iron around his wrists and ankles left deep red gashes burned into his skin. Aidan did not perceive the damage they had done, or what he looked like. He had been without food and water for too long. His skin seemed to hang on his brittle bones. *How much longer before death claims me?* He wished it to come quickly.

If he had been aware, he would have heard the footfalls approaching his cell. He would have heard the taunts and laughter at the person they were leading to him. The scornful voice of Myrick, as he addressed the other prisoner, would have filled him with dread. In his state, he did not hear the door of his cell when it opened. He was not aware of someone being shoved forcefully into his prison. Sounds of the person falling, scraping their knees and gasping went unheard in his self-imposed hell.

Chapter 2 - Alexa

When I left our protected estate outside Verona, I had only one objective foremost in my mind. I gave no further thought to those I had left behind. Only Liam's anger at my escape followed me, as I crossed the distance to where Aidan's presence acted like a beacon. I blocked everyone else's displeasure, their recriminations at how easily I had fooled them. Nothing would be gained by giving my attention to their fears.

Focusing on Aidan, on what little I could sense from him, overwhelmed me. Alarmed at his condition, I hastened to reach him. Worry that I would be too late gnawed away at me. The threads binding us together were unraveling, coming apart. Close to panic, I reached out to him, but was met by a dark empty void where his mind should have been.

Whatever state he was in, I knew it to be of his own choosing. Arriving at his location, I allowed myself to be caught. Brought before the hideously scarred, immensely pleased Myrick, I scanned with my senses for where they were holding Aidan. His body was near, but the emptiness of his mind alarmed me. Biding my time until an opportunity presented itself, I returned my attention to the vast hall I stood in, knowing there was little I could do at that time.

Myrick appraised me mistrustfully when the guards brought me before him. His sharp eyes studied me for any sign that I might attempt to fight back. Probing my mind, he ran up against an impenetrable wall.

In his arrogance, he assumed it meant I was incapable, powerless against him. If he knew I had planned that, the sneering smile would have been wiped off his face.

Fooling them into thinking I had been careless had been the easy part. They rightly assumed I was searching for Aidan. Leaving obvious traces of my movements, I let them corner me near Abbey Wood. The old ruins of the abbey, on the outskirts of Greenwich, were isolated and free of human prying eyes.

I gave a show of resistance before allowing myself to be taken. Seizing me, two warlocks cast a spell to hold me within what they presumed to be an impenetrable shield. I feigned fright as they led me into the tower, where I could faintly sense Aidan's signature. The guards immediately took me to Myrick for inspection. The vast throne room they led me to, appeared to be well guarded. Brought before the traitorous warlock and the man he had given his allegiance to, Myrick showed no fear in coming face-to-face with me.

Elsam, on the other hand, was more cautious. The man kept himself at a relatively safe distance from me. His watchful eyes strayed over my face, wondering what all the fuss was about. Paranoia ran deeply within him. Elsam did not trust anyone around him. His elite guard, chosen from his most loyal followers, watched his every move, wary of how he would react to me.

The tension in the room was electrifying. It was obvious that Myrick and Elsam were at odds. The two men despised each other, but they were bound together in their unholy alliance. Each had their own plans, their own machinations in play. Myrick thought he could influence Elsam. He had no idea how close Elsam was to ending his pitiful life.

Hearing their thoughts, knowing how close to unraveling they were, almost made me smile. I lowered my head so they would not catch the glint in my eye. They asked me no questions, only congratulated themselves on apprehending me. Elsam readily gave over my care to Myrick. He thought I posed no danger to him. How wrong he was. Only one thing kept me from attacking. Aidan needed my help. Whatever Myrick planned to do with me, I could see the gears in his mind turning. He would take great pleasure in trying to break me. Let him try, I thought.

With Elsam's interest in me waning, Myrick summoned the guards to remove me from the throne room. They took me down, one level closer to Aidan, locking me up in a dingy cell. As much as I would have liked to go to Aidan immediately, I needed information from my captors. I probed their minds endlessly without their knowledge. Their plans, their strength, would be beneficial in the days to come.

After a third night alone in my prison, they were moving me somewhere deeper in the dungeons. Why the move, I had no idea. I could have easily read their minds, but I needed to hide my powers. Three guards arrived in my cell, grabbing me and tying my wrists tightly behind my back. Pushing me out, they led me down the narrow passage towards a stairwell.

With one guard in front and two behind, we descended the stairs, all the while the tension of the cord binding my wrists cut painfully into my flesh. With a slight use of my power, I loosed it a bit, while the guards behind me never noticed a thing. Each step I took increased the knowledge that I was measurably closer to Aidan. His nearness filled me with concern though. Moving closer to Aidan should have been a welcome relief, but what I sensed from him made me feel the complete opposite. I needed to get to him urgently, before it was too late. His signature was rapidly fading, giving me almost nothing to hone in on.

The stairs ended, bringing another narrow passage before me. This underground corridor stunk of humid rot. Stepping around the puddles of water that had accumulated from overhead dripping, I did my best to appear nonthreatening. I needed to maintain control over my increased abilities. It was proving difficult not to strike out at the guards around me. Concentrating on finding Aidan, saving him was all that kept me in check. Trying to probe his mind was impossible. He had cut himself off from everything. I sensed no thoughts. It was as if he had ceased to exist.

Nearing the only door on that level, a guard held me back, while another unlocked the massive wooden door. Footsteps behind me alerted the arrival of Myrick. Glancing down the dimly lit corridor, I watched the warlock approach. Myrick ordered one of the guards to unbind my hands once he had reached us. It was a test to see what I would do.

While he uttered veiled threats and taunted me, I rubbed my wrists, seeing the ugly bruising that was forming. His nasal inflection was driving me crazy. By force of will, I kept myself under control. I knew enough not to respond to his malicious remarks. Any comment I made would have given him reason to believe he had rattled me.

In any case, I was more worried about the tingling sensation spreading around the marks left by the cord. Feeling my wrists self-healing, I placed my hands behind my back. The subtle move went unnoticed by Myrick, who gave me a final smirk before ordering the guards to lock me up. He did not wait to see his instructions carried out. In a swoop, he pivoted and strode away, going back down the corridor where we had come from. The guards, responding to his order, unceremoniously tossed me into the cell. The large door banged shut behind me.

I landed with a thud, falling heavily on the jagged stone floor. Skidding on my knees, the harsh fall made me gasp. My thin cotton dress ripped as I landed. Crimson red stains spread across the cloth covering my kneecaps. I had blood seeping from cuts on my knees. My hands were not in any better shape. Along with the healing bruises on my wrists, I now had cuts on my palms from trying to stop my fall. It would not be long before they too started to mend. Keeping it a secret would be challenging. My jailers could not know I was beyond their ability to keep me imprisoned.

Finding Aidan remained my solitary reason for being. My eyes struggled momentarily to adjust to the all-encompassing darkness around me. It did not take long before I could distinguish my surroundings. I had been thrown into a room smaller than my previous prison. I wondered why they had brought me there. Were they watching me? I sensed no one keeping watch over me. My sight broke through the blackness, seeing only one other person present in the confines of the cell.

All I knew was that Myrick had managed to trick me somehow. Coming into my cell the night before, with a woman the same height and build as my own, he demanded that I change out of my clothes at once. The young woman with him helped me out of my outfit. My jeans and shirt, along with my leather coat were folded neatly. She took the items away, leaving me with the cotton dress I now wore.

Whatever they had planned, I was sure it was not good. Sometime later, I heard the explosion that ripped through the ship in the distance. I heard the wretchedness of Liam calling my name. The unbearable anguish of my parents tore my heart. I could do nothing for them. I needed to stay my course. Numbing myself to the agony they were all going through was all I could do. How long I cried for what they assumed happened to me was lost to time. Curling into a ball on the floor, I let the tears fall unhindered. I could not hold them back. Hours later, Myrick returned, ordering the guards to take me to the new location.

My eyes adjusted easily to the lack of light in the cell. In the shadowy room, a bulk of something or someone drew my attention. In front of me, the non-moving object emitted a harsh, raspy sound. I moved closer to it, sensing what it was. Or, I should say, who it was. When I was inches away, I found myself facing the person I had been searching for.

Unseeing eyes were staring at a point behind me. I saw no recognition on his face. My vision blurred with tears at his condition. I crawled closer to him on my hands and knees, ignoring the pain from the latter. Touching his face, I saw no indication that he knew I was there. I called out his name and got no reaction.

Inspecting him further, I saw the marked differences his incarceration had had on him. His muscles were less defined, his loss of weight had eaten away at his mass. His beautiful face lay hidden behind unkempt facial hair. His ebony hair, oily and limp, fell almost to his shoulders. Dirt had accumulated on his cheeks and chin. Emerald eyes lacked the spark I had grown accustomed to. Running my hands down his torso, I shivered at the response within me. Even in that condition, he was the most captivating man I could ever hope to meet.

Resisting the pull his presence had over me, my hands continued their exploration, searching for any other hidden damage. Feeling no other wounds under his clothing, I took in the rest of him. His wrists had red welts where the metal cuffs hung. His ankles were in no better condition. The metal dug deeply into his skin, cutting into muscle to the bone. I hesitated to cure them, worried it would give me away. Continuing to hide my abilities from Myrick and Elsam was imperative if I hoped to escape with Aidan. I knew I could get us both out whenever I wanted. Their feeble spells were no match for me, but I needed Aidan aware before getting us out.

I had no idea how to reach him. Touching him elicited no response. I held his face in my hands, willing him to look at me. His eyes never made contact with mine. Taking him in my arms, I held onto him, crying silent tears for what I had let happen. His stiff body, arms hanging by his sides, gave me no comfort. I longed for him to come back, to be the man I had so carelessly rejected. His blood in my veins hummed in his presence. It had been months since he had gifted me with his blood on my birthday. The drop was a reminder of the link that joined us. His heartbeat drummed to the same rhythm as mine. It recognized the owner of the drops that ran through me. Letting him go, wiping away my tears, I watched as his eyes stared off.

What could I do to bring him back? The returning painful reminder of my injured knees made me wince. Leaning on them had started fresh blood seeping. I sat back on my heels to take the pressure off of them while I rubbed at my swelling kneecaps. My hands came away bloodied. I stared at them as an idea formed in my head. Would it be possible? I had to try. I had given the vial of my blood to Elron to use to retrieve the Kaemorra. I would have to use the fresh blood from my wounds. I brought my bloodied hands in contact with Aidan's wrist, allowing the wet drops to mingle with his. My fingers tingled where they touched him. I felt a shiver race up his arm.

I waited for another reaction, staring deeply into his eyes for any movement. The vacancy of his stare was unnerving. There was no life in his eyes. After what seemed like hours, I heard what sounded like a moan escape his lips. I waited further, praying silently for him to wake from whatever hell he had placed himself in. It was his doing. No, I admitted to myself, it was my doing. He would never have ended up there if not for me. I had almost given up when he dragged in a deep breath. His lungs expanded, then released the air in a long, mournful moan.

Hearing the pain-filled exhalation, I rejoiced in the sound. It gave me hope. It was minutes before I got another reaction. He trembled slightly, as I held his hand. Speaking his name, I waited for him to look at me. Minutes passed without any other sign of his recovering. Losing hope, I pulled him down so he lay on the floor. I managed to stop his head from banging on the hard stone, as his body collapsed on his side. The chains overhead rattled in response to his movement, breaking the deathly silence around us. I positioned myself lying in front of him so I could watch him. Supporting my head in the crook of my arm, I somehow managed to fall asleep.

"Alexa." My name coming from his lips, softly murmured, brought me awake.

I lifted on my elbow to see if he was aware of me. His eyes still stared unseeing. Maybe he was dreaming. Could someone dream with their eyes open? I doubted it. How long had he been without sleep? The fact he said my name, at all, brought a smile to my face. He was still thinking of me. All was not lost. I sat up, looking down at him. I would wait as long as it took. If any dangers presented themselves, I would handle them. Aidan needed to get his strength back.

The unlocking of the door made me stand up. Watching for any dangers, I saw a guard enter with a tray of food. He placed it on the floor, near the door, and pushed it towards me with his foot. Without a word, he exited. The sound of the lock turning reverberated throughout the room. I went to the tray, picked it up and brought it to where Aidan lay. I sat down in front of him, making sure I had a clear view of his face. I wanted to catch any change in his condition.

I ate a piece of the bread from the plate, leaving the rest for when Aidan woke. He would need to eat, to regain his strength. Tired, I lay down again facing him. I put my arm around his waist, drawing closer to him. My other hand went to his cheek, feeling the softness of the beard that covered it.

"Please wake up, Aidan. Come back to me." I begged him softly.

A deep breath broke from him. A sigh followed. Glowing emerald eyes turned my way, recognition filling them. The pain I saw in their depths made me gasp. What had I done? How could I have caused this? He was in so much harrowing, agonizing anguish. Tears fell unheeded from my eyes. I swore that I would make it up to him.

Aidan tore his eyes away from me. He drew away, trying to return to oblivion. I could not let that happen. I brought my lips to his, pressing the softest kiss on them. My hand caressed his cheek. His gaze landed on my lips, which trembled in grief over what I had done. Keeping my eyes open, I stared into his, as I placed another kiss on his unmoving lips. My eyes begged him to respond.

"No, don't leave me. Please stay. I need you." Tears flowed from my eyes.

"Alexa." Was all he said before his lids fell, his eyes closing, as sleep finally, blessedly, claimed him.

Chapter 3 - Thalia

Thalia was spent, past exhaustion, but sleep eluded her. Her mind could not stop reliving the explosion that took her daughter. A mother should not outlive her children. *How am I to go on?* Nothing could replace her beautiful Alexa. Grieving her had overtaken Thalia's life. She pushed away everyone who tried to console her. Alone in her room, in the dark, she had been in her bed for days.

Every time she closed her eyes, tried to lose herself in the insensibility of sleep, she saw flames, heard the explosion, all over again. Rider, her husband, lost to his own grief, stayed away from her. He blamed himself. Thalia could not exonerate him, or anyone else, for the events that led to her daughter's death.

Liam had remained on the dock, staring incomprehensibly at the inferno that blazed across the horizon. Attempts to have him transport away almost caused him and Elron to come to blows. He would not leave the place. Thalia watched Liam's eyes go from a dazed mournful sea green to a dark mossy murderous green. They had no choice but to leave him. He was probably still there.

Elron tried to get him to transport back to Deis-dé, but it had been in vain. Liam, lost to his own grief, searched for an outlet for his rage. Thalia had no idea where everyone else was. Rider transported her to Deis-dé soon after the devastating events. She had fallen, broken on the marble floor of the main room, unable to fathom that her daughter was no more. *How did I let this happen? What kind of mother would put her child in so much danger? I should have kept Alexa hidden, kept her away from this infernal prophesy.*

It fell to Elron to inform the others of what had transpired. Thalia and Rider were both too shocked to speak aloud the words that would make it all too real. Bet was inconsolable at losing her friend. She sunk down on a chair, her legs going numb at the news. Stunned, she stared at Elron, begging him to tell her it was untrue.

Eliana had gone rigid, her eyes narrowing at what she heard. She held her hand out to stop Asher, who tried to go to her side. Thalia blamed Eliana most of all. She was the reason her daughter had been thrown into the calamity in the first place. Eliana left the room without a word. Her husband followed her, unsure of what she meant to do.

Rina and Tory entered the room soon after. Thalia could not bear to hear the news repeated. Leaving them, she went to her bedroom, wishing to be left alone. Anger at everyone and everything was quickly replacing her grief. Rider came to her, wanting to go through their loss together. They had to support each other, he tried to explain.

Thalia was past caring if Rider would get over losing Alexa. She pushed him away. Feeling her scorn, he left her alone, as she desired. She was as she wished, alone, trying to block out the awful reality. Closing her eyes gave her no peace. Slumber was elusive. She knew she had to rest, but her mind would not still.

"Get up." Eliana pulled the covers away from Thalia's body. Too engrossed in her thoughts, she had not even heard Eliana enter the room.

"Go away. Leave me to my grief." Thalia screamed at the

woman.

"You have nothing to grieve. Get up and come downstairs." Eliana had made it to the door, when she stopped to see if Thalia was following her instructions.

Thalia was incensed at the cruel remark. She had just lost her daughter. Eliana met her cold contempt with a slight smile.

"Alexa is alive. If you wish to hear what I know, you will get yourself out of that bed and join us in the main room." Eliana turned and left.

Thalia's mind took a second to register what Eliana had said. *Could it be true, or is the woman playing with me?* For the first time in days, Thalia had a reason to get up. Making a quick stop in the bathroom, where she combed her hair and splashed water on her face, she then hastily took the stairs down to the lower level.

On entering the room, her eyes landed on Rider who had his back to her. He gave no sign he was aware of her arrival. Seeing his stiff back, she regretted how she had treated him. She silently stepped next to him, placing her palm on his rigid back. Rider reacted by turning to face her. He held his arms open, and she wasted no time walking into them. Held firmly against him, their sighs left them in unison.

"I'm so sorry, Rider." She murmured, as his hand held the back of her head with her cheek pressed against his chest.

"It will be all right. Thalia, I love you. There is nothing to forgive. It was my fault." Rider's body quaked with guilt.

"No. Never think that!" She pulled away to look into his pained eyes. "I don't blame you. Not really. We should have gone through this together. You were right. I lost myself to blinding rage over what happened. I love you too, Rider. Life without you would not be worth living."

Rider pulled her back into his arms, holding her firmly in his grasp. Her pent up emotions broke free, as Thalia cried for the first time since the explosion. Scalding tears ran down her cheeks. Rider simply held her while the tension left her body.

"Everyone take a seat." Eliana strolled in, taking an armchair for herself.

Thalia took Rider's hand and together they sat on a sofa facing the woman. She waited anxiously to hear what Eliana had to say. *Can it be true? Can Alexa be alive?* Hope steadily built in her. Rider squeezed her hand in anticipation.

Elron escorted Bet into the room, seating her in a chair, while he stood behind her. Thalia could see Bet's red-rimmed eyes had only recently stopped crying. Tears still clung to her eyelashes. Sniffing, she wiped at her face to clear the remnants away. Elron put his hand on her shoulder, giving her added courage.

Asher came in next, followed by Rina and Tory. As they all took seats to hear what Eliana had to share, Thalia studied Asher. He in turn had eyes only for his wife. There was a marked difference in how he was looking at her. The anger had left his face. In its place, Thalia saw renewed respect for his wife. One could only wish it meant that they had somehow come to an understanding between them. *Could he put aside the fact that his wife left him stranded as a statue for centuries?* Thalia could only hope for their sake and their children's that they could get past it.

"I have consulted with the Kaemorra. As I stated, Alexa is alive. She is presently with Aidan, trying to revive him. We must let her accomplish this before we try to reach her. I am most worried about Liam. I have been unable to communicate with him. He has blocked anyone from contacting him." Eliana looked at her husband, as she spoke of their son.

Asher seemed to be concentrating, trying to link with Liam. His attempt was futile. Liam did not wish to receive their communications. Seeing that Asher was also unable to reach him, Eliana continued.

"We are at a crossroads. I see only one path we can follow. What the Kaemorra has shown me, leads me to conclude that we have little choice. My spies have informed me that the Daimon have already possessed most of the coast overlooking our homeland. Elsam wants to make sure that we cannot launch an attack from there."

"Wait." Asher broke in. "What exactly did the Kaemorra show you?"

Eliana hesitated before answering. What she had to say made her shiver slightly. Everyone could see the trepidation she was experiencing. Whatever she had seen, it was enough to render her fearful. The seconds ticked by, as they all waited for her answer.

"War. We are going to war with the shadows and Daimon." She all but whispered.

"What?" Elron bellowed, making everyone jump.

"I know. It is something we haven't done in over a thousand years. They have to be stopped. Their alliance with Elsam has to be broken." Eliana tried to calm them all.

Asher took to his feet, pacing. The shadows were almost impossible to defeat. Their strength came from them not having corporeal bodies. Only light could draw them back. As they did not attack during daylight hours, but only in the depths of night, how could they to defeat them? The Daimon on the other hand were easier to combat. The Sidhe race had special swords made of an enchanted metal that would banish the souls of the Daimon if they came in contact with their enemy.

"I have called on our army to amass on the coast of Loch Maree in the highlands. They are gathering as we speak. Asher, I need you to lead them. As their king, they will swear fealty to you and fight to the last. We all will have our own individual tasks if we are to succeed." Eliana informed them.

"We have to find Liam before all hell breaks loose." Elron spoke up. "He has to be made aware of what is going on. He has to be told that Alexa still lives."

Eliana closed her eyes at Elron's statement. Whatever she foresaw in the future jolted her eyes open. Rising to her feet, she reached Elron and placed her hand on his forearm. Their silent communication halted when Bet rose to her own feet. Seeing the expression on her face, Elron shook his head at her.

"Love, please, for once do not think of anything but your safety." He implored her. "Where I go, you cannot follow."

"Bet has her own mission to accomplish. One that will have no dangers attached to it." Eliana eyed her daughter.

Bet, curious over what her mother planned for her, forgot to argue. Thalia had been silent until then. She wanted, needed, to know of the dangers to her daughter. Rider, holding her hand, sensed her unease at all that had been discussed. Before she could broach the subject, Elron interrupted her train of thought.

"Help me get ready, Bet. I have to leave within the hour." Elron waited for her to join him.

When they left the room, silence descended. Thalia could see that Eliana was preoccupied with the coming battle. She had to maneuver her army, her subjects for the oncoming conflict. Still, her own mind was focused on her daughter.

"Thalia, I need you and Rider to reach out to your kind. The witches and warlocks will have to be made aware of what is to come. I count on them to aid us in this crisis." Eliana addressed Thalia.

"I will do all I can. Can you tell me more about Alexa, please?" Thalia's voice broke on speaking her daughter's name.

Eliana nodded and smiled gently. She joined Thalia on the couch and took her hand. Rider was also impatient to hear about Alexa's condition. Squeezing Thalia's hand, Eliana started speaking.

"Alexa was captured as she meant to be. She has not been harmed. They have placed her in the same cell as Aidan. She is trying to get him to recover. My son has cut himself off from life. He is fighting her nearness, but he will come back to himself. She will get them to safety within the next few days. Those who hold her are unaware of how powerful she is. Do not fear for her. Myrick and his cohorts are no match for her. She will meet up with you where I am sending you."

Eliana imparted the information with a grin.

Thalia blessed the goddess for keeping her daughter safe. Knowing she was not in danger was all she could hope for. Now, they needed to go ahead with what Eliana asked of them. They had to meet the council of witches to get their support.

"Asher you need to meet Ronan, our general, in the field tomorrow morning. I have some instructions for you to take to him. Please see me in my room in an hour. I have to consult with the Kaemorra again. Thalia, Rider, Godspeed to you. Let me know how your meeting goes." Eliana had reached the door. There she turned to address the other two forgotten people in the room.

"Rina, reach your mother. Tell her that all she has foreseen has come to pass. I am relying on her to rein in the gods' interference. You may need to use your powers of persuasion to have them do as I ask. Tory, find your parents. They are integral to our success. Forgive them. Only they have the answers to your history. You have to learn of your origins to understand what you must do. Now, excuse me. I have much to think on and plan."

Rina and Tory were left speechless in her wake. Eliana had effectively imparted information they both had been unaware of. Why she had not gone into detail, they were left to wonder. She breezed out of the room, not giving them a chance to inquire. Thalia giggled at their stunned faces, showing for the first time in days that a heavy burden had been lifted from all their shoulders.

Chapter 4 - Liam

The Daimon prince, Manar, had arrived under the cover of darkness less than an hour before. Liam spotted the royal Daimon's entrance into the tower from where he spied, unseen, near the outcrop reaching up from the shore. Only steps away from him was where he had last seen Alexa. Blinded by his grief, he remained, waiting for a chance to retaliate for her death. Attempts to communicate with him by his family, he had refused, while he scanned for an opening.

He would make them all pay for taking her away from him. Myrick, he would capture and make suffer each day for the rest of his miserable life. So far, there had been no opportunity to gain access to the structure. It was well guarded. Manar's sentries joined with Elsam's guards at the main gate. From what he could see, they were not pleased with each other's presence. Jostling for dominance, it would not take long before they turned on each other. It might give him the opportunity he sought.

Movement from the shore drew his attention down to the beach. Black inky shapes glided along the water's edge and onto the grainy sand. Liam dropped down behind the rocks, keeping still as the shapes moved nearer. He knew not to come in contact with the beings traveling towards him. The last time he had been touched by one, he had been rendered unconscious for weeks, and then had fallen under their control. They had even driven him to attempt to kill Alexa. His mind had been consumed with their evil thoughts.

The shadows possessed no bodies to fight with. Their attacks, once their shapes passed over someone, were worse than any physical blows. The victim's mind would erode, go insane from the whisperings that took over. There were five of them slithering along the grass towards the tower. Once Liam was sure they were far enough away not to see him, he peeked over the rocks at their retreating forms.

Reaching the gate, one of the shadows lifted off the ground. Its form morphed into what looked like a human body. Spindly arms and legs stretched out from a round-shaped black mass. The only color from within the darkness was its two red glowing eyes. Liam recognized the leader of the shadows. Erebus, sensing someone nearby, fixed his two red orbs on where Liam stared fixedly back at him. Their eyes collided, each surprised to see the other.

A subtle movement of Erebus's finger had the other shadows moving towards Liam's direction. Liam instantly transported away from his hiding place, materializing on the other side of the field, behind a massive oak tree. Keeping out of sight, he waited for them to lose interest. A piercing screech broke the silence. Erebus had called his minions back. Liam waited a minute more before peeking out from behind the tree. He caught a brief glimpse of Erebus disappearing inside the building, keeping to the shadows away from any light within the structure.

Breathing a sigh of relief, Liam continued to watch from his safe distance. The mix of races guarding the front door posed a problem. He might have been able to take Elsam's guards, but he could not risk confronting the Daimon and shadows. He would have to wait. Sitting down, he used the tree to support his back. The trunk was large enough to completely hide him from view. Now that he had nothing to do, his grief over the loss of Alexa assailed him anew. His heart ached. He ignored a ringing in his ears, alerting him to an incoming communication. No one could offer him relief from the blame he had placed on himself. He had done nothing to save her.

Four days. It had been only four days since he had watched her disintegrate before his eyes. It felt like a lifetime. The explosion stole his breath. Liam could do nothing but watch the destroyed materials of the boat rain down upon the sea. He heard none of his friends' cries over Alexa's fate.

Thalia, Rider and Elron did not exist in his shell-shocked mind. They tried to get him to leave with them. Liam had nowhere to go. *Where could I go to escape? Alexa is gone.* Revenge, avenging her was the only thing he lived for. The ringing was back. He shut it off again. He did not want to speak with anyone.

"You fool, answer when we call." Elron plopped down next to him.

"How did you find me?" Liam was startled to see him appear so suddenly.

"You forget who trained you." Elron admonished him. "Let's get out of here."

Liam refused to move. He had to stay. Finding a way into the tower remained his sole objective. Elron would have to bodily remove him.

"Listen to me. You do not know all the facts. Come with me

now if you ever wish to see Alexa again. Dying will not help you achieve that goal." Elron pushed him.

What is he talking about? Liam froze, stunned at Elron's words. *Alexa is dead. Dying may be the only way for me to ever see her again.* Still, Elron seemed cheered. *Does he know something I do not?*

Curiosity took hold of him. He could always return after listening to what his friend had to say. His mind opened to Elron's suggested location. Liam followed him into the void of space, materializing in Deis-dé. In the main room, Elron motioned for him to sit. Liam preferred to pace.

"Are you ready?" Elron smirked at him.

"Get on with it. I need to go back." Liam spoke impatiently.

Elron laughed out loud at his friend. He was taking great pleasure in taunting Liam. When it looked like Liam would depart, he spoke.

"Alexa is alive."

Elron did not anticipate the fist that landed, catching him squarely on the jaw. He staggered back a step before righting himself. His hand rubbed at his cheek that flamed red.

"You only get one of those." Elron warned Liam in the silence that fell.

Liam's eyes flamed at Elron. *Why? Why would Elron torment me like this? What did he hope to gain? Is all this to keep me here?* Liam attempted to transport, but something held him back. He tried again, only to have his ability blocked.

"Enough." His mother all but yelled.

Liam watched her enter the room. She touched Elron's arm, as she passed by him on her way to her son. She shook her head at Liam, who obstinately tried to transport again. She blocked him again. Angrily, he sidestepped her to reach the doorway. He never made it. Elron planted himself in front of Liam.

"Don't even think about it!" Elron threatened him. "I am not lying to you. Alexa is alive."

"I saw her get on that boat. I saw it explode with her on it." Liam's voice broke.

Why are they cruelly teasing me with hope? Liam made it to one of the sofas, where he numbly dropped. His chest hurt to draw breath. His mother sat down slowly next to him. Taking his hand, she half turned him so he faced her.

"My dear son." Eliana cupped his cheek with her hand, heartfelt emotion in her voice as she spoke. "I would not lie to you about something so painful. Alexa is alive. She was never on that boat. Myrick tried to trick us into believing she had perished. Alexa is still in the tower. She has been reunited with Aidan. Your brother needs to revive before they can come to us. Do not fear for her. She is safe."

Can I believe her? He felt no subterfuge from his mother. She appeared to truly believe the information she was imparting. Liam, on the other hand, was not ready to drop his defenses. His anger was all that held him together. A burgeoning hope steadily built within him, as his mother kept her gaze fixed on him. He saw she was sincerely seeking his acceptance.

"How? How is this possible?" Liam choked out the words.

Eliana grasped his hand with both of hers. Before she could say anything, they were interrupted by the appearance of Thalia in the doorway. Thalia did not appear to be mourning her daughter. Liam's mind registered the fact that Thalia seemed like her old self. Slowly, realization that what his mother and Elron were telling was the truth took hold of him. His relief was immediate. Taking a deep breath in, he released it along with his anguish.

"Eliana, we are ready to leave. I will contact you as soon as we have news." Thalia spoke to his mother. "Liam, I'm glad to see you back. It's wonderful news, isn't it?" Thalia smiled at Liam.

Liam had still a ways to go before fully absorbing the fact that Alexa was alive. He simply nodded at Thalia, at a loss for words. Rider arrived behind her, so they could depart to wherever they were headed. Rider acknowledged them all by a slight incline of his head. His mother responded likewise. Liam watched Rider take his wife's arm, and then they were gone.

"We have much to discuss, my son. Elron, you know where you must go. Please take care of that little matter. I'll make sure Bet is unable to follow." Eliana addressed Elron, who quickly did as she asked. "Liam, come with me please." Eliana stood, waiting for Liam to follow.

Once Liam was on his feet, she guided him towards the stairway leading down into the lower levels. Down the spiral stairs they went. He followed his mother down to the second level below the manor. There was only one room, covering the expanse of the size of the structure above them. In the center, behind a protective shield, the Kaemorra gravitated above a square, marble pedestal. The crystal spun slowly on its axis. Its fiery glow pulsated, casting out rays that had the room saturated in crimson.

To his right, there was a stone bench, large enough to seat them both. Twelve marble sculptures, interspersed throughout the room, acted as support beams. Each was fashioned to represent one of the gods. The one closest to him was a striking representation of the goddess of the hunt, Artemis. The bow and arrow in her hands were poised to fire. The Sidhe had always called her by the name of Scadi.

"Sit." His mother broke into his examination of the room.

Doing as she asked, Liam went to the bench and sat. Intrigued over what she wanted to discuss or show him, he followed her with his eyes, as she made her way to the Kaemorra. The crystal hummed at her nearness. Spinning faster, its glow increased as her hand passed over it. A beam broke from it, sending images playing out in the vastness of the room. Liam's eyes misted because of what the Kaemorra forced him to confront.

The smiling face of his mate, Mara, made his heart stop for a second. She appeared before him just as he remembered her. Her chestnut hair, long and flowing, billowed in a wind he did not feel. Her face held a soft smile upon her lips. Eyes like emeralds glowed at what she was seeing. The sweetness of her presence became unbearable for Liam. Seeing her brought his pain over her loss back full force.

"Watch!" His mother ordered him, when he turned away.

Liam had no choice but to return his gaze to the scene before him. Even that glimpse was worth the anguish he felt. She was beyond beautiful to him. He knew each contour of her body. From the shapely legs, all the way up to the willowy arms that had held him. His eyes narrowed at what else he saw. *Where is she?*

The bubbling waters of the river she knelt beside were unknown to him. They had never been there together. He could name every place he had visited with her. The red sediment- covered riverbed, with the molten lava covered mountains in the distance was unfamiliar. The trees surrounding the area were lifeless. Contorted, blackened trunks and twisted bare branches were rooted in a scorched soil. The fast moving waters of the river reflected all the death around her. *Why is she smiling?*

The Kaemorra, as if hearing his question, showed him more. The scene developed further, spreading out to show more of the landscape. Mara was on her knees on the shore by the river. She held a photo of him in her hand. It was an old one, taken when they had first met. Worn and wrinkled, the picture held proof of how often it had been scrutinized. Her hand trembled while holding it.

Liam could almost feel the hot, arid air she breathed. Mara was covered in sweat from the incredible heat rising from the water. Looking closely, Liam saw the waters of the river gurgle and surge as if boiling over. Above her, the sky burned a fiery red with black clouds swirling. *Where is she?* An answer gnawed away at him, but he could not bring it into focus. What surprised him was she seemed so alive. The image projected by the Kaemorra stilled. The beam returned back into the spinning crystal. Liam almost groaned at losing the vision of her.

"You never told me." His mother whispered.

No one knew, except for Aidan. Liam had been forced to tell his brother when Aidan had not recognized what was happening with

Alexa. He still did not want to discuss it. Any reminder of her loss, he had managed to block in order to survive.

"Liam, she is alive. I don't know why or how, but she lives. Have you not felt her at all?" Eliana was astonished.

"What?" Liam asked, dazed at what she had just said.

Eliana went to her son, sitting down next to him. She did not touch him. She knew that Liam was going to be shocked at what she had to say. *How could I have no knowledge that Mara lived*? As her mate, they were eternally joined. Something kept them apart on purpose.

"Liam, Mara is alive. She has been all this time. I need you to tell me everything that happened. There has to be a reason why you don't feel her." Eliana spoke softly, trying to be as gentle as she could be with her son.

Liam could only stare back at her in stunned silence. It was so long ago, but every second of that traumatic day was burned in his memory.

Chapter 5 - Aidan

Aidan was dreaming. *What else could this be, but a dream?* He was home. The waves lapped at the lakeshore he stood beside. Across from him, the mountain range, at once familiar, rose like a rug of forest green. The majestic summits peaked above the pillow clouds floating lazily by. On the tallest peak visible to him, the citadel, the palace he had grown up in, stood proudly over the floral gardens that were resplendent in their illuminated colors. The glimmering effect of the shades of flora lit up the stark white walls of his home.

The sun welcomed him with its warmth. It was the sounds that had held him so enthralled. Birds chirped happily, flying, soaring above him. Bees buzzed and butterflies hummed. It was as if he had never left. *How can this be?* Aidan did not care. He wanted to stay in that setting, whatever it meant, forever.

A whisper in the breeze made him turn towards the direction it came from. It came again. His name was being spoken by someone in the distance. *Who could be calling to me?* The voice held a pleading tone, making him want to reassure whoever it was. *Aidan, come back. Don't leave me.* Taking a step towards where he thought the plea was coming from, his environment changed, replaced by the gardens of the citadel.

The voice was forgotten, as memories of his childhood took hold. He remembered the path in front of him, as if it were yesterday. It led to his secret hiding place. *How many hours did I spend there to escape mother's attention?* Without thought, he walked the cobblestones, rounded a corner and dipped under the rose trestle that was brimming with its white-colored flowers. A left turn, five steps across the patch of grass and he brushed through the large hedge blocking him. Once clear, he was atop of the world. Standing on an outcrop of a ridge, the location gave him an all-encompassing view of the deep valleys, the lush meadows and the shimmering sea that surrounded the island.

Aidan lay down on the carpet of grass. Just as he had done when he was a young boy, he closed his eyes, savoring the tranquility. A fluttering sensation grazed the skin of his cheek. A scent of orchids invaded his senses. *Where did I encounter this exquisite scent before?* It beckoned him to be somewhere, do something. Unwilling to relinquish the peace he had found, he ignored everything else. *Just a little longer.*

His attempt to clear his mind from the unwelcome presence of someone trying to communicate with him was foiled by the answering response. *No, you have to come back now.* Startled at the clarity of the plea, Aidan sat up. *Who is it? Why are you interrupting my serenity?* In answer, a form took shape in front of him. From within sparkles of white light, Aidan identified the woman who intruded on his secret place. *Why is she here?*

Alexa fully materialized, gazing around at her surroundings. Her eyes took in the magnificence of the view. A shy smile graced her lips, as her eyes found his. Aidan had tried hard to forget her beauty, her allure. The hunger he felt for her tore through him. Needing to escape, he tried to rise to his feet, to go anywhere but where she was. Held by an invisible force, his body refused his wish. Alexa dropped to her knees, her hand reaching for him. Aidan shut his eyes, willing her to vanish.

With his eyes closed, a faint drumming reached his ears. The steady beat of his heart was accompanied by a second almost imperceptible pulse. Aidan focused on it, captivated by its rhythm. The increasing crescendo of the two drum rolls merged into one thundering, continuous beat. Aidan's heart understood the significance before he could grasp its meaning.

"Aidan, do you hear it, feel it? Listen." Alexa's voice whispered in his ear.

Aidan's eyes popped open. His body shivered in response. The merging of their blood traveled through his system, reawakening hope. Alexa's heart lay open to him. Where he had been able to only hear her thoughts previously, he now also saw into her heart. He understood what it meant. Alexa had completed their joining. Somehow she had found him, found a way for their bond to forge fully. What he glimpsed staggered him. There was no Liam residing within the walls of her heart. *How did I not see it before?*

"Aidan, I need you to wake up. I need you aware before I can get us to safety. You must be able to protect yourself. I can't have eyes everywhere. If we are attacked, I will have to fight them myself. That may leave you unprotected. I can't lose you now. Please, please wake up." Alexa begged him.

Aidan's eyes flashed with something akin to regret over wasted time. He had abandoned her. *How could she still need or want him? Why had she placed herself in danger over him?* Protecting her became his reason for being. He would wake. Already he could see the cracking around the edges of his dream world. The colors were becoming muted, losing their brilliance. Alexa was the first to go. She faded gradually from his sight. The seamless transition between his environment and utter darkness took seconds. Aidan knew waking would soon follow.

His moan, escaping his lips, pierced his ears. His emerald eyes fluttered open. Aidan lay on his side on cold, hard stone that was past freezing. His clouded breath billowed in the frigid room. Lying next to him, Alexa had cuddled into his side for warmth. Her eyes were closed, her breathing even. Aidan let her sleep in peace.

He took the opportunity to reacquaint himself with her face, the feel of her body and the sweet scent of her. He lay perfectly still so as not to wake her. The effort it cost him made him wince in pain. His wrists were inflamed and bleeding. His ankles were in the same condition. The iron binding him had done incredible damage to his skin.

"Aidan?" Alexa's questioning whisper had him staring into two steel silver eyes.

In response, he gathered her in his arms, bringing her closer to him. His lips descended to meet hers in a bittersweet kiss. This was where she belonged, in his arms. He felt her answering response to his exploration. His hand traveled down her spine, reaching her waist. With his other, he cupped her cheek, marveling that she was with him. Their tongues joined greedily together, dancing in exquisite pleasure. All too soon Aidan drew back. Agony filled him over his flesh rubbing against the iron. Alexa moaned softly at the loss of his lips. Realizing he was in pain, she shifted so she could sit up.

With a flick of her wrist, the irons binding him fell away. She reached with her hands to encircle his wrists. Tingling spread through him as he stared, awed, at the healing flesh. Within seconds his wrists showed no evidence that there had been any marks on them. She repeated the action with his ankles.

Aidan could see clearly that there was a change in her. Her aura was a different shade than the last time he had seen her. Her power seemed increased tenfold, if not more. She placed her hand on his chest and he immediately sensed an increase in strength. They had much to discuss, but first they needed to get away. *How can I get us out of here?* Alexa laughed softly on hearing his thoughts.

"Eat. They brought food not long ago. Once you're finished I can get us out." Alexa grinned.

Alexa pushed a plate over to him. The unappetizing block of hard cheese and stale bread did not elicit any hunger pangs from him. Still, he ate what was there. He wondered what she meant when she said she could get them out. *How far have her abilities grown?* Alexa had risen to walk around their prison. His eyes followed her trek around the cell. She appeared to be listening, concentrating on something outside their walls. A smile broke out on her lips, making him question what or who had caused it.

"We need to go. Elsam has ordered Myrick to kill us. You will need your sword." Alexa grabbed his hand to pull him up. "They can't know yet how powerful I am. It must look like it was you that recovered and transported both of us out." She continued.

Once on his feet, he noticed there was no more pain from his wounds. Movement was easy and unhindered. Looking at his wrists he saw nothing to show that moments before they had been bleeding, ripped open. Even his strength was increasing as time passed. He felt his sword materialize in its sheath on his back. His hand reached for it automatically.

Alexa stopped him before he could unsheathe it. Shaking her head, she removed her hand from his and placed it on his shoulder. Aidan recognized the effect of being transported. Their prison walls vanished, replaced by an eerie silence that covered the darkened night. Wherever they were, the enchantment over the area blanketed them in its protection.

Tall trees, hardly moving, rose up high above them. They stood beside a lake, where a boat was tied on a small pier. Alexa shivered from the cool night air. Her thin cotton dress was too little to offer her protection from the cold. Aidan moved closer to offer her whatever warmth he could.

Before he could wrap his arms around her, she was dressed warmly in black jeans, a cream colored turtleneck and brown leather jacket. Traces of the dirt that had covered her were also gone. Her hair was tied back, exposing her long neck, drawing his eyes to the beat of the vein that drummed there.

Aidan did not have to look down to see she had changed his wardrobe as well. Warmth from his black leather coat wrapped around him. His shoulders lay bare of the hair that had grown to reach them. He ran his hand over his head, feeling the cropped length of his hair. Alexa's hand cupped his now beardless cheek, her fingers tracing his jaw.

Staring into her brilliant eyes, Aidan needed time to process the changes he sensed in her. He grabbed her hand, locking their fingers together and brought it to his lips. Her knuckles were cold, her hand frozen. She turned away, her attention drawn back to the boat waiting for them.

"We need to talk." Aidan spoke, while making a sweep of the area.

"Yes, in a bit. We have to reach the other side of the lake. They have attempted to block my access, so we'll do things their way. It will ease their minds." Alexa responded.

"What?" Aidan was lost as to what she meant.

"I can't frighten them. If they understood what I can do, they might get scared. People always fear what they can't explain. Come." Alexa chuckled at his confusion.

Aidan did not know how to respond to that, but her smile forced one from him. *Could they not put off what she needed to do here?* He was besieged with questions. There were so many noticeable changes in her. Until they discussed what took place while he was held in the tower, he could not make sense of what she was saying. Seeing he was not moving, Alexa hooked her arm through his, pulling him towards the small motorboat tied to the pier.

Once they climbed in, Aidan untied the line and pulled the cord to get the motor running. Alexa pointed to where they needed to go while Aidan steered them towards it. She sat facing him, observing him with a slight smile on her lips. Her eyes were warm, filled with an emotion he recognized. He smiled back at her in response. There was nothing hidden between them any longer. Words were unnecessary to convey their feelings. Aidan knew she was completely and utterly his. They belonged to each other.

His attention was needed to maneuver the boat. By force of will, he diverted his gaze from her to focus on where he steered. Scanning across the lake, he drove them towards an area where he could beach the boat. The only sound in the night air was the motor's whine. They reached the other side, where Aidan guided the boat to the shore. There was no pier on that side of the lake. He cut the engine, then jumped out to haul it through the murky waters and onto the limited beach.

Once the boat was secured, he helped Alexa climb down. Grabbing her by the waist, he lifted her, letting her glide down his body till her feet touched the ground. She smirked at his intentional actions, while he continued to keep her firmly within his arms. The words of devotion died on his lips on seeing her eyes flash in response.

"So, you have made it." Someone remarked, interrupting Aidan from any further flirtation.

"Jasper." Alexa said, while still staring into Aidan's eyes.

"Come, we have much to discuss." Jasper turned to lead the way.

The leader of the warlock clans had appeared under the canopy of trees to their right. Without waiting to see if they followed, he disappeared into the forest. Aidan released Alexa, but not before placing a promise kiss on her lips. Her sigh was all the answer he needed. Following after Jasper, they entered the forested area. The path was lit by floating candles high above the branches. Aidan kept Alexa close to him, continuously scanning the area for any danger. He almost laughed out loud at the ridiculousness of his protecting Alexa. She could probably take care of both of them.

Jasper receded from view as he rounded a corner. Alexa continued on as if she had no cares. Beside her, Aidan had no choice but to follow wherever she went. Rounding the bend, they both felt the energy field erected around an open field before them. Jasper was nowhere to be seen. Continuing forward, they passed through the field's blue haze, entering a world few could see.

A village appeared out of a dense fog. The inhabitants, dressed in flowing robes and turn of the century costumes, milled about. A farmer's market was full to overflowing with fresh produce. In the distance, across a moat, a fortified castle towered over the area. The castle's four turrets each flew a flag of the different elements used by witches and warlocks. Alexa continued down the road after Jasper's retreating figure.

Aidan kept his guard up, as whispers reached his ears. Alexa's name was being spoken in reverence. The people had stopped and were openly staring at her retreating back. Words reached him, but he did not understand their meaning. *Chosen, the one, can she do it?* He picked up his pace to keep in step with her. All the while, his senses were alert to everyone around him. Alexa walked on as if she heard none of the whisperings.

Crossing the drawbridge over the moat, they passed under the massive gate into a central courtyard. Across the empty yard, a short distance away, marble steps led into the keep. The large stone structure had been expanded several times, as evidenced by the differing colored stone facades.

Aidan had been too preoccupied with the immense building to notice when Alexa broke off into a run towards two people standing by the castle's main door. Seeing it was Thalia and Rider, he gave them a moment before approaching. Alexa's parents wrapped her in their arms. Thalia was crying, tears of joy, while Rider seemed overcome with emotion. Aidan knew he had missed a lot, but now thought he did not know the half of it.

"Aidan. Welcome. We are so glad to see you are well." Rider spoke first.

Thalia regarded him with less exuberance. Before he could figure out why, Jasper walked over to join them.

"The council meeting is starting. Follow me."

Chapter 6 - Elron

Scourie Bay, to the north of the town with the same name, was brimming with activity. Elron counted five barges and six long boats in the calm waters. The caravan park he found himself in had only one structure. Empty of visitors, there were no campers or motor homes to make use of the amenities building that offered toilets, showers and laundry services.

He huddled inside it, out of sight, next to the window facing the bay. From what he could see, the Daimon were coordinating their attacks from there. All along the seashore, towns had fallen silent, their inhabitants too frightened to leave the safety of their homes. Some had already been possessed by Daimon, who made use of the controlled bodies to menace the rest. Isolated from the outside world, their plight had not become known yet. He wanted to keep it that way.

Elron spied from the window, trying to catch sight of the leader of the group. The Daimon were an unruly gang. Without someone to lead them, they would quickly dissolve into anarchy. So far, whoever was in charge had not made an appearance.

Elron had spent the last hour crouching, watching the comings and goings of those who came ashore from the window facing the bay. His right leg was numb from maintaining his position. Moving away from the window, he used the wall next to it to keep himself out of sight. Standing up, he stretched his cramped body, feeling the pins and needles travel up his leg. Shaking it only increased the unpleasant, prickling sensation.

He stilled as a sound came from outside. *Have they found me?* Listening closely, Elron waited for any noise from outside. Seconds passed with no other sound. Lowering himself back down, he ducked beneath the window ledge. He slowly peered up to steal a glance outside. He saw no one. From outside, pebbles crunched under someone's feet. There was someone there after all. Elron just managed to duck out of sight, as a Daimon came into view. He could not risk being discovered. His enemy emerged from the other side of the building. *How did I miss sensing him?* The crunching sound moved off, back towards the shore. Elron peeked out again to make sure he would not be found. The Daimon continued down the slight slope to join the others. Sighing in relief, Elron saw no other Daimon in sight.

He needed to be more careful. His queen was relying on the information he would garner from his mission. He continued to keep watch, as day turned to night. On the beach, as full darkness fell, a bonfire was lit. The flames reached high, lighting up the night sky. Elron could see clearly the hideousness of the faces of those that drank and brawled openly on the beach. Even though they were masking their appearance in human form, Elron could see past their disguise.

The Daimon had black, charred bodies. Their frames made up the bulk of their body, which stood at over seven feet. Resembling komodo dragons, their reptilian appearance made their legs seem stunted. The claws at the end of their feet were razor sharp and lethal. They were matched in their death-dealing by the talons that grew out of their hands. Their round faces held no human features. Instead of a nose, two holes protruded in the center of their faces. Their ears grew away from their heads, built into the horns that twisted on either side. The mouth was an oval opening, with no lips, and their tongue a thorn-covered muscular organ. It too was deadly. In the darkness, the only thing that stood out was their two glowing red orbs, their eyes.

"Silence!" A booming voice called out.

On the beach, the Daimon cowered, their previous joviality forgotten. Elron saw them all drop to their knees. Squirming, they waited for further orders. From the nearest boat a figure appeared on the bow. Surrounded by royal guards, the Daimon in the center looked out upon his men. Manar, their royal prince, scowled at the group. Elron now knew who was in charge. It caused him to question why it required his presence.

"Tomorrow we will move out. Their island is unguarded. Once we take possession, Elsam will have to deal with us. His concessions will become void and we will make our own terms. The dawn of a new era is upon us, one that will have the Daimon rule. Prepare yourselves for battle. Board your ships and await my orders." Manar left the bow, his guards falling into step around him.

The remaining Daimon on the beach quickly moved to do as he asked. They boarded the ships one by one. All that remained of their presence on the beach below was the blazing fire they left to burn. Elron was not surprised that the Daimon would not honor any deal they had made with Elsam. That they meant to take over their homeland, though, was a cause for concern. He had to return to let his queen know what he had discovered. Maybe they could circumvent the

Daimon. Leaving the site, he re-materialized in Deis-dé.

Eliana, seated on a red upholstered chair next to the fireplace, seemed lost in contemplation. At first, she did not acknowledge his presence in the room. Elron moved to stand a few feet in front of her. There he dipped to one knee waiting for her. Deep in conversation with someone, her finger rose to indicate him to wait a moment longer.

"Please rise. You do not need to show such courtesies to me." Eliana waved for him to get up.

"My Queen." Elron stood. "I have news that may not be welcome."

"Elron, whatever it is, I will not blame the bearer. Please sit. I know of Manar's plans. I have already alerted Asher to prepare. What else did you notice?" Eliana pointed to a chair next to her.

Elron sat as she commanded. His thoughts went over all he had seen. Without speaking, he opened his mind to her, so she could readily observe the images that spanned his. Eliana's brow furrowed at what she saw. When she broke the link, she rose to her feet.

"They are still as unruly as they have always been. It is their fatal flaw." She remarked.

"Will we persevere?" Elron wanted to know.

Eliana cast her mind to the future, her eyes glazing over while she concentrated on the passages of time. So many outcomes presented themselves to her. There were only a few that gave them a win. She would need to advise Asher of what to do. Returning to the present, she nodded at Elron.

"Yes. There is a way. Leave me please. I need to speak with

Asher. Bet is upstairs resting. See her before you join our army on Eruva. Asher will already be there." Eliana turned away from him, already reaching out to her husband.

Elron took the stairs two at a time to the upper level. Bet had tried to contact him a number of times, but he had not responded. Expecting her to be royally pissed, he was surprised by the welcome he received. On entering the room, Bet ran to him, wrapping her arms around him and showering him with kisses. *Who is this woman?* He thought. *Where is my wife?* She should have been furious with him for ignoring her calls.

Instead, she was showing no signs of being upset. Well, he was not one to argue. Giving in, he captured her lips in a toe-curling kiss. Her moan brought an answering one from him. Lifting her off the floor, he dropped her unceremoniously on the bed where he joined her. Losing themselves in each other, the hours passed seamlessly one into the other.

Many hours later, Elron lay sated under Bet. She was draped across his chest with her hair tickling his nose. Too relaxed to move, he blew the offending strand away. Bet giggled, as she felt the slight breeze. Rising to her elbows, she took her weight off Elron and flicked her hair behind her.

Smiling down at him, her eyes were softened with her love. Elron felt blessed. There was no other way to look at it. His son or daughter moved within her. Where their bodies touched, the rippling brought a tender smile to his lips. He caressed Bet's cheek, in awe that she was his.

"Bet, I have to go." He whispered.

"I know." She answered. "Just a minute more."

Bet lay down to cover his body with hers again. Her arms gripped him tightly, fear of what was to come breaking her calm. Her soft sigh escaped her in a tremor. Elron wrapped her in his arms, giving her all the time she required. After long moments passed in silence, she let him go. Getting to her feet, she held out her hand for him to take it. Elron slipped off the bed and took her in his arms. With her cheek pressed up against his chest, Elron could have stayed there forever.

"I will be back. This I promise you. You are my life, my reason." Elron spoke softly over her head.

"You better! I can't go on without you." Bet answered back.

Elron let her go, retrieving his clothes from where they had been discarded on the floor. Once he was dressed, he had no more words to give. Giving her a final smile, he faded from the room. Bet's eyes shimmered with unshed tears at his leaving.

He found himself back on the island he had left a little over a week before. The terrain had not changed. Bleak and overcast, the valley he arrived in was rain-soaked and frigid. As far as his eye could see, the Sidhe army spread out across the landscape. Prepared for battle, dressed in armor, they stood at attention facing the sea. They would remain in that alert position until their king or general issued orders.

Elron looked around for Asher, his king. In the distance, he saw a large tent situated on the hill rising above the valley. That was where he needed to go. Disappearing from his position, he materialized several yards away from the tent opening. He did not want the guards to attack him, fearing he was an enemy. Seeing him, they immediately blocked the entrance while unsheathing their swords. One of the men recognized him, and alerted the others to resume their positions.

He marched to the entrance, entering the large tent and finding the king and the general bent over a table, studying a map. Asher turned his head to see who had entered. Elron dropped to a knee in his king's presence. Ronan, the general, raised an eyebrow at the gesture.

"Stand up. You do not have to bow to me." Asher ordered Elron.

"Yes, Sire." Elron addressed the man, getting up from the floor. Now that they were in battle, Elron felt the need to act his station. Asher was his king.

"You either call me Asher or Dad. You are family." Asher returned his attention back to what the men had been looking at.

Elron was at a loss over being so ordered. He knew he would find it difficult to address the king so familiarly. Ronan tried in vain to hide his smile at Elron's discomfort. Giving him a pointed glare, Elron then ignored the other man, as he made his way to the table. On it, a map of the island was spread out with marks showing where their army was positioned. The Daimon army was positioned at the old port, where their main city had been located. It seemed the only plausible place they could launch their attack.

"Eliana has advised me of what you have learned. Ronan and I are at odds over where their attack will come from. Do you have any insights to add?" Asher fixed his stare on Elron.

The port was too obvious a place. The Daimon may be unruly,

but they were not stupid. They may not know he had heard their plans, but they would expect resistance nonetheless. Elron scanned the map, looking at alternatives. If he were to raid the island, he would come from above and push any threat into the sea. Elron pointed to the mountaintop to the east. He placed a tack on the map then drew a line to the coast lying further east.

"If I were planning an invasion, I would land there." Elron pointed to the marked coast. "From there I would travel over land to the top of this mountain. The summit gives a clear view over this area and down to the port. Their objective will be to drive us into the sea. From there we would offer no resistance."

Ronan was about to object when Asher raised his hand. The king studied the marks Elron had made. What Elron advised was more or less what he had been thinking. They could protect both options. If they turned half their forces to the east, the other half could still keep watch over the port. Their army numbered in the thousands. The Daimon could not afford to match their numbers. Their race was dwindling.

"Ronan, half to the east, half to the port. We conceal ourselves. Watch, but give no signs that we are present. Let them come in thinking no one is here. Elron, I give command of the forces facing the east to you. Ronan, you command the rest. Let us prepare, for in the morning we are at war." Asher stated.

Chapter 7 - Tory

He tried very hard not to stare at the behind that swayed provocatively in front of him. Rina had insisted on taking the steps first. Forgoing her usual long flowing dresses, she wore tight-fitting, low-rise jeans, with the tiniest camisole he had ever seen. Leaving nothing to the imagination, her curves were outlined for everyone to see. Her exposed skin was everywhere.

Each step up, pulled the waistband of her jeans down, exposing the cleft of her behind. Tory's perspiration had nothing to do with the temperature. Ignoring what he glimpsed in front of him grew impossible. His eyes could land nowhere but on her. Tory may not have been an innocent when it came to women, but Rina was way out of his league. He should not be imagining her in his arms, beneath him. His body hardened at the mere thought of what he would like to do with her.

In just a few months, he had matured beyond his years. He had lost his humor, his naïveté. As if in response, his body filled out with well-formed muscles that flexed and extended with his movements. His face had lost its youthful appearance. A strong jawline, chiseled cheeks replaced his fresh-faced innocence. Since finding out he had been placed with the Sidhe for some unknown reason, he had struggled to comprehend who he was.

Everything was a mess. Tory was five-hundred-and-sixty-three-years old. In all that time, he thought he had belonged somewhere. His family, those who had raised him, his brother Elron, were not related to him. Tory belonged nowhere. He was foundering. Looking for answers had brought him there, following Rina up the seemingly never-ending steps. Her presence made it impossible for him to concentrate on anything other than her. Having her near, envisioning her lying naked in his arms, consumed him.

"Are you all right back there?" Her voice snapped him out of his fantasies.

"Mmm…" Was all he could muster in response.

The spiraling, rock-carved steps he climbed were steep and slippery from the early morning dew. Tory had one hand on the mountain wall to his left, the other he used to balance himself so as not to drop off the edge. They were about a thousand feet above the ground and they still had another seven-hundred-and-twenty feet to go. The view would have been awe-inspiring if there had been time to stop and enjoy it. Keeping one foot moving in front of the other took all his concentration. Maybe not all of it. Rina remained impossible to ignore.

The island of Santorini with its horseshoe shape, spread out below the ridge he was climbing. The center of it had collapsed into the sea from a volcanic eruption over three-thousand-years before. Its tallest mountain, Profitis Ilias, was a popular hiking destination. Tory had no idea why they were climbing it that early in the morning. He could have easily transported them where they needed to go.

Dawn had hardly broken when Rina had woken him from his sleep. Sometime during the night, he had kicked of his sheets and lay naked atop the bed. Well-defined muscles were slack in their repose.

Opening his door, she cast a look inside to make sure he had awakened.

He should have been embarrassed, should had covered himself, but for some reason he froze under her stare. *Did I imagine an interest?* Tory was pulled away from coming up with an answer by his foot slipping on a step. He righted himself before he lost his balance. Looking down, as stones cascaded down the mountainside, the ground rose up to meet him as vertigo developed.

"Tory, do you need help?" Rina had stopped her climbing.

"I'm fine. Let's keep going." He avoided looking at her.

After a moment, Rina resumed the climb up and Tory followed. Keeping his eyes on the steps, he attempted to clear his mind. Counting the steps occupied him until they finally reached the top. An old monastery, its walls cracked and crumbling from past earthquakes, sat atop the mountain. Rina continued to its central courtyard. There she sat on one of the stone benches, waiting for him to join her. They were alone. *What are we doing here?*

They had left Deis-dé two days before. Rina had been trying to communicate with her mother for most of the first day. As night fell, they sought shelter at a hotel in Athens. *Why Athens?* That was another question he had received no answer to. Rina asked him to transport them there without explanation. She used her wiles with the night concierge to procure them a suite with two bedrooms. Seeing the man lean closer to her, an irrational anger slammed into Tory.

Before he could act, Rina moved next to him, hooking her arm through his. She led him into the elevator, where an uncomfortable silence descended. Exiting onto the twenty-first floor, Rina led him to their rooms. There she left him without a word. She went into her bedroom and closed the door softly. Tory stared at it for close to five minutes before he retired to his own.

In the middle of the night, he awakened to voices outside his room. Their pointless whisperings were unnecessary, as Tory could hear their entire conversation. Rina related Eliana's request that the gods not interfere with what they were doing. Her mother shared how the gods were in an uproar.

Rhea's recent actions, allowing Meredith to speak with Alexa, had not gone over well with the other gods. That Meredith bequeathed her powers to Alexa had incensed many. They were split into three groups: those who wanted to help, those who wanted to stop Alexa at any cost and those who could not care less. Rina begged her mother to intervene, to do something, anything.

Tory got out of bed, disturbed by the tone of Rina's voice. He had never seen or heard her so frightened. The sound of him opening the door stopped their conversation. When he walked into the living area, the two women gawked at him. It took him a moment to realize he stood before them naked.

Rushing back into his room, he grabbed his jeans and slipped them on. He breathed out before returning to them. Rina's mother held back laughter at her daughter's blush. Rina glanced anywhere but at Tory. For some reason, it pleased him to see the faint flush on her cheeks.

"Come. Join us." Her mother smiled at him.

Moving to the armchair across from them, Tory sat down. Both women were on the elegant paisley-covered couch, their legs folded under them. Rina gripped a yellow throw pillow across her chest, her fingers toying with the seam. *Is she nervous?* Tory cleared his throat to get her attention. Once her eyes turned to him, his breath caught at the shy, uncertain look she gave him.

"Rina." Her mother spoke. "There is not much I can do. Unless..."

"Unless what?" Tory asked, breaking eye contact with Rina.

He focused on Rina's mother, who took the pillow away from her daughter. Rina had unraveled enough thread from the seam to create a small hole. Putting her finger under Rina's chin, her mother lifted her daughter's head to look at her face. She must have seen something there because she laughed out loud. The reaction it elicited from Rina was instantaneous. She angrily pushed her mother's hand away, turning away from being studied.

"Excuse me, unless what?" Tory interrupted the two.

Rina's mother controlled herself, patting Rina's shoulder. Returning to what they had been discussing, she answered Tory.

"Unless I get my father involved." She stated.

Rina jumped to her feet in response. She looked livid for some reason. Her mouth opened to speak, then quickly snapped shut. Shaking her head, she stalked out of the room, entered her bedroom and slammed the door shut. Tory sat stunned. Her mother snorted. The door to the bedroom opened again. From the doorway, Rina looked about to say something. Exasperation kept her unable to speak. Her hands fisted, her body shook. She turned around and slammed the door closed again. Tory stared at the shut door, not knowing what to make of Rina's reaction. He turned to Rina's mother, hoping she had an explanation. If he recalled correctly the woman's name was Melia.

"This might take a while. Yes, that is my name. How wonderful you know it." The other woman told him. "Tell me about yourself."

Tory did not know what to do. *Is Rina all right? Why is she so angry? Who is Melia's father?* Melia waved her hand in front of his face, snapping her fingers to get his attention.

"You're not fully Sidhe." Her softly voiced statement made him turn her way, intrigued by what she might offer as an explanation.

"No, I'm not sure what I am." He answered her.

He kept one eye on the closed door, worried about Rina. The fact that she had said not fully Sidhe was not lost on him. *Does that mean I do somehow belong to my adopted family*? He leaned forward in his chair, curious over what she might tell him. *Can she help me figure out who I am? Could it be that I share parts of myself with the people who raised me*?

"Mmm, you do have a smidgen of Sidhe in you. Some parts warlock. Surprising. It is rare that the two ever mix. The rest seems to phase, distorting. I have only ever heard of this once, so many years ago. It will come to me." Melia was studying him like a lab rat.

"You will not contact your father. There must be another way." Rina had reappeared in her doorway. Once she uttered her statement, she slammed the door shut again. The interruption pushed away any questions he would have asked. His eyes narrowed on the shut door, unsure what to make of Rina's actions.

"Why is she so angry?" Tory wanted to know.

Melia shrugged her shoulder. She patted the couch seat next to her for him to go over. Once he was seated, she took his hand in hers. A puzzled expression covered her face. He never found out what it was that bewildered her. Rina came out of her room, stomping over to where they sat.

"Why him, why grandpa?" She muttered.

"My dear, I think he can help." Her mother told her. "Now, your friend here needs you. Try to be gentle with him. I like him very much."

Melia released Tory's hand while rising to her feet. She straightened her stark- white, pearl-buttoned shirt, smoothed out her pleated rose-colored skirt before gliding over to her daughter. Facing Rina, she placed her palm on her cheek. Tory could tell they were communicating. Rina raised an eyebrow at what her mother told her. She tilted her head to the side, turning skeptical eyes on Tory. Unnerved at the force of her stare, Tory broke eye contact with Rina. Melia, having said all she had to say, removed her hand from Rina's cheek and backed away from her daughter.

Once she put distance between them, she started to glow brightly while her body started to shrink. Tory shielded his eyes from the piercing light, watching as Rina's mother's feet left the floor. Melia ascended towards the ceiling, her body shrinking, losing its form. When she hovered but a foot from the ceiling, she transformed completely, creating a single point of light that whisked by him.

Out the window she went, floating upwards to join the night

stars. Tory found himself alone with Rina, wondering what they had discussed about him. She gave him no answers that night. She simply told him to get some sleep and went back into her room. At least that time she did not slam it.

And now there they were on top of a mountain. Rina awakened him from a deep sleep, ordering him to follow her with no explanation. The knock on his door had woken him from an intense dream, one that inevitably featured her. He could vividly recall the feel of her. Locked in a passionate embrace, their lips touching, Tory was harshly brought back to reality. When she called out again, he could only mumble that he was up. He had to stop the thoughts of her. Rina could not possibly view him in that way, after all. She still had not told him why she had brought him there. He could tell she was hiding something from him. *What did her mother tell her? Will she ever be straight with me?*

"It won't be long. We just have to wait." She turned her face away so he could not see her expression.

Tory rose from the bench, leaving her side. He strolled over to the fountain in the courtyard. Walking around it, his irritation started to develop into full-blown annoyance. He hated being in the dark. Most of all he hated being lied to. He knew she had brought him there for a reason. *Why keep it secret? What is the purpose of us being here this morning?* Glancing at her, he saw she was studiously avoiding looking at him. She was tense, nervous. *Should I be worried?*

"Why are we here, Rina?" Tory faced her across the distance.

She still would not look at him. No answer came to his question. Shaking his head, rolling his eyes in exasperation, he took a step towards her. He would force an answer out of her if it was the last thing he did. Anger rapidly grew to replace his annoyance. Hearing his footsteps, Rina finally looked at him.

In her eyes he saw a mix of emotions. Pain was the predominate one. *Did I do something to cause it?* Uncertainty was the next impression he got from her. As quickly as he identified the baffling emotions, her demeanor changed, resuming her usual serene expression. *Did I imagine it?* She even offered him a slight smile. Tory blew out a heavy breath. Exasperated yet again, he resumed his walk around the fountain.

"They're here." Rina spoke, rising from her seat.

Tory saw no one. *Who is here?* He halted his steps on hearing her speak. He scanned the area, but there was no other person present. Then, out of nowhere, time seemed to still. Rina appeared to be moving in slow motion. Where there had been just him and Rina on the mountaintop, two other people were standing near her. They appeared to phase in. Their bodies winked in and out before fully materializing. Once they were fully in view, time resumed its normal path. A man and a woman were gazing at him. It was the man that spoke directly to him.

"We are Conall and Elethea. We have come to take you home."

Chapter 8 - Alexa

Jasper led us towards the main archway that gave way to the interior of the castle. Passing under the twenty-foot-high, gray-stoned arch, we found ourselves in a large, empty ante-chamber. At the far end, in front of me, a heavy red curtain blocked the way into what could only be the main hall. On the right side of the room, the same gray stone constructing the castle's walls was used on stairs, which swept up to the second floor landing.

 Scents of jasmine, mixed with others I could not identify, seemed to cling to the air. A memory rose in my mind of my mother. She often smelled of a similar mix of scents during the summer solstice. I did not dwell on the memory, as my eyes wandered around the space, taking note of the room's features.

Looking up, I was filled with wonder at what I saw. A clear glass dome overhead gave a pristine view of the twinkling night stars outside. I could make out some of the constellations that filled the cloudless sky. My eyes tearing from the beauty of it, I looked around to view the rest of the space.

Along the walls of the rectangular room, flaming lanterns gave enough light to see the mosaic tiles of the four elements arranged in the center of the floor. The tiles forming each of the four elements were made up of the colors that identified them. Green for earth, yellow for air, red for fire and blue for water. The circular border that surrounded the emblems was a patchwork of shiny black stones. Varying sizes and tints of blue-gray flagstone covered the remainder of the floor.

I had no further time to examine the other intricacies of the ante-chamber. While I took in the marvel of the entrance, my parents and Jasper had continued to make their way to the main hall. For a moment I forgot what we were there to do. Standing in the center of the entrance hall with Aidan, who faithfully remained by my side, it was not difficult to sense his unease at our being within those walls. He held himself rigid, ready for anything. He had questions. So many of them. I lifted the wall around my mind a little bit higher to block the cacophony of his thoughts.

The answers to his questions would have to wait. As much as I would have liked to reassure him, there was no time. I offered him a smile, placed my hand on his arm and gently tugged at him to follow the others. We reached them quickly, where they were stopped in front of the red velvet curtain.

We lined up behind Jasper, waiting for him to guide us into the next room. Aidan came alongside me, taking my hand once he reached me. Placing a soft kiss on my knuckles, he returned my grin once our eyes met. Promises lay between us. We had so much to discuss, so much time to make up for. Regretfully, I was once again reminded that it would have to wait. Mom cleared her throat to alert me to what Jasper was doing.

Facing the heavy curtain, Jasper passed his hand in front of it. A pinkish thin current of energy left his finger, drifting towards the velvet covering. The vapor the energy created slowly traced the symbol of a five-pointed star in front of the fabric. Once the pendulum was complete, the pinkish hue transformed into a brilliant crimson, matching the shade of the curtain. It blazed brightly for a mere second before the outline of it completely exploded away. I stared at the fabric magically pulling back on itself, folding in pleats, opening the way for us to enter.

Squaring my shoulders, preparing for what lay ahead, I readied to face the attendees inside. The signatures of those in the next room, I could sense, were many. With little difficulty, I differentiated the energies of each individual present. Jasper passed through the opening first, followed by my parents. I stepped through the entranceway, entering into a vast room, where dozens of witches and warlocks waited for us.

Their thoughts immediately bombarded me. Some were pleased, some were anxious. Others were fearful of what I represented. With a mere glance, I identified each one's elemental power. Jasper moved past me, brushing by me from where I had stopped, blocking the way of my parents and Aidan. Behind me, I could feel their nervousness. They were all apprehensive about facing the assembly.

Stepping out from behind a group of witches, a delicate-faced young woman came forward. She exuded power. Water. I saw the flow of her energy spike, as she approached me. She came to within feet of me before stopping. Keeping some distance between us, her bluish-hued eyes were glued to mine. Her hand slowly raised to reach out and touch my arm.

Once she had her fingers on my skin, she enveloped me in a calming wave of soothing relief. Accepting her energy while she studied me, I observed her, intrigued by the aura she emitted. Shades of blue covered her from head to foot. She was a fair bit shorter than I was. Auburn waves of hair fell to her waist, framing her unlined pale face.

She removed her hand on sensing my returning calmness. Next to her, a young man, at least a foot taller than her, regarded me with interest. Fire. His spark was strong, but his powers were much weaker than hers. Where she was diminutive and fragile looking, he was immense and brawny. Their relationship was easy to ascertain. He was her husband. I wondered how she did not douse the flames I saw running through his veins with the amount of water she controlled. Aidan, who had stepped next to me while the woman touched me, lightly touched my arm. *It's fine, they are no threat.* He relaxed slightly on hearing my thoughts.

"Welcome. My name is Rydia and this is my husband, Blayze." Her melodic voice hushed the room. "Please join us." Her hand beckoned me to follow.

The train of her sea foam colored dress trailed behind her as the people in the room stepped aside, clearing the way for her to glide to the end of the hall. She made her way to a massive rectangular oak table that was set with platters of food. The dinnerware was plain white, with gleaming silver utensils arranged around the dishes. Crystal stemware glasses were filled with wine. I saw water jugs appear suddenly at intervals along the expanse of the table. There were forty red velvet upholstered dining chairs around it.

Rydia reached the far end of the table and took a seat to the right of the head of the table. Her husband sat on the opposite side facing her.

Aidan fell into step next to me, as I followed them. My mom and Rider trailed behind us. I lost track of Jasper, and had no idea where he had disappeared to.

Aidan pulled out my chair as I sat, then made sure I was comfortable before finding his own seat across from me. His eyes never strayed from me. Prepared for anything, he was ready to jump over the table to protect me. I watched his eyebrow raise at my attempt to hide a smile. Lowering my head, from the corner of my eye, I saw my mom sit down next to me. Her hands were clenched together in her lap, her body stiff and her face inscrutable. Rider, who took the chair next to Aidan, did not look any more comfortable in the surroundings. I knew we were waiting for someone, as the head seat was not yet occupied.

Around me, the other witches and warlocks approached the table, their eyes studying me as they each sat. They could not hide their suspicions or their distrust. I tried to block their thoughts, to still my mind from their many questions. One of the witches in particular was making me uncomfortable. When our eyes met, her cold stare challenged me to respond.

Kesia, that was her name. She exuded strong earthy powers. Her dark brown hair was rolled up in a bun atop her head. Sharp features marked her oval face. Her eyes, the color of moss, were glaring at me. I tore my eyes from hers, refusing to acknowledge the hatred I felt from her. What had I done to elicit such a response?

Silence fell around the table. I kept my gaze on the tabletop, feeling theirs focused solely on me. Clenching my fists, I fought back the energy that wanted to make its presence known. It would not do to have them even more unsure of me. Struggling to regain my equilibrium, I was thankful when my mom took my hand under the table. Her power flowed through me, calming my errant emotions. Under control again, I heard a shuffling of footsteps coming from the other end of the room. My mom squeezed my hand to reassure me, then released it. Her head turned to watch the person coming nearer.

Her emotions slammed into me. She sat with her back straight, her hands folded on her lap, holding her breath. I turned my own head to see who had caused the deep upset within her. I tried to figure out why my mom suddenly fought to hold back resentment. The person I caught sight of was hooded, unidentifiable. Whoever they were, my mom was not pleased to be in their company. That it was a man was obvious. He progressed slowly to the head of the table, limping profoundly. His left leg seemed to drag behind him as he advanced. Once he was seated, his hood was pulled back to reveal someone I never thought to see again.

"We may start. Rydia, please commence." My long-thought-dead grandfather spoke. He ignored both me and my mom's presence, staring ahead unblinkingly.

I glanced at my mother, who refused to meet my eyes. Why had she told me her father was long gone? I now realized she never said he had died, just that he was no longer with us. I only ever saw pictures of him. He was never a part of my life.

His presence there threw me. I did not know what to do with the information. He had not looked at me once since sitting down. I sensed nothing from him. His signature, thoughts, emotions were all completely hidden from me. He faced forward, wrinkled and gaunt, ignoring his daughter. She must have known he would be there. Why did she not warn me?

"Thalia has come with a request for the council. Before we begin, I would like to welcome Aidan and Rider. We have not had representatives from the Sidhe in our council chamber for centuries. I hope this will be a new cooperative beginning for our two races." Rydia inclined her head, while looking directly at Aidan.

Aidan nodded at Rydia. My grandfather scowled at her remarks. His left eye twitched slightly. Rydia went on as if she had not taken notice. I went to stand, to confront him, but my mom grabbed my elbow to stop me. She subtly shook her head for me to stop.

"Thalia, the floor is yours." Rydia stated.

Mom took a moment before rising to her feet. She steeled herself for what lay ahead. I could feel Rider tense beside her. Mom schooled her face into neutrality, showing none of the conflict inside her. Once on her feet, she looked everywhere but at her father. I resented his attitude. What had my mother done to deserve his scorn?

"Thank you, Rydia. I will not speak for long. Our request is a simple one. You all are aware of what Elsam has begun. If we do not join with the Sidhe in this battle, all we hold dear will be lost. Elsam has the Daimon and shadows working with him. Releasing them, unhindered, on earth will be devastating to all of us. I have come here to request that the council agree to have witches and warlocks join in the fight. Only together can we overcome the death and destruction that is sure to come." Thalia sat once she had finished speaking.

Rider winked at her when she was back in her seat. Having him there greatly bolstered her, and I knew she was grateful for his support. Everyone around us broke into argument over what must be done. From wanting to help, to choosing to stay out of it, they all voiced an opinion. I waited for an opening to speak. They had to be made aware of what would happen if they did nothing. What I foresaw was death and destruction. There would be none of us left alive if Elsam stayed unchecked.

"Enough!" My grandfather's voice boomed to silence everyone. "We have heard their request, now we must vote. I cast mine as a No. We cannot get involved in Sidhe affairs."

Stunned at his pronouncement, I simply stared at him. Could he not see what their staying on the sidelines would do? He was in the process of standing when he froze in mid-action. I could not help it. Instinctively, my power wrapped around him, stilling his movement. I had heard enough. I rose to my feet to address them all.

"This is not a Sidhe affair. This involves all of us. Do not think that Elsam will leave any of you alive. He cannot afford to have anyone oppose him. He will come for you." I tried to reason with them.

"And what will you do then? Will you rule over all of us? Do you think we do not see the power that has been bestowed on you?" The woman Kesia accused me.

"I have no wish to rule. I just want my life back." I fought back the anger building in me.

They all regarded me as if I had sprung a second head. Did they not realize that I wanted to find an end to this nightmare and reclaim my life? I had no wish to lead these people. I wanted to get as far away from them as possible. My grandfather mumbled something from his frozen position. Chagrined at what I had done, seeing the fury in his eyes, I released him.

Sitting back down, I waited for them to start arguing again. Grandfather's cold stare settled on me once he took his seat. I kept my eyes on Aidan across from me. His lopsided smile almost made me giggle. His thoughts transmitted to me. *Try not to frighten them too much, Alexa.* The corners of my lips twitched, as I struggled to control my smile. To gain some control, I resumed listening to the council arguing heatedly over what to do.

"I for one will be voting Yes." A regal-looking woman spoke. Her name was Solana and her aura was a pure white light. Her mastery of the air element was impressive. She was tall, lithe, had platinum-blond, short-cropped hair and was absolutely stunning. Her icy blue eyes were trained on me.

"I too will be voting Yes." Rydia added.

My grandfather was flummoxed at being overridden. He looked to Kesia to vote his way. She appeared to be debating how to answer. At the other end of the table, another woman captured my attention. Her fiery red hair was a sign of which element she controlled. Fire breathed life into her. Her name was Nyria. I saw a blood-orange, heated, aura flame around her. Her thoughts until then had been quiet, but were full of a need to fight now. I knew which way she would be voting. Only my grandfather and Kesia stood in our way.

"Caden, we must fight." Was all Nyria said to my grandfather.

Now it lay with Kesia, and what she decided. My grandfather would have no choice but to accept the council's verdict. The vote had to be unanimous. Kesia was still undecided. Her worry lay in what I would do, what I was capable of doing. I felt a twinge of jealousy in her. She was put out that the goddess allowed Meredith to give me her powers. Being attuned to the earth, she felt it should have been her. I would have gladly traded places with her.

"It may already be too late. The battle has begun. The Daimon have struck hard on Eruva. Your island is overrun by them." Caden, my grandfather, spoke.

Chapter 9 - Elron

Sleep did not come for Elron, who lay on a cot inside Asher's immense canvas- wrapped tent. With enough space to allow ten men to sleep, plus a section for their meetings, only he seemed to be awake within the chilly interior. Soft snores escaped the men closest to him. Behind a draped enclosure, a few feet away from him, the king himself breathed heavily, blissfully lost to dreams. Every now and then a muffled snort escaped him.

Where Elron's cot was unwelcoming, uncomfortable and hardly big enough for his frame, Asher lay on a double mattress with an elaborately carved headboard made from maple wood. Under the two blankets and royal crest-embroidered comforter, the man made Elron wish he too could be slumbering in such splendor. With the heavy curtains around the king's bed pulled shut, blocking his view, he left it to his imagination to picture Asher in his bed, serenely dozing while his own mind raced.

He felt it in his bones. The time would soon be upon them. Seconds trickled by, while he listened for the sound of marching steps. The Daimon were somewhere out there. Their Sidhe scouts reported the docking of the longboats to the east of the island, as he had predicted. They stayed long enough to watch the large contingent of Daimon fighters disembark. The numbers in their force were larger than Elron had anticipated. The Sidhe fighters, long without battle, were nervous and uncertain of the upcoming fight. Elron would have to guide them, embolden them. His men were strong warriors.

Why are the Daimon holding back? It had been hours since their arrival. Elron had expected them to attack quickly. It was unlike them to hold back. *Why the wait? Are we being spied upon? Are they looking for a weakness in our defenses?* Asher ordered more men to face the east. The port to the west was being protected by a quarter of their forces. Elron was second-guessing the decision. He had an uneasy feeling about it. If they were hemmed in on both sides, they would lose any advantage. He had no reason to believe the Daimon were planning something so elaborate. They did not have any skills in strategizing. But, the feeling of something not being right would not leave him.

"I can hear your mind spinning in my dreams, Elron." Asher pulled the drapes aside, exposing the bed and its tangled bedsheets.

Knowing any attempt to get further rest was impossible, Elron sat up on his cot. His bare feet landed on the cold, hard ground. Grabbing his boots, he pulled them on, and stood to meet Asher. The king had already made it to the table, and was holding the map they had been perusing earlier in his hands. *How can I explain the trepidation I feel?*

His senses were screaming of approaching danger. Every one of his nerve endings were warning him of something. He had no idea of what. Maybe if he had Alexa there, she would know. As it was, he had to rely on himself to figure it out. The powers he had inherited were new and unknown to him. His mastery over them was almost non-existent. Elron's abilities were still governed by instinct. His instinct right now was telling him they were in deep trouble.

"I have a bad feeling. I just wish I knew what it meant." Elron addressed Asher.

Asher threw the map back on the table and motioned for Elron to follow him. Together, they stepped out of the tent, walking a few steps to the base of the closest hill. Somewhere out there, the Daimon were watching them. Elron's skin tingled in awareness of their presence. His eyes searched the summit of the hill for any sign of them. Not seeing anyone, he turned to speak to Asher.

"They are there, up over the hill. I can sense them. Why have they not attacked?" Elron asked.

Asher scanned the hill with his eyes. There was no easy answer to Elron's question. Eliana had not given him any indication on how the attack would come. The Kaemorra did not show her anything that would help them. He tried reaching out to her, to communicate with her, but he was met with a wall blocking him. The Daimon had blanketed the area with their shields. They were on their own.

"What are your senses telling you, Elron? Why the apprehension?" Asher asked in return.

Elron could not point to one thing in particular. If he had to go with his gut, he would turn their forces back towards the port. Asher was waiting for a response from him. The arrival of Ronan, their general, stopped what he was going to say.

"Sire, a scout has returned with information." Ronan waited for Asher to return to the tent.

Elron needed to hear what the report was. They all returned to the tent, entering to find a young, fresh-faced scout waiting. Asher found a chair and pulled it over to the table filled with maps and documents. Once seated, he waved at the scout to report. Elron did the same as Asher. Once he too was seated, the young man spoke of what he had seen.

"Sire, the Daimon forces have split. I saw three barges carrying off half their men. They rounded the island where I lost sight of what direction they went. If I had to guess, I think they went south." His out-of-breath voice told them.

Elron did not have to guess where they were headed. They must have seen their men turn towards the east. Rising from his seat, he hastily ran out of the tent, down the slope of their camp and stared out at the inlet of the port. His breath left him, as three barges rounded the curve, sailing towards the shore. He turned back to the tent, seeing Asher standing with Ronan at the entrance. Before he could make it back, a battle cry erupted from the hilltop. Thousands of Daimon filled the hillside. Ronan wasted no time grabbing his battle horn from where it hung at his side, bringing it to his lips and blowing the alarm.

Sidhe warriors responded instantly, readying for battle. In their glinting armor, their swords in hand, they took up their positions to meet the attacking enemy. Elron yelled orders at his men to split up. They had to guard both sides. The Daimon meant to box them in. From the hilltop, Daimon rained down the slope. In no particular formation, they came down in a mad rush. Elron kept his eyes on the shore, where the barges were spewing out additional Daimon. So many of them.

Elron judged that their enemy's forces more than matched their own. It would be a long day. He steeled himself for the work that lay ahead. Unsheathing his sword, he braced himself, as the first wave of Daimon reached their camp. From the corner of his eye, he saw Asher re-enter the tent with Ronan. The two men had planning to do. The elite guard posted to the king took position around the tent, protecting him with their lives if need be. Elron had only the fight to deal with.

Quickly dispatching the two Daimon who had reached him, Elron yelled at his men that they only had to scratch the Daimon. Their sword's enchantment would do the rest. Nicking the arm of a Daimon who took a stab at him, Elron watched the hideous scaly body of the man evaporate into a dark billowy cloud. The wind then did the rest, dispersing the essence of the Daimon back into the hell it had come from.

All around him, other Daimon were also being destroyed. The field was covered with their unholy blackened vapor. Surprised at their numbers, Elron was engrossed in fighting the Daimon coming at him from all sides. He did not see Manar, the Daimon prince, step off a barge and make his way to him.

The young scout who had given them his report minutes before was surrounded by five Daimon. He was able to get his sword in contact with two of them, before a Daimon positioned behind him, and stabbed him through the heart. The shocked eyes of the young Sidhe found Elron's. Elron could do nothing but watch the Sidhe fall to his knees, watch uselessly as the essence of his life left him, taking his body from that plane to the next. One moment he was there, the next his body vanished, as if he had never existed.

Elron wasted no time in dwelling on the man's death. His forces were being overtaken by the Daimon. There were too many of them. His arm swung his sword at anything near him. Cutting through the enemy, he managed to clear his way back towards the tent. Asher needed to be evacuated.

He did not see the knife that cut into his sword arm. The suddenness of it caused him to drop his sword, as pain shot up and down his arm. Whirling around, unarmed, he faced the Daimon who had wounded him. Ducking out of the way of the blade he saw coming down at him again, he used his shoulder as a battering ram to drive the Daimon back. His sword was lying out of reach on the ground. The two men faced each other, assessing each other's strength.

Elron recognized Manar, and the deadly intent in his eyes. He needed to reach his sword. Manar gave him no opportunity to make it to where it lay. Elron was forced to back up, away from the advancing steps of the Daimon. A triumphant sneer formed on what appeared to be Manar's mouth. The jagged teeth showing through his mouth hole were sharp and stained with blood.

"It is time to meet your maker." His slithering voice threatened.

Manar was a foot away from Elron. He made a stabbing motion towards Elron's torso. Elron managed to avoid the serrated blade. Jumping back, he landed unbalanced on the dead grass at his feet. He lost his footing, falling hard on his back. Manar was on him in a second. Elron had just enough time to grab the Daimon's arm before he could stab him again. Using all his might, he held onto the arm with both his hands. Manar growled, his foul breath almost causing Elron to draw back.

Struggling to free himself from under Manar, he threw his hips up to disengage him. The Daimon fell onto his own back. Elron jumped to his feet, looking for his sword. Seeing it, he attempted to bypass Manar to reach it. Manar was quick to wrap his arms around Elron's calves, forcing him down to his knees.

Manar's blade had missed him again. Seeing the attack coming, Elron barely had time to twist his body to the side at the last moment. Manar swore bitterly at missing his mark. His blade had embedded itself completely in the ground where Elron had been.

Using the opportunity, Elron dove to his sword, his hand wrapping around the hilt. Getting to his feet, he saw Manar struggling to remove his knife from the ground. Elron was almost upon him when the knife broke free. Like a raging lunatic, Manar launched himself at Elron. The two went down hard. A large rock slammed into Elron's back. He grunted in pain, his legs going numb.

Elron's badly injured arm throbbed. He barely managed to keep hold of his sword, but the effort cost him. His injury had worsened. The cut on his arm opened, exposing muscle and tissue. Manar wasted no time in lifting his blade and attempting to drive it into Elron's chest.

Only chance allowed Elron to avoid the death it promised. Manar was pushed off of Elron by another falling Daimon. Driven to the ground by the other Daimon, Manar growled in frustration. Elron rolled away from the two, putting distance between them. He saw a fellow Sidhe warrior stab the Daimon that had barreled into Manar. Its essence blackened the area, hiding Manar from his view.

Elron slowly, painfully got to his feet. His sword arm hung

loosely at his side. With blood seeping down his arm, he could barely hold onto his sword. The other Sidhe moved on to fight another Daimon. Beyond the clearing smoky cloud released by the dead Daimon, he saw Manar rise slowly to his feet.

The Daimon prince faced him from across the distance, his knife ready to do its worst. Elron kept his eyes glued on Manar, while he transferred the sword to his other hand. Lifting it to point at Manar, he waited for his attack. Manar snarled and ran full tilt towards Elron. Stepping out of the way, Elron's sword missed its mark. The two circled each other. Elron, pained from the wound on his arm, tried to keep vigilant, alert to Manar's next mode of attack. Unfortunately, it was at that moment Asher stepped out of the tent.

Elron saw glee take over Manar's face. The Daimon saw an opportunity, forgetting about Elron, who was slow and unsteady on his feet. Manar raced towards Asher, who had no time to respond to the threat. Elron chased after Manar, tried to intercept him, but the split second it took him to respond made it too late for him to stop the inevitable outcome.

He watched helplessly, shocked, as Manar drove his knife into Asher's chest. Time seemed to stand still. The king's eyes blinked, then blinked again. They lost their focus, as he fell listlessly to his side. Elron reached him, forgetting the danger Manar still posed.

Bending over Asher, he tried to stop the flow of blood from the gaping wound. His hands were drenched in crimson red from the lifeblood draining from his king. He saw his own life ending when a shadow fell over him, as Manar readied to drive his blade down into

Elron's back. Elron had no time to react. His hands were occupied in maintaining the pressure on Asher's wound. The fatal stab never came.

Manar was forced back by the arrival of Ronan. The general had exited the tent when Asher failed to return inside. Seeing the king bleeding, unconscious on the ground with Manar standing behind Elron, Ronan reacted without hesitation. Manar's knife was poised threateningly to drive into Elron. Ronan unsheathed his sword, rushing over to intercept him before he could harm Elron.

Manar had no choice but to focus his attention on the threat, and positioned himself to face the attack from their general. Ronan's blade sparked, as their two weapons came into contact. The two seemed poised to enter into a lethal battle where only one would emerge victorious.

Elron needed to do something to keep Asher safe, to move him for treatment. They did not have time for the battle to be over. His mind wished Manar and his men gone. The instant the thought entered his mind, the scene before him flickered. Elron saw the space where Manar stood become encompassed by a swirling portal. Ronan jumped clear, falling on his back and rolling away.

Unceremoniously, Manar was dragged into the opening, screaming his frustration. The battlefield was being emptied of Daimon, as they were all pulled into the twisting doorway to another location. When all Daimon were gone, just as suddenly as it had appeared, the portal snapped shut.

Ronan lay on the ground, his sword still in his hand, looking stunned at the Daimon's disappearance. He looked over at Elron, who simply shrugged. At times like these, he welcomed the powers he possessed, even if they were unpredictable. Elron returned his attention to Asher and his wound. There was not much he could do there. They had to get Asher back to Eliana. Elron would question how and why Manar vanished later. *Was it only my wish to have the Daimon gone, which had opened up the portal*? He would examine it at a time when he was not pressed to get his king to safety. For now, they only had one option.

"Get the men out of here! Retreat back to Loch Maree. Await instructions there. I will take Asher back to Deis-dé." He ordered Ronan.

Chapter 10 - Alexa

My grandfather's words, the unemotional ease with which he proclaimed the attack on Eruva, stunned me for a moment. Needing to know what was happening, I left my body in the crowded room, casting my mind to the battle that raged on Eruva, the Sidhe home world. Unmindful of the others around me, I left the room for what seemed like minutes. My mother later told me it had been well over fifteen. When I eventually returned to my body, I was still in the main hall of the castle, with the witches and warlocks keeping a watchful, unnerving eye on me. The warning of impending disaster had truly shaken me. I needed to see it for myself. I gave no thought, no warning, as I left the room in search of confirmation.

Floating high above the battle, the scene below played underneath me like a silent movie. The fight was going badly. Just as my grandfather warned, the Sidhe were outnumbered and outmaneuvered by the Daimon. The fighting raged on while the bodies of the fallen Sidhe held my attention. I saw hundreds of fallen Sidhe, their essences leaving their bodies, reshaping into ghostly images of their former selves.

They marched across the landscape, gliding towards an opening between our world and what I glimpsed as a separate kingdom. Through a haze, their spirits entered a world unseen to those still fighting around them. I watched them float towards the barrier that separated the worlds. On the other side, a pristine blue flowing river ferried them towards a shore where two tall warrior women stood aside to welcome them. The dead Sidhe climbed out, one by one, led by an armored fighter towards an enormous, towering temple that awaited them. I felt no fear in the men that fell in line, striding forward to the gold-leafed gates that lay open before them.

Tearing my eyes away from the scene, I looked down at the terrain below me. Daimon were everywhere. The hill above the Sidhe camp was overrun with them. From the port side, barges were releasing thousands more. In the middle of the fray, Elron was battling a Daimon unlike the rest. Immediately I knew who he was facing. The Daimon prince Manar was larger, fiercer than all the others. I sensed in him a viciousness, a trained killer who took pleasure in each and every kill.

Elron was wounded, weakened from his blood loss. I could not do anything to help him. Helplessly, I watched them face each other. Elron was not using his powers. He was unaware that with a mere thought all the fighting could be over. Warning him was beyond my ability. Because of my distance from him, all I could do was watch.

In shock, my eyes widened as I observed Manar's blade enter Asher. Shock, bewilderment covered Asher's features. His essence was close to joining his warriors in the other world. With his face etched with pain, he crumpled to the ground, unmoving. Barely breathing, Elron reached him, giving no thought to his own safety. He kept both his hands on Asher's wound, trying to staunch the flow of blood. Manar approached him from behind, seeing his opportunity. Only the arrival of Ronan saved Elron. Engaging Manar, Ronan was no match for the Daimon.

It would not be long before he was maimed as well. Elron could see the outcome as clearly as I. He finally made use of his abilities to dispatch Manar back to his barge. His expression was baffled. Elron had no idea where the Daimon went. Or for that matter, that it was he who had made the Daimon disappear. Ordering a retreat, he transported away with Asher, leaving Ronan to carry out his orders.

From my vantage point only death and destruction remained. Ronan communicated the ordered retreat to his men. I saw them all transport away to safety. Many lives had been lost. The remaining Daimon, disembarking from their ships, found their objective had been reached. I watched Manar and his other men reappear from wherever they had been sent by Elron. Celebrating their victory over gaining control of the abandoned island, Manar for some reason did not rejoice. He seemed to be fearful all of a sudden.

Returning back to my body, I shuddered at the losses we had incurred. It took me a moment to realize the hushed silence that had fallen over the room. Kesia was regarding me suspiciously. My grandfather, on the other hand, was studying me openly with a bemused expression. He seemed to be aware of what I had seen. It was the first time he had actually looked at me. I gave him a hostile look. Anger slammed into me at his unwillingness to help us. He had let it happen. He and Kesia to be precise. Their willful inaction had allowed the Daimon to take possession of the Sidhe home world. How many more had to die before they joined with us?

It was the immense distress, fear and fury I sensed in Aidan that tore me away from the rage overtaking me. He was half-leaning over the table, his hand tightly gripping mine. His expression bore the same emotions coursing through me. I realized he had made contact with me, touching my hand, the moment I left the room. That allowed him to see everything I had. He had seen his father get stabbed.

I could offer no assurance that Asher was going to make it. He may well be dead already. His wound was too close to the heart. Giving Aidan's hand a squeeze, I gently let go of him and lay both of my hands flat on the tabletop. I took a deep breath, the decision already made for me by those present. They would not help us, therefore we had nothing more to do there.

"We have wasted enough time. We need to go." I pushed my chair back to stand.

My mom followed my lead. She ignored her father, who reached for her. Aidan was by my side before I had a chance to take a step out of the room. Rider met my mother, whose face showed her scorn at her kind. Her fellow witches were frozen, unsure how to respond to my statement. I saw no need to try to convince them. They had more than voiced their opinions. I appreciated that some were willing to aid us, but the rest of them, I could do without. I would have to find another way to battle Elsam on my own.

Aidan joined me, draping his arm across my shoulder, walking with me towards the curtained doorway. His touch let me know how proud he was of me. I leaned into his side for support, wishing I could comfort him somehow. Even with being struck with worry over his father, he nonetheless pushed it aside to fortify me. The raised voices around the table, the arguing breaking out, did not stop me from leaving. We were at the exit when my grandfathered called out.

"Wait." He bellowed from across the room.

Aidan was the one to stop me. I would have kept going. I did not turn around to see what my grandfather had to say. The man had done nothing but irritate me since our arrival. I owed him no respect. His actions towards my mother, the hurt she tried to bury was more than enough reason to keep him at arm's length. I could feel his deep-seated hatred for my father. He was so much like Rider's mother, who hated my mom. What had my parents done but love each other?

"We have not finished." He said.

I slowly turned to face him. Burning rage colored my eyes red. He was standing, leaning over the table with his hands braced upon it. What I must have looked like, with my eyes flashing and my body quaking made him back down. He retook his seat, waiting to see what I would do. My mom's eyes caught mine. She subtly shook her head. She was right. We had no time for this. We had to get to Deis-dé, make sure Asher was fine and plan our next move. These people were on their own. I felt no loyalty to them.

Giving him no response, I turned away, resuming my original decision to leave. Aidan pulled the curtain out of my way, as we passed through the doorway. He held it long enough for my parents to pass. Dropping it back down, he followed me out of the ante-chamber to the courtyard outside. The drawbridge was a few feet in front of us. Before I could take a step onto it, Jasper appeared beside me, his hand grabbing onto my elbow. Aidan bristled at his touching me.

"Alexa, stubbornness is not what will get these people on your side." He removed his hand before Aidan could react.

"Jasper, you mean well, but these people believe they are above all the other races. They will not help unless it is for their own benefit. I cannot work with them. They will face the danger alone." I answered him.

He let me go. I could tell he was not pleased, but he did not block our way when I continued. Aidan and my parents stepped in beside me, as I continued over the drawbridge. Daylight was fast approaching. We had lost a whole night with the council. If only they could understand that we all had to work together, I would gladly have stayed. The races were more intertwined than they realized. I stopped at the opposite end of the drawbridge. Turning back to look at Jasper, I offered an olive branch.

"You know where we are going. If my grandfather has need of us, you can contact me there. I cannot promise anything, but know this, in order to survive, the races have to come together. There is not one that is above the other. Their very existence is because of the balance they all hold on the earth. If one race dies out, the rest will quickly follow." I imparted my warning.

Jasper inclined his head, acknowledging my words. Having said what I wanted, I transported all of us away. The fact that their protective shield was so easy for me to breach should have alarmed Jasper. Instead, I saw a pleased smile turn up the corners of his mouth. He knew all along that I had the ability to come and go as I wished.

The world around me faded, replaced by the main room of the manor in Deis-dé. My eyes were drawn to the oatmeal-colored rug now stained with copious amounts of blood. The deep red marks were still wet. Whose blood it was, I could not tell. It could be Asher's or Elron's. Both men were injured.

"I'll go find the others." My mom left the room, searching for anyone that might need her healing powers.

Rider went after her. Alone with Aidan, I wondered why he did not go looking for his father. He came to me instead, wrapping his arms around me. I held him onto him, burrowing into his arms, marveling that with all he had to deal with, he was comforting me. He pulled back to look into my eyes. The black specs in his were dancing, swirling furiously in reaction to our closeness. Slowly, gently, he brought his lips down to mine, giving me the sweetest, most tender kiss. As our lips parted, I gazed at him in wonder. Why had I fought him for so long? Hearing my thoughts, he smiled down at me.

"Go. Your dad needs you." I told him.

"In a minute. I just want to hold you a bit longer." His answer made me smile.

I let him draw me fully into his arms. With my cheek pressed up against his chest, I inhaled his familiar scent, luxuriating in the feel of him. My arms wrapped around his waist, holding him close. I sighed with contentment. Lifting my head, I stared into his beautiful emerald eyes, watching the ever-present black specks swirl within his pupils.

Passion, unexpectedly and thrillingly, exploded between us. Seized by a hunger I had never experienced, I clung to him. My fingers gripped the muscles on his back. He pulled me closer. His one arm was wrapped around my waist, supporting me, while his other brought his hand to the back of my head. With his fingers tangling in my hair, his lips descended, crushing into mine. Our tongues danced, stoking the fire between us. A moan escaped us. Whether it was mine or his, I could not tell. I wanted more. Dizzy with desire, my heart hammering in my chest, my hands found their way under his shirt, exhilarating in the way his back muscles tensed, rippling in response to my touch.

"Mmm… Can this wait?" Liam broke the spell. Unashamed, somewhat peeved at the interruption, I felt Aidan still under my hands.

Aidan's whole body tensed on hearing his brother. His eyes found mine, searching for any sign that Liam's presence had affected me. Finding nothing in my gaze, but the still smoldering desire for him, he turned his head towards Liam. He did not release me, but did move me to his side so that we could both see his brother. Liam looked like hell.

Unshaven, disheveled, he was ashen and edgy. His eyes darted around the room, unfocused. Aidan had no idea what Liam had gone through. He did not know that the shadow had possessed him, that he had been driven to try to kill me. Touching his mind with mine, I gave him an abbreviated version so that he would not be too hard on Liam. The two brothers needed each other. Especially now, with their father hurt.

"Liam." Was all Aidan said. I knew he heard my thoughts. He had questions, but pushed them aside.

"I need Alexa for a moment." Liam spoke. "Father is upstairs. He is not doing well."

Aidan was suspicious of what Liam wanted with me. He did not want to leave me alone with him. He had nothing to worry about. After what had just happened between us, I knew there was no one else for me but Aidan. My hand cupped his cheek. I turned his face towards me, so he could see into my eyes. Communicating with him that it would be all right, he finally left me to go see his father. I knew it was difficult for him to leave me alone with his brother. Distrust over Liam would take time to overcome. I sensed something in Liam I never felt before. Distress, guilt, uncertainty, heartache were fighting for dominance in him. There was also a smidgen of hope running through him.

"I need you to try to find someone." His strained voice asked of me.

I took a seat on the couch, waiting for him to continue. His expression went from hopeful to despairing. Of course, I would do anything I could to help him. I beckoned him over to sit beside me. Haltingly, he found his way to me, seating himself on the other end of the sofa. He was tense, making my nerves edgy over what was bothering him.

"Mara is alive. I have failed her." His anguished words confused me.

"Liam, start at the beginning. I can't help you if I don't understand." I asked him.

For the first time, Liam spoke of his mate. Hearing his tale, I listened to the details of how they had met and fell in love. It had been centuries ago, but his continued love for her could not be denied. What he thought he felt for me paled in comparison.

Liam had met Mara on an expedition to Norway. His mother

had sent him to retrieve an artifact she had lost there years earlier. She told him it was imperative it not fall into human hands. Charged with the mission, Liam went alone. He searched for days before finding himself near a village that did not appear on any of his maps.

Mara had stepped out from under the trees, her presence jolting him by his response. She was exquisite. Across the expanse of the open field between them, they stood frozen, their eyes glued to each other. In an instant he knew he wanted her. In the next breath he had to have her. Liam would have let no one stand in their way.

Captivated by her, he saw the same emotions seize her. How long they stared at each other across the distance, Liam could not say. Time had simply stopped for the two of them. In the space between them, threads of light stretched out. He saw them wrap around her, returning back to him to grab a hold of him. Liam knew what that meant. He met her mid-field. Afraid she was an illusion, he hesitated to touch her. It was her hand that made contact first. Holding his cheek, she took a step closer to him. Mesmerized, Liam just stood there, speechless, staring at her.

He spent years with her. From that moment on they were inseparable. Her village accepted him as their own. His mother's mission was forgotten. The time with Mara had been the happiest of his life. They married in the presence of the entire village. All that they built together came to an end ten years to the day later.

He was out hunting with Mara's father. Guilt at being absent from her, at her facing the danger alone, still ate at him. Their village was attacked mercilessly by some beings. They never found out who was responsible. When he returned to the smoldering remains of his home, a lone body lay charred beyond recognition in the living room.

He lost her essence. The remains had to be her. Why else would he have lost their bond? She was nowhere to be found. Pain. All he felt was unbearable pain. He left the village even though Mara's father wanted him to stay. He could not be around them, where every corner of the place held memories of her. He wandered for close to seventy years before returning to Deis-dé. There he remained for another twenty before reaching out to his mother. He never spoke of what he had lived through.

"Why do you think she is alive, Liam?" I had to ask.

He told me of how his mother had seen her through the Kaemorra. She was somewhere he could not find her. His only hope lay in my ability to see beyond our world. I was not sure I would be able to locate her. Even if I did, I had doubts we would be able to return her to our plane of existence.

"I'll do what I can for you, Liam. Do you have anything of hers that I can use to get a sense of her?" I needed something of hers to focus on.

Liam reached inside his pocket and drew out a ring. The elegant gold circle was inscribed in Sidhe. *Where you go so shall I.* The simple words brought tears to my eyes. I carefully took it from his fingers. The moment I touched it, a vision of a woman developed in my mind. Liam was right, she was beautiful. I closed my eyes, to follow the vision where it took me.

Chapter 11 - Solas

He had been searching for his mother for most of the morning. Vanya warned him the night before that she was going to attempt to communicate with Eliana. He fought with her over it. It was dangerous and foolhardy to think that Elsam would remain clueless to what they were up to. The man was becoming more paranoid with each hour that passed. Solas wanted to help Vanya in any way that was safe. There was no mistaking his intense dislike of his biological father.

The years since his release from prison had not softened Elsam. If anything, he had grown harder, more intractable. Solas had been avoiding his presence as much as he could. Fearful of what his father would do if he realized how much Solas hated him, the young man had been pretending to be occupied with strategy. How much longer he could keep his feelings in check he was not sure. It was making him jumpy. He lived in fear of when the end would come. For it was inevitable that Elsam would learn of their subterfuge.

The corridors of the tower were near to overflowing with Daimon. He did not trust them. Their eyes followed his every step, while he trudged the halls looking for Vanya. *Where could she be?* She was nowhere to be found. Solas rounded a bend and seeing that part of the corridor was empty, stopped to think. She had to be somewhere. He tried linking with her, to communicate. Only emptiness was his response. She must be keeping herself silent. Growing unease took hold of him.

"Well, young prince. What are you doing here alone?" Myrick appeared suddenly.

Solas watched the man come nearer. Myrick looked pale. Elsam was treating the warlock extremely poorly lately. Since Aidan and Alexa's escape, Elsam had blamed Myrick for allowing Aidan to regain enough strength to transport himself and Alexa away. Myrick in turn took it out on everyone around him. More than one Sidhe had been injured by the man. Elsam had no more use for Myrick. If he could have, he would have killed him outright.

Only the fact he held sway over the other warlocks kept Myrick alive. Elsam allowed him limited powers inside the tower's walls. His father had effectively rendered him useless. Even with his abilities in check, Solas knew Myrick was still a danger. Pretending to be unaffected by the warlock's presence, Solas tried to go around him. The other man moved to block his escape.

Solas, standing at six-foot-one inches, towered over the other man. His clear emerald eyes narrowed, trying to ascertain Myrick's motive for stopping him. A curl from his ebony hair fell to cover his right eye. Brushing it aside, he pulled to his full height trying to intimidate Myrick with his size. Sinewy muscles flexed, preparing to bodily remove the warlock from his way.

"Let me pass." Solas tried to inflect authority in his voice.

Myrick grabbed Solas's arm. His eyes narrowed, searching Solas's face. Solas kept his eyes steady, refusing to give the man any hint of how his touch nauseated him. He knew Myrick was trying to rankle him. Snatching his arm back, he tried again to get around the warlock.

Angry welts developed on his skin from Myrick's talon- long nails. Rubbing at the offending marks, he started to walk away.

"Young prince. Do you know where your mother is, I wonder?" Myrick sneered, a hollow laugh escaping him.

Solas stopped in his tracks. He took in Myrick's face, looking for a sign that he knew anything. His hands went clammy at what he saw. The warlock's face held a gleeful malice. Solas had to get away from him, to find out what had happened to his mother. He took off down the hall, away from the man who was laughing at his retreat. Urgency made him speed away. His last hope was to seek out his father, to see if he showed any signs of having harmed her.

His mother was the only person that ever truly loved him. Growing up, he had no idea who he really was. She made sure he lacked for nothing. Vanya provided a loving, stable home for him. Her work took her away a lot, but she made sure he had everything he could possibly desire. She hired tutors, made sure he had the best education, and hired the best fighters to train him. Whenever she was home, she devoted all her time to him.

The fateful day his world had fallen apart, she appeared to him with tears streaming down her face. It was then she had told him of his ancestry. Elsam had been released from his prison days earlier. Vanya had loved the man all those centuries he had been incarcerated. When he was free, after she told him of Solas's existence, Elsam blamed her for his capture and imprisonment. Her bruised face was evidence of how he had reacted.

Learning that Elsam was his father had stunned him. He knew

from his history lessons who he was. Vanya tried to reconcile the two, but Solas instantly became resentful of his father. He could not forget her tears, her bruises or the fear in her eyes.

On the run, having nowhere to go, when their island became visible, Solas had no other choice but to follow where Elsam went. His mother was too afraid to resist his father. When Elsam started plotting his rise to power, Solas listened, waited and came up with a plan of his own. If he could, he would find a way to rid the world of the menace Elsam represented.

Vanya warned him, tried to reason with him. He would not be swayed. When word came that three prisoners were captured, Vanya finally came round to his way of thinking. He saw her worry over the young woman that had been brought before Elsam. Crumpled on the floor, her eyes shut, Solas felt an affinity with the young woman. Bet, that was her name.

Vanya tried to help her. Solas questioned why his mother suddenly decided to go against his father. *Why for this woman?* His world was further altered at what she then related. Bet was his half-sister. Eliana, the queen, was his natural mother. He had two other brothers he knew nothing of. Staggering from the information, he had for a moment wondered where his loyalty lay. Vanya explained the circumstances that had brought him into her life. His own mother had abandoned him.

It took Vanya's faith in her queen to restore his resolve. Vanya hated herself for aligning with Elsam and betraying Eliana. Understanding the reasons why he was given to Vanya to raise, Solas gave his all to defeating his father. His chance meeting with his brother, Liam, trying to help when Alexa was captured, had further emboldened him. Liam had been as much in the dark as he had. Solas wanted to be acknowledged by his true family. Whether he lived or died, he wanted them to know he was on their side.

He had no opportunity to see Aidan. Elsam made sure to keep Solas away from his younger brother. While Aidan was held in the deepest dungeon, Solas had been ordered to keep away. Vanya tried to communicate with Eliana about Aidan's capture. Unable to reach her, Vanya kept an eye outside for anyone coming to rescue him. She made him promise that if anything happened to her, he would go find his family. He was unsure of how he would be received if he tried to reach the queen.

Pushing away the memories, Solas arrived at the great hall before he knew it. Sidhe warriors lined the walls, while Daimon shuffled around inside under their watchful eyes. He hated those beings. His father was a fool for thinking they were aligned with him. He scanned the room for Elsam. Trying to appear unhurried, untroubled, he strode towards the empty throne. His father was not present.

Solas was having a difficult time keeping his panic under control. He felt eyes following him towards the door hidden behind the throne. The Daimon were suddenly agitated, excited about something. From the corner of his eye, he saw the Sidhe warriors become alert, expecting an attack.

The door in front of him sprang open. His father stood before him, staring stoically back at him. He waved Solas aside, brushing by him to go to his throne. Solas was left to stare, disbelieving what his eyes were seeing. Inside the room, from what little the opening allowed, he saw blood dripping down the back wall. It pooled on the floor, creating a puddle of crimson gore. Pushing the door all the way open, he stepped into the room. On the floor, a body lay mangled. He slowly advanced further into the room, as if in a dream. His feet led him to the body of the woman who lay unmoving on the floor. His brain refused to acknowledge who it was.

Kneeling down, his fingers checked for a pulse. Finding none, he collapsed on his knees beside the dead woman. Vanya's open eyes stared unseeing back at him. Tears blinded him at finding her dead. Her arm lay in an unnatural position, twisted and broken. His hand shook when he gently shut her eyes. A tear rolled down his cheek, where it quivered on his chin, before dropping down to mix with her blood on the floor. Taking her hand, he brought it up to his lips and placed a soft kiss on it.

He silently prayed she had not suffered too much. Lifting her hand to his cheek, he held it there a moment, wondering how he could have let it happen. He should have been there to protect her. The coolness of her skin brought home that she was truly gone. An intense, blinding rage took hold of him. Kissing her hand again, he placed it back on her chest. He would avenge her death if it was the last thing he did.

Standing up, he breathed deeply to regain control of his emotions. He could not afford to let Elsam see how infuriated he was. Somehow he had to make him believe he was uncaring of her death. He made it back to the door, trying to contain the rage that boiled relentlessly over within him. His attempt made no difference, at that moment the arriving Daimon prince was taking up his father's attention. Manar stood at the other end of the room, bloodied and armed. His sword pointed at Elsam, who had risen to his feet.

"We shall have new terms, you and me." Manar crowed.

Elsam stepped down from his dais unconcerned. Solas would side with Manar, if it meant Elsam's demise. But, it would not solve all his problems. Joining his father, Solas stood beside him, watching and waiting to see what would happen. Manar approached them, sauntering steadily closer. His men, the other Daimon, fell behind him, as he neared Elsam. The Sidhe guards, in response to the danger, formed a line of defense in front of Elsam. Solas waited to see what his father would do. His bellowing laugh surprised Solas. Turning to his father, he watched while Elsam continued laughing.

"You fool. You have played well into my hands. Thank you for assuring the island was free of Eliana's troops." Elsam's words resulted in an immediate response from Manar.

Infuriated at Elsam's statement, the Daimon prince attacked full force. He ran towards Elsam, bringing his sword out of its sheath, aiming it at Elsam. His father, still laughing, easily avoided the pointed end of the blade. Solas unsheathed his own sword, prepared for the Daimon's attack. Manar kept his focus on Elsam. He did not pay attention to Solas at his rear.

Elsam was still laughing crazily at the mayhem that broke out. Sidhe and Daimon were locked in mortal combat. Manar went after Elsam, bypassing the group fighting in front of him. Elsam vanished from where he stood. Appearing next to Solas, he pushed his son towards Manar. Solas was at a disadvantage. He stumbled from being forced forward. Manar took a swipe at him. Missing his mark by inches, the Daimon prince prepared to take another stab at Solas.

Solas knew then his father was aware he had been working with Vanya. Elsam wanted him dead. If he prevailed over Manar, his death would come at his father's hand. There was only one course open to him. He had to escape. Avoiding the sword coming his way, he swiveled around to see his father. Their eyes met. Solas put all his disgust and venom in his stare. Elsam seemed thrown at the look his son gave him. Raising his sword, Solas pointed it at his father.

"What you have done will be avenged. By my hand, you will die." Solas shook with rage.

Elsam's expression changed to match his son's anger. He would have met him with deadly intent if not for Manar getting between them. The Daimon was torn over who to go after first. It gave Solas the opportunity he needed. He reached for the knife strapped to his side. Drawing it out, he threw it with precision at Elsam. He watched the blade cut through the air, its aim true.

At the last second before it found his father's heart, it fell away. Behind Elsam, Myrick had his hand aimed at Solas. A blue-toned current released from the warlock's hand. It never reached Solas. Solas was not there when it arrived where he had stood. Solas vanished, transported away. The infuriated screams of his father trailed after him through the darkness. The blast had passed through where Solas had been, destroying, obliterating his father's once majestic throne.

Chapter 12 - Tory

Tory remained rooted by the fountain, distrustful at the appearance of the two beings. Their proclamation that they meant to take him home almost drove him to transport away. Whoever these people were, Tory stubbornly refused to believe anything they were telling him. Shaken to the core by Rina leading him to Conall and Elethea, a sense of betrayal filled him. Rina spoke not one word of explanation, nor showed signs of regret. She continued to sit on the stone bench, a short distance away, keeping her eyes downcast.

The man, Conall, was speaking, droning on, but Tory was not listening. He was considering his options instead. He could always leave. There was no counting on Rina to intervene. She was allowing them to persuade him without question. She plainly knew something. *What is she not telling me?* He was wounded at her willingness to see him gone. Whatever closeness he thought had grown from their relationship, she obviously felt none of the emotions he did. The drumming of his heart pounded in his ears, threatening to explode with each second she avoided looking at him. *Who are these people, really? What do they want of me?*

"Master, your time here is at an end. Your parents await your return." The woman Elethea pressed him.

Any other time, he would have been intrigued to have the answers she promised. Who he was, why he had been placed with the Sidhe were questions that haunted him. Ever since finding out he was not related to the parents who had raised him, Tory welcomed answers.

Now, he was not sure that it would make any difference. He belonged there. His loyalty lay with his brother Elron, the Sidhe and his queen. They had been there for him. Whoever his real parents were, they would have to wait until he completed the mission queen Eliana had sent him on.

"I will not go with you." He answered Elethea. Turning to Rina, he fixed her with a cold stare.

"As for you, I will continue on alone. Your services are no longer required. You can go. We have wasted enough time here, when we could have been searching for my parents."

His dismissive, brutal words finally forced Rina to lift her head. Tory refused to acknowledge the anguish on her face. He needed to get away from her, before he said what was truly in his heart. Betrayed. He felt betrayed by her. She had led him there, knowing what had awaited him. She had wasted valuable time, when she knew he needed to find his parents.

He turned away from the grief in her eyes, while she blinked back tears. Tory steeled himself against reacting to her wounded look. He did not trust its authenticity. She had misled him, lulling him with a sense that she had cared, with her beauty and allure. Treachery was all she offered.

"Your parents are not lost. They are waiting for you." The man Conall broke into the tense silence.

"My parents are those who raised me. I have a brother that I will not abandon." Tory harshly answered the man.

Tory had to get away from these people. He urgently needed to locate the only two people who had loved him, unconditionally, through each day of his life. He owed them everything. Seeing no other way but to return to their family home, to look for any clues, Tory readied to transport there. His intent must have shown, alerting the woman, Elethea, who blocked his escape.

Unable to shift away, Tory tried to leave the only other way available to him. He moved, stepping around Elethea towards the path leading down the mountain. Two steps were as far as he got. His face was scrunched up against an invisible wall. His body bounced off the field blocking him. Stumbling back, his jaw clenched in anger.

"Please listen to us. Master, please come home." Elethea begged him.

"Stop calling me Master!" Tory clenched his fists in frustration.

Elethea turned to Conall for guidance. She was not sure how to proceed. The man seemed to be debating how much to say. They must have sensed that Tory would not be responsive to anything but the truth. So far, they had given him no reason to trust them. Conall calmly approached Tory. His feet stopped, as his face suddenly registered alarm. Conall's body winked in and out, fading slightly from Tory's view. Elethea was losing her own cohesion. Tory could see right through her.

"We do not have time left. Tory, we cannot stay any longer. You have the power to come back anytime you wish. When you are ready, you will know what must be done. Your parents protected you in the only way they knew how. You must trust that we mean you no harm.

Rina, we leave him in your hands. Explain it all to him." Even as Conall was uttering those words, both Conall and Elethea were fast losing their shapes. With his final words to Rina, they both faded completely from view.

Tory took the opportunity to transport away with a clear mind of where to go. He abandoned Rina on the mountaintop, not wanting to hear anything she had to say. He found himself back outside his home, where he pushed aside any guilt at leaving her. She had hurt him in ways he was not ready yet to interpret. His heart lay broken from her deception.

Standing next to his mother's rose garden, the walkway in front of him led directly to the house. The ache in his chest grew with each step he took towards the front door. He entered, going directly to his father's den. The silent, darkened, empty room held no easy answers. Needing light, he went to the window to pull back the drapes. Outside, the sun peaked out from fluffy, lazily drifting clouds. Melancholy covered him with its sorrow and dejection.

Drawing in a burden-heavy breath, he turned to take in the room. He and Elron had gone over it once already, back when Elron was searching for his own beginnings. It was then they had found the letter from his father addressed to Elron. Now, he needed to go over it all again. There had to be something else there, some way to find out where they had gone.

The bookcases held his father's favorite books. His father loved, thrilled at reading any human spy thrillers and mysteries. Tory's preferences always ran towards the human imaginings of the paranormal, and the skewed views they represented. He and Elron had a good laugh at some of the descriptions of their race. Lumping all faeries together was amusing. Their race was unlike anything ever written about.

His fingers brushed over the book spines, as he slowly walked along the bookcase. He knew he was procrastinating. Afraid to find anything else to throw his life further into disarray, Tory was putting off his reasons for coming there. Screwing up his courage, he moved over to the hiding place where his father kept the key to the safe.

In the bookcase, the book titled, *Ways to Throw Caution to the Winds*, brought a smile to his lips. His father's whimsical humor always entertained the family. What better place to hide the key. Lifting the book, Tory opened it and pulled the key out of the hollow on the inside cover. He made his way to the floorboard behind his father's desk, and used the heel of his foot to kick it loose.

Sitting down on the floor, he inserted the key in the keyhole. He hesitated to turn it. *Am I ready for what I might find? Do I really want to know more?* Only the pressing need to find his parents compelled him to unlock the safe. Drawing back the door, the first things he saw were the documents he and Elron had previously perused. He pulled them out, dropping them onto his lap. He would have to go through each, one by one.

Hoping for a clue, he could not put any aside. Tory made himself comfortable, stretching out his legs and bracing his back against the wall behind him. He went over the first couple of documents, which dealt with council business. His father's position on the queen's council afforded him an inside look at how involved his father had been in its day-to-day operations. He never imagined how trusted his father was.

The pile of documents already read, grew next to him. He was starting to read a letter written on the queen's personal letterhead, when a sound alerted him to the presence of someone outside. The voice calling out to him was easily recognizable. Her persistence made it impossible to concentrate on what he was reading.

Outside the energy field protecting the house, hiding the property, Rina was shouting for him to let her through. Without him, she was incapable of penetrating the field. He would have left her out there, if it were not for the fact she may have been attracting attention.

He got to his feet, still debating on whether to go get her. He placed the documents in his hands on the desk, taking his time sauntering outside. Reaching the end of the pathway, where the property line ended, Rina stared back at him from beyond. She looked harried, panicked. Her eyes teared at seeing him.

Reaching out, his hand grabbed hers and pulled her through the protective shield. Once on his side, Rina for all appearances looked lost. She tried to say something, her lips parting, but no sound came out. Tory did not have time for that. He left her there, still uncertain, going back into the house, the den and looking through the documents he needed to study. If Rina followed him, he did not notice.

Grabbing the documents he had put aside earlier, he took a seat on his father's leather desk chair. He resumed reading, ignoring Rina, who stood in the doorway. Concentrating on the letter he held in his hand, he was aware of her entering the room, going to the sofa and taking a seat. With his heartbeat increasing from having her near, he fought back the rising conflicting emotions she brought out in him. He was not ready, may never be ready, to trust her again.

Letting go of the breath he had been holding, his eyes focused on the letter he held in his hands, dated some three hundred years before. In it, the queen was thanking his father for his service. Reading on, the words that stared back at him gave him pause. *How long had the queen known he and Elron were not who they appeared to be?* In the letter, the queen was advising his father to keep it secret a while longer. Tory was the one she was most worried about. She was insistent that he not be told until she was ready.

"Tory." Rina cut into his thoughts.

She was leaning forward on the couch, her hands clasped together, nervous of saying the wrong thing. Tory continued ignoring her while he read on. Time dimension, time traveler were words he could not make sense of. *What do they have to do with me?* Finishing the letter, he had more questions than answers. He added the letter to the completed pile, then picked up the next one from the desk.

The remainder of the documents were standard council meeting notes. They mentioned neither him nor Elron. He dropped them on the floor, and dug into what else was in the safe. His mother's jewels, necklaces and rings, he left where they were. Only one other object was inside the safe.

"Tory, don't. You have to listen to me first." Rina raced over to him, grabbing his hand, stopping him from removing the object from the safe. She appeared panicked for some reason.

Tory yanked his hand away from her. Her touch brought emotions to the surface he wanted to wipe out. It hurt too much to have her near. His whole body ached. He wished her away, anywhere but there in the room with him. Just as the thought finished, he watched her body slightly waver, as if she would dematerialize.

Her hand grabbed onto his arm, her eyes widening in surprise. He stepped away from her, her hand falling away on seeing the bitter look he gave her, shaken by what almost happened. *Did I do that? Did my thought almost make her disappear?*

"Listen to me, please." Rina reached for him, grabbed his hand and refused to let go. "Please, Tory." She begged.

Torn over trusting her and anything she had to say, Tory collapsed on his father's desk chair. She knelt in front him, her hands going to the armrests, where they kept him prisoner on the seat. He had nowhere to go. Tory knew that whatever she said, the object in the safe was involved somehow.

"I'll listen. But, then I want you gone, Rina." His voice shook at uttering the words.

Rina sat down on the floor in front of him. He could see he had hurt her, but fought against wanting to comfort her. Whatever friendship they had developed was broken. He saw no way for them to go back to their easy camaraderie. She had misled him. He thought she was helping him find his parents, when instead, she led him on a wild goose chase. He waited for her to have her say, so he could return to his task.

"I'm sorry, Tory. I should have spoken earlier. The truth is, I was afraid to tell you. My mother only let me know a few nights ago. I could not process it immediately. I am as much at a loss as you are. I care for you, Tory. Maybe too much." She hesitated before continuing. Tory said nothing in response.

"Your parents, your real parents, have only recently made their world safe for your return. You were in grave danger if you had stayed with them. There were outside forces trying to gain control of where you come from. Your parents did the only thing they could. Placing you with the ancients gave you a chance at survival. How you ended up with the Sidhe was not something they planned. They need you back, Tory. I will miss you more than you know. I don't see a way out." Tears flowed openly, running down her cheeks.

Tory could not fully understand what she said. *Where do I come from? What danger had there been? And why now, when I am needed here, do I have to go back?* He could not go anywhere while the race he considered his people were in their own danger. He had to help the Sidhe, his brother and those he cared about.

"I have unfinished business here. When everything is settled, only then, can I think of what you are trying to tell me. I believe you are still hiding something from me, Rina. I can't put my trust in you." Tory got to his feet, throwing Rina off balance. She just managed to right herself, rising to her feet while Tory crouched down to retrieve the object in the safe.

"Don't touch it if you want to remain here." Her voice stopped him from picking it up.

Inside the safe, an hourglass lay on its side. The intricate design carved into the wooden base was exquisite. The wood held together two glass bulbs connected by a thin neck to allow the sand to flow through. With it lying on its side, it looked like time had stood still for it. Tory raised his eyes to Rina's when she uttered her warning. He removed his hand from the safe on seeing her expression. Rina was positively petrified of him touching the object.

"It will remove you from this time." She whispered.

Chapter 13 - Alexa

I wanted to help Liam in any way I could. I really did. But, once the ring landed in my open palm, I immediately let it drop out of my hand. The second it touched me, I was overwhelmed with the darkness it projected. It was not the ring itself, but where its owner was that had caused me to flinch away. I received an image of the vast, bleak world she was imprisoned in. The purplish-black sky, the lava rolling, burning rivers, the putrid atmosphere was vile, repulsive. The poor woman had been breathing those fumes, feeling the stifling heat for years.

What I sensed from her was an unassailable hope. I glimpsed her fierce spirit refusing to be broken. Her mind was full of love, trust and belief that Liam would find her, save her from the hell she lived in. How many centuries had she endured isolation from human contact? How could I tell Liam without causing him more guilt to contend with?

While I struggled with the knowledge of what I saw, Liam reached down to retrieve the ring from where it had landed. Reverently, his fingers gently lifted it, holding it out to me again. His eyes begged me to try again. I did not have to take the ring to know where she was. I knew instantly. The only reason I took it from him was so that I could understand why. Why had she been taken there? Who had stolen her from Liam?

My fingers wrapped around the gold band, enclosing it in my palm. I fought the urge to drop it again. Images assailed me. Her heart was full of love for Liam. I saw their meeting, watched them wed, living their happiness. Her love for him was beyond the boundaries of the ordinary. Theirs was an unending, eternal bond. They were joined in the same way Aidan and I were.

Then a stranger came to their village. The accepting inhabitants welcomed the man, offering him food and drink. I watched the way he eyed Mara. Her nervousness was infectious, as I felt her growing apprehension. She tried to keep her distance, but the stranger found ways to get her alone. Mara had been able to rebuff his advances, for a time. She prayed for Liam's return. Liam was regrettably away, hunting with Mara's father.

The stranger grew more bold, refusing to take no for an answer. Her pleas that she was married fell on his deaf ears. In a fit of anger, the stranger burned the village to the ground. If she refused him, she would be made to watch all those she loved killed. Mara did not know what to do. Waiting for Liam was taking forever. The stranger offered her a choice. Come with him, or be responsible for the end of her people. Mara gave in, believing that Liam would eventually come for her and save her.

The stranger took her into his hellish world. Imprisoned within the sunless, shadowy place, he assured her that one day she would love him back. When enough time passed, she would forget her husband and see that she was his. Mara managed to hold him at bay, knowing his selfish, controlling desire for her would keep her safe. His need to possess her kept him from harming her.

With each passing year, the stranger returned on the anniversary of the day he had abducted her, but her answer was always the same.

She would never love him. Her heart belonged to another. I could tell he was growing frustrated and annoyed at her constant refusal. It would not be long before he took what he wanted, whether she was willing or not. We had to save her. Time was running out for her. I returned to the present, opening my palm to let the ring drop into Liam's waiting hand.

"What did you see? Do you know where she is?" Liam asked.

How much to tell him? He would be distraught to learn she had been waiting all that time for him. The guilt of thinking her dead, believing he loved me, not searching for her, would be crushing. I could not hold back any of what I had learned. He needed to know all of it.

Softly, gently, I recounted all I had learned. I described in detail, so he could fully understand Mara's resolve to remain faithful to him. I tried to make him understand none of it was his fault. His reaction to what he heard was the difficult part. Once I apprised him of what I had seen, he blamed himself. Any attempt I made to console him was met with more recriminations against himself.

"Liam, concentrate on finding her and getting her back. I want to tell you where she is, who has her, but you need to think before you act." Internally I reached out to Aidan, asking him to come to the main room. I needed him to be the voice of reason. His responding, *I'm on my way*, let me breathe a little bit easier.

Liam was agitatedly pacing when Aidan walked in. I mentally told him what was going on while my eyes anxiously followed Liam moving around the room. Aidan pushed back his shock at the image I had painted for him. He rushed over to his brother, blocking his path, understanding fully what Liam was experiencing. He knew the bond would drive Liam to do something dangerous. I stayed silent while the two stared at each other. Liam was the first to break eye contact. Aidan did not allow Liam to speak.

"Liam, sit down. Let Alexa finish and then we will plan a way for Mara to be rescued. I know you feel responsible, but it's not your fault. How were you to know? You never once felt her presence." Aidan led Liam to the couch.

I reached out with my mind to silently thank Aidan for being the voice of reason. The next part I had to tell Liam would be even more difficult. His response would necessitate our interference. My mind touched Aidan's to warn him to be vigilant. Liam would most likely attempt to leave.

"Manar has her." I blurted out. "Liam, stay!" I said, feeling his urge to take off.

Aidan allowed Liam no room to maneuver. Holding onto his arm, Aidan forced Liam back into his seat. I leaned forward to get his attention. There was more. Liam went still on seeing my face. He braced himself for what else I would reveal.

"What?" He controlled the rage in his voice.

I glanced at Aidan to make sure he was ready. I paused in telling Liam the worst part. Fear of his reaction made me hesitate. Liam schooled his face into neutrality. He did not fool me for a second. His outward appearance was in contrast with the inner boiling anger rising within him.

"He is in love with her. Or what he takes to be love. His hope is that she will forget you and come to love him. Liam, all this time she has remained steadfast in her love for you. I feel he is losing patience. He has kept her prisoner in the deepest part of their realm. She sees no one. Only once a year, he visits her to see if she is willing to accept him. He has never revealed his true form to her. She doesn't know what he is. The worst part is that his father is unaware of what he has done. If Manar's father discovers her, he may very well kill her outright. I know you want to rush off to save her, but you cannot enter their land. You have to trust me. Wait. Let me see what I can do." My pronouncement brought out Aidan's protective instincts. He would not allow me to place myself in danger.

"No way. You will not do this alone!" Aidan said through clenched teeth.

Both of them were ready to fight me over what I wanted to attempt. I gave them no opportunity. I was gone from the room before they knew it. There would be hell to pay for my actions later, but it was the only way I could see we could save Mara.

Going from our world to the one Mara was imprisoned in was not easy. I struggled to find an opening. My eyes searched the field blocking me. I studied the bubble of energy protecting the entry. It looked like the whole world was encompassed by a globule of some type of liquid. I quickly gathered enough energy to create electricity around my body. When I was completely surrounded by it, I stepped up to the barrier and attempted to penetrate it.

The electric current hissed, sizzled as I fought my way in. Finally, with a flashing snap, I made it through. Inside, the Daimon realm was just as oppressive as my vision foresaw. Sweat filmed by body within seconds upon entering it. The acrid smell burned my throat. I had to act fast before I suffocated in the fetid atmosphere. My breathing was labored, difficult, as I scanned the area.

The distance I needed to cover was negligible, but it posed a problem. There was a scalding, flowing river of lava between me and Mara. I attempted to transport myself over it, only to have my way blocked. Something or someone was hindering my attempt.

I did not have long to wait to find out who was the cause of my being unable to transport. A roar of laughter came from my right. The deep timber of it identified whoever it was as a male. Was it Manar? Had I somehow stepped into a trap? Trying to exit the hellish place was unfeasible. Something was keeping me in place.

Struggling for breath, I watched as a figure neared me. The scaly reptilian body of the Daimon grew in size, as it climbed up on its hind legs to face me. It had no humanity in it. The red glowing eyes pierced me with their stare. I should have been weak with fear, but felt none.

"And what have we here? Are you lost little one?" His voice rang out.

"I have come to retrieve the one your son imprisoned." I answered him back showing no fear.

I was face-to-face with Manar's father. He seemed at a loss, unsure how to respond. He had not expected me to stand up to him. The king of the Daimon was surprised, both by what I said and my lack of fear. I also knew he had no idea Manar had been holding Mara. His kingdom was vast. That part of his land was farthest from his capital.

Manar chose that place because he knew his father seldom kept an eye on it. He scanned the area, his attention drawn to the place where Mara was. His red eyes became slits, as they narrowed. Before I knew it, he transported both of us to the other side. Mara was but a foot away from me.

"Will you let me take her? She does not belong here." I hoped it would be that simple.

The Daimon ambled closer to Mara, barring my view of her. I was surprised by how she was being held. Manar had created his own little fairy-tale world. Mara was laid out on a jeweled pedestal acting as a bed. Over her, a clear glass dome covered her from head to foot. Flowers, dead and withered, cascaded down the base of the pedestal. Inside, she lay unmoving, in a deep sleep. The only sign she still lived was her chest evenly rising and falling. I would have laughed at the sleeping beauty scene if not for the Daimon reaching towards her. I was afraid of what he would do to her.

"Manar did this?" The giant of a Daimon roared.

Trying to draw his attention away from Mara and back to me, I carefully walked closer to him. I hesitated to speak, to answer his question. His reaction so far had surprised me. He did not seem upset at my being there, or that Mara was present. More likely, it was his son he was angered by. Could I use that to my advantage?

"Who are you, little one? How did you enter my kingdom?" I had gotten his attention. Now, I wondered if it was wise.

The Daimon openly studied me. He was baffled. His keen eyes considered me, trying to ascertain who and what I was. I saw recognition spark an interest. He moved closer, stopping when I took a step back.

"My name is Alexa. I think you know who I am. I have come only to retrieve the woman being held by your son." I tried to sound surer than I felt.

The Daimon threw his head back and roared with laughter. His reptilian legs stomped away from me, still laughing softly under his breath. I stepped over to Mara while he was preoccupied. She did not look harmed. I attempted to lift the glass dome, but it would not budge.

"I see my son has involved us in things I expressly forbade him to do. The human world does not concern me. Where is he? Ah, yes, there he is, the young rascal. I will have to teach him a lesson." He seemed to be talking to himself, so I did not offer any response.

The Daimon was using his abilities to locate his son. What he had in store for him was not my concern. That was between them. Mara had to be removed from under the glass, if I hoped to get her out. The fact that it was sealed, had me looking for some way to force it open. I saw nothing around me to help me achieve that goal.

"Go. The woman stays here." His words startled me.

"I can't leave her here. Why can't I take her?" I sounded panicked even to my ears.

The Daimon returned to Mara, gazing down at her. His expression was hard to read. With almost no humanity in it, what he was thinking had no effect on his face.

"You can have her after I deal with my son. Tell the one who is waiting for her that I will not harm her. Olar, the king of the Daimon, is bound by his word. Now, go." His promise did little to ease my mind.

How long would we have to wait? How much longer would Mara have to endure that place?

"Not long, Alexa. It will be over quicker than you think." With those last words, I found myself back in the room, next to Aidan, who looked thunderous.

Chapter 14 - Eliana

Eliana expected she would feel nothing for the son staring hollowly back at her. Oh, but she was wrong. Emotions were a funny thing. Out of the blue, they rose up to surprise you. The last time she saw him, he was a small squirming bundle in her arms. With little concern over his well-being, believing her actions to be the best course in protecting her kingdom, she had readily placed him in Vanya's care. Any affection or tenderness towards the innocent child, resulting from her youthful dalliance with Elsam, she had kept at bay. She could not afford to be taken in by his sweet smile, nor by the tiny fingers wrapped around her forefinger. All that had been so long ago. But, it felt like yesterday.

There was no question that Vanya had taken great care of him. Through the centuries, the memory of his existence had faded in obscurity. Now, there he was, looking so much like Aidan that she wondered how she could ever have let him go. Her fingers itched to touch him. Her heart thundered in her chest, while her eyes filled with unexpected tears. Only his haunted look stopped her. Solas felt no love for Eliana. His sorrow was for the woman who had raised him. Vanya's death had utterly destroyed him.

Eliana had been alone in the basement of the manor in Deis-dé, watching through the Kaemorra as Elsam tortured her long-ago friend mercilessly. Her death after hours of the brutal inquisition came as a welcome relief to the battered woman. She spoke not one word against

Eliana or Solas. In fact, through it all, she uttered not one word. Her endless screams from the savage abuse still rang in Eliana's ears.

Eliana was thankful that Solas had not been present to watch his father viciously exact his vengeance on Vanya. He did not need to know all she had endured. Vanya would have wanted him to be spared. Keeping him safe was all Vanya ever strove for. How incensed she would have been to see Elsam's attempt to have Solas killed. It infuriated Eliana beyond reason. That Elsam could so blatantly feel nothing for his child, forced Eliana to examine her own feelings. Solas was hers. In the end, he was her son and she had to take responsibility over what became of him.

Her need to find him forced her away from her ailing husband. She reluctantly left the still-unconscious Asher in Thalia's capable hands. Asher was not responding well to treatment of his wound. A black spidery web of venom was spreading across his torso, expanding outward from the gash near his heart.

The puncture wound from Manar's sword refused to close. Blood continued to seep out, steadily staining the bed covers where he lay unmoving. The sight of the webbing on his exposed chest, the way it fanned out unhindered with each passing moment, punctuated the gravity of the situation.

Thalia, uncertain what poison was spreading through his system, tried in any way possible to stem its spread. The woman kept her thoughts to herself, refusing to acknowledge what became increasingly obvious as time progressed. Eliana undeniably knew the prognosis was dire. Asher was in grave danger. All the magic in the world might not save him. Even Thalia started to believe nothing she did would pull Asher away from death's door.

Eliana had no doubts about leaving him in Thalia's capable hands. She was the only one skilled enough to save her injured husband. Thalia's healing abilities were matched by none other. Eliana completely trusted she would do everything to save Asher.

Hope though was quickly leaving her. Ignoring the probable outcome of his demise by finding something else to focus on, Eliana directed her attention to locating Solas. Instead of standing around helpless, her time would be better spent in finding and fixing the broken bond with her son.

It took her hours to figure out where he had gone upon escaping from his father. She finally found him in a broken-down cabin not far from where Meredith's home was located in Scotland. In the barren room, the frigid air chilled her to the bone. Solas sat on the dirty floor, facing the unlit fireplace, which bore only spider webs and dust. Her arrival briefly brought him out of his catatonic state.

Catching sight of her, he ignored her, resuming his silent vigil. Eliana knew she needed to tread carefully. She wanted him to come back with her to Deis-dé. Slowly making her way to him, he seemed to brace himself, his back stiffening on hearing her steps. His head turned her way, while his eyes uneasily followed her progress to him.

"Solas." She whispered, unsure what to say to ease his pain.

"Mother." He answered, one brow rising.

Eliana could not be certain if she heard sarcasm in his voice. His features remained inscrutable. Only the muscle of his jaw clenching showed any sign of some inner conflict. Whatever emotion he was experiencing, he carefully masked. Once she stood in front of him, she sat down on the floor, fighting the urge to reach out for him. *How can I explain to him the unbearable guilt I feel over casting him cruelly aside?* She should have handled things differently.

In hindsight, so many options presented themselves to her. Any one of them would have let him be a part of her life. Sensing her emotions, Solas rose to his feet, crossing to the other side of the room, where he kept his back to her. Staring across the space that separated them, seeing his rigid posture, Eliana's vision of him blurred as tears gathered.

"She was everything to me. I had a good life. Better than most. I know she betrayed you, but in the end, she died for all of us. I will come with you. I have nowhere else to go." His words held no emotion in them.

Eliana got up off the floor. Mindful of his hurt, that he had no reason to trust her, she went to him, hesitantly putting her hand on his shoulder. His back flinched, trembling at her touch. Eliana walked around him, so she could look at his face. Unable to avoid her, his features lost their blankness as his defenses crumbled. The tears he had been holding back since finding Vanya's bloodied body broke free.

Sobs escaped him. Eliana gathered him in her arms, letting him cry out his pain. Only for a moment did he try to pull out of her embrace. When Eliana refused to release him, his head dropped onto her shoulder, where he buried his face in its hollow. Having him in her arms, touching him, her own tears fell unhindered. He shook with the force of his anguish. She said nothing, for nothing would ever make Vanya's death right. Taking advantage of the moment, she transported both of them back to one of the free bedrooms in Deis-dé. He would need privacy to deal with his loss.

"I don't want to see anyone." His voice trembled, realizing where she had brought him.

"You can stay in here as long as you need. Only I will know. You will be welcomed, Solas. Your siblings will be happy to get to know you. I will be happy to have you here. I know it is too soon to talk, but I am sorry. I did a great disservice to you. We will have to discuss it at some point. For now, rest. You have a private bathroom and extra clothes in the drawers. I will make sure you are not disturbed. Call for me when you are ready." Eliana went to the door, where she stopped with her hand resting on the knob.

Gazing back at him, she gave him a slight nod of encouragement. Knowing Solas would need time alone to grieve and come to terms with his new family, she reluctantly exited and shut the door softly behind her.

Leaving him was the hardest thing Eliana had done in a while. She remained with her back pressed against the closed door, listening for any movement within the room. On hearing the water run in the bathroom sink, she sighed in relief that he had not taken off. Now she could return to Asher.

Stepping down the corridor to her husband's room, her senses perked at another arrival in the house. *What has that girl done now?* Whatever it was, she was in great distress, her breathing ragged and heavy. Eliana instantly knew where she had been. Idiotic stunt that it might be, Eliana was nonetheless curious over what she might have discovered.

Taking the stairs, she descended, arriving in the main room in time to see Aidan lying Alexa down on the couch, on her side. Eliana observed Alexa struggling for breath. Her time in the Daimon realm had been too long, too toxic. Her lungs were full of their poisonous air. Racked with coughing fits, she lay curled in a fetal position.

Eliana could see the restraint both her sons were exerting. Their concern over her kept them in check over voicing their anger at her dangerous actions. Once she recovered, Alexa would feel both of their wraths.

"I'm fine." Alexa said between coughing fits.

Alexa was not fine. Not at present. Eliana could see she needed help. She walked over to her, grabbed her by the arms and forced her into a sitting position. With Alexa upright, Eliana held her hands over Alexa's chest, finding and forcing the poison out of her. A vile breath left Alexa, who gave a final hawking cough while Aidan patted her back. He waited for an opening to have his say.

Liam on the other hand was not as put off by her visible struggle. He stared daggers at Alexa. Torn between wanting to know what she had found out and wanting to berate her for putting herself in harm's way, Liam did the only thing he could while she rested. He paced. He seemed to be doing a lot of that lately. Aidan on the other hand had no trouble putting his dissatisfaction into words.

"Have you gone completely out of your mind?" He admonished

her.

Alexa bristled, her eyes narrowing at his tone. Lifting her head, she glared up at Aidan, who refused to back down. Aidan knew Alexa was much more powerful than she had been before his capture, but he was not aware of the full extent of her capabilities. The two of them needed to have a chat, and soon. But, now was not that time.

Eliana cut in, before things deteriorated further. Their focus should be on what Alexa had gleaned from her visiting to the Daimon world. They all knew she took a great, maybe foolish, risk in crossing over. There was no disputing that. Dealing with it would have to wait. Eliana knew she had met Olar, but why the Daimon king let her go unharmed was a mystery.

"So you met Olar. Do you know how lucky you are to still be living?" Eliana met Alexa's surprised stare.

Alexa shrugged her shoulders, making light of the danger she had placed herself in. Aidan breathed deeply to control the fury he still felt.

"He was pleasant enough. Actually, he was nice to me." Alexa said.

"While you were making nice with the Daimon king, did you happen to see Mara?" Liam's voice dripped with sarcasm.

Alexa laughed. Seeing his outrage, she covered her mouth with her hand to stop any further outburst. Liam advanced on her, ready to do her bodily harm. Aidan intercepted him before he could reach her. Grabbing his arm, Aidan kept him from acting out his frustrations. Alexa fought to control the giggle stuck in her throat. Eliana shook her head at them.

"Alexa, please control yourself and tell us what happened." The queen ordered her.

Alexa did as Eliana asked, and told them everything that she and Olar had discussed. The two men stared at her, as if she had grown another head. With a heavy sigh, Liam dropped down into an armchair facing Alexa. Mara was still in danger. He did not trust that Olar would release her. *Why did he need her? What purpose would she serve in dealing with Manar?* Liam wanted to go get her right that minute. Only, he had no way to get her out. Alexa left her there and only she could go back.

"How could you bargain with her life like that?" Liam accused her, at his wits end. Aidan was the one who answered him.

"I don't think she had much of a choice, Liam. I'm sure Mara will be fine."

How could he possibly be sure of that? If it were Alexa stuck in that place, what would Aidan be willing to do to get her back? Liam's stomach churned, feeling sick at having failed Mara yet again. He covered his face with his hands, lost as to how to help her. Eliana reached across and pulled his hands away. She held onto them, wanting to offer him a solution. She saw no way out, other than to wait and see if Olar fulfilled his promise.

"Liam, he will release her. Olar is usually true to his word. If he promised Alexa he would return her, he will." Eliana told him.

"The magic word there, Mother, is usually. How long before I know if he means to let her go. And, why does he need her? Why can't he just deal with his son without her?" Liam had no faith in Daimon promises.

Eliana had no answers to his questions. All they could do was wait, hope that Olar freed Mara soon. Her attention went to Aidan, who had his head tilted to the side, concentrating on something not related to their current conversation. Instantly, she knew what he sensed. Catching his eye, she shook her head to stop him alerting the others. Aidan had sensed his brother Solas upstairs. Eliana had promised to give Solas time to grieve. Thankfully, Aidan did not speak of what he had found.

"Alexa, go up and rest. Aidan, please take her. She is still weak from the effects of the Daimon air. Liam, come with me. I need to consult the Kaemorra. A lot has happened that we all need to discuss. Tonight we have decisions to make. I will see you all later." Eliana waved at Liam to follow her.

Leaving Aidan to make sure Alexa rested, Eliana led Liam down to where the Kaemorra was housed. A long history existed between the queen and Olar, the king of the Daimon. Liam needed to understand that history and what it meant for Mara. Eliana hoped once he saw the past, he would understand the future. Her added worry over what she sensed from Asher's deteriorating health, hurried her steps. Once Liam was informed, Eliana would have little time to sit with her husband.

Chapter 15 - Elsam

He sat on the top step of his dais, his hand gripping a mangled piece of his broken throne. His dark mood had everyone steering clear of him. Elsam's plans were falling apart. It seemed like his throne's destruction bespoke an unfavorable omen. Blasted apart by Myrick, who missed his intended target, the throne lay scattered in pieces behind him. Elsam, incensed at the loss of his seat of power, blamed the warlock for all that had gone wrong. His once-majestic chair was nothing but rubble, just like his alliance with the Daimon.

The Daimon had all vanished at the same time as his son. Manar managed to escape while Elsam seethed over his son's defection. Myrick had failed him once again. The warlock showed himself to be useless, completely incapable of following simple orders. Solas should be dead, just like his dear departed mother. Elsam wanted them both rotting in hell together. They had deceived him for the last time. *How much of my plans have they already shared with Eliana? How much does she know?* Solas would surely apprise Eliana of everything Elsam intended to do. Or, everything that had been done to undermine him.

His only chance now lay with the shadows. Elsam thought that the Sidhe possessed no weapons to fight against those beings. He was unaware that Alexa knew their weakness. His plans relied on the shadows being able to overcome the queen's army. The alliance with the shadow overlord, Erebus, continued tenuously at best. Elsam was not ready to give up what the overlord demanded as payment for his aid.

The Kaemorra's value to Elsam would never allow him to relinquish it into the hands of the shadows. *Why does Erebus covet it so?* Elsam could not understand Erebus's demanding it as payment. The gemstone could not be wielded by him or any of the shadows. Only a Sidhe could use its powers. The shadow overlord had sent a message that he would arrive later that night, under cover of darkness, to discuss terms. Elsam needed to come up with another form of payment, one that did not mean giving up the Kaemorra. That was the one thing he would not, could not, give up.

The great hall was deserted. Elsam sat alone seething. Fearing his reprisal for their lack of foresight, his guards were standing outside, barring the entrance. Dropping the piece of the throne still in his hands onto the floor, Elsam pushed himself up. He had one thing to take care of before Erebus arrived. It would give him great pleasure to exact his revenge.

Striding from the room, he made his way to the corridor outside. The guards, who were positioned in front of the door, immediately moved aside to let him pass. Wordlessly falling in step behind him, they tensely made their way down into the dungeons. The smell of the flammable fluid lighting the torches on the stairs permeated the air with its sticky, oily stench. Smoke billowed, filling the stairway with the noxious fumes. Deeper and deeper they went. His prisoner was being kept in the lowest level under the tower.

Elsam stepped off the last step, onto the dirt-covered, rocky ground of the dimly lit corridor. At the other end, a thick wooden door stood between him and the warlock being held prisoner. The guards accompanying him kept their distance, trailing several feet behind him as he approached the door. As he marched down the corridor, Elsam motioned for one of the guards standing at attention in front of the locked door, to open it. The man moved instantly to do as he was commanded.

Taking the ring of keys from the peg on the wall, they clinked as the guard's hands trembled to find the right key for the keyhole. Any other time, Elsam would have relished the fear he instilled in his men. It was not one of those times. It only made him wonder if they were up to the coming events.

Finally, finding the right key, the guard unlocked the door, pulled it open and stepped aside. The door creaked loudly on its hinges, allowing Elsam to enter. The sudden sound cut into the silence, reverberating, echoing up and down the cell. From the now-open doorway, Elsam had a clear view of Myrick, who hung nearly senseless from the ceiling.

His hands were bound in chains, looped around a meat hook and his feet dangled loosely a yard above the floor. Unable to use his powers, he was bruised, bleeding from multiple wounds. He had been tortured for hours. Elsam was pleased with the results. His orders to not hold back, to punish Myrick severely, had been taken to heart. He would reward those who had participated.

Myrick squinted against the light entering the darkened cavern. His prison cell was the same one Aidan had been held in. The irony of it was not lost to him. What you sow, so shall you reap. These were words he should have been accustomed to by that time. His arrogance had led him there.

Thinking that Elsam would reward him, think him to be irreplaceable, Myrick threw his lot in with the wrong side. His need to pay back Rider for the hideous scars on his face, drove him past redemption. In the past, he went by the name Paul, and Rider had been his best friend. Thalia's choice was what had driven a wedge between the two men.

Myrick saw her first, loved her first. Losing her to Rider had made him bitter. Watching them be blissfully happy together was more than he could stand. The damn prophesy presented him with a way to make them both pay. Rider somehow learned of Myrick's betrayal.

Having tasked Myrick with protecting his wife and daughter, the warlock spied on them and passed information on to Elsam instead. Confronted by Rider, the fight between them ended with Myrick being marked for life by the scar that crisscrossed his face. What Rider remained clueless about was the obsession over Thalia driving Myrick. Thalia was to be his once Alexa was out of the way.

Myrick waited for the end to come. Elsam would kill him. There was no other possible outcome. Myrick would not beg for his life. The wait was becoming unbearable, however. *How much more would he have to endure before Elsam finally ended his misery*? Wanting to exact the maximum agony from Myrick, Elsam unleashed other warlocks on him for hours.

Using their powers, the warlocks rendered him unconscious before removing themselves from the cell. When he had regained his senses, they returned to torture him yet again. They used the same spells and torture practices that he had used on Bet and Rider. Thalia had been spared injury only because of Myrick's longing to gain control over her. He could not bear to have her harmed.

"Tell me Myrick, did you let him go on purpose?" Elsam's voice boomed in the room.

Myrick did not answer. Any response he made would only anger Elsam more. Yes, he had let Solas escape. His timing and aim were deliberate. He cringed, recalling having been forced by Elsam to kill Vanya. It had been the final straw. He could not continue his alliance with Elsam. Somewhere within him, something had broken. Seeing her bloodied body, gasping for her last breaths, forced him to realize how far he had fallen. Redemption for his acts would be hard to win. Elsam's order to kill his son was reprehensible.

Myrick could not do the same to Solas, as he had done to Vanya. The boy had to be spared. Elsam knew the moment Myrick had lost his nerve. Another death on his conscience was too much for Myrick. *How did I end up here?* Myrick welcomed the final judgment over his life. He wanted to be free of the guilt gnawing away at him. Wishing he could go back and change things, undo the damage, was beyond his capabilities.

"It doesn't matter. He will be found and made to pay for his sins against his father. As for you, well, you won't be around to see it." Elsam continued.

Elsam stepped aside as another warlock entered the room. Myrick knew the man well. So, the end had arrived. Myrick waited, closing his eyes, for the final moments of his life. The attack never came. His body convulsed, as an energy beam seized him. The interior of the cell flooded with a piercing white light. Myrick could not open his eyes even if he wanted to. The blinding light made it impossible for him. Gradually, the light faded. He felt his body falling. Dropping onto the ground, he opened his eyes to find he no longer occupied the cell in the dungeon. Realizing where he had been taken to, his arrival at the new location did not fill him with any confidence his position had improved.

Deep under the tower, inside the now-empty cell, Elsam screamed in frustration. He knocked the other warlock, still in his presence, to the floor. Rushing out of the cell, he continued screaming orders while pushing the guards out of his way. *Where did Myrick go? Who took him? Why?* Elsam was close to losing his mind. Feeling forces outside his control were mocking him, he strode into the great hall, making for his throne. He had forgotten it was destroyed. Gnarling deep in his throat, he continued past the rubble, entering his office.

"Clean that up!" He ordered his guards. "Get me a new throne, now!"

He slammed the door on their shocked faces. Dropping down in his chair, he slammed his fists on the desk. Nothing was going right. At every turn forces were working against him. He refused to believe his cause was lost. He would win, one way or another. Eliana had the Kaemorra. What she intended to do with it was beyond his power to know. He needed to get his hands on it. Without it, he would never get the power he craved. She had kept him away from the throne, gave away his son, and used his own imprisoned witch to keep the Kaemorra from him. He should have killed Meredith when he had the chance. A knock on the door made him clench his fists. *How dare they interrupt me?*

"Go away!" He yelled, as the knock came again.

"Sire, Erebus has arrived. He awaits you outside." A guard hesitantly spoke through the door.

Elsam took a deep breath. Trying to regain his composure, he dragged his hand through his hair. Standing, he straightened his clothes, and rolled his head around his neck. His need of the shadows was the only reason he plastered a smile on his face. He left his office, walked out of the great hall and exited into the black night outside. Erebus needed the cover of darkness to meet with Elsam. The shadow overlord had taken human form, standing just to the right of the tower's entrance. Although he had what looked like arms and legs, his body was nothing but a black blob.

"I hear you have had some trouble with your people." Erebus grinned at Elsam.

Elsam's smile wavered. *How much does the shadow know? Does he know I lost my alliance with the Daimon?* Recovering, Elsam grinned back at Erebus. He strolled over to take a seat on the marble bench next to the door.

"Nothing I can't handle." Elsam said.

Erebus laughed. His guffaws irritated Elsam. Waiting for the overlord to finish laughing, Elsam schooled his features into neutrality. Erebus waved his spindly arm and four other shadows rose from the ground to surround Elsam. Their presence presented an obvious threat. He could not risk being touched by them.

"Manar has run home to daddy, who, let me tell you, is not very pleased with his son right now. Did you know, he did not advise Olar of his plans? You have lost one alliance. Will you gamble to lose another? Are you ready to give me what I want?" Erebus waved his hand again. The four shadows moved closer to Elsam.

"Enough!" Elsam bellowed. "You know I cannot give what I do not possess. If you want the damn thing, you have to help me."

Erebus laughed again. With a flick of his wrist, he waved off his followers. Elsam took the chance to stand and try to go back into his tower. Erebus quickly blocked his way. He eyed the Sidhe, looking for any sign that he would dishonor their agreement. Elsam tried to keep his eyes steady, but the twitch in the corner of his left eye gave him away. He was nervous, untruthful.

"You are on your own." Erebus started to melt back into the ground.

"Wait!" Elsam spoke, panicked at losing his only remaining alliance.

Erebus remained half a shadow below the ground and half above it. His head turned and waited for Elsam to speak. The seconds it took for Elsam to come up with some way to maintain the shadow's help, were too many for Erebus. He did not trust the Sidhe. Sliding down fully into his shadow form, he and his men moved away. Elsam watched them go, frozen by how badly things had gone.

It took him several minutes to move. Keeping alert, in case the shadows returned, Elsam finally entered his tower, feeling alone and deserted. All his allies had abandoned him. He should have been worried, but it was a minor setback, he tried to reassure himself. *After all, I still have my ace in the hole*. Properly motivated, the delusional woman would come through for him.

It still surprised him how easy it was to fool her. Elsam had only loved one woman in his whole existence. Agatha had been his for too short a time. Vanya tried to fill the void, but she was unworthy of him. Her sniveling declarations of love grated on his nerves. Elsam could love no one but Agatha. This other woman also believed he cared about her. He would use her to get what was rightfully his. When he had dominion over all the races, he would discard her like all the rest. She would be lucky if he let her live.

Chapter 16 - Alexa

"Aidan, please stop fussing. I'm fine." I nearly slapped his hand away.

He had carried me up to a bedroom, refusing to let me walk. Depositing me softly on top of the violet comforter, he left me for a moment to retrieve the extra pillows from the chair by the window. The room was one I had not seen on my previous visit. The decor colors clashed loudly. Purple, yellow, brown. What had the decorator been thinking?

Aidan returned with a stack of forest-green pillows and went to work on placing them behind my head. It was at that moment that I tried to stop his unnecessary concern. His response was to ignore me and unfurl the throw at the foot of the bed in order to cover me.

When he decided I was finally comfortable, I found myself cocooned in the warmth of a paisley blanket, half-sitting, half-lying on the bed. My arms were imprisoned under the throw, which was tucked in under me. I felt ridiculous. Yanking my arms out, I pushed myself into a seated position. Aidan observed me suspiciously.

"I'm not going anywhere. You can relax." I snapped.

His face broke out in a smile at my frustration. I turned away so he would not see how my lips fought against answering his. The bed moved under me, as he sat beside me. Glancing back, I saw him still grinning. Avoiding his eyes, I pretended to arrange the blanket around me. His hands captured mine, stilling the nervousness overtaking me. I peeked up at him from under my lashes.

"Alexa, you need to rest. Will it be better if I leave you alone? I could come back later." Aidan studied me.

"No. No." I insisted. "Only…ah …well… Can you just stay with me?" I wanted to slap myself. Why did I sound like such an idiot? This was Aidan. Why was I suddenly nervous?

His raised eyebrow, his lips twitching to break out in a laugh, made me blush a vivid red. I could feel the heat, as it spread over my face inch by inch. Humiliated, I ducked under the blanket so he could not see my face. My groan was echoed by a laugh that did escape him then.

"Come out." He continued softly laughing, while pulling the blanket away from me. "I'll just lie next to you."

It was unnerving, the sudden shyness striking me. We had not been alone together since I had found him. With all the things needing our attention, finding time to be alone had not presented itself. Now that we were, I was overcome with uncertainty. Aidan was so much older than me. His experience, both in life and love, far outmatched mine. How many women? I refused to finish the thought. Sensing my predicament, Aidan lay down next to me, pulling me down so that my head lay on his chest. His arms held me gently, understanding what I was going through.

"No, there were no women that could compare to you. I wish I could say there were none, but there were none I loved." Aidan whispered.

I sighed. I could not hold it against him. Snuggling closer to him,

I opened my mind so he could feel what I was going through. His response was to hold me tighter. *Tell me everything I missed*, he wordlessly asked me. I relived all that occurred since he left Liam's room on the day he found me crying over him. I let him into my mind, so he could follow the journey.

From my leaving for Crete, to Meredith's giving me her powers, he said not a word. When I started in on letting myself get captured so I could save him, he tensed. He hated that I had placed myself in danger for him. He felt he did not deserve it after abandoning me. The blame was half mine for not accepting him. *These powers, are they as strong as I sense*? He wanted to know. Yes, they were barely controllable. I was in a constant battle to keep them under control.

"Thank you for sharing it all with me. Now, I really think you need to sleep. I feel your energy is completely drained." Aidan half rose on his elbow to stare down at me.

I was tired, but I did not want to lose time when I could be with him. Still my eyelids were heavy from fatigue. Maybe I could take a half hour to get some rest. Aidan gently dropped a kiss on my lips. My insides quivered in response. Seeing the black specs in his eyes gather speed, I was again seized by my lack of experience.

"It will happen when you are ready, Alexa. We have all the time in the world. Relax, sleep." He gently spoke, my blush reappearing at his knowing look.

A soft knock on the door, the knob turning, took my attention away from the embarrassment I was feeling. Bet's head peeked in once the door was pulled back a few inches. Seeing we were watching her, she opened the door fully.

"Hi Bet. Come in." I waved for her to come closer, glad to have someone else to focus on.

Bet wandered over to us and took a seat at the foot of the bed. Aidan, clearly not pleased at the interruption, would have preferred that I sleep. Snatching one of my pillows, he put it behind his head, so that he could sit up.

"How's Elron?" I asked her. In my vision he had been badly hurt.

The man himself appeared in the doorway. His injured arm, wrapped in a bandage, was held in a sling. Blood from his wound had seeped through the stark white gauze, as it continued to trickle out. He could not hide the pain it inflicted on him, evident by his drawn, ashen face. Trying to find the cause of the wound not healing remained hidden from me.

Coming over to join Bet, he lifted her up, sat down and positioned her on his lap. His uninjured arm wrapped around her. The only person I had no news about was Asher. I reached out to find him, seeing his condition rapidly deteriorating. Afflicted by a poison I knew I could not heal, his breath came out ragged and stressed. Was Elron also in danger? Why could I not see what ailed him. It was obvious something was wrong. Aidan squeezed my shoulder, sensing how rapidly my concern grew.

"Your father? How is he doing, Bet?" I asked, trying to shake my disquiet over Elron's condition. I could only hope he would be fine.

"Well, your mom has helped him a great deal, but he isn't

healing. All we can do is wait." Bet answered, worry replacing the smile she gave Elron when he sat with her.

Aidan had been silent while we spoke. His thoughts were not on his father, but somewhere else. It was the second time I had noticed his mind wandering. I scanned the house again, finding there was a room I had no access to. Blocked from me, it appeared that the room was shadowed, hidden on purpose. I nudged Aidan with my arm to get his attention. His eyes met mine, unsure of relating what he knew.

"You can forget about trying to hide it. I know he's here." Bet told Aidan. "Should we go see him?"

Solas. Instantly I knew who occupied the room hidden from me. I closed my eyes to catch his essence. What I felt was so brutally painful, I quickly shut the link between us. Vanya was dead. In that short instant that I linked with Solas, I saw all he had lived through the past few days. He felt alone in the world. His misery over Vanya's death was part of the loss he felt. His own father had tried to kill him. The only family who remained had never been a part of his life. His wariness of their reaction, of their accepting him, kept him isolated.

"Bet. Give him time. Please go easy on him." I counseled her. "He has lost everything. Vanya is dead. Elsam has tried to have him killed. We are all he has left."

Bet stared back at me, looking affronted. Elron felt her stiffen in his arms. I knew how volatile she could be. My warning came not because I felt she would do something on purpose, but that she might say something to cause Solas more pain. Before I could explain what I meant, Aidan got up from the bed.

"The person to speak with him should be me. I think I know some of what he is feeling." His look warned Bet to stay put.

He did not wait for me to offer any input. He kissed me before departing. I saw him stride across the room, exit and turn the corner out of view. He left our link open for me to follow his signature down the hall to Solas's room. Bet and Elron were not so lucky. Bet left Elron to go to the doorway, where she hesitated to go after Aidan.

"Bet, if you want, I can let you see what is going on." I stopped her.

I offered my idea with no way of knowing if I could actually pull it off. Sitting up in the bed, I gathered my power, my hands tracing a circle over my lap. Within the imaginary circle a globule resembling a water drop formed. It hung in the air, suspended, clear and translucent. Elron was visible through the crystalline globe that hovered over the bed.

Intrigued, Bet came back to my bed, returning to sit next to Elron. Her finger lightly poked the outside wall of the watery globe. Enthralled, she watched as it indented at her touch, but maintained its cohesion. I passed my hand over it, concentrating on where Aidan had gone. Inside the walls of the sphere, Aidan's image materialized as he approached Solas's room. When he stopped in front of the door, his head tilted to the side at sensing me. He knew we were watching.

Aidan did not bother knocking. He opened the door and stepped inside. Solas was not in sight when Aidan scanned the room. He could hear him in the bathroom. The sound of the shower turning off, the curtain rattling across the rod at being pulled open, filled the bedroom.

Aidan waited for Solas. He appeared soon after with a bath towel tied across his hips. Seeing Aidan, he said not a word. Instead he went directly to the cabinet, removing a pair of jeans and a black T-shirt. He returned to the bathroom, closing the door so he could dress.

It was several minutes later that the door re-opened. Solas, his wet, shoulder length, ebony black hair dripping, stepped out to face his brother. It was eerie how similar they were. Only about an inch shorter, Solas was also just slightly less filled out than Aidan. It was hard to miss that they were related. Aidan's first look at Solas, made him aware of how delicately he must approach him. Solas had no reason to trust him. Aidan, himself, was unsure of Solas being there.

"I'm Aidan." He said. "I assume you already know that."

Solas sighed. He went to the bed, where he sat down on the edge. Aidan pulled the chair that rested by the desk closer. When he sat, he still had no idea what he should say. I nudged him, touching his mind, telling him to be gentle. Solas had more reasons to fear Aidan than Aidan to fear Solas. He had nowhere else to go. Aidan let me know he would try his best.

"I want you to feel welcome here. Anything you need, just let me know." Aidan tried to put him at ease.

Solas just stared at Aidan. Unsure that the words were said in earnest, he gave the impression of waiting for more. He lowered his head and emitted a deep sigh. *Why should they accept me?* Bet itched to take off to the other room. Elron held her in place, waiting to see what else transpired. We watched Solas get up, pace around the room.

"I'm truly sorry over Vanya." Aidan continued. "She was a good friend to my mother in the past."

Solas raised his head, studying Aidan to see if he could detect any sarcasm in his features. What he saw made him bow his head. His sorrow filled the room, had him fighting back tears. Aidan waited for him to collect himself. Bet's better nature, wanting to comfort, had her racing out of our room before we could stop her. Elron and I remained where we were. There was no point going after her. We saw her enter the room, going directly to Solas. Her arms gathered him, holding him, while he stiffened.

"You have nothing to fear here. We are your family." She tried to soothe him.

Solas's eyes met Aidan's, bewildered at Bet's arrival. Aidan shook his head, grinning back at him.

"This is Bet. Always unpredictable. Good luck in keeping her away." Aidan laughed at Solas's reaction.

Bet shushed him. She hooked her arm through Solas's and leaned into him. Aidan could not help the laugh escaping him, at his brother's expression. Solas looked befuddled, confused. Bet grinned from ear to ear. I had seen enough. The poor man had no way of dealing with those two. Letting go of the crystalline globe, it dissolved from sight. I got up and with Elron following me, I found Aidan no longer laughing at his brother's expense.

"I want all of you out. Now." I insisted. "Bet, go with Elron. See if your father needs anything. Aidan go find your mother and Liam. Now!"

They all were shocked at my tone, but they moved to do as I

asked. Aidan's hand brushed mine on his way out. His mind touched mine briefly, telling me he only agreed to leave because he knew I wanted to see Solas alone. When they were all gone, Solas waited for me to leave as well. I closed the door, returning to take the chair that Aidan had vacated. His eyes were so much like Aidan's, only the black specs I was familiar with were absent. He looked apprehensive of me, scared of what I represented.

"There is no way I can understand what you are going through." I started. "We are all here for you in any way that can help. Solas, you do belong. Never think otherwise. Your brothers, and yes, as you already saw, your sister, Bet, are all ready to accept you. Your mother has many regrets. Let them in, know that you can trust that they will do right by you."

Solas dipped his head, tearing his eyes away from me. I could see it would take time to convince him. Involving him in our family and what lay ahead was the right thing to do.

"We will soon have an additional guest. Please, come with me. We need your help." I held out my hand to him. With reluctance, he took it. I led him out, down the stairs to the main room, where everyone but Asher and my parents awaited. In the busy room, the new arrival showed signs of being in the same condition as poor Solas.

Tory looked forlorn, unapproachable where he stood stiffly by the patio doors. I could see his turmoil, the deep hurt he tried to hide, although no visible signs of harm showed on him. I glimpsed his inner conflict and the rage he just barely kept under control. Rina was at the center of a betrayal that ran deep within him. What had she done to hurt him so?

Concerned over Tory's emotional state, I left Solas standing in the doorway to enter the room alone. I carefully made my way to Tory, who refused to look at me. When I reached him, he moved away, his jaw clenching to control his emotions. At a loss to understand what had transpired, I watched Tory go rigid when Liam spoke.

"Where's Rina?" Liam wanted to know.

Hearing her name, Tory's face transformed. His features hardened further, his eyes blazed with anger. I bridged the distance, touching his arm to steady the fury gripping him. Shocked at his response, as he yanked his arm away from my touch, I tried to get a read on him. It was difficult to get a complete picture of what had caused him to act that way. His thoughts were all over the place. Without answering Liam, he stomped over to where Eliana sat on a sofa. Approaching her, he stopped to stare heatedly down at her.

"Why?" His voice thundered in the room.

Eliana lowered her eyes at his tone. Clearly, she knew what he was asking about. The rest of us were in the dark over why Tory glared down at her. From the corner of my eye, I saw Solas remained standing uncertainly in the doorway where I had left him. He was unsure if he should participate in the discussion. Bet noticed him as well. She went to him, pulling him into the room and into a chair. I returned my attention to Tory, wondering what made him so angry.

Studying him, trying to see past his defenses, I caught sight of what caused his outrage at Eliana. She had known all along he was not Sidhe, and had kept his existence secret. How much did she know of where he came from? Why did she send him off to find his own way, if she had the answers? I was curious myself. Had she learned nothing from her past actions? I thought there would be no more secrets among us.

"Tory, I have known you are not full Sidhe. Where you came from I can guess, but not why you were sent to us. These questions are ones only your parents can answer. It is the reason I asked you to search for them." Eliana gave Tory her full attention.

Tory was not appeased by her response. Suspicious, unconvinced over what she told him, he stomped away, going back to the patio doors, where he stared out at the gardens. His whole body remained tense from trying to control his anger. Elron followed him, stepping next to him to offer his support. The two brothers, even though not related, were close. As much as they fought, or tried to pretend they were different, the two held a strong bond. Elron did not attempt to touch Tory. He simply spoke to him softly.

"I know how you feel. Believe me, I too need answers. Anger will not solve anything."

Tory tried to gain control over his emotions. Closing his eyes, he took steady breaths to calm himself. Elron silently waited for Tory to master his emotions. Letting go of a final deep breath, Tory turned to face his brother. Nodding that he was ready, Elron placed his hand on Tory's shoulder. Agreement passed between them. Together, they came back to face and question Eliana.

"My Queen, we need you to tell us everything you know." Elron told her.

Eliana closed her eyes for a second before she rose from her seat. All eyes fell on her. She visibly struggled to find the words to give them the answers they demanded. Hesitating, she took several steps towards me. Her eyes found mine, seeing my curiosity matched the others. How much did she know? Would she even tell us the truth? Grimacing upon seeing my skepticism, she turned towards the two brothers, speaking directly to Elron.

"Elron, your parents, those you were raised by, came to me soon after they received you. They asked me to keep your origin secret. They never told me the real story of why you were brought to them. This we have discovered only recently. I only knew you would be a catalyst to getting the Kaemorra back. I knew your adopted parents were not Sidhe. They were found wandering near our island by some of our scouts. Both were preparing to leave this land, to end their lives. They were alone, tired of their existence. I offered them a home, somewhere they could continue. They accepted my offer. Arriving on our island, we masked their origins, letting all our citizens believe they were Sidhe. I know nothing more than that."

Elron dropped down onto the couch, still not any closer to fully understanding everything. He knew his mother Agatha was an immortal, that she had placed him with his adopted parents to keep him from Elsam, his father. How he was to be a catalyst was something only I and Eliana knew. We had not spoken one word of it to the others. I still felt they would oppose what actions I took.

Elron fidgeted in his seat, trying to find a comfortable position. I saw him wince, his left hand going to the wound on his right arm. His face clouded, at what I assumed were unanswered questions. The bandage around his arm was completely drenched in blood. The wound though, was the least of his preoccupations. He glanced at Tory, his expression puzzled at what little information Eliana had imparted. Still, it was more than he previously knew. Tory waited to see what she would say about him. Eliana faced him, preparing to cast light on his origins.

"Tory, I don't know much about you. Why you were placed with the same family, I do not know. Your parents, your real ones, are unknown to me. I sent you to find the ones who raised you because only they know. I knew you were on our island, but your signature is baffling. I often felt you were not present, even when you stood in front of me. I cannot offer you anymore. I too would like to know who, what you are. You need to find your parents." Her words gave him no comfort. He was still an unknown.

I searched his signature to see what I could see. It was true that what I saw was intriguing. Tory appeared to be there, but not there. His essence fazed in and out continuously. Before I could remark on it, Tory seemed to come to a decision.

"I will find them. Alone. If anyone sees Rina, keep her away from me." His words worried me. What had she done to him?

Not waiting for an answer, Tory transported away. Elron sighed into the silence he left behind. Bet went to him, touching his injured arm. The sight of the bloodied bandage had her nearly panicked. Eliana noticed it as well. She commanded the two of them to follow her.

Bet helped Elron stand and once he was on his feet, she guided him after her mother, who strode from the room. Solas, who remained uncertainly in his seat, itched to leave us as well. I nodded at him to go if he wanted. He did not wait to be told twice. He launched off his chair, disappearing up the stairs, back to his room. Aidan knowingly grinned at me. Solas would have to acclimate to us slowly.

Tory's state was continuing to baffle me. I wanted to find Rina, to understand what had happened between them. Aidan spoke in my mind, that he too was curious. Would I be able to bring her there? I had never tried to transport someone into Deis-dé. Opening up my mind further, I focused on finding her.

A nudging alerted me to Rina's signature somewhere in Scotland. She leaned against the side of a house facing an overgrown, weed-infested garden. I felt remorse cloud her mind, as I probed it. Grabbing onto her essence, I tried pulling her to us. With some difficulty, I managed in the end to grab hold of her after a few attempts. She materialized, dazed and confused to find herself in the room with us.

"Where's Tory?" Were the first words out of her mouth. She was anxious for an answer.

"What happened, Rina? What did you do?" My words accused her. I only knew that Tory was hurt by something she had done.

Rina paced, wringing her hands. Clearly agitated, she appeared desperate to find Tory. I stepped in front of her, blocking her movement. Her eyes met mine, clouded with guilt and grief. She effectively hindered my attempt to gather more information by reaching into her mind. Watching tears form, I put my arm around her shoulders and led her to a sofa. Once we were both seated, I grasped her hands, which were shaking.

"Rina, please tell us what happened. Why is Tory angry with you?" I did not mention his hurt.

Rina glanced around, catching sight of Aidan curiously observing her. She tore her eyes from his, subtly shaking her head as if to clear it. With a deep rugged breath, she began to explain what they were up to. Her mother Melia was the one who told her to take Tory to Santorini.

There they were met by a delegation of his people. Tory was asked to return with them, but he refused. He wanted to stay, to help the rest of us complete the prophesy. Tory saw her actions as a betrayal, because she wanted him to leave. I could tell his leaving was the last thing she wanted. Did she even realize the extent of her feelings for Tory?

"Who are his people, Rina? Who were the people that came for him?" I asked her instead.

Rina hid her eyes under her lashes. She dropped her head, so I could not see her expression. Would she keep the information from us?

I held onto her hands, applying pressure for her to answer my question. Her head lifted slightly, so she could look at me.

"It was Elethea and Conall, the beings that aided you in the past. I cannot tell you more. Only my mother knows who they are exactly." Rina's answer was not the whole truth. She knew more than what she was willing to tell us.

Who were these people? How could they be in the past and the present? I knew I would not get further answers from Rina. She was already on her feet ready to go after Tory. I rose with her, holding her arm, wanting to tell her to give Tory time.

"I cannot. I need to find him. He must understand why I did what I did." Rina spoke before I uttered a word.

I sighed, defeated in finding a way to help them both. Rina refused to acknowledge the reasons why she was agitated at Tory avoiding her. I saw plainly her feelings for him had grown beyond friendship. Opening my senses, I found where Tory had transported to. Nodding to Rina, I accepted that they needed to find their own way. I let go of her, focusing my energy on sending her to him. She vanished, giving me a thankful look before she completely left us.

"Alexa, I need to speak to you in private. Please follow me." Eliana's appearance in the doorway interrupted what I was going to say to Aidan.

Curious at what she wanted of me, I glanced at Aidan. His face showed the same curiosity. He inclined his head for me to go. I could always tell him what Eliana discussed with me later. I joined her by the doorway, ready to follow her. At that moment, my mother found us.

Coming down the stairs, she was panicked.

"Eliana, come with me. Hurry! Asher…" She could not finish her statement.

Eliana's head lifted, anguish filling her face at what she sensed. What she gleaned with her senses propelled her up the stairs. Not knowing what caused the commotion, I closed my eyes to find the cause. My heart stopped. Blinking back tears, I turned to Aidan. He knew immediately the cause of my reaction. He took off at a run up the stairs.

Liam, who had entered from outside, breezed by me, following Aidan. I caught sight of Bet standing on the upper floor landing. She was rooted, frozen next to Elron. I raced up the stairs to them, not knowing what I could do over the inevitability of what I foresaw. I watched through my tears as Solas went to her side. He took her elbow, leading her down the hall to Asher's room.

"What will we do now?" Elron asked me.

"We need to look at your arm. It hasn't healed. Let me see if I can do something about it. Come with me." I held my hand out to him.

Chapter 18 - Elsam

Elsam stayed his hand from striking the idiotic woman lying naked atop him. He tried his best not to flinch from her fingers tracing lazy circles on his bare arm. With her head on his chest, her hair fanned out across his body, making him itch to push her aside. She continued to place brief, nauseating kisses wherever her lips could reach.

Elsam was irritated beyond belief by her continued presence. *How long would she stay this time*? Staring up at the ceiling, he counted to ten. His room was dark. He had made sure to pull the drapes so no light from outside could penetrate the room. It was bad enough he had to touch her, he did not want to have to look at her as well.

His bedroom was sparsely furnished. A king-sized bed dominated the otherwise undecorated room. Only a chair and a side bureau were off to his right. There was no need for anything else. Once he gained possession of the Kaemorra, returned to his rightful place on the throne, then he would reward himself with all the opulence of his new station.

Until then he would have to put up with the inconveniences he was forced to undertake. He almost gagged at what some of those burdens forced him to do. He promised himself this would be the last time. After today, he would not need to see that foolish woman again. At least not in that position. He would make excuses the next time she arrived, expecting him to accommodate her.

Elsam felt the mattress shift, drawing his attention back to her.

Lifting up on her elbow, her eyes sought his, expecting to find the same contentment she was experiencing. He schooled his features into neutrality, not showing how repulsed he was to be in bed with her. His need of her and her powers were essential to his plans.

Any information she brought him more than made up for having to make love to her. She had already reported to him that Alexa received no help from the warlock council. That in itself was worth the hours he spent pleasuring the insipid creature. Seeing her lips pucker, descending to meet his, Elsam recoiled. Unable to take anymore, he grabbed her shoulders to stop her.

"I have business to attend to." He rolled out from under her, rose hastily out of bed and grabbed his robe from the chair.

The silly woman reached for him again, expecting him to come back to her. Ignoring her outstretched arm, Elsam pulled on his robe instead. He left her pouting, striding purposefully away from her into his bathroom. He made no attempt to stop the door slamming shut behind him. Stepping up to the vanity, the mirror revealed what he already knew.

Disgust and anger fought each other on his features. It would be impossible to put himself through having to be near her again. He hoped she would be gone when he emerged. Wanting to wash any evidence of her away, he grabbed a quick shower. While toweling off, he managed to block her from his mind. There were other complications needing his attention.

He actually did have business to attend to. A response to the call he made to Erebus, the shadow leader, was still pending. Elsam had not heard back from him yet. To say their last meeting did not go well was an understatement. Erebus had all but called off their alliance. Elsam thought it too early to say his plans were completely falling apart. There still remained time to regain control.

Ready to make the concession Erebus demanded, Elsam had reached out to the shadow lord to set up another meeting for that night. Making Elsam wait for a response was a tactic, one that Erebus thought would place him in a better bargaining position. Elsam's ire grew with each second he was kept waiting.

A knock on the door made him grimace. *Is she still here? Can she not take a hint?* He pulled the door open, ready to tell her to get lost, but found one of his guards instead. Glancing at the bed, he was pleased to find the woman was gone. The Sidhe facing him could not meet his eyes. He must have seen the witch in his bed. Striding past him, Elsam went to his closet for clothes.

"Sire, Erebus will arrive within the hour. Darkness is almost upon us." The man reported before hastily leaving the room.

Elsam pulled clothes out of the closet, dressed quickly and exited into his throne room. His men had replaced the destroyed seat with one that hardly benefited his position. Plain, with no adornments, he ignored it. There was no way he would sit upon it. They would have to procure him a better one. The throne room was deserted when he entered. His jaw clenched at perceiving the desertion of some of his men.

Half his forces were gone. The remaining stayed because they had nowhere else to go. Loyalty towards Elsam was an afterthought.

None truly believed in him. He would show them all. He would prevail. The traitors would soon find they had chosen the wrong side. With his forces down to a minimum, the shadows would more than make up for any men he had lost.

He left the room, catching sight of no one about while making his way outdoors. Taking a seat on the stone bench, he scanned the horizon for any movement. Erebus, along with his men, would soon be there. What his plan entailed, he hoped would placate Erebus. Agreeing to hand over the Kaemorra to the shadow overlord once he possessed it, could be a lie that would come back to haunt him. But, for the moment it was the only way to appease Erebus.

Elsam had no intention of handing over the precious crystal. Elsam's only objective was to have the shadows help him in claiming Eruva for himself. Once he rose to the throne, Erebus would find himself unable to set foot on the island. The protection the Kaemorra would afford, would effectively keep the shadows out.

Elsam waited impatiently for Erebus to slink his way to their meeting. He did not have long to wait. From across the field, he watched shadows move along the grassy knolls. The largest of the inky black shapes approaching him, rose on hind legs once he reached Elsam. Erebus took on the appearance of a man, though he lacked any facial features. The face that stared at Elsam was a black void in the darkness. Two red eyes were centered in the unformed face.

"Why have you called for me?" Erebus's voice hissed.

As the shadow advanced towards Elsam, he in turn pulled his body as far away as he could to avoid any contact. Elsam did not trust the creature. Coming up against the wall of his tower, Elsam could not retreat further. Erebus stopped, waiting for Elsam to answer.

"I agree to your terms." Elsam spoke.

Erebus was silent, staring at the Sidhe in front of him. The red orbs seemed to narrow. The silence stretched, as Erebus stared at Elsam, searching for signs of deceit. Elsam kept his face open, not showing any of what he intended.

"You would not be planning to cheat me? Would you, Elsam?" Erebus asked. What was supposed to be his head leaned to the side, coming within inches of Elsam's face.

Elsam had nowhere to go to avoid the shadow. His head pressed against the stone wall behind him. He fought to control his anger at being put in that position. A muscle in his cheek twitched with fury. Erebus backed away, slinking to the grass-covered ground on the walkway. His laugh at Elsam's fear sounded in the night air. Elsam left his seat, taking a step away from the wall. He stretched up to his full height, hands clenching at his sides, while Erebus mocked him.

"I will have the crystal, Elsam. If you cross me, there is nowhere you can go to hide. I agree to your terms. My men will join with yours. Tell us where and we will come." Erebus's shape fell to the ground, slithering off into the night.

Elsam would have screamed his frustration, if not for the guards who appeared in the doorway. Keeping his temper, he turned to see what had brought them there. Both Sidhe were watching the fading forms of the shadows in the distance. Their faces showed disapproval at being forced to work alongside the shadows.

"What is it?" Elsam drew their attention.

The younger of the two guards turned his eyes to his liege. He could not hide his internal struggle. His men were at the end of their rope because of how Elsam had proceeded with his plans. It took the other Sidhe to voice what brought them out of the tower.

"We have not found any trace of Myrick. It seems he has been shielded from us."

Elsam had tasked his men in finding the warlock. He still wanted to see him tortured and killed with his own eyes. The arrogance of Myrick, his saving Solas, not alerting him to what Vanya was doing, were actions that necessitated the ultimate punishment. Even that small pleasure had been ripped from him. *Who had taken him? Why was Myrick saved?* The witch he was forced to sleep with did not know anything. *Is she hiding things from me? Am I unduly paranoid lately?* Elsam lacked information and no one could clarify for him what had happened to Myrick.

"Continue the search. Apprise me if he is found." Elsam dismissed the guards.

It took the older Sidhe to grab the elbow of the younger to pull him away. Both entered the tower whispering between themselves. Elsam gave them no notice. His eyes were scanning for any other shadows that may be present. Seeing none, he too entered the tower. Making his way to his room, he passed the throne room again, giving a final order to the guard stationed within it to procure him a decent throne.

In his room, he was displeased to find the witch still there.

Where had she been hiding? How much had she seen of his meeting?
The only thing that gave him relief was that she was fully dressed.
Hoping she would leave, he put up with her wrapping her arms around
him. Kissing her back, he watched her face with open eyes. She gave no
indication she was aware of his plans. She stepped away from him,
giving him a sultry smile.

"I'll see you soon." She blew a kiss at him.

Elsam hoped he gave her an acceptable smile back. She left
through the secret passage in the wall of his room. Alone, he shook his
head at what he was forced to do in order to advance his plans. The
woman would be trouble. His mind went to Agatha. She deserved
better than his using the witch. *Would she approve of what I am doing?*

Agatha always kept her own council. She neither agreed nor
disagreed with what he planned. At times he thought he saw
disapproval in her eyes. That he loved her beyond reason was a fact. He
still missed her. Shaking himself out of his remembrances, he went to his
desk.

On it lay the scroll he had procured at great expense. The paper
was old, the ink faded. He knew where he needed to be on the summer
solstice. There he would wait for Alexa. She would bring him the
Kaemorra. She stood no chance against him and his army. The little
witch would find herself greatly outnumbered. A smile broke from his
lips at what he intended to do to her.

Chapter 19 - Witch Council

Caden, the head of the council, kept his eyes on Myrick, who struggled against the warlocks dragging him to face his judgment. Myrick visibly showed signs of torture at the hands of Elsam and his followers. The scars ran deep. They joined with the one crisscrossing his face, marking him for the traitor he was. As head of the council, Caden could have ordered their healers to look after him. Seeing the scar running across Myrick's face, he suppressed a smile, giving grudging respect to the man who had married his daughter.

Rider may be an unacceptable choice for Thalia, but he did well in marking his anger on Myrick's face. The newer marks covered exposed skin and were angry red welts. Caden forbade anyone in their encampment to aid in Myrick's healing. He wanted the man to suffer for his treachery against his kind. His condemnation was for more than the path Myrick chose.

There were additional reasons to abhor the man's actions. Caden held back his personal need to exact vengeance for the dangers Myrick had subjected his granddaughter to. Coming closer, Caden saw Myrick fighting the bonds holding his wrists together. His attempts were futile. The powers that held them in place could not be outmaneuvered. Caden had worked the spell himself. Myrick's powers were no match for Caden's abilities.

The audience chamber had fallen silent upon his entrance. Myrick's eyes showed his panic. Off to the side, Rydia, the water elemental, standing next to her husband Blayze, twitched nervously. The fire element in Blayze responded to her by sparking where his hand touched her back. All around Caden, the witch council members awaited for him to pass judgment.

Nyria's own fire element was dangerously close to erupting. Her narrowed eyes stared at the man being brought forth before them. She refused to acknowledge the look Myrick gave her. He was on his own. Any loyalty she owed her father was gone. He had abandoned her, along with her mother, long ago. That man was a stranger to her.

Across the room, Kesia, the earth elemental, looked serene, unaffected by the proceedings. Her eyes were focused on a witch standing near Caden. She long suspected the other of betrayal. She focused her energies to try and read what more she was hiding. The other woman was clever. She gave nothing away. Kesia had the proof needed to have her accused of treason. However, she would wait. It was only a matter of time before Caden gave his permission.

Solana was not far from Kesia. The air element she governed was held back by force of will. Her anger at the council for not supporting Alexa was making it difficult to maintain the illusion of control. The winds would have risen in the room if she had allowed them. Reigning them in was taking all her concentration.

Myrick finally arrived before Caden. The warlocks who had dragged him stepped to the side, giving their council leader clear access to the prisoner. Caden lifted his hand, pointed it at Myrick, and let his power drive Myrick to his knees. Falling, Myrick groaned as his kneecaps hit the floor. His head lifted to stare at Caden.

He waited silently for Caden to pronounce his punishment. Whatever the verdict might be, Myrick was ready. Everyone he ever cared about was lost to him. He had loved Thalia. His driving need, the actions he had taken, were due to her not returning his affections. She had chosen Rider above him. The pain of losing her had driven him mad.

Elsam had promised him she would be his. Blinded by his hatred for Rider, he had believed Elsam's promises. Casting a furtive glance at his daughter, he saw even Nyria could not look at him. She stared off, her face rigid, showing no emotions. He did not blame her. Dragging a deep breath into his lungs, he returned his gaze to Caden.

"Myrick, I leave the sentencing to the council members. If it were up to me, you would be dead already. There will be a vote tomorrow morning. Do you have anything to say in your defense?" Caden questioned.

What could I say to defend the complete betrayal to my kind? There is no defense. Myrick stole a glance at his daughter once again, deciding the only thing he could do was offer information. Elsam needed to be stopped. Myrick knew of his plans. The Sidhe thought himself clever, but the walls within his towers were thinner than he thought. The stone walls gave away their secrets when commanded. Elsam believed Myrick to be blocked from using his powers within the tower. The warlock was not as powerless as Elsam had thought.

"On the summer solstice, Elsam will be in Asserbo awaiting Alexa. He found a scroll that spoke of where she would be headed. He plans to ambush her and reclaim the Kaemorra. Whatever you do to me is immaterial to you warning her and saving the Kaemorra. Elsam cannot be allowed to reclaim it." Myrick told the assembled.

Caden did not show any signs of what he would do with the information. The rest of the witches and warlocks responded to his statement by breaking into vociferous discussions. They immediately started arguing for or against getting involved. Caden held his hand up to silence them. He would not discuss it in front of Myrick. He inclined his head to the guards, giving them permission to remove Myrick from the room. They grabbed the warlock, pulling him from the floor.

Myrick turned his head back, his eyes landing on Caden. His worried glance met Caden's steely gaze. Myrick saw the fury in the other grow, as he attempted to reach inside his mind. The warning he would have imparted was left unsaid. Myrick was pulled roughly out of the room before he could tell Caden more.

"We will convene a meeting to discuss this in an hour. Prepare your arguments." Caden spoke, then left the room.

Nyria approached Kesia, worried over what Myrick had said. Her father's warning needed to be verified. If Alexa were in danger, if Elsam knew of her plans, it may be too late to stop him. Nyria wanted to prove herself. She did not want to be stained by her father's betrayal. Her whole life, she had tried to distance herself from his actions. She had constantly presumed that others viewed her with suspicion.

Nearing Kesia, she found the other witch was focused on a group of their members, who were whispering, their voices rising as they tried to make their points. Nyria gave them no heed. She needed to convince Kesia. She was a holdout from their last meeting with Alexa.

Kesia must be made to see their involvement was necessary.

"Kesia, we must speak in private." Nyria said.

Kesia briefly glanced at Nyria before returning her attention to the other group. Her eyes narrowed, concentrating hard on what they were discussing. What held her interest, Nyria could not say. When one of the witches broke from the group to exit the room, Kesia moved to intercept her. As she made her way towards the other woman, Kesia gathered her earthly energy, creating a spinning rising cloud of dust to encircle her. Drawn from the particles on the floor, the dirt effectively kept the other witch confined. Kesia glided over, grinning maliciously, to confront the woman.

"Where would you be going? What has you so riled?" Kesia asked her.

The witch pushed against the force of the energy, unable to break free. The commotion got the attention of the other members of the council. They were slowly coming over to see what was happening. Kesia stared them down. Their steps faltered under the look she gave them.

"Let me go." The witch yelled above the sound of the winds driving the dust around her.

"Not until I know where you are going. Tell me, how long have you been consorting with Elsam?" Kesia accused her.

The other witch blanched at the accusation. Her eyes traveled to a man staring incomprehensibly back at her. Returning her angry stare to Kesia, she fought harder to release herself. It was plain that Kesia had spoken the truth.

"What is she talking about, Rydia?" Her husband Blayze strode closer.

"It's a lie. Kesia is trying to come between us. Don't you see that?" Rydia responded. "She has always wanted you for herself."

Kesia laughed. *Really! That is her defense?* Blayze shook his head, his disbelief plain on his face. He took a step back wondering how he had missed her lies, he turned his back on his wife. *Kesia is telling the truth. My wife has betrayed us to Elsam. Why?*

"I think, my dear, you have it wrong." Kesia spoke. "I was never interested in Blayze. It was you who I would have liked to know better. I see it is now an impossibility."

Nyria, hearing the terse words spoken to Rydia, stared shocked at Kesia's pronouncement. She would never have guessed what Kesia had divulged. *Oh well, one never knows. What are we to do with Rydia now?* Nyria asked herself. They could not let her go. Blayze left the room, not giving his wife a backward glance. She was on her own. The other members were too stunned to offer any solutions. Rydia panicked, fighting harder to free herself from the wall that surrounded her. She knew her situation was perilous. Unable to break free, she stopped fighting the field and stared back at Kesia.

"Kesia, darling, please. You know how I feel about you. Why didn't you tell me? We can be together." Rydia tried to worm her way out.

Kesia laughed. She threw her hands up, shaking her head at the attempt to use her feelings against her. *Is the woman completely without honor?* Kesia's mirth was replaced with hatefulness. By force of will she kept herself from striking out at Rydia. Nyria placed her hand on Kesia's arm to draw her attention away from the other woman.

"I'll call Caden." Nyria said. "He'll know what to do with her."

Caden entered the room within minutes of being called. He showed no surprise in seeing Rydia held against her will. The rest of the congregation left it to him to state what to do with her. Rydia's fearful expression did not affect his decision. Probing her mind, he drew every last bit of what she had done out of her. Anger blossomed, his cheeks reddening, incensed at the depth of her betrayal. *Must I probe the minds of all my people to assure myself of their allegiance?*

Caden had had enough. Releasing his link to her, he shuddered from the images he had seen. Rydia knew she was in deep trouble. There was nowhere she could go to escape what was coming. Caden asked Kesia to let the field drop. Once Rydia was free, Caden drew his hands together, clapping them together loudly in the room. Instantly, Rydia collapsed. She would remain immobile until he could decide what to do with her. Wanting her out of his sight, he called the guards to remove her from the room.

"Place her in a cell in the lower levels. The rest of you, I hope none of you are as treacherous as her. Meeting, half an hour!" He left the room, his heavy steps alerting the others to how angry he was.

Chapter 20 - Alexa

Overwhelming grief descended upon us in the days that followed. Asher's death hit us all hard. Eliana could not eat and barely slept. Consumed with guilt, the despair that washed over her kept her in a fog. While Aidan and Liam made arrangements for his funeral, I spent as much time with their mother as I could. Nothing I said or did brought her any comfort. She answered questions posed to her in a monosyllabic tone. Her dull eyes stared untiringly at something unseen.

When I took rest, my mother replaced me to keep Eliana company. Only two days before, my mother had called her to Asher's bedside. When Eliana had arrived, his condition had greatly deteriorated. He fought to drag breath into his lungs. The raspy sounds he had made were hellish to hear. Eliana fell to her knees beside his bed, grabbing his hand, willing him to open his eyes.

Asher never regained consciousness. While she caressed his cheek, I watched a single tear travel down Eliana's face. It was minutes later that Asher released his last breath. Eliana lost it then. Collapsing onto the floor, she was inconsolable. As she sobbed uncontrollably, Aidan lifted her into his arms, carrying her to her own room. I followed after them, my own tears blinding me. I bypassed Bet, Elron and Liam, who remained rooted to the spot in shock.

Off to the side, my mother was being embraced by Rider. Her tear-stained eyes caught mine when I passed them. What I saw almost made me stop. She was blaming herself for not being able to heal Asher.

I would have gone to her, if I could have. The controlled, unemotional wall surrounding Aidan forced me to follow after his wake. He instilled in me the greatest fear.

Asher's funeral, attended by only our small group in Deis-dé, was brief. Placed on a raft, the king lay on a bed of the luminous flowers from the gardens. Asher had been dressed in his ceremonial robes and his eyes were covered by two bronze coins. These were payment to enter the kingdom of the dead. While the raft floated on the calm lake waters, Aidan stoically walked up to his father. In his hands he held Asher's sword. Pulling Asher's stiff fingers apart, Aidan placed his father's sword in them. The fingers closed around the hilt, seeming to know the object belonged there. Aidan let the sword drop, positioning it to stretch down Asher's body. My eyes brimmed with tears seeing Aidan almost lose his composure.

Staring down at his father one last time, Aidan closed his eyes to control the grief devastating him. I knew he needed a moment alone with his father. Stiffening my back, I fought against the urge to go to him. When he made his way back to me, the walls around him were firmly back in place.

We were all dealing with our sorrow in our own way. I stood silently beside Aidan, holding onto his hand, feeling nothing from him. While my mom cried quietly on Rider's shoulder, Elron was supporting Bet. She stared forward, dry-eyed, unfocused on the proceedings. Since Asher's passing, Bet had shed not one tear. I wondered when she would let herself feel again.

Keeping close to Elron, her hand on her extended belly, Bet

showed no emotions. Liam, on the other hand, stood apart from us. His body language was not difficult to put into words. He was angry. He had put the blame squarely on his mother. She was the one who set them on that course. I did not believe for one second that she had wanted that, or ever thought it would be her punishment.

Eliana let no one console her. Guilt over lost time, all she had let happen were driving her to isolation. She silently watched Rider light a torch, walk to the raft and release the mooring. Before it floated out to open waters, he brought the torch to the kindling under Asher's body. Erupting into flames, the raft was quickly overcome by the spreading fire. We stayed while it was consumed, traveling away, taking Asher into the afterlife. Eliana left soon after the somber service, retreating below the manor, seeking the Kaemorra for answers.

Why had she not seen this coming? Why had the Kaemorra not warned her? These were the same questions we were all asking. Why had Asher's wound from Manar's sword not healed? I had been unable to see the cause of the worsening blackened wound. My mom, with all the healing powers at her disposal, had been unable to stop whatever had spread through Asher's body.

My thoughts went to Elron, whose wound appeared to be infected with the same poison. The increasing size of the bandage around his arm was proof he was afflicted with the same venom as Asher. I needed to do something, anything for him. Thinking of what that could be, the search for a remedy was put off by the added strain of trying to keep everyone from falling apart.

Aidan hid all his pain inside, while Liam raged for hours. Bet remained mute, refusing to acknowledge her father's passing. Mom used her tranquilizing power to get her to sleep. Elron stayed with her, keeping watch, in case she needed anything. I reached out, searching for Aidan and found him outside. His emotions were unchecked, letting me experience his agony. Getting him to open up, to let himself grieve, was my sole purpose in seeking him out. He needed to let his feelings out.

How much longer could he go on like that? I left the room, exiting into the garden, taking the path that led to him. I did not know which gave him more torment. The fact he had lost so much time with Asher while he was in statue form, or the distance that grew between them. Even he could not distinguish. It was all too much for Aidan. Guilt was swallowing his grief. None of it was his fault. It was his mother who had put us on the road we were on.

"Aidan." I called out to him.

"Over here, Alexa." He answered immediately.

He was under the tree near the stream we had been to months before. It was the spot he had brought me to, to escape his mother. He tried to smile, but it did not manage to reach his eyes. I did not need him to hide what he was feeling.

"Aidan, talk to me." I implored him to open up.

Dropping down next to him, I took his hand, willing him to open up. His eyes stared out across the water, clouding at what I asked of him. Ready or not, he needed to discuss what he was feeling. I would not take no for an answer.

"I failed him. I failed all of us. If I was not missing all those months, I would have been with my father in the fight against the

Daimon. He would not have been injured." Aidan took all the blame.

I shook my head. No, it would not have made any difference. Explaining that to Aidan would do little to make him feel better. I could see he was using guilt to stave off his pain.

"How's Elron?" Aidan changed the subject.

I snuggled into his side, trying to come up with an answer that would not cause him further worry. My hand lay on his chest, over his heart. Its beat steadied me in telling him how bad it was. Elron was afflicted with the same symptoms as Asher. His wound was a growing, blackening, spreading web on his arm. How to treat it, I did not know. My mom had no knowledge of what it was. Liam suggested that the only way to save Elron may be to cut off his arm. Elron would rather die than have that happen. He was a warrior. Bet's pleading could not sway him.

"It's getting worse. We don't know what is spreading within him." I told Aidan.

Aidan was silent at the news. I sensed him start to withdraw from me, pulling his emotions behind an impenetrable wall. Instead of allowing him to hide, I leaned away to look into his eyes. I could not let him do that.

"Aidan. Don't do this. It's not your fault. I need you now more than ever. Let me try to ease your pain. Please, let me in. There is nothing I wouldn't do for you." I begged him.

I felt him shudder at my words. His beautiful emerald eyes found mine. Suddenly, I was awash with anguish, torment, a driving need to hurt something, someone, anyone. Aidan's emotions flowed into me, their strength causing me to flinch. His fingers were squeezing my hand hard. I must have moaned at the pressure because he dropped my hand. He attempted to pull back, but I would have none of it. I straddled him.

My hands grabbed his face, keeping his gaze focused on mine. Staring into eyes that pooled with tears, I felt my own respond. His tears mixed with mine, as we shared our loss. Finally, Aidan calmed enough for me to release him. He did not let me go far. Pulling me into his arms, he held me, breathing shallowly against my cheek. I felt a soft kiss on my neck, his arms tightening, pulling me closer.

"You smell of orchids." He murmured.

I smiled, sensing he was calmer. His mood though was changing, developing into a baser one. I lifted my head to stare at him, finding a mischievous smile on his lips. An answering need rose in me. I let my lips find his. Softly I kissed him. His hand tightened on the back of my neck, drawing me closer. His tongue gently pried my lips open, searching, finding mine. My breath caught at the exquisite pleasure I felt.

One moment I was straddling Aidan, the next I found myself prone on my back with him lying atop me. Tingles spread through me at the contact of our bodies. Ready for what was about to happen, I was surprised when Aidan sat up. He cleared his throat before speaking.

"This is not how it will happen." He took my hands to pull me up. Once I was sitting next to him, he clarified. "When we make love, it will not be on damp grass, not due to grief. I love you, Alexa. I want it to be perfect for you."

I remembered Liam telling me that when the bond formed completely, I would wonder why I put up so much fuss. Well, it seemed he was right. Staring into Aidan's eyes, seeing his earnest look, I did wonder. Eliana told me that the bond was there for two people who belonged together, that would love each other no matter what. Aidan was that person for me. My heart hurt in my chest with the love I felt for him. Tears blinded me at what he was offering. Seeing them, he looked back at me with worry. My hand found his face, as I blinked the tears back.

"I love you, Aidan. I can't believe how stupid I've been. So much wasted time." I explained.

He grinned, pulling me into his arms. His lips never found mine. A sensation of travel overtook me. Aidan faded from my arms, his eyes panicked at me disappearing. The scene around me changed to one I hoped not to have to relive for a long while. The gaseous, noxious fumes made me gasp.

Finding myself back in the Daimon world, I tried unsuccessfully to return to Aidan. Olar was blocking me from leaving. Behind me, Mara lay still, asleep in her glass enclosure. The Daimon king's laugh, as he approached me, made me take a step back. Coming closer, I saw he held another Daimon in his claw-like hand.

"We have some business to attend to." He spoke, all the while dragging the other Daimon with him.

When he was steps from me, he tossed the other to the ground near my feet. The Daimon landed heavily where Olar had dropped him. He kept his head down, quivering in fear. At his full height, Olar dwarfed me as he came nearer.

"This pup Alexa is my son. He has gone against my wishes in involving us in your world." Olar hissed at his son. His anger with Manar kept the other Daimon silent.

"Why have you brought me here?" I tried to sound unafraid.

He laughed again at my show of defiance. Walking up to the glass enclosure, he laid his hand on it. I trembled slightly, scared that he would harm Mara. His red-orbed eyes turned to me. His round mouth seemed to form a smile. Leaving Mara, he glided over to his son. Yanking him up by the scruff of his scaly neck, Olar stared into his son's face.

"Manar, what do you have to say for yourself?" He growled at his son.

Manar said nothing. Fear of what his father would do to him held him back from answering. Seeing that fear, Olar laughed again. He let Manar go, letting him stumble from the force of being pushed aside. I forcibly kept myself from retreating, as Olar made his way to me.

"My son will be punished. He will remain in our realm for the foreseeable future. He has much to learn in the ways of our world. I have barred him access to yours." Olar stated. "I see he has caused much grief to you and your friends. Although I cannot restore the king, I can aid the other who is afflicted with our poison. Here, take this." He extended his claw, offering me a flask containing some kind of liquid.

I took it from him, studying the blackish liquid within it. Instinctively, I knew it was the remedy to the poison that had killed Asher. I glanced up at Olar, ready to thank him for helping with Elron.

He held up his claw to stop me.

"He has to drink all of it. He may not appreciate the taste, but it will kill what is within him. Tell Eliana I am sorry for what my son has done. Her husband's death will be avenged. Now, one final thing." He turned to look at Manar.

The other Daimon must have realized what Olar meant to do. He hissed at his father. I stayed out of their way. Olar marched up to Manar, grabbed him again and tossed him towards Mara. Manar had eyes only for the woman who was a prisoner in the enclosure. He stilled, panicked at what his father would do to her. I also worried that Olar would exact revenge for his son's sins. Mara was an innocent in all this. I would have voiced my opinion, but Olar cut me off.

"This woman does not belong here. She is not of our kind. Manar, you will release her. If you do not, I will kill her." Olar's words brought me out of my silence.

"No, you can't do that. Let me take her." I pleaded.

Manar snarled at my suggestion. Olar pushed me aside, grabbing his son again. Bringing his son's face inches from his own, he stared menacingly into his eyes. Manar must have seen the resolve in his father's face. He nodded, turning his face away from his father. Dropping him again, Olar and I watched Manar unsheathe his sword. Once in his hand, he lifted it, bringing it down hard on the lock that kept the glass fastened to the base where Mara lay. The lock smoked, hissing angrily before dissolving. Manar pushed the glass off, letting it smash in a thousand pieces where it landed on the ground. His claw lightly traced Mara's face. I could almost believe that he did love the woman. Olar gave him no time to grieve her loss. I saw Mara fade, disappearing from where she lay. Manar fell to the ground in torment.

"Go, she is back with her bonded. Alexa, know this. My kind will always bear allegiance to Queen Eliana. Tell her what was forged long ago remains." Olar told me.

I felt the sensation of travel taking hold of me again. Returning back in Aidan's arms, as if I had never left, he clearly appeared relieved by my arrival.

Disoriented at being thrust unceremoniously back to Deis-dé by Olar, waves of nausea kept me from moving. My head swam and my stomach heaved. I struggled in the arms holding me tightly against a firm chest. Panic hit me. It took me a moment to realize it was not my panic, but Aidan's. His hands gripped me firmly, afraid that I would disappear again without warning.

Needing space to catch my breath, to stop the rolling of my stomach, I tried to pull away from him. A moan escaped me, alerting him that something was wrong. He took in my pale, green-hued complexion. He gave me enough room so I could lower my head down between my knees. I closed my eyes, focusing on swallowing back the vile heave threatening to escape. It was no use. I needed to stand, to regain my equilibrium.

Freeing myself from Aidan's arms, I managed to climb unsteadily to my feet. Using the trunk of a tree to steady myself, I held on for dear life. Aidan followed me, giving me something else to focus on, as I swayed on trembling legs. His hands came to rest on my shoulders, supporting me from falling. I kept my eyes on his, using them to stop the world from spinning. In the back of my mind something was nudging me to remember something important. It took several seconds to recall Olar's releasing Mara from his kingdom.

What had he done with Mara? Did he harm her in any way? Breathing deeply seemed to drive the last bit of queasiness from me. My mind was solely focused on Mara and where she might be. Alarmed, I tried to locate her. Her signature seemed so faint, I wondered if it was my imagination. I needed to know for sure.

Pulling away from Aidan, not giving him any explanation, I took off in a run back to the manor. Aidan sensed the foreboding taking hold of me. He followed, keeping up with me all the way back through the gardens and into the main room. Inside, I found Mara laid out on one of the sofas, alone. Relief filled me at finding her unharmed. Even though she remained unconscious, she was gratefully alive. Her chest rose and fell, as her breath struggled. The sound of labored wheezing filled the room.

I sensed the toxins in her system, recalling how I myself had struggled to cleanse my lungs after spending mere minutes in the Daimon kingdom. The poor woman spent centuries breathing in their noxious fumes. Running to her, I placed my hand on her chest, just as Eliana had done with me, trying to heal her. I drew as much of the fumes as I could out of her, knowing the rest would be up to her. She would have to fight to come back to us.

Aidan stood over me, patiently waiting for an explanation. I could see he held back, giving me time to look after Mara first. Whatever discussion we would have had was interrupted by Liam entering the room. As Mara's bonded, he must have felt her arrival. I glimpsed no pleasure on his face at her being safe. What I saw was a man tormented by guilt, a belief that he had failed her when she needed him most. After several moments where he silently gazed at her, he left the room, going out into the gardens. Aidan took a step to go after him, but

I stopped him.

"I'll go. Please find your mother. Oh, and give this to Elron. He must drink all of it." I placed the flask Olar had given me in Aidan's hand. Miraculously, I had not dropped it.

Aidan's fingers wrapped around mine, taking the flask without question. Without releasing me, he lifted my fingers to his lips, where he placed a tender kiss on my knuckles. His eyes promised me so much, I could not help the smile that rose onto my lips. I stepped into his waiting arms, breathing in his familiar scent of sandalwood with a hint of citrus. He held me, exhaling a deep breath, content to have me safely back in his arms. Only the urgent need to find Liam gave me the strength to lift my head away from his chest and look up at him. Planting a soft kiss on my waiting lips, Aidan stepped back.

"Go. I'll find the others." He told me, giving me room to pass by him.

Reluctantly, I left him. At the patio doors, I stopped to glance back. Aidan had not moved from where I had left him. He nodded for me to go, then turned to leave the room and find his mother and Elron. The gardens were deserted when I stepped outside. Liam was nowhere in sight. Where could he have gone? I opened up my senses, searching for his signature, finding him in the forested land to my right.

Liam's essence was like a beacon, drawing me to him. It was impossible to dim the force of his energy. Increasing my pace, I made it to where he had gone, to find him pacing back and forth. Stepping past the tree line, I found him swearing loudly at the heavens. I stopped, giving him time to notice me. When he did, his expletives stopped.

Unable to meet my eyes, he turned away, sitting down heavily next to a tree. I struggled to block his conflicting emotions. Sorrow, remorse, joy and overwhelming guilt fought for dominance.

"Liam, you could not have known. Mara needs you now. The past will work itself out." I sat down next to him.

"How will I explain that I never once looked for her?" His guilt was more profound than I had thought.

What could I say to ease his recriminations? Liam had thought her dead. There had been a burned body who he had assumed was her. Could he have known Manar had taken her? No. I did not believe that. Their bond had broken due to her being in the Daimon realm. It would have been impossible for Liam to think anything other than she was gone.

"Listen to me. Mara never gave up on you. Don't you dare give up on her. She will need you to recover. Liam, your love for each other will help you both through this." I told him.

Liam sighed deeply. Closing his eyes, he drew in a deep breath. Getting a hold of his emotions, he stood, ready to face the woman he felt he had abandoned. I rose with him, taking his hand, walking alongside him back to the manor. Entering the room, we found Eliana seated next to Mara. She made room for Liam, who went directly to the sleeping woman.

"Where's Aidan?" I asked her, hoping she had news of Elron.

Eliana got up from her seat to meet me by the patio doors. That gave Liam the opportunity to take her place. Sitting on the edge of the sofa where Mara lay, I saw him touch her face with his fingers, his emotions too much for me to bear. He leaned over her, gathering her in his arms. His face showed so much sorrow, it was heartbreaking.

"Liam, take Mara upstairs to your room. Make sure she is comfortable. Stay with her." Eliana told her son.

He instantly did as he was told. Gently lifting her up, he cradled her in his arms. He stole a glance at me before leaving the room. I knew he was replaying my words to him. Mara would need him to recover. Left alone with Eliana, I saw she was somewhat more herself. She was handling her grief in the only way she knew how.

Keeping busy was her way of coping with the heavy loss. I relayed to her Olar's message, not understanding what he meant by their alliance. She made no attempt to explain. Instead she approached me with a baffled look on her face.

"I need to speak with you, Alexa. Please come with me." Eliana said tensely.

I wondered what she could possibly need of me. She turned, expecting me to follow. Leading me down into the basement, I entered the room that held the Kaemorra.

Upon stepping into the room, the crystal pulsed at my presence. Its spinning seemed to increase, as I made my way to it. I hesitated to touch it. The object I had been compelled to search for, been driven to find, called to me. Hesitantly, I reached out to place my hand on it. Jolted by the sudden vision I glimpsed, I drew my hand away. For an instant, I was surrounded by mighty warriors who were valiantly battling all around me.

"Come. Sit with me." Eliana walked to the only available seat in the room. The bench was a cold marble slab, just feet from the Kaemorra.

I joined her, waiting for her to let me know why she had brought me there. With her head tilted to the side, her attention was on the rotating crystal. What did the vision mean? She turned to me, knowing that I had glimpsed something from the future.

"When Elron and Liam found the Kaemorra, they also retrieved a scroll, a letter with vital information. The language it was written in is one I haven't seen in a long time. Alexa, the meaning of it, the instructions on it, have made me question your existence. I am at a loss to understand who you are, who you are meant to be." She seemed genuinely confused by what was written in the letter.

Once she finished speaking, she stood and walked over to the Kaemorra. Appearing to be deciding how to explain, I heard an unsteady breath leave her. Whatever the letter said, I sensed it would add another layer to the ever-growing ones encircling my life. Just when I thought she was lost to the images the Kaemorra projected to her, her voice startled me. Breaking, fearful, her tone brought out my own insecurities.

"The text is in ancient Norse. Alexa, it seems it is a calling to raise Freya's army. Why it was found with the Kaemorra, I can't understand."

I rose from my seat and stepped over to her. The image of the picture I had seen in the estate's library formed steadily in my mind. In it, a woman resembling me, surrounded by warriors emerging from the deep waters around her, waited for them to answer her battle cry.

Casting a glance at the Kaemorra which pulsed, infusing the room with its red aura, the crystal glowed more brightly. From within it a projection was cast out from the rapidly spinning crystal. I saw myself standing inside some sort of cavern. With arms spread out, my lips moved, saying words that made no sense to me.

Risa eôa hefna minn drengr. Slàtra vàrr andskotti.

Captivated by the scene unfolding, I paid attention to what the Kaemorra showed me. As the image of me uttered the words, the floor under my feet heaved, rising up as if reaching out to me. The violent shaking it created cracked the floor. Steam rose up, clouding the area around me. From below, I saw arms reach up, then shoulders, bodies of warriors ascending. Their fierce eyes met mine, glinting a deep red as they marched out, turning to face the enemy. In the distance, Elsam's men were surrounding us. I never saw who claimed victory. At that moment, the Kaemorra returned to its restive spinning. The vision fell away, leaving me staring at Eliana.

"So now you know. You must memorize the words. You will need them when we face Elsam in Asserbo." Eliana softly whispered.

The words were already stored in my mind. I knew they were meant for me. The summer solstice was a little over a month away. I needed to find Aidan. Asserbo was an unknown to me. Where it was, how to reach it and how we could defend ourselves, while I finished this once and for all, required planning.

"Eliana, we will be ready. You know what I must do. Please, when the time comes, make sure it was not in vain." I implored her.

"There will be no repeat, Alexa. I will make sure of that. Do not lose hope. I believe all will work out in the end." She gave me a slight smile, making me question what she could possibly mean. I somehow knew I would lose everything when the end came.

Chapter 22 - Tory

Distracted by his continued brooding over Rina, Tory made a quick cursory sweep of the area. As far as his exhausted eyes could detect, the land before him gave away none of its secrets. There appeared to be no hint that the Sidhe had ever inhabited the once resplendent sanctuary.

Scanning in all directions, he found himself alone, bitterly cold and dreading what he would discover. His life had taken a sharp turn into the unknown. All he knew, understood of his existence, now lay shrouded in mystery. *Who am I? Where am I from?* Tory wished for answers. Refocusing his attention back to the matter at hand, Tory gazed out across the wide expanse in front of him.

In the far distance, across miles of deadened grass, a familiar mountain range climbed high above dark threatening clouds. The summit of the highest peak was hidden from view by an ominous veil of darkness surrounding it. A violent storm raged unmercifully, creating thunder and lightning, which struck with impressive force at intervals, growing in intensity.

The rising wind from the east would soon carry it down to his location. There was nowhere in that abandoned land for him to escape the ravaging power coming his way. Already splatters of raindrops were falling around him. *Should I leave, return later once the storm has passed?* It would delay him from finding answers, but he saw no other option.

The island, even in its present condition, felt like home. He knew Elron had visited their home world recently. The whole time he was there, Elron had seen nothing to indicate anyone else had set foot on the island in centuries. Tory had arrived there on a whim. More needing to put distance between himself and Rina, than any concrete reason that he would find his parents there.

Tory sought refuge in a place he hoped Rina would not think to look. Thinking of her brought renewed anger at her deceiving him. The intense, uncontrollable emotion created an unwelcome side effect.

A violent, uncontrollable shiver ran through him. Trembling from the impact, losing his balance, he fell down hard on his knees. His body toppled over, causing his hands to slam hard on the ground. As he tried to gain control over the shiver wracking him, he watched his right hand phase in and out, fading somewhat from his sight. The effect was troubling and was but one of a number of altering traits he was experiencing.

Fearing what it meant, he clenched his fist, concentrating all his energy into stopping the effect. *What is happening to me?* Tory cleared his mind of any and all thoughts. He suppressed his emotions. Abruptly, he felt the shaking cease. His hand returned to normal. Sitting back on his heels, he tried to even out his breathing. He felt he had aged centuries in the last few months. Gone was his easygoing self. In its place was a man who saw nothing to make life cheerful. The weather raging around him matched his mood. The wind had picked up, while torrential rain fell from the sky unhindered.

"Tory." The voice was unwelcome. Recognizing who it came

from, Tory fought back the rising exasperation her continued intrusions produced.

"Leave! I don't want you here." Tory refused to look at her. *Why does she continue to follow me?*

Rina ignored his request. Instead, she came nearer until she stood next to him. Still on his knees, Tory tried hard to ignore her. He caught a brief glance of her before tearing his eyes away. Her clothes were completely drenched, hiding none of her alluring features from the little he glimpsed of her. He closed his eyes against her beauty. It was unbearable to watch her and not want her. He rose to his feet, readying to depart.

Before he could make his escape, her hand caught his forearm, her eyes pleading with him to stay. They stood in silence, while around them the noise level of wind, thunder and lightning grew in strength. *How can she not feel the cold?* Rina was not dressed for the harsh weather assaulting them. He pushed down the need to offer her his coat, to put his arms around her for protection against the elements.

"Come with me, Tory. I will tell you all I know. Your parents are not here. I know where we can find them." Her words, admitting to having answers and not sharing them, incensed him.

Why now? Why did she not say anything before? Tory would have left her, but his need for answers outweighed everything else. He pushed down his indignation over her actions, for the moment. Seeing her visibly blink back tears, he steeled himself against her. Her hand instinctively reached out to touch him.

Stepping away, Tory shook his head at her. He could not let her off that easy. As much as he would have liked to forgive, take her in his arms and forget everything, his distrust made it impossible. Rina let her arm drop back to her side, waiting for Tory to come to his decision. She was not unaware of how little faith she instilled in him.

"Where? Where are you taking me?" He finally asked.

Calmly, without answering, she did then reach for him. The slight tremble of her hand where it touched him, marginally pleased him. Her fear of being rebuffed indicated her nervousness. Tory briefly experienced remorse at putting her through the distress. Remembering all her lies gave him the strength to hold himself rigid under her hand. Rina lowered her eyes from his. Wrapping their fingers together, she showed him where she wanted them to go.

Tory wasted no time in transporting them. In an instant, they were back at the estate outside Verona. Arriving in the garden, next to the fountain, they were alone. Rina still held onto Tory, trying to catch his eyes. His heart thundered in his chest from having her near. He removed his fingers from hers, unable to take her touch a second longer.

Leaving her, he entered the house, going straight into the main room. He sat on one of the sofas that materialized as soon as he walked into the vast room. There he waited for Rina to follow, so she would finally share what she knew. Once she did, he would leave. There was nothing more to be gained by having her with him.

Rina appeared in the doorway, entering the room hesitantly one slow step at a time. She made no attempt to join him on the sofa. Taking an armchair facing him, Tory marveled at how he was keeping it together. Her presence was too painful, reminding him that there was no way for them to be together after all her deceptions.

"So, tell me what you know." He told Rina, his voice hollow and resentful.

Rina's head snapped up to get a better look at him. What she saw must have hurt her deeply. A single tear drifted down her cheek, while Tory chastised himself for caring. Rina regained control of herself, sitting stonily in her chair, staring at a spot behind Tory. He saw that her clothes were now dry, but still clinging deliciously to her frame.

The jeans hugged her hips, showing him curves he would have liked to trace with his fingers. Her camisole was low cut, exposing the cleft of her breasts. His body responded to her without hesitation. Forcing his gaze away, he waited for her to speak. From the corner of his eye, he saw her lips twitch, fighting a smile. He was aware that she knew how her nearness affected him.

"The hourglass, in your parents' safe, the ones who raised you, was given to them so that when the time came, it would return you to your people. If you touch it, you will leave this time. Your real parents are of a race this world is unaware of." She kept her voice level, not showing any emotion.

More questions of who he was were taking hold. *Who are my parents? Why did they send me here?* Tory was curious, but not ready to leave for wherever they were. His time there was not done yet. He felt it with certainty. There was something he needed to do before leaving. What that was he had no idea.

"You have to do better than that. You know more. Tell me or let me go." Tory went to rise.

Rina's look held him back. She leaned forward in her chair, grabbing his arm and pulling him back to take his seat. Tory exhaled, frustrated at her not giving him full answers. *What is she keeping from me?*

"Listen to me. I will tell you all I know. My mother has only given me partial answers. I will help you all I can. Tory, I care for you. No, don't say anything. We cannot be, but that does not mean I don't feel for you." She said when Tory would have disputed her.

Tory grasped only three words from her statement. *What does she mean, we cannot be? Why?* He broke off his thoughts of being with her. She was right. He could not trust her after everything she had hidden from him. He would listen to the rest of what she said, then he would find his parents.

"Your people are a race of travelers. They have the ability to pass through time, to travel through it. They never let themselves be seen by others. They come and go, only to observe. Sometimes they interfere when they feel one race needs guidance above another. Why you were put here, I don't know. I can only guess." She continued.

"What is your guess? Why do you think I was put here?" Tory wanted to know.

Rina rose from her seat to pace in front of him. He was left to wonder if she would continue to hide things from him. His suspicion was unfounded. Rina continued, filling him in on what she thought his purpose was.

"I think you will be the catalyst in what Alexa needs to do. You have to remain here for that."

"What do you mean?" Tory was puzzled at what he could do.

"The fact that you can manipulate time, that you were placed alongside Elron, must mean that you have a role to play. We need to find your parents to get the truth from them." Rina explained.

Tory would have liked to know where to find his parents. *Does she know where they are? Will she help me?* He was hesitant to accept her aid after all she had held back. But, she was helping now. Could he trust that she was being honest?

"Tory, I will help you." Rina must have sensed his reluctance.

Tory leaned his head back against the sofa's pillows. Closing his eyes, he fought the feelings rising in him. It would be so easy to go to her, to hold her, accept everything she was willing to give him. Her words of their not being able to be together were playing in his mind. *Why do I want to dispute them? What harm could it do if we were involved?*

His emotions rose to the surface, forcing him to decide. He would not accept it. Getting to his feet, he went to her. When he was in front her, he grabbed her and hauled her into his arms. Too stunned at his actions, Rina was momentarily frozen. Coming to her senses, she fought to escape him. Tory only held her more firmly against him.

"Stop. There are so many things I could say right now. The only thing that is clear to me is that I will not let you go. What you said makes no difference to me. If I have to stay here and never go home, I am willing to accept that." He told her, while she squirmed to escape him.

Rina went still in his arms. Her eyes found his, seeing he meant every word. He felt her heart beat faster. His body tensed at what his instincts were telling him. *How could it be that this woman possesses my heart? How did this happen?* Tory understood that it would be impossible to leave her behind.

Whether he wanted it or not, she had become necessary to his existence. He would not leave her. Now or ever. He brought his lips to hers, silencing what she would have said. It took a moment for him to feel her capitulation. Her arms wrapped around him, giving in to the sweetness of his kiss.

"I see we have come at a bad time." A man's voice broke them apart.

Tory did not release Rina on hearing the intrusion. Looking over her head, his adoptive father smiled serenely back at him. Rina squirmed to escape Tory's arms, which continued to hold her captive. Releasing her, Rina stepped away from Tory, giving him room to go to his father, who embraced his son. His mother waited her turn. Once they had hugged, said their hellos, Tory launched into an endless array of questions. His father stopped him, telling him what he knew.

"My son, I will tell you what you want to know. The time has come for your involvement. Rina is right, you are to be the catalyst. For that you need to embrace who you are." His father explained.

Tory sat with his adoptive mother beside him. The woman was elegant, even with the age lines around her eyes. Rina saw no resemblance to Tory. It was obvious they were not truly related. Tory's mother was short for a Sidhe. His father also was well below the usual six-foot height associated with the race. They appeared aged, older than what they should be. *How long had they been in the world?* Longer than Rina herself it seemed.

"Your real parents are the governors of your world. You were placed with us during a civil war that broke out among your people. Your parents did not think you safe. By placing you with us, they thought to protect you while they tried to regain control. Once it was safe you were to return." His father spoke, while continuing. "Your world has been at peace for centuries now. We were asked to keep you with us a bit longer. Your parents saw the destruction that would take over this world. They left you here, knowing you would be the only one to help Alexa complete her mission." He finished.

"How can I help her? What must I do?" Tory asked him.

"For that I need to show you. Rina, please come with us. My son will need you." The answer offered clarity on what Tory was meant to do. Tory would have to follow to where they were leading him to gain perspective.

Elron's wound, bandaged once again under a clean white dressing, had shown a marked improvement since drinking Olar's remedy. Following my instructions, Aidan had found him soon after I asked him to, making sure Elron swallowed every last drop of the liquid. The persistent bleeding, along with the spreading black ugly marks on his upper arm, ceased almost immediately. I was alone with him, debating whether to admit to him what I was planning. I would need him to do as I asked without question. Not sure if the time was right, or if it was too early still, I studied him as he repositioned himself, trying to get comfortable.

I sat on a chair near his bed, watching his face for any sign of what to do. Would he agree to it? Unaware of my inner struggle, Elron lay back on his bed, keeping a watchful eye on the door. His hand rubbed absentmindedly back and forth over the bandage on his arm. We had not spoken one word to each other since Bet went off in search of food for the ravenous man lying back against his pillows. The silence broke every once in a while when a growl escaped his empty stomach. I failed to stifle a giggle when I heard another one fill the room.

"It's not funny. I would eat you if you had any meat on your bones. When was the last time you practiced your sword play?" He glowered at me.

I ignored his question, knowing any response I gave him would displease him greatly. The truth was, practice had long been forgotten.

It had been weeks since I even glanced at my sword. Thankfully, at that precise moment, Bet entered the room taking his attention away from my answer. Seeing all the food she was carrying, Elron lifted himself up to a sitting position. He stared, practically salivating, at the food she carried, anticipating feasting on the assortment of enticing aromas reaching him.

Bet struggled to balance the weight of the tray, holding onto the many overfilled dishes. When she neared the bed, I helped her position it over the man waiting impatiently in extreme hunger. With the tray on his lap, he started to eat, stuffing food in his mouth, forgetting us and anything else while he lost himself to gorging. We let him eat, Bet and I exchanging an amused look, while we discussed other matters.

"Has anyone seen Solas recently?" I asked Bet.

Bet shrugged her shoulders at my question. As if I did not have enough to preoccupy me, I nonetheless added Solas's well-being to my long list. Thinking he was in our way, I was not surprised he had made himself scarce. I ached for him. He not only had lost the only mother he had ever known, his father was a monster who had tried to have him killed. Now he found himself among strangers.

Even though we were family, he was finding it difficult to relate to us. Eliana, most of all, tried to include him as much as possible. Where he spent his days, what he occupied his time with, were questions no one seemed to know the answers to. His adeptness at hiding his signature from me gave me no clue to his whereabouts.

"I should find him." I said.

"He's fine. I just checked on him. He'll join us shortly." Aidan strolled into the room, making his way to me.

On reaching me, he lifted me up off my chair, cradling me in his arms. Startled at finding myself held close against his chest, I draped my arm across his shoulder to hang on. Aidan's smile almost undid me. The black specs in his clear emerald eyes increased their swirling, reacting to our closeness. Bet loudly cleared her throat before Aidan could claim my lips.

Pulled back to the present, I grinned at him. It was not the time for what I so wanted from him. Aidan narrowed his eyes at my thoughts. Luckily, that time I did not wish to hide them. With me still in his arms, he took my place on the chair, sitting down and positioning me over his lap. His arm wrapped around me to keep me balanced. My heart lurched in my chest at having him near. The responding increase of his heartbeat met mine head on. He smiled, before turning his attention to Elron.

"How's the arm? Is the poison gone?" He asked his friend.

Elron answered back something unintelligible with his mouth full. Bet translated his mumbling for us, confirming that the wound was healing nicely. Elron, hearing her speak for him, glanced up, giving Bet a reproachful look. She simply shook her head and giggled at Elron's reaction. He resumed his eating without missing a beat.

Olar's remedy drew out whatever poison Manar's blade had transferred into the cut on his arm. My receiving the cure had been too late to save Asher. The poison had worked its way into Asher's system too rapidly. There was no guarantee it would have helped him, even if I had received the remedy sooner.

Asher's death remained a raw, heavy blow to us. We were all dealing with his passing in our own way. Aidan shared some of his pain over the loss of his father with me. Eliana refused to speak of it at all. Every attempt I made to console her, she brushed aside, changing the subject. How she managed to function without her husband I could not hazard a guess. If I lost Aidan, surviving would be impossible.

My love for him had grown into something far greater than I had anticipated. Bonded or not, I could not envision a future that he was not a part of. Losing him could ultimately destroy me. What I planned to do would inevitably take him from me. I had a spark of hope that we would find each other again.

"Alexa, stop. There's nothing you could have done." Aidan had followed my train of thought and tried to reassure me.

I lowered my eyes to the floor, knowing I would inevitably betray his trust in me. Clueless to the exact course I had laid out for us, certain it would not be something he would ever agree to, Aidan nonetheless had his suspicions. He pulled me closer, holding me tightly, sensing I hid vital information from him. Motion from the bed drew my attention to more pressing matters. Elron, who had polished off every last morsel on the plates, lifted the tray from his lap and placed it to the side.

Bet quickly removed the tray, depositing it on a table by the window. She returned to lie down next to her husband. Lowering herself down on the mattress, her protruding belly had definitely gotten bigger. Her body barely fit next to Elron. Stretched out alongside him, her back was almost off the bed. Only his arm around her managed to keep her from falling off.

"So, I need information on Asserbo." I spoke once I saw she was comfortable.

Aidan nodded, knowing there was little time left in planning our strategy. Within weeks I would follow through on what I meant to do. Keeping it a secret from Aidan taxed me. My mind erected walls to keep him from finding out. The energy it was taking was immense. I could tell he was aware of the power it was taking out of me.

"Yes, we should go to the library to find maps and information on the place." Aidan lifted me in his arms, letting me slowly brush his chest to let my feet touch the floor. His suspicions at what I held back colored his eyes a deep green. Black specs in his pupils danced in response to the dread consuming him. I placed my palm on his cheek, trying vainly to reassure him. My touch only made it worse. Aidan would try his best to stop anything he saw as a danger to us.

"I'll come with you, if I may?" Solas interrupted us, standing in the doorway, looking pensive over what he had walked in on.

Bet struggled to get up from the bed when she heard Solas's voice. With Elron's help, they both got to their feet together, anticipating our need to get started. Waiting for Aidan to decide whether Solas could join us, I personally saw no harm in their brother helping. Elron's wariness of Solas was baseless. He more than once voiced his concern in Solas knowing our plans. Even so, I understood Solas had every reason to find a way to thwart his father, to avenge Vanya's death. Aidan was of the same opinion.

"Yes, please join us." Aidan accepted Solas's help.

Bet left Elron's side, went to Solas and hooked her arm through his. Leading him out, Elron followed closely behind them. Aidan held me back from going after them. Instantly, I bolstered my walls, so he could not see into my mind.

"Alexa, what are you planning? Why do I sense you are holding something back?" He asked.

I attempted to leave his arms, to put some distance between us. He would have none of it. Forced to stare into his eyes, catching the worry that clouded them, I hesitated. What I meant to do was not something he would ever understand. My vision was all I had to go on. It was the only way I could find to save us all. With Eliana's help, things could be set right. Finding myself imprisoned in his arms, with no way to avoid answering, I gazed back at him.

"I hope you know that I love you, Aidan. There is nothing I wouldn't do for you. Please, let it go. I have to see this through in my own way. It's not that I don't trust you. I just can't explain. Please." I begged him to let me handle it.

His eyes searched my face, while his mind tried to penetrate my wall. He was worried, as well as dubious. I could offer him nothing further to allay his fears. I willed him to trust me, to know that what I did was for everyone's benefit. My heart ached at what I would lose. Tears suddenly blinded me at the thought. Seeing them, Aidan stepped away from me, giving me room to back up.

"All right. I won't press you. I love you, Alexa. Please, whatever it is you must do, know that I will also love you." Aidan cupped my cheek with his hand, placing a gentle kiss on my lips.

I wanted nothing more than to step back into his arms and forget about everything else. A tear rolled down my cheek. How could I have ever doubted we belonged together? I had wasted so much time fighting him. We had weeks remaining to us. I would take the time we had left to make up for it.

"Let's go see the others. We will need our parents' input as well. Come." He brushed the tears from my eyes, then took my hand to walk me to the library.

Chapter 24 - Caden

Caden stood outside Myrick's cell, leaning against the wall, his face masking his inner contempt and disgust at the man on the other side. With arms folded across his chest, Caden had been watching Myrick pretending he was unaware of his presence. It took all his will not to step through the field keeping Myrick from escaping and doing him bodily harm.

That traitorous excuse of a man had done his best to harm his daughter and granddaughter. Pushing away from the wall, he looked down the corridor to make sure they were alone. No one was about. The only thing he had caught sight of was the energy suffusing the area.

The enchantment barring the use of magic in the lower level of the castle, where they held their prisoners, shimmered faintly. Caden detected the fleeting increase to its power, as something fought to penetrate it. The field hissed, sparking briefly under the attempt Myrick made to find a weakness. The man was still trying to find a way of escaping while seated across the room.

Resting on a cot, his back braced against the wall, with his feet off the floor, Myrick showed no sign danger surrounded him. Anyone would have thought he was unconcerned with the predicament he found himself in. Caden knew differently. Myrick, his head bent down, face hidden behind the veil of his long tangled hair, used his time to test the strength of the field. He would find no escape.

"You might as well stop." Caden finally spoke. "You have

nowhere to go."

Myrick slowly lifted his head, his eyes finding and focusing on the other man. Giving no response to Caden's statement, Myrick swiveled away from the wall, dropping his feet to the floor in order to sit up straight. The two men eyed each other silently, appraising each other.

Caden was pleased to see Myrick drop his gaze first. *He should be afraid of me*, Caden thought. *He has much to answer for.* His hatred of the man went beyond the crimes against his kind or the betrayal to his people. He would have killed his grand-daughter without any hesitation. The thought that he would have at one time accepted Myrick as his son-in-law over Rider, now sickened him. Maybe Thalia made the right choice after all.

Caden took his eyes off of the hideously scarred face in front of him. Rider had done well in marking Myrick for his treachery. His son-in-law's knife had left a grisly reminder of the actions Myrick had undertaken. It gave Caden a modicum of respect for his daughter's husband.

Caden turned his attention to the cell Myrick had been placed in. It was one of the more comfortable ones. Along with the cot, a reading desk and chair sat within the space. He would have put the man in the deepest levels, where the cells were nothing more than dark, subterranean caves.

"Why have you come, Caden? I have nothing to say." Myrick spoke up.

Caden focused on his prisoner, narrowing his eyes as anger

shook him. Myrick would answer his questions whether he wanted to or not. Caden had ways to force everything he needed to know out of him. Caden held back his smile at seeing Myrick's left eye twitch at the resolve he must have seen in him. Nervousness forced Myrick to his feet. He paced around the cell, all the while trying to weaken the field keeping him from using his full powers. The laugh escaping Caden halted his steps.

"Myrick, you are as insolent as ever. I would like nothing more than to end you here and now. But, you will tell me all you know. Then it is up to the council to decide your fate. I have made my recommendation. Whether they give you leniency is up to you. Are you ready to atone for your actions?" Caden almost grinned at Myrick's reaction to his words.

Myrick gave up, sat down on the cot, ready for what lay ahead. The sound of approaching footsteps alerted him to someone else's arrival. Caden stepped off to the side to let the woman appearing come closer to the bars. Her expression gave nothing away. Myrick felt a shiver run down his back on seeing who it was. He had no way to protect himself against her powers.

"Kesia, I leave him to you. Find out everything. And I mean everything. I don't care what remains of him once you are done." Caden instructed her.

Kesia's earthly powers went beyond calming and stabilizing those around her. She possessed the means to force loyalty, to enter the mind of others and extract their deepest thoughts and memories. With a powerful mind like Myrick's, she would have to probe deeply. The damage she may do if he fought her was incalculable. There was a chance that he would become nothing but an empty shell.

"I will find out all we need to know, Caden. One way or the other, he will tell me everything." Kesia assured him.

Caden gave a final disgusted look at the man in the cell before turning away. Leaving Myrick in Kesia's capable hands, Caden left them to return to other pressing matters. He made his way further down into a lower level, finding he was not the only one seeking out the other prisoner being held there.

Blayze was in the corridor in front of the cell that kept his wife prisoner. His anger pulsed out of control in a deep red aura, which surrounded him and lit up the space he occupied. Deep in the cell, Rydia had retreated to the furthest corner. Her own aura of deep ocean blue was fighting to maintain itself. Blayze had almost entirely evaporated her water strength with his fiery one.

"Blayze, that's enough." Caden strode over to him. "We still have not questioned her."

Blayze fought to regain control. A muscle worked in his jaw, his eyes flashing crimson at the hurt and betrayal he felt. Caden slowly, carefully placed his hand on the man's arm. He used his own power to center Blayze, helped him to batten down his emotions. From the corner of his eye, Caden saw Rydia tense as a final wave of Blayze's fury hit her. She sank to her knees from its force. Blayze breathed deeply, and with Caden's aid, let his energy drop completely.

"Good, good." Caden told him. "Please, let me handle this. Go alert the others. I need to see everyone in an hour's time."

Blayze gave a final blistering look at his wife before doing as Caden asked. *I will have a say in her punishment*, Blayze promised himself. What Blayze planned for her would give him immense pleasure. Knowing that Caden needed to get the whole truth out of her, he would wait, listen to what was shared and then exact his revenge. *The woman will pay dearly for what she did to me.*

Caden waited to make sure that Blayze was out of earshot before facing Rydia. He watched as she rose to her feet, going to sit on her cot. *Did she care at all about the damage she had caused?* Looking at her, he saw no evidence of remorse. Once she was seated, she lifted her eyes to his.

"Get it over with. Whatever you mean to do with me. I will accept my punishment." She told him.

"I don't think we need to delve too deeply into your motivations, Rydia. Obviously you believe that Elsam cares for you. That man has only cared for one woman, and that woman herself betrayed him. Why do you think Agatha is no longer living? The woman he loved gave herself to death in order to escape him. I know much of what went on back then. I have my own contacts that inform me of what goes on in our world. You have been lied to, manipulated by Elsam. You thought we were unaware of your actions. My dear, we let you connive with that man while keeping track of you. I know everything you ever discussed with him. Oh, and every illicit thing you did with him. A simple spying spell is all it took to confirm what you were up to." Caden informed her.

Rydia, stunned into silence, could only stare back at Caden. Her mind broke into a cacophony of turmoil. *How long? How long was I under suspicion? Did Blayze know? Had he known all along? Is what Caden telling me true? Did Elsam really use me? I can't have been that stupid.* Every thought transmitted itself to Caden. There was nothing she could hide from him.

"Not to worry, Rydia. I have a plan to thwart Elsam. In a way, I should thank you. I know everything he plans to do. I will be sure to fill in Queen Eliana as well. As for you, once we convene our meeting and let everyone in on what is to be done, Blayze will be given the pleasure of sentencing you. I see no one better to mete out your punishment." Caden felt a rush of exhilaration on seeing the panicked look on her face.

Not giving her time to respond, he left to go to his office. They all needed to prepare. Hopefully, Kesia would be finished interrogating Myrick and would apprise him of what she learned before they started. Till then, Myrick's sentence would remain pending. He was not sure how to make the man pay. The council would need to be involved. Maybe the others would offer an idea.

Entering his office, he sat behind his desk, waiting for the hour to be up. He could not concentrate on any business other than what lay ahead. His mood lightened somewhat at seeing Kesia standing, looking triumphant in his doorway.

"Come in. Take a seat." He motioned her in.

Kesia entered the room, taking a chair on the other side of Caden's desk. She always marveled at the barren feel of the room. Caden's office was immense, but the furniture in it was sparse. The only things in the room were a desk, two chairs and a sofa. The walls held no frames, the floor no carpet. Gazing around, she wondered if the leader of the council was aware of what that said about him. The man had no roots, no personal effects showing where he came from.

"What did you learn?" He brought her back to the present.

"Did you know the man believes himself to be in love with your daughter?" She started.

Caden waved the statement away. Myrick did not love his daughter. He was obsessed with her. He always had been. When she chose to marry Rider, it broke Myrick. His actions since then were to punish Thalia for choosing what he believed was the wrong man.

"He did redeem himself somewhat in the end. By letting Solas escape, he showed some backbone." Kesia continued.

"I know that Elsam plans to ambush Alexa and her party from what we learned spying on Rydia. Myrick told us as much himself?" Caden asked her.

Kesia rose from her chair to walk about the room. She was never good at sitting still. Caden followed her movement with a keen eye. She did learn something more. He was sure of it.

"Myrick was not aware of all of Elsam's plans. Elsam hated him, abhorred his presence. He put up with him simply due to his need of the other warlocks in his employ. Myrick's days were numbered." Kesia went on.

Caden stood up as well. It was time for the meeting. Walking around his desk he went to Kesia, waiting to see if she had more to say.

"Caden, Vanya's death is deeply troubling him. He feels culpable in what happened to her. His remorse makes it difficult for me to mete out a punishment. We have to tread carefully here. The only other thing I managed to get from him is that Elsam's deal with the Daimon has fallen through. Olar has banned his son from this world indefinitely. The only ones Elsam has on his side are the shadows. What he promised them is sure to cause them to turn on him. He will not give them the Kaemorra. If we can alert them to this, it may break their alliance." Kesia finished.

Yes, it was something to think about. But, would the shadows return to their world, or would they strike out on their own? That was an unknown.

Chapter 25 - Liam

Worn out from lack of sleep, Liam rubbed his hand over his face, fighting to stay alert. The darkened room, the buzzing silence did not make his task any easier. His dry, tired eyes, felt heavy. They inched down, shutting out the room's feeble light. Nodding off, he jerked awake at a sound coming from the bed. Rubbing his eyes, he studied Mara, but found no change in her condition.

Since bringing her up to his room, she lay unconscious, unmoving, under the pale blue comforter on his bed. Her raspy breathing had eased somewhat, but her not waking, the lack of movement under her eyelids, had kept his gaze fastened on her still form, waiting for any change.

Liam blinked hard to stay vigilant, afraid he would miss signs of her recovery. Sitting slumped on an uncomfortable wooden chair, he waited while the woman he loved lay unresponsive. It was all he could do. How much longer it would take was anyone's guess. But, wait he would. He owed it to her to be there when her eyes finally opened.

Guilt over not looking harder for her, for assuming she was dead, while she spent centuries imprisoned by Manar, increased with each hour that passed. His heart ached over trying to replace her with Alexa, believing he loved his brother's mate, while Mara fought for their love. She had never given up on him.

How will I explain why I never looked for her? Why would she stay with me after she finds out about Alexa? These thoughts continuously ran through his mind. Having Mara back, the bond that existed between them was as strong as ever. He could see the threads of light binding them, felt the energy that bonded them together. Liam was consumed with regrets and a feeling of having betrayed her. All he could hope for was that Mara would forgive him, would allow him to make it up to her. He would spend the remainder of his days proving his love.

"Liam, there's no change, is there?" Alexa crept closer, aware of Liam's internal castigation.

Liam did not respond. He could not take his focus away from Mara. Alexa sat on the bed, bringing her hand to Mara's forehead. Her soft sigh was all the evidence he needed to know that the woman he loved still struggled. *Can she hear us? Does she know I am here?* There were no answers to his questions.

"Have you slept at all, Liam? You need to rest. You are not doing her any favors exhausting yourself." Alexa studied his face, seeing a muscle twitch in his cheek.

He would not sleep. His guilt, anger at himself was consuming him. *How can I rest knowing I have let her down?* Alexa slipped off the bed, went down on her knees, blocking his view of Mara. She touched his cheek, forcing his gaze to hers. She sensed in that brief touch all his internal turmoil. Liam grabbed her hand, pulling it away. He did not need pity or understanding. Liam had no excuse for what he had let happen. He tried to move so he could resume his watch over Mara. Alexa made that impossible. From her position in front of him, her body blocked Mara from his view.

"Alexa, please. You need to let me handle this my way." He

implored her to move.

"She will wake, Liam. It won't be long. I can feel her coming back. Seeing you like this will only confuse her. You need to get a grip on yourself. Rest, lie down next to her if you must. Know that she loves you. She will forgive you anything." Alexa insisted.

If only it were that simple. His uncertainty over whether Mara would absolve him lay at the core of his doubts. Seeing there was nothing she could say to get him to ease up, Alexa rose to her feet. Her fingers gently lifted his chin so he would see her. Looking down at him, she gave him a gentle smile, while her touch tried to calm him. Her energy flowed through him, alleviating some of his anxiety. Once Liam relaxed partially, she walked over to the other chair in the room, picked it up and returned to place it next to him. His eyes returned to Mara.

"We are days away from the summer solstice. Aidan has found as much as he could in the library on Asserbo. I know where we have to go, what I have to do. We will need you." She spoke quietly. "The only thing I am fearful of is the timing. It will be after dark. Elsam, along with the shadows, will be waiting for us."

Alexa paused to give Liam time to absorb what she meant. With the shadows present, it would be difficult to complete their mission. *How were they to combat them? Would Alexa be able to create enough light with her powers to drive them back?* So far, it was the only way they could get them to back off.

"I have a way to rid ourselves of the shadows. I can't go into it with you right now. Elsam and his warlocks are what I am worried about. We will have no help from the witch's council. I was unable to convince them and my grandfather to get involved. I can't be everywhere at once." Alexa finished.

Liam would be there. He owed it to her, his brother and his people to assist in any way. Alexa must finish this once and for all. What she meant to do, she still guardedly kept secret. Liam trusted she would do the right thing. Any twinge of suspicion over her holding back explaining her plan, he brushed aside. She would not risk their lives. Her love for Aidan, their bond, would force her to keep everyone safe.

"I don't know much about Asserbo, other than that it was a sacred site for Freya's worshipers. What did Aidan find out?" Liam was now curious.

The man himself appeared in the doorway, as if he had been summoned. Liam wondered if Alexa had called him. Aidan strolled into the room, finding nowhere to sit except on the bench in front of the window. Once he was seated, he answered Liam's question.

"I must admit that we know nothing more than before. Asserbo is an old fortress, later used as a monastery. Originally it was a site dedicated to Freya's followers. There is not much left of any of the structure. We will find nothing but ruins in its location. I believe, just like you found with Elron in Kobberdam, that the way will show itself to us." Aidan explained.

Liam remembered the lighted path leading them to the Kaemorra in the forested area around Kobberdam. Anything was possible. His eyes were drawn back to Mara. *Would she be awake before he left? He was conflicted suddenly on what to do. How could he leave her? Then again, how could he not go on their mission?*

"Liam." Alexa pulled his attention to her. "She will be fine. We will leave you now." She waved to Aidan to come along with her. Once they were at the door, she left him with a final command.

"Rest."

Left alone with Mara, who still showed no signs of movement, he unsteadily rose from his chair. Stepping silently, he made his way to the other side of the bed where he could lie next to her. Easing his weary body down, he carefully stretched out making sure not to stir the mattress too much. *Does she know I'm here?* She gave no sign showing she was aware of him next to her.

Bunching the pillow under his head, he kept his eyes fastened on her face. Fatigue made it impossible for him to keep his eyes open any longer. Lying down, he felt tiredness wrap itself firmly over his entire body. Maybe he could close his eyes just for a bit.

The sound of strangled coughing brought him out of a deep sleep. It took him several moments to remember where he was. Under him, the bed shook from the racking sounds escaping the woman beside him. He rose up on his elbow, so he could see her better. Her eyes were open, her unwavering gaze locked on him.

Even as she fought to regain her senses, her fingers gripped his hand, her expression shocked, hardly believing Liam lay beside her. Another series of hawking sounds erupted from her. Grappling to sit up, Mara clutched at Liam. He helped her to lift herself into a sitting position, as her coughing continued. Her lips moved, trying to say something in between the wheezing sounds escaping her.

"Don't try to talk. Just breathe normally. Most of the gaseous fumes are out of your body, but it may be a while before all of it is gone." Liam whispered.

Terror-filled eyes met his over her being powerless to catch her breath. Each inhale sounded raspy, agonizing to Liam's ears. Unable to do anything but hold her, he hoped his presence would reassure her. His arm wrapped around her back, pulling her closer to his side. Her head dropped to his chest, doing as he had instructed. Mara attempted to breathe evenly.

After several minutes, the sound of her gasps of air gentled, giving Liam some measure of relief. Lifting her head, she peered up at him from under wet lashes. He saw the onset of tears developing, the attempt at a smile. Easing her back down on her pillow, falling down next to her, he tried to think of something to say. He came up with no words that would explain his abandoning her. Mara seemed to understand his predicament. She turned, lying on her side to face him. Her hand cupped his cheek, her fingers brushing the stubble.

"Mara." He whispered. "I'm so sorry." Was all he could get out.

She did smile then. A full, breathtaking smile rose to her lips. Her gaze softened, showing him the love she held for him. *Do I deserve it?* Whether or not he did, he did not care. He would take what she was offering. Her offer of forgiveness was more than he deserved. Entering his mind, her thoughts reminded him of why he had fallen in love with the woman.

Mara absolved him of all she had suffered. She knew everything that occurred since she was taken. Manar made sure to tell her where he was, who he was with and what he was doing. She knew about Alexa.

His sharp intake of breath warned her he would chastise himself again. She quickly assured him she did not blame him.

Liam could not believe his luck. He felt humbled by her total devotion. After all the years they had been apart, she still loved him unconditionally. There was only one way to honor her. He would love her until his last breath. He would never leave her side. Liam vowed to the heavens that Mara would be his only priority going forward.

"Don't promise that which you know you will have to break soon." Her raspy voice warned him.

Chapter 26 - Elsam

Elsam found it hard to concentrate on pressing matters needing his attention. He was consumed with how ineffectual he appeared while sitting on the new throne his guards had procured for him. Like a spoiled child he found it wanting and not up to his standards. Anger boiled inside him. The gold leaf on it was tarnished, faded from years of neglect. There was not one jewel on it. *What had they been thinking in presenting me with this as a replacement? Did they do it on purpose?*

His guards wisely kept their distance while he stewed. His order to contact Erebus for another meeting gave them the opportunity to find themselves elsewhere. Receiving a reply, they drew straws on which of them would bring the news to Elsam. The two who were presently reporting to him could not meet his eyes. They addressed him, keeping their eyes downcast. The one who stood closest to Elsam seemed extremely nervous. *What am I to make of it? Have they lost confidence in me?*

"What news have you brought me?" He barked at the Sidhe, looking for any sign of what the other might be thinking.

The guard visibly flinched at the harsh tone, frightened to have to give Elsam the news. His eyes strayed to the door at the end of the hall, clearly indicating he would rather be anywhere but there. The moment it took the terrified guard to speak was enough for Elsam to rise stiffly from the throne. Jaw clenched, Elsam stepped down from the dais to stand directly in front of the Sidhe. He forcibly restrained himself from striking the man.

"Sire, Erebus has agreed to your request of a meeting. He will be here once the sun has set. His message was to be relayed word for word. He said, tell your idiot of a master, I will deign to see him again." His guard said haltingly, his voice shaking.

At having given his report, the man took a step back, expecting the worst. Scared to death of Elsam's reaction, he braced, waiting for the expected violence. His head lowered to stare at the floor, expecting Elsam to explode at any moment. *At least they still fear me*, Elsam thought to himself.

The guard before him remained silent, awaiting his next orders, or any other response from Elsam. That he wanted to escape out of his presence was obvious. Elsam could almost hear the increased hammering of the man's heart. Fed up with having to put up with everyone's shortcomings, Elsam strode back to his throne. Falling down onto the decrepit seat, he battened down the fury over Erebus's words.

"Leave me." He bellowed.

The Sidhe did not hesitate to immediately do as he was asked. Relieved to make it out unscathed, he hurried before Elsam changed his mind. Elsam watched him stride purposefully to the other guard, grab him and move quickly towards the exit. Both guards retreated out of the room, out of his sight.

Alone, Elsam wondered what else Erebus would exact as payment for his allegiance. There was no other reason for his agreeing to a meeting at that late date, other than to seek something else. Elsam needed the shadows. The loss of the Daimon, of Manar, had depleted his resources. He struggled to hold the warlocks on his side. Many saw his actions against Myrick as a betrayal. His guards had been ordered to keep an eye on them. Elsam did not trust anyone anymore.

"Sire, may I enter?" A voice from the doorway drew his attention.

The warlock standing there was now in charge of the others. With Myrick gone, he was the highest ranking of those who remaining. Elsam hardly knew him. The gray-bearded man was old. His plain brown robe covered him from neck to ankles. Beneath it, the warlock's frail body was hidden from view. Elsam waved the man in, wondering what he could possibly want. The warlock advanced slowly towards Elsam. His movements were proof that age had ravaged the man. His left foot dragged behind him, as he made his way to Elsam.

"What is it?" Elsam tried to sound conciliatory. He could not afford to antagonize the man.

"I have a concern." The warlock stated.

Elsam eyed the man suspiciously. He did not have time for anymore grievances. Whatever the warlock's problem was, the fact that he needed him and his followers, stilled his caustic response. He took a deep breath, calming himself before asking what the issue was.

"What can I help you with?" Was all Elsam said.

The warlock was not deceived by Elsam's tone. He knew the man was close to unraveling. It was the reason he had come to see him.

"I believe that we are at a disadvantage. Myrick has been captured by the council. I am sure by now he has told them everything of your plans. Have you come up with any contingencies for this?" The man asked Elsam.

Elsam was not aware that it had been the council who stole Myrick from his clutches. Hearing the warlock's information, Elsam felt a moment of alarm. *Why would they spare him? What were they up to? Do they know something I don't?* Elsam had been ready to end Myrick once and for all. The man's lack of commitment lately had made him a handicap. His failure to kill Solas was only one of the most recent derelictions of his duties. *What was the council up to?* They had agreed not to aid Alexa. Rydia informed him of that at their last meeting. Now, even she was not answering his calls.

"I am sure that we have nothing to worry about. Myrick was not totally involved in my planning. He knew little of what we are to do." Elsam answered.

The warlock did not appear appeased by what Elsam said. He turned towards the door, where Elsam saw another warlock waiting. Waving at the man to approach, they waited for him to near the dais. That man was young, appearing to be less than twenty-years old. Elsam had a sense of something more in that man. He was not a warlock alone. Something else flowed in his veins. Rattled that he could not put his finger on it, the new arrival gave him no time to try to figure it out.

"I sense a change in time. Something is at play that I cannot foresee. We must tread carefully." The man stared right at Elsam, not afraid of him at all.

Ridiculous, was all Elsam could think. These warlocks took too much stock in their inaccurate predictions. So far, everything had progressed as Elsam wanted. Nothing would stand in his way. *Did they* not see he was the future's protector? He would rule.

"Gentlemen, there is no outcome where we will not be victorious. Leave aside your concerns. Know that I have everything under control." He placated them.

The warlocks cast a glance at each other, not completely confident in Elsam's pronouncement. Bowing, they turned away to leave. Seeing them lean in and whisper between themselves, not being able to hear what they were discussing, Elsam waited for them to be out of the room before he clenched his fists. *How dare they question me? When I finally attain my throne on Eruva, they will be punished for their insolence.* He needed to calm himself before meeting Erebus. The shadow lord could not see him agitated. Appearances were everything at that moment.

Rising from his throne, he left the room, exiting out of his tower to await Erebus. The night was warm, spring clearly making its presence known. He kept close to the stone wall with his back almost pressed up against it. The overhead lantern cast its glow down over him. No need to risk Erebus's touch.

Elsam wondered what the shadow overload could possibly request as added payment. As far as he knew, they had sealed their agreement days ago. Promising to hand over the Kaemorra should have placated Erebus, even though Elsam had no intention of actually giving up the powerful crystal. *Does the overload suspect my lies?*

Impatiently he waited for Erebus to arrive. *I should be spending my time laying out the orders for the assault at Asserbo.* His men, Sidhe and warlocks alike, were more than enough to stop Alexa from whatever she planned. Sure in their strength, he saw no possible outcome other than his complete victory.

It would give him immense gratification to end the girl once and for all. Hidden from him for years, she was now out in the open. Alexa would soon learn she was no match for him. A slow grin blossomed on his face at what he planned to do to her. When he had finished with her, she would wish she had never been born.

"You should not stand out in the night alone, Elsam. So many wish to do you harm." Erebus's shadow form lifted slowly off the ground, rising to face Elsam.

Once the shadow overlord took a more pronounced human shape, he stealthily advanced on Elsam. Stopping before him, only inches separated the two. Elsam could not move from where he stood. His back was pressed against the wall, with no means of escape. Only the light from overhead gave him enough room to halt Erebus's touch. The malice Erebus was projecting kept Elsam frozen. Narrowing his eyes at the attempt to frighten him, Elsam straightened to his full height.

"Move back, Erebus! Speak of what you want and leave me. There is much I need to do before we leave for Asserbo." Elsam tried to sound unaffected.

"There are rumors, Elsam." Erebus laughed at the Sidhe, taking a step back. "I wonder if they are true."

Rumors? What rumors? Does Erebus know something I don't? Elsam had no idea what the overlord was speaking about. As far as he knew, everything was progressing as planned. Almost everything at any rate. There were one or two troubling issues to mull over. Rydia for instance. *Why does she not respond to my call?* The other was Myrick. *Why did the council help him escape?* These thoughts crossed his mind in seconds. He returned his attention to Erebus, watching for any clue on what rumors he was alluding to.

"It seems that your lovely Agatha deceived you. Do you know you have a son? Any ideas on who it might be?" Erebus stared directly into Elsam's eyes, seeing the Sidhe gripped in shock over what he had imparted. Anger quickly replaced the confusion coloring Elsam's eyes. He seemed about to lash out at Erebus.

"Do not speak of her. Her name should never pass your lips." Elsam hissed in rage.

Erebus moved away from Elsam. The Sidhe had no awareness of the existence of the child. Agatha had hidden him well. Erebus held back his exaltation at having something to hold over Elsam. *What more can I exhort from the Sidhe?* He must plan his next moves carefully. The knowledge of who Agatha was, how she outmaneuvered Elsam, gave him leverage.

"It seems as if I know more of your lover than you do. What will you give me for the answers I have? How much do you wish to know the identity of your son?" Erebus sneered.

Elsam held back attacking Erebus. Touching the overlord was out of the question. Fury at what he was suggesting tore through him. Only by force of will did he not strike out. Agatha loved him unconditionally. She would never betray him. She was the only woman he had ever loved. Keeping her memory pure, her image forefront in his mind, was all that had sustained him all these years. *How dare Erebus try to take that away from me?*

"You know not of what you speak. Agatha is beyond reproach. She would never hide things from me. Our child was killed by the humans. If there is nothing else, go. Leave me. I have much to do." Elsam took a step to the door.

Erebus quickly blocked Elsam's move. The Sidhe stepped back, keeping his body under the light from the overhead lantern.

"Your child lives. Agatha let herself be killed rather than continue to be involved with you. She was an immortal. Did you not once wonder on her powers? She hid your child from you. Her sister Meredith kept you from him. You have been made a fool of. When you are ready to learn what I know, contact me. It might be useful if you hope to achieve your place on the throne." Erebus dropped his form back through the ground, not giving Elsam a chance to respond. Once he was nothing but a shadow, he slithered away across the darkened field.

Elsam watched his retreat, silenced by the words the other had left him with. It was not true. He refused to believe Agatha had betrayed him. Entering the tower, he made his way to the throne room. Once there, he sank down onto the throne, gripping the armrests in frustration. He could not see any reason why Erebus would lie to him. *Can it be true? Does my son live?* Approaching footsteps interrupted his thoughts. Seeing it was the lead warlock, he waited for the man to speak.

"I have been contacted by the council." The man informed Elsam. The worried face of the warlock was all Elsam needed to see to know that the council had come to a decision. A decision that would not sit well with the warlocks working with him.

It had been less than an hour since I sensed the first twinge of someone reaching into my mind, attempting to communicate. Since then, a steady stream of unsettled, mostly incoherent messages from Rina began to assail me, culminating in one massive headache behind my eyes. The resulting queasiness from the unpleasant effect of her contact drove me to the couch, where I dropped down next to Aidan.

My legs were shaking, my entire body trembling. Aidan, sitting next to me, experienced every bit of the dreadful consequences of her transmissions. With the fingers of one hand clutching my arm, our bond permitted him to listen in on every word Rina had shared with me. His other hand absentmindedly massaged my neck, while he attempted to ease both of our discomforts.

We sat on one of the loveseats in the main room, Aidan's face as pale as mine. I had had enough. Searching for her signature, finding her across the expanse of space, I pulled her without warning to our location.

She materialized, surprised and unbalanced at finding herself in the same room as us. Caught off guard by her changed surroundings, her eyes traveled around the room before settling on me. I swallowed back the nausea and breathed deeply to ground my equilibrium. Rina's sharp eyes caught my dilemma.

Making her way to where we sat, she stood behind the seat facing us, giving me time to regroup. It also gave me time to wonder where she had been. The landscape around her had not been welcoming. Recalling the glimpse I had gotten of a fearful Tory, seeing Rina vanish before his eyes, I reached out to grab him too. Without delay, I pulled him into the room to join us. Aidan's fingers stilled, from where they were pleasantly kneading my shoulders, upon seeing our guests. He removed his hands and gave me a lopsided grin. When I felt in control of my rolling stomach, I motioned Rina closer.

"Rina, please sit." I patted the empty seat next to me. "Take a breath and start at the beginning." I told her.

Rina moved towards us, but did not sit down. She stayed on her feet in front of me, agitated, unable to keep still. Tory followed her to where she stood, intent on helping her relax. I sensed a change in their dynamic, a certain acceptance of their involvement. Tory rubbed her arm, drawing her troubled eyes to his face. The look that passed between them confirmed my suspicions.

Aidan noticed the exchange, but made no comment. His hand reached out to mine, grabbing it and bringing it to his lips. Placing a soft kiss on my knuckles, he gently replaced my hand on my lap before rising to his feet. Leaving my side, he reached Rina and Tory, breaking into their silent interaction.

"Tory." Aidan tapped him on the shoulder to get his attention. "Why don't you both sit and tell us what has been going on."

Tory had started on hearing Aidan speak next to him. Nodding his acquiescence, Tory guided Rina to the available chair in front of where I sat. Once they were both comfortably seated, Aidan returned to retake his own seat. I in turn stared at Rina, seeing she could barely sit still. On the edge of her chair, one of her legs unconsciously shook from stress.

Tory began their story by telling us what he had so far learned from his parents. He came from a race of travelers. His placement with the Sidhe on Eruva, though done for his safety, also had to do with our present situation.

"I am supposed to be a catalyst in what you mean to do, Alexa. I can't know how unless you tell me what your plan is." Tory explained.

"You never told me what exactly that is either." Aidan's misgivings were ones that would be difficult to appease.

I could not tell him yet, if ever, what path my vision had shown me to take. His remaining oblivious to what I had foreseen was imperative. Any path that would separate us would be one he would fight against. I could only trust Elron and Tory with this. They were both involved in the result I hoped to achieve. In time, I would explain to Elron what I needed from him. Tory, I was unsure of. We needed to find out why he had been put there. There had to be a reason.

"Rina, what has your mother been telling you?" I changed the subject, drawing a quizzical look from Aidan. I sensed his frustration at my changing the subject.

Rina seemed unaware I had spoken to her. I repeated my question to her, putting emphasis on her name. Hearing me call to her, Rina started. She looked at me blankly, her thoughts a million miles away. I reached out to her, touching her arm, feeling the shiver that ran through her. Her dazed expression cleared, focusing on me and my question.

"The gods are in an uproar over Rhea allowing Meredith to speak with you. They are aware of what she did. Giving you her powers goes against all they hold dear. Some blame Rhea for all the problems. Cronus is holding Meredith prisoner once again. He will not allow either of them further contact with you." Rina spoke in a hushed tone, fearful of the gods hearing her.

At that point, expecting any further help from those beings had not crossed my mind. They could fight among themselves all they liked. Other worries were preoccupying me. Asserbo awaited us.

"Alexa, they mean to stop you. They want the powers that Meredith bestowed upon you back. You must be careful. Until they decide what to do about you, you must be vigilant. They are still debating on how to circumvent you. It won't be long before they decide." She warned me.

My powers hummed in response to the veiled threat. They responded by increasing the energy surrounding me. Engulfing me, wrapping me within its protective force, I knew Meredith's power would keep me safe. With her added strength to mine, I could combat them. Let them come. Rina caught the response her words had engendered, how my energy pulsed. She seemed awed by the strength I possessed.

"By the time they get around to it, this will all be over." I told her.

Tory took my comment to mean our meeting was over. He rose to his feet, pulling Rina up with him. I agreed with his assessment. The time had come to send them back to his parents. He had to find out how he was to help me. Having told us all they knew, both were eager to return to the island to complete their mission. I searched for where his parents were, keeping the link open to send Tory and Rina there.

"Tory, find out all you can and contact me. We leave for Asserbo in two days. Your being there is crucial." I told him.

Without waiting for him to answer, I transported them both promptly to the island. Aidan eyed me skeptically, battling to keep his questions to himself. He knew I would not answer. All I could do was reassure him.

"It will all work out, Aidan. Have faith in what I do. I would never risk what we have. I will be with you always." I said.

Aidan seemed mildly appeased by my response. Getting up from the loveseat, he pulled me up, took me in his arms and fiercely clutched me against his chest. His heart thundering loudly, his fear of losing me tore through me. Wrapping my own arms around him, I held onto him, opening up for him to sense how much I loved him. Everything I did was for that man. We had but one chance for us to always be together. I love you beyond life, Aidan, my mind whispered to him.

A soft wispy sigh escaped him. Kissing the top of my head, drawing me closer, his desperation eased somewhat. I lifted my head to gaze into his most beautiful emerald eyes. His silky, long black eyelashes hooded his eyes, clouding his desire. Watching the black specs in his irises swirl with his emotions, mine rose to meet his.

Fascinated, I watched him slowly dip his head to find my lips. The soft pressure he first applied rapidly evolved into a desperate crushing, soul shattering kiss. Passion exploded between us, blinding me with its force. Rising up on my toes to meet him, I luxuriated in the feel and taste of him.

"Sorry. Can we come in?" Liam's voice barely registered over the sound of my drumming heartbeat. Would we always be interrupted? Aidan and I so rarely got a moment alone. Before we left for Asserbo, we needed some quality time together. I would find a way for that to happen, I promised myself.

Breaking away from his embrace, I stared into Aidan's eyes. He brought his forehead to rest on mine, his breath both rugged and uneven. He smiled upon hearing my thoughts. We will continue this later, I promised him.

Aidan loosened his hold on me, but kept me within his arms. We were both able to see his brother waiting by the doorway. Liam hesitated to enter after what he had interrupted. Embarrassment kept him rooted to the spot. In his arms, he cradled Mara, who, weakened from her ordeal, had little strength to move about on her own yet. Her fingers patted his shoulder to bring him out of his stupor. At her urging, he carried her over to the sofa, gently depositing her on it. Making sure she was comfortable, he sat next to her.

"How are you feeling, Mara?" I asked her.

She regarded me without speaking for several moments. I watched her appraise me, trying to understand what had attracted Liam to me. Whatever she gleaned in those seconds, she correctly concluded she had nothing to worry about. A tentative smile rose to her lips, as she brought her gaze back to Liam, who appeared nervous at having us both in the same room.

"I am much better, thank you. If not for you, I would still be in that hell." She put us all at ease.

Liam covered her hand with his, squeezing it gently, glad that the moment of unease had passed. He exhaled the breath he had been holding, while Mara briefly laughed at his relief. Her attention was taken by Aidan, who led me to the other sofa. She seemed fascinated at the contrast between the brothers. As I sat, I noticed her complexion showed a marked improvement from the last time I had seen her. Her cheeks were rosy. The yellow tint of her skin had faded back to a natural tone.

"Have you finalized the plans about our arrival at Asserbo?" Liam wanted to know.

Aidan simply nodded at me to take over that particular conversation. He and I had studied the maps of the area for hours last night. Asserbo Castle lay in ruins in the northern most point of Denmark, outside a small town by the same name.

At one time it had housed a monastery. The fortress had passed through many hands before it fell into disrepair, and was later abandoned at the start of the eighteenth century. Since then the drifting dunes around the area had basically decimated the fortress. Few tourists made the long, out of the way trek to visit the site. Even fewer people remained who knew of its link to the old Norse gods.

"We should arrive during daylight. The summer equinox is the day after tomorrow. We cannot risk being there at night. I fear the shadows would have the advantage. Trusting my powers to protect us all is risky. I can't be everywhere." I spoke to Liam.

Outlining what I found to be our best hope in defeating Elsam and his cohorts, I continued to give Liam further information. The land where the ruins were located sat closer to Sweden than the Danish capital. Its isolation from any nearby towns would give us free rein over the site.

Once we arrived, what we would find, I could not hazard a guess. I informed them Eliana made me memorize a phrase, in old Norse, believing it would call Freya's warriors to assist us. Not taking anything for granted, I had stored the words in my mind. The image of me in the book we had found on the estate in Verona, surrounded by warriors rising from the waters, made anything possible.

I knew I needed to be in a particular room with Aidan, Elron and I assumed Tory. How he would act as a catalyst in me undoing Elsam's plans, I still waited for him to advise me on. I hoped he would contact me soon. From what I saw on the maps, there were no rooms of the fortress left standing.

"I believe the way will show itself, just like when we retrieved the Kaemorra from near Lake Kobberdam." Liam spoke.

Elron had related the details of their excursion to me, and how a path lit their way to finding the Eruvian crystal. We could only hope that we would be guided in some similar way. I still needed to speak with Elron, to tell him what I expected of him. The man was spending all his time with Bet. I had not seen the two of them for days. After finishing, I would track him down. I needed his complete acceptance of my plan. Aidan's hand gripped mine, his look questioning what I was thinking. Thankful that he could no longer read my thoughts unless I allowed it, I spoke to Liam again.

"I'm sure that will be the case. Eliana has spoken with Ronan. The general and his soldiers are awaiting orders at Loch Maree. Asher's death has emboldened them to fight to the last against Elsam. They will meet us in Asserbo when needed. With the Daimon no longer aiding Elsam, his strength will be greatly diminished."

Liam frowned at my assessment. My mentioning his father brought a pall over the room. We greatly missed Asher. Our mourning for him had taken a backseat to everything else going on. At times like these, I would have welcomed his experience and guidance. How Eliana continued to go on under the strain of his loss, I had no idea. She seldom joined our discussions now. I knew she felt extremely guilty over her actions. The lost time with her husband must have been unbearable.

"I know father would not want us to wallow in our grief. We will avenge him by defeating Elsam. Go on, Alexa. Do you have anything more to add?" Liam broke the silence.

There was nothing else I needed to say. I shook my head to indicate that I was finished. Eliana would stay behind with Bet. The two could not be placed in danger. Bet, due to her pregnancy, and Eliana because of what she would inevitably have to do. Mara would also have to stay here in the safety of Deis-dé.

Unsure if my parents would join us in Asserbo, or for that matter what the council would ultimately decide to do in the end, I did not include them in the mix. The council refused to believe they were in danger. Without their participation, I could not guarantee their safety. I had barely finished the thought, when my mother appeared in the doorway.

"Alexa, your grandfather has called us to a council meeting. We must attend immediately."

Chapter 28 - Tory

Tory spent five minutes cursing, picking up and throwing rocks, all the while stomping angrily in a circle around Rina. When he and Rina had rematerialized back on Eruva, they had found no trace of his parents. They were no longer on the island. He needed answers and the only ones who could provide them had vanished, again. Giving in to his despair, Tory sank down on the rough ground, pushing away Rina when she came to him. Swatting at her when she tried to pull him to his feet, he dropped his head, closing his eyes in frustration.

"Tory, we will find them again. They can't have gone too far." Rina hesitated to reach for him again.

Tory's mood would not be placated. He raised his head, giving her a blistering look. *My parents are gone. They will not be found again.* His certainty in this only increased his churlishness. He picked up another rock, throwing it viciously into the distance.

Rankled over his predicament, he slammed his palms on the dirt beside him. Rina knew to give him space. *How am I to know what to do? How can I help Alexa?* His thoughts were centered on the unknown. With no clue as to who or what he was, being useful to anyone seemed laughable.

Rina tried to approach him again. She lowered herself to sit next to him, leaving enough space between them so as not to draw his ire. For long moments, she made no sound or movement. Glancing over at him, his continued irritation kept her from speaking. *What can I say to him anyway*? They were at an impasse. Without his parents they were adrift. Rina contemplated what more she could do or say. She opened her mouth to offer a solution, but none came.

Biting her lip, she saw a change in Tory's expression. Following his piercing gaze, she stared at the two individuals who had materialized before them. Conall and Elethea, the two who had tried to get Tory to return to his people, coalesced before them. Tory got to his feet, prepared to argue with the two. There was no way he was leaving with them. When they spoke, it halted his words.

"We have been asked to aid you in your quest." Conall told him.

"There is not much time left. We have much to tell you." Elethea added.

Tory would have left if it had not been for Rina. These two beings had all but ordered him to abandon his friends. No argument they presented would convince him to do that. Rina stopped him from transporting away by quickly rising to block Tory. She grabbed onto his arm, keeping him from moving. He stole a look at her and saw her determination. Rina wanted him to hear what these beings had to say. *What could they possibly have to say to help me? Will they clarify who I am, what I am? Will it help me in any way?*

Elethea lifted her hand, pointing to the barren field to his left. Tory's eyes stole in the direction she indicated, finding a campsite taking form. The two beings strolled over to it, expecting Tory and Rina to follow them. Rina, who still held his arm, gently tugged Tory towards the campsite. Seated on pillows that had materialized, Elethea waited for them to take a seat. Conall stood, and from what Tory sensed, was communicating with some unknown entity.

His misgivings on who Conall was in touch with were temporarily brushed aside. Rina pulled on Tory's arm, causing him to stumble forward to where she guided him. Keeping a careful watch over Conall, expecting the worst, he dropped down on a pillow at Rina's urging.

"There is someone who wishes to speak with you. She will be here momentarily." Elethea glanced at Conall, who nodded back.

Time ticked away while his anxiety grew. *Who are they talking about?* Tory, nervous and apprehensive, waited for a better explanation. Activity over Conall's shoulder had him squinting in distrust. The empty field behind Conall was suddenly lit up by a spreading, intensely bright beam of white light.

From above, he watched what seemed like a dazzling star descend. When it neared the illuminated field below, it blinked in and out, slowly taking the form of a woman, as it settled on the ground. Her eyes latched onto Tory, her gaze keeping him captive while she moved over to him. When she stood before him, he was left speechless.

"I have only a few minutes before they notice my absence. Tory, you must listen to Conall. He will explain everything to you. Alexa is depending on you. I will remove the block placed on your powers. You will understand once all is revealed." Rhea, the goddess herself, spoke quickly, her eyes scanning the sky.

"I have to go. They know I am no longer in the heavens. I have to help my daughter through this. They mean to strip her of her place with us. Without her powers they view her as obsolete. Know that you are an important piece of the puzzle." She passed her hand over his head.

An unknown energy passed through him, growing infinitely in intensity. His body appeared to phase for an instant. Watching his hand almost dematerialize, his panicked eyes found Rina's. She simply stared back, not knowing what Rhea had done to him. He glanced back at the goddess, whose focus remained fastened towards the heavens above. Without further comment, she resumed her light form, rising up into the clear blue sky. She vanished as quickly as she had appeared.

Tory's hands shook while he tried to control the energy seeking release. *What has she done to me?* Suddenly, clear as day, memories of his youth assailed him. The place he abruptly remembered, beckoned him to return. He recalled the land of his people. *How did I forget it?* His people were incorporeal. They existed as a form of energy. Their primary existence lay in the power to affect time, to rewrite history. *Why am I here away from my home?*

His home. Those words replayed in his mind, causing him to experience a loss he did not comprehend. His home world was nothing like that one. There were no lands, no objects, nothing that could be touched. His people existed in a state of perpetual energy.

"You remember." Conall said.

Rina blinked back tears, sure that she would lose him. He did not belong there. At some point he would return to his people, leaving her broken on that side. Tory, seeing the direction her thoughts were taking, took her hand in his, trying to reassure her that nothing would tear him away from her. If only she could believe him.

"Tell me everything you know." Tory demanded of the other being.

Conall did as Tory asked. He started by repeating how Tory came to be on that world. His parents, wanting to protect him from an uprising in their land, sent him to the Sidhe for protection. In order for him to stay there, they removed his ability to time shift.

With the uprising they had faced resolved, his parents wanted him to return. What they failed to mention was that he had a choice on what to do. Remaining there could be possible, as an emissary with the humans. If he did stay, the only stipulation placed on him was that he not use his powers to affect their development. He could only observe.

"How am I to help Alexa? What must I do?" Tory wanted to know.

Elethea took up where Conall had left off. Once she explained to him what he must do, Tory had a moment of doubt. *Is it possible? Can I really do what they say?* Elethea assured him that his powers made him more than capable of it. At Asserbo, with Alexa and Elron, he would be the one to put things right. Dubious over their claims, Tory found it difficult to believe he possessed that strong an ability.

"I know you can do it. Trust in your powers, Tory. I will help all I can." Rina spoke up.

He regarded the woman he loved, knowing under no circumstances would he ever leave her. He belonged there with her. If it were possible, he would visit his true parents, see his world again, but knowing in his heart where he belonged gave him peace. Rina, seeing his love and commitment to her, bestowed on him a knee-weakening smile.

It warmed his heart to see her beautiful face light up. Only the need to finish with these beings kept him from going to her.

"I have to advise Alexa. She asked that I tell her what we found out." Tory rose to his feet.

Conall and Elethea stood up as well. Their time there had come to an end. They had to return to their world.

"Do you wish us to say anything to your parents?" Elethea asked.

Tory thought about it. *What can I possibly say after such a long time?* They had been absent from his life for centuries. The fact that he remembered them at all was astounding.

"Tell them I hope to see them soon. I have not forgotten." He finally said.

Rina came to stand next to him, linking her arm through Tory's and leaning into him. His heart hammered in his chest at having her near. Elethea's knowing look met his, understanding that Tory would not be leaving that earth any time soon. Her head turned towards Conall, nodding to him that the time had come for them to go. The two beings phased in and out for a second before they completely vanished. If Tory had blinked, he would have missed their departure.

"Can you reach Alexa?" Rina softly asked him.

Tory ignored her question, choosing instead to reach for her. Enfolding her in his arms, he stared deeply into her eyes. His hand reverently cupped her cheek. *Does she know how she makes me feel? Does she have any idea that there is nothing I would not do for her? How can I love her so deeply so soon?* It was barely a week ago that he had wanted her to leave him alone.

Seeing her acts as a betrayal, he had wanted nothing to do with her. His arm wrapped around her waist, pulling her firmly against his body. Her quickening heartbeat gave him all the proof he needed she felt the same for him. His lips found hers, gently at first, before giving in to the passion taking hold of both of them. Her sweet moans of pleasure, echoed by his own, filled the air around them. Reluctantly he felt her pulling away. Breaking the kiss, she tried to step back. Tory refused to relinquish her.

"Alexa." She breathlessly spoke.

"When this is over, we will take a long holiday, just you and me." He promised.

Seeing a sweet blush overtake her face, he smiled, pleased to see she knew exactly what he meant. He let her step out of his arms, giving her space to compose herself. Focusing on Alexa, his new power found her in the distance. His instincts detected Alexa's surprise at his manner of contacting her.

Before his eyes, he saw her shimmering form appear as if through a window. It was as if he had opened a space between the vast distances between them, like a pane of glass to where she was. Even though she remained in Deis-dé, he opened a path for them to communicate.

"Tory, how did you do this?" Her voice rang out, looking out at the scenery in bewilderment.

As succinctly as time allowed, Tory filled Alexa in on what they had learned from Elethea and Conall. Alexa knew these beings well from the past, when she traveled there with Liam. They were the ones who had provided the book she had been searching for. When she heard how he would help her, she simply nodded. She understood exactly what he meant to do. Having foreseen it in her vision, all the pieces were falling into place.

"I will see you in Asserbo the day after tomorrow. I have to go. We have a meeting to get to. Let me know when you have arrived, Tory." Alexa said.

Tory let his power drop, releasing Alexa to fully return to Deisdé. His plan, necessitated one other stop before leaving for Asserbo. He needed to retrieve something from his parents' home in order for him to help Alexa.

"Go. The item can no longer harm you. I have something to do as well. I will meet you in Asserbo." Rina told him.

He did not ask what she needed to do, believing in his heart that whatever it was he could trust her. Striding over to her, he cupped her cheeks and placed a gentle kiss on her lips. Suddenly reluctant to leave her, she took the matter out of his hands by taking her leave, vanishing before his eyes.

The drawbridge leading to the keep of the castle, lined with guards keeping a watchful eye, lent an air of being under siege. An atmosphere of readiness and protectiveness gave a different impression from the last time we visited the council. In the village on the other side of the castle, people were scarce. Where it had been filled to overflowing with shoppers previously, the market place came across as being abandoned. Stalls were closed, the owners missing.

Crossing over the bridge, we were met by a delegation of witches. Taking position on either side of our group, they guided us into the keep. Accompanied by my mother, Aidan and Rider, my steps were unhurried as we made our way towards the imposing castle. My mother had insisted Rider join us. He would have foregone being there, but she would not let her father dictate to her. Stubbornness seemed to be a family trait.

"Wait here." One of the witches blocked us from entering the main room.

I would wait. My curiosity at being summoned had been piqued. My grandfather masked the area effectively, giving me no clue as to why he had called. The council's motives, their decisions, in the end made no difference to my plans. Time allowed me to revisit that place. We would be leaving for Asserbo tomorrow.

In the meantime, I had time to spare in accepting the invitation. Tomorrow would come soon enough. Coming there would not delay our departure. I smiled upon seeing my father's anxiety. He did not want to be there. My mother wore an exasperated expression on her face. All in all, everyone equally showed their displeasure at being back. Aidan at least hid his own emotions, simply staring off, rubbing my back with his hand.

The curtain barring the way into the main room fluttered aside, allowing Kesia to come through. Her eyes found me, then assessed the people with me. Seeing Aidan, her eyes narrowed, unhappy to see him. Too bad, I thought. Where I go, so does he. She would just have to live with it.

My mother walked over to her and tried to pass into the main hall. Kesia blocked her from entering. Extending her arm out, she caught my mother before she could step through. Instead Kesia dropped the curtain to close the entrance after coming into the small hallway we occupied.

"They are still debating. I can take you to a room where you may be comfortable. I don't know how much longer they will be." Kesia spoke directly to my mother.

"I want to see Adam, I mean Myrick. Can I visit him?" My mother asked her.

Kesia studied her, trying to figure out what she could possibly want from the warlock. Caden had not forbidden visitors to Myrick. She would allow it. Her curiosity over what would be discussed had her readily giving her permission to the request. Thalia's husband, Rider, said not one word, but his fixed stare on his wife convinced Kesia the man wanted to see Myrick as well. Kesia watched him, while she decided. Aside from containing his immense anger at Myrick, Rider had a few choice words for the warlock.

"I don't see why not. Follow me please." Kesia led the way to a corridor off to the side.

I followed behind my mother, keeping up with Kesia's long strides. At the end of the corridor, we arrived at a stairwell. Down the steps we went, deep into the bowels of the castle. We descended two levels before Kesia stepped off onto the third.

Along the walls leading down another corridor, I glimpsed the magic keeping the prisoners locked in their cells. Light provided by lanterns floating from above, barely lit the way. We passed cell after cell, before Kesia stopped in front of one. She kept herself out of the way, allowing us access to the warlock within.

"Come to see me at your mercy?" Myrick's voice echoed through the corridor.

My mother stared, without expression, at the man behind bars. What she thought at seeing the prisoner she kept hidden from us. Rider, who stood closest to her, gripped her arm, pulling her back to a safe distance from the cell. I watched my father's jaw clench with fury. His eyes had gone a deep forest green. Mom patted the hand that still held her, pulling his fingers away. She stepped closer to the cell, not afraid of Myrick.

"We used to be friends once, you and me. It does not seem that long ago. I have tried for years to understand why you betrayed us. Why Myrick? Could you not be happy for me?" Mom asked him.

Myrick turned his back to her. He returned to his cot where he dropped on it, his gaze staring down at the floor. From across the cell, I saw a broken man. It was not just the scar that marked his face, but dejection that consumed him. I searched his mind, finding that he felt some remorse over his actions. He loved my mother. That love, and the rejection of it, had led him down his path.

Through the years, he had tried to harm my father, tried to hurt my mother for her choices. My birth, proof of their union, had been too much for him. He then joined with Elsam to exact revenge. Only recently had he seen the error of his misguided alliance with the other Sidhe. The warlock's eyes landed on mine, flinching from my reading him. Trying to block me, he found it impossible. My abilities far outmatched his own.

"You do feel regret, don't you?" I asked him. "What would you do to make amends for your actions?"

Myrick stayed silent. I could feel him fight to not give anything of what he felt away. His mind though lay open to me. He turned his face away from me, hiding the hideous scar that ran across it. My father had given him that. Rider had been his best friend. I glimpsed a longing for their former friendship to be restored.

Remorse clung to the man like a veil of punishment. He believed he belonged in prison, believed any verdict against him would be too lenient. He had for all intents and purposes given up. He awaited a death sentence to ease his conscience. Pitying the man came as a surprise to me. Deep within him there was a glimmer of something good and redeemable. I hoped what I was about to do would in some way comfort him.

Giving Myrick back some of his former self became my focus. Gathering my power, the current entered my body with more ease than ever before. Controlling it, I concentrated my energy on the broken man inside the cell. Forcing his face my way, his eyes snapped to mine, showing fear and confusion. His attempt to fight me was futile. His head inched my way until I had a clear view of him. Closing his eyes, he struggled under my power. While keeping him still, I lifted the index finger of my right hand out towards him.

From across the distance, my finger moved to trace along the line that marred his face. I watched as the air shimmered around him. In my mind, I envisioned what I wanted. Along the path my finger traced, his scar became less pronounced. Fading with each pass I made, his face transformed before our eyes. Before me sat a man as he had been.

I dropped my hand at seeing the end result. The scar had completely healed. His features were no longer ugly, difficult to look upon. Myrick actually was rather good looking. That face I remembered. It brought to mind happier times when the man had played with me in my youth. Our family had been close to Adam once.

"What have you done?" He said, stunned at my action.

"Only what you have longed for. Your scar is gone." I replied.

His hands traced his face, realizing that I spoke the truth. He shook his head, trying to understand why I had done it. Incomprehension kept him mute. His mind loudly protested what I had done. The scars were part of his penance over his past actions. My removing them brought him no relief. My motivation came not without a price. I wanted to know everything he knew of Elsam.

Preoccupied over the removal of the scar, I got easy access to his mind. Before he knew it, I entered his head to find what I needed. Realizing what I searched for, he gave no resistance. He let me in, allowing me to learn everything of my enemy. When I became convinced there remained nothing more to learn, I let his mind go.

"Adam, thank you." I told him. Broken, alone, he stared fixedly at my mother.

"Thalia, I have wronged you greatly. I can't go back and change things. Rider, my old friend, whatever happens to me, I deserve. I wish to be left alone now." Myrick lay down on his cot, turning to face the wall.

Mom, tears welling, could find nothing to say. For so long, she had regarded Myrick with loathing, but seeing him defeated brought her no pleasure. Rider took my mom's arm, turning her away from Myrick. He too seemed moved by the state of his once friend. Starting down the corridor, I followed them with Aidan by my side. *You did right by him, Alexa. I too felt the good in him*, Aidan's thoughts assured me.

Behind us, lost to her own musings, Kesia kept up with us. Her thoughts on how powerful I had grown did not appear to be alarming her. Her attitude towards me had changed, I sensed no animosity coming from her. As we passed one of the cells, my curiosity piqued at who it held. Why was Rydia imprisoned?

"Your grandfather will have to answer that one." Kesia answered my unspoken question.

We reached the stairs and climbed them back up to the

entranceway. Kesia immediately led us through the passage into the main room. Only my grandfather along with Rydia's husband Blayze were present. The council meeting had ended. In his agitated state, Blayze showed every sign of being on the brink of losing control of his powers. His essence hummed, growing increasingly unstable. His mind lay open to me. What I glimpsed made me shudder. Right under their noses, Rydia consorted with Elsam against her husband and her kind. Her betrayal now drove him into a dangerous state.

With a few steps, I reached him, placing my hand on his arm. It took a second for him to notice me. Spinning towards me, eyes the color of red embers met mine. I let my energy flow to him, covering him with as much calmness as I could. Slowly, regaining control over his emotions, his eyes changed from a deep crimson red to a cool icy blue.

"I need to know what has happened." I spoke to my grandfather.

His response was to turn away and walk to his chair at the head of the conference table. There, he sat down, waiting for us to join him. Blayze took a deep breath, pulling away from my touch. He left my side to join my grandfather. Sitting down next to him, he kept his eyes averted from me. His embarrassment over his wife's actions only added to the deep hurt consuming him. I could do nothing more for him other than what I had already done. Maybe he would be better able to control himself.

Aidan approached me, gently taking my elbow to walk me over to a seat. *What's happened?* Aidan wanted to know. Filling him in, he absorbed the information without any comment. Still, I could tell he felt for Blayze. Mom and Rider were not up to date on the events leading up to the meeting. My grandfather's reasons for calling us there were partly due to Rydia's betrayal.

With no time to fill them in, I hoped my grandfather would not gloss over what had occurred. His people were giving me no reason to trust them. Kesia followed after us, silent and aware of my misgivings. Once we were all in our respective chairs, my grandfather finally spoke.

"We have been remiss in keeping our defenses up. It seems we have been betrayed by one closest to us. Rydia had been consorting with Elsam for some time. We luckily became aware of her actions and used her to gather information. As you can imagine, some of us are more affected than others." His eyes took in Blayze, who still stared down at the table.

Consorting was an interesting choice of word. I could just imagine what that entailed. It bewildered me how easily women succumbed to Elsam. Why did he have that effect on them? The time I spent in his presence, I found nothing enticing about him. Maybe it was just me. What did I know anyway? It seemed that he could easily sway some women to do his bidding. First Vanya and then Rydia. I brought his image to mind, noting that he had a certain magnetism about him. His extremely good looks, if you ignored the aura of entitlement he projected, could be construed as alluring.

"Has she spoken at all? Has she told you anything that would help us?" I wanted to know.

My grandfather nodded to Kesia, giving her permission to continue. She bit her lip, uncertain of sharing what she had learned. Her glance strayed to Blayze, worried at what he might do. I could appreciate her apprehension. Tension covered the man's features. He was barely keeping himself under control. Shifting my attention to the others around me, they each showed their own strain. My mother, sitting across from me, stared at her father. He had not once looked her way. So much tension moved through the room, for differing reasons, that my control wavered. Aidan, sensing the slip, rubbed my back to center me. The motion grounded me.

"Kesia." I prodded her to speak. She steeled herself before starting, taking in Blayze, who now clenched his hands together on the table.

"Rydia has been Elsam's lover for months." She stole another look at Blayze, seeing how her words angered him. She waited for him to control his emotions before continuing.

"Whatever she told him of our plans, it makes no difference. We did not include her in anything of importance. Our last meeting was a show. I'm sorry if we made you feel unwelcome, but we could not show our hand." The last she spoke directly to me.

Blayze glared at her, understanding that he too had been left out. *Was I under suspicion as well?* Blayze wondered. I saw nothing but loyalty to my grandfather in the man. They were worried Rydia would have seen their subterfuge if they included Blayze in what they planned.

"Thalia, I wish to speak with you alone." My grandfather finally spoke to my mother.

Startled, she reached for Rider's hand, afraid of what she thought would be a confrontation. I sensed no hidden meaning in my grandfather. He genuinely wished to speak to his daughter. Seeing her worry, he rose from his seat, taking a step to the door on the far side of the room.

"Rider, you may join us." He said, striding to the door, opening it and entering the other room.

Rider helped my mom get up to follow after her father. Leaving me with Aidan, Kesia and Blayze, I expected the meeting to be over. Kesia had other plans for us, as she rose from her chair. Surprised to find her smiling at me, I stayed seated. I sensed nothing but affection from the woman. Had our last meeting really been a show for Rydia?

"Come, we have much to discuss. We will help in any way we can." Kesia strode out of the room, leaving me to wonder what had just happened.

Chapter 30 - Alexa

We were given all of two minutes to catch our breath once we transported back to Deis-dé. Eliana summoned us to another meeting as soon as she sensed our return. As we were already in the main room of the manor, Aidan and I took our seats while we waited for the others to arrive. My parents remained standing near the fireplace. They spoke in hushed whispers, which were pointless. I could hear every word they spoke as clear as day. Mom remained ambivalent of her father's involvement.

What they discussed in private, she had not shared with me. With the powerful protection over his office, my grandfather effectively blocked me from hearing their conversation. Whatever they had discussed, it had put Rider at ease. My dad reassuring my mother proved my grandfather had not raised anything between them to cause further angst. I turned my attention to Aidan, noticing his focus on the door where sounds of approaching footsteps could be heard.

Bet, aided by Elron, came in first. Well into her pregnancy, she waddled into the room with Elron's help. Exasperation marked her features. Swatting at the hands holding onto her arm, she left his side to find a seat on her own. Elron kept pace with her, trailing after her, not letting her get too far.

Catching up with her, just as she sank into one of the sofas, I hid a smirk at her rolling eyes. Elron, completely ignorant of the fact that his over-protectiveness was creating her frustration, went about positioning the pillow behind her back. Treating her like a china doll was not going over well with Bet.

I held back my amusement over her reaction to Elron's well-meaning attempts to get her comfortable. Sinking back on the sofa, the weight of her extended belly drove her deeply into the cushion beneath her. She glared at Elron, yanking the pillow he was in the process of placing behind her back from his fingers. Settling back, she gave me a pointed stare to keep my comments to myself. Elron briefly glanced my way.

While Bet squirmed in her seat to find an agreeable position, he shook his head to silence me. I held back what I would have said. Bet felt put out at having to miss all the action. The decision that she needed to stay in Deis-dé, while we went to Asserbo, had not gone over well. Pointing out to her that in her present condition she would hinder us, would only anger her further. She knew the truth of it, but did not want to be reminded.

"You will need to leave soon." Eliana breezed into the room, breaking me out of my musings.

She looked regal, in command again. Dressed in a long flowing rose-colored sheath, she glided into the room, her eyes directly latching onto mine. The deep lines under them spoke of the lack of sleep, the continuing grief over Asher's death. I ached for what she had to endure. Aidan's hand squeezed my shoulder, feeling my heartache at the loss of his father.

Turning to him, his own eyes were clouded with sadness over the remembered passing of Asher. I gripped his hand, squeezing it back, while gently smiling at him. We will get through it together, I promised him. Eliana gave no sign to acknowledge she knew where our thoughts had gone, even though she must have been aware.

She had been accompanied by Liam and Mara, who had traipsed in behind her. Since her recovery, Liam barely left Mara's side. His lightened mood over the guilt and recriminations he had experienced upon learning she lived all those years he believed her dead, pleased me. I knew it had much to do with Mara not judging him.

Her easygoing nature gave him exactly what he needed. Her unconditional love relieved him of any blame. After everything she had endured, being kept imprisoned by Manar, she never once lost faith in Liam. Liam endeavored, going out of his way, to try to make it up to her.

Liam led Mara to a chair near Bet. Once she was seated, he stayed standing by her side. Eliana went straight for her usual chair. Resembling what a throne might look like, the red velvet wing chair sat near the fireplace, giving her an unencumbered view of the entire room. She settled on it, letting her arms rest on the padded velvet armrests. I heard her voice in my head. *It begins*. I stared at her, understanding exactly what she meant.

From that point forward, what I meant to do could only be shared with the two people I needed to complete what my vision had shown me. I knew everyone would follow me, do as I asked. Still, I felt renewed resistance from Aidan. His aura shifted, clouding over, under the suspicion and misgivings he experienced.

"Has anyone heard from Tory?" I asked the room.

Aidan had been silent beside me the whole time. As much as I kept my thoughts hidden from him, he exerted the same blank slate back at me. There was a distance between us, one that I had created. I wished I knew what he hid behind his deepening, camouflaged emerald eyes. I reached out my hand to take his. My fingers wrapped around his, squeezing them, giving him reassurance. He allowed a brief smile before turning serious.

"Tory has not been in contact with anyone, yet." He answered my question.

Trust me, Aidan. Everything will work out. Please do exactly as I ask. I let my thoughts reach him, hoping he would allow me to keep my secrets. His eyes met mine. Worry showed on his face. As I felt tears gather, he lifted my hand and placed a kiss on it. *Whatever you need, I will do, my love. Know that I cannot lose you. Promise me we will be together afterward.* His words were like a knife to my heart. I could not promise anything. So much could go wrong. We will. I love you, Aidan. Know that everything I do is for our love. I lied back to him. Did he believe me? I hoped he did.

"Has the Kaemorra shown you anything new, Eliana?" I broke my contact with Aidan to get any new insights from her.

"No, it has been uncharacteristically silent." She informed us. *You know what must be done*, she added to me alone.

"There is a room within the old walls of Asserbo that I need access to. So far, from what I've seen, there are no standing structures at the site. I presume that when we arrive the same thing that occurred at Kobberdam with Liam and Elron will happen. Once the goddess shows us the way, I will need Elron, Aidan and Tory with me. I need you all to do as I say." I let them know.

"What do you need of me?" Elron asked.

"Bring the blade Agatha gave you, Elron. We will need it. Tory must be with us. Someone must find him. We have no time to waste." I pressed him.

I could feel Elron already trying to reach his brother. Wherever Tory had gone, whatever he was doing, he remained silent. Elron received no reply to his calling. His frustration showed in the way he held himself. Fists clenched by his side, his jaw rigid, he would have thrashed his brother if he could find him.

"One hour. You must leave in one hour." Eliana spoke.

I nodded that I understood. She rose from her chair, leaving us to consult with the Kaemorra once more. At least that is where I assumed she was going. With Eliana, one never knew. My gaze landed on Bet, struggling to rise from her seat. Elron took pity on her feeble attempts, helping her by taking her hands and pulling her up. That time she readily accepted his help. Once she was upright, she made her way to me.

"I wish I were coming along. But…" She pointed to her belly, leaving the rest unsaid.

I smiled at her. "Take care of the little one. That is your job for now."

She scrunched up her face at my statement. Elron arrived to take her elbow, guiding her back to her room for some rest. When they were gone, I turned to Aidan. His concentration centered on my mother, who had a peculiar look on her face.

"Alexa, may I speak to you alone please." She said.

Aidan's eyes narrowed. Rider raised an eyebrow, not understanding her motives either. What could she possibly have to say to me that required them to leave? Rising from her chair, she approached where I sat with Aidan. Rider moved to join her. Mom stared down Aidan, who seemed to be refusing to leave. I sighed. Patting his hand, I asked him to go. Not happy at my request, he almost refused. Nodding at him that it would be all right, I sensed the moment he gave in. I watched as he and Rider exited the room, leaving me alone with my mother. She took Aidan's place beside me, gathering my hand in hers.

"I know what you will do." I started at her remark.

Would she try to stop me? Did she mean to try to dissuade me? What she said next put me at ease.

"It will be all right. It must be done. Your grandfather will be waiting with his followers to help in any way they can. I will make sure that when the time comes, you and Aidan will find each other. You two belong together." Her words comforted me.

"Mom, how?" I was curious how she knew.

"Alexa, there is little that happens that I do not see. As much as Eliana relies on her Kaemorra, I too have my means. There has been so little time to show you, tell you of the wonders that our kind experience. There will be time. When all this is finished, we will have the time that we missed out on." She promised.

Seeing my belief in what she told me, she got up, patting my shoulder. I could only hope she would do everything in her power to keep her promise. Nodding in response, understanding my goals, she smiled briefly before leaving me alone in the room. When she disappeared out of sight, I felt Aidan's arrival before I saw him. Appearing at the doorway, he gazed at me, trying to see what my mom and I discussed.

"Just encouragement, Aidan. Nothing to worry about." I told him.

Whether he believed me, I could not be sure. But, he let it go. I sensed in him a pervasive need to safeguard me. One moment he stood in the doorway, the next he stood in front of me. Pulling me to my feet, he enfolded me in his strong arms. So little time remained.

I hesitated to touch him, afraid that if I did I would break down. My arms instinctively reached up to wrap around his neck. He needed that. I let him hold me, hearing our heartbeats drum to the same rhythm. Drawing me closer, I laid my head to rest against his chest. That man was all I needed. I burrowed deeper in his embrace, exulting in the feel of him.

"I love you, Alexa." He whispered.

"And I you." I answered back.

His deep sigh ran through me. Leaning away from me, he planted a kiss on my waiting lips. I had been fighting the inevitable for so long. As he softly explored my lips, our tongues melding together, the realization of how much I had to lose hit me. I belonged with Aidan. I would make sure we had the future we deserved. He reluctantly ended our kiss, releasing me slightly, gazing lovingly down at me.

"Let's get ready. Liam and Elron are waiting for us. We need to look at the maps of the area one final time before we go." He told me.

I braced myself for what lay ahead. Taking his hand, I let him lead me out of the room, to where our friends were waiting.

Chapter 31 - Tory

Tory continued to struggle coming to grips with what he had discovered. His contemplation consumed him to the point where he had not spoken one word since leaving the island. Their return to the only home he had ever known, did little to soothe him. All around him were reminders that he did not belong there. Rina wisely kept her distance, giving him the space he needed to come to terms with it all. She had spent the previous two days tending to his parents' weed-infested gardens.

At night, she made sure he took time to rest. The familiarity of the place should have given him some comfort. Instead, he found that every corner held signs of his not belonging. Knowing where he came from, that the people who had raised him were not his real parents, that he had no blood relation to Elron, everything around him brought that fact clearly into focus.

How many hours have I spent eyeing the hourglass placed in my father's safe? For the third time he found himself drawn to the office because of the thing. Each time he left, an emptiness, spiraling out of control inside him, drew him back. He only knew the sun had been rising when he entered the room that time. The daylight hours were now almost entirely gone. In the dimming light, his gaze never wavered from the jewel encrusted hourglass. Fear made it impossible to reach out and touch it. *What will happen if my fingers make contact with it?*

These were questions that were impossible to answer unless he did in fact reach in and pull it out. He knew that soon he would have no choice but to do exactly that. The hourglass's vital importance to what he would have to do, gave him no out. Once more he found himself sitting on the floor beside the safe, staring down into its depths.

Time seemed to be standing still, as the hourglass lay on its side, the sand within it lying dormant. Tory sensed an affinity to the object. It beckoned him to take it in his hands. His heritage, his entire reason for being, drew him to it. His people existed for just that purpose.

Tory slammed the door of the safe closed, refusing its call. With it out of his sight, he breathed in to clear his head. Time was running out for him. Elron had contacted him, telling him he must get to Asserbo in one hour. *I am not ready for what is to come.* Whether he could pull it off was another matter. These newly formed powers he was experiencing were unruly. Only by force of will did he keep them in check. *If I release them, what will they do?*

"The hourglass will guide you." Rina entered the room, finding him in a state of confusion.

His uncertain eyes landed on hers. She stared back unflinchingly. Leaning against the door jam, she folded her arms across her chest, waiting for him to say something. Dressed plainly in a pair of cargo pants, topped off with one of his T-shirts, dirt clung to the clothes from her foray into the gardens. A smear of caked dried earth covered her left cheek. Even in that messy state, he found her to be the most beautiful sight he had ever beheld. Losing her would be his end. He had to make sure she would be waiting for him when all this ended.

"I wish I had your confidence." He answered her, getting to his feet.

He rounded the desk, meeting her where she waited at the doorway. Facing her, he hesitated to touch her. If he did, nothing would be able to drag him away from her. He needed to keep his distance. Steeling himself, he brought his eyes to hers, seeing she understood. As if of its own volition, her hand came up, her fingers tracing along his jawline.

"I wish I could go with you, but this is something you must do on your own. Know that I will be waiting, Tory. Time has no meaning for us." She whispered.

He knew exactly what she meant. His lonely path stretched out in front of him. Bringing her along would only place her in danger. He could not in good conscience do that. She would remain there, out of harm's way. Tory stepped back, watching her hand fall back down to her side. The time to go had arrived. Retrieving the hourglass remained the last thing he needed to do. From the couch next to him, he picked up his backpack. Stepping back to the safe, he sat back on his heels and pulled the door open. As if waiting for him, the hourglass called to him to pick it up.

"I love you, Tory. Be safe." Rina did not wait for his response. She stepped away out of view.

Tory closed his eyes, wishing he had spoken of his own undying love for her. He would make sure she heard it every day when he returned. His heart hammered in his chest as he opened his eyes, reaching in to pick up the hourglass. His fingers grasped it, feeling a surge of energy make its way through him. The room around him faded slightly. He felt removed from the space around him. Quickly placing the hourglass in his backpack, the sensation faded away. Tory stood up, hefting the pack over his shoulder.

There was nothing more for him to do there. He took a moment to scan the room, to capture the image of it in his mind. That was home. It did not matter that he did not share blood with the Sidhe. It would always be where he belonged. Letting the acceptance of it take hold, he dematerialized from the room, leaving it for his destination of Asserbo.

Chapter 32 - Aidan

Asserbo. Aidan saw nothing but a vague outline of where the monastery used to stand. Few stones lay on the ground to outline the existence of any previous structure. The ground, covered by grass that appeared well-tended, showed no markings to guide their group. In the distance, the currently vacant charter-house, a building for the caretakers of the site, cast a long shadow under the full moon's light. All the tourist attendees had departed for the day.

The parking lot in front of the building lay empty of any vehicles. The two-lane road leading from the tourist information center to the ruins themselves joined in the silence covering them. Aidan could see the sun setting on the horizon. The summer equinox, arriving well past sundown, made their foray onto the site fraught with danger. It was unfortunate for them. They would need to keep extra vigilant of the threats that were sure to come. He had sensed no imminent danger so far. To the extent that he could discern, they were alone.

A wooden drawbridge faced him. It allowed one to cross over a watery moat onto the site bearing scant markings of where the monastery used to be. Alexa had transported them all there earlier. Standing steps away from him, he saw only her back, as she scanned the area before her.

Not for the first time, the unease gripping him almost made him transport her away. She would not speak of what she had planned. His surety that he would not like it had him keeping a close watch over her.

Wherever she went, he would follow. Her back suddenly stiffened on hearing his thoughts. Giving no other response, he watched her straighten, start walking towards the drawbridge. Liam and Elron followed after her. Aidan had no choice but to do so as well.

Crossing over the drawbridge they all stopped, waiting for something to appear to them. Only silence greeted them. Alexa stepped further onto the site, making her way to its center. When she stopped, she turned to look over where the rest remained. She looked baffled over what to do. Aidan had nothing to offer to guide her. Only she would know what was required. Sensing someone coming, he instantly went on alert for any dangers. He unsheathed his sword preparing for battle. His brother and Elron were equally on guard. Advancing towards Alexa, they all surrounded her, ready for battle.

Steps away from her, a form was taking shape. He visibly relaxed when he saw who it was. Tory materialized before them, holding a backpack and his sword. What struck Aidan were the changes he saw in the young man. He no longer seemed his usual easygoing self. Tory had aged well beyond his years, matured into a man, since he had last seen him. His essence appeared different also. His aura continuously phased in and out while he studied him, baffling Aidan over what it meant.

"Tory, do you have it?" Alexa asked him.

Aidan, curious over what she asked about, watched her draw closer to Tory. She approached him, standing in front of him, so that Aidan lost sight of him. Whatever he communicated to her, Aidan saw her relax. Aidan could only guess that Tory had replied to her in the affirmative. She had what she required to complete her mission. Aidan knew that Elron possessed the other object instrumental in achieving her goal. The blade that Agatha bequeathed to him was strapped to his side.

Since Alexa had rescued him from his imprisonment in Elsam's tower, Aidan had grown wary of her keeping secrets. He longed for the days when she was unable to hide her thoughts from him. Having their bond completely formed, she effortlessly blocked his attempts to see inside her mind. She allowed only her love for him to escape the wall she had built to keep him out.

More than once, he had tried to get her to talk of what she had planned. She never once gave him any clue. That their love grew daily was what he clung to. His instincts to grab her, take her away from there, were screaming at him. He knew of nowhere where they could be safe. It did not stop his longing for the impossible. They had so little time left to be alone. His certainty that Alexa meant to do something drastic he could not refute.

Sensing his inner conflict, he found her looking at him, with a slight smile on her lips. He took some measure of reassurance from that look. *She would not jeopardize their love, would she?* No, he did not believe she would. He understood that whatever happened, she would do her best to make sure they came out of it together. He would give her the benefit of the doubt, for now. His gaze followed her as she resumed walking around the site, looking for a clue on what to do. Liam came to stand next to him.

"Any ideas what we are searching for?" His brother asked him.

Aidan simply shook his head. They would have to wait. In his inner jacket pocket, the Kaemorra lay dormant, waiting for Alexa. His mother had given him the crystal to keep until Alexa asked for it. It sat heavy against his chest, the pressure of keeping it safe falling onto him. Aidan deeply felt the immense burden over what lay ahead. They were led to this place by the goddess herself. *Where is she? Why does she not show herself?*

Aidan grew impatient over the delay. Alexa's destiny had been set centuries ago. His was tied irrevocably to hers. His very life depended on her accomplishing her goal. He saw Alexa look up at the sky, asking the very same questions. The two brothers kept watch, anticipating that it would not be long before they were needed.

As suddenly as the thought passed his mind, the ground beneath his feet shook. A rumbling sound echoed across the site. Rushing over to Alexa, he grabbed her elbow, steadying her from the ongoing trembling. The others joined them, balancing themselves against the heaving ground at their feet.

All around them, walls started to rise, growing ever higher. Surrounded by the bricked walls surging from the ground, they found themselves enclosed inside a room of the monastery. Overhead a wood-rafted ceiling covered them. Aidan knew that the whole complex was being recreated in a perfect reconstruction of its former glory. He also knew that there were twenty-five rooms in total to the structure. Somewhere, in the center of the complex, it housed a chapel. Below them lay a vast network of tunnels that were used by the monks to escape persecution.

"We need to get to the underground. There is a room I need to find." Alexa breathlessly whispered.

Awed by what had taken place, she studied the room, searching for a way out. Aidan could not deny his own fascination over the transformation. The temple rose around them in breathtaking beauty. The room they were in was decorated with fine tapestries on the walls. Conchs were lit along the walls illuminating the room. The furniture, although sparse, drew the eye with its elegance. An antique burr walnut desk with a matching chair set off to the side, near the only window, gave him a view outside.

Darkness confirmed the arrival of night. Aidan appreciated the antiques in the room, though they had no time to spare. The way to the underground could be reached through the chapel. Liam, Elron and Tory exited the room on their way to it. Aidan held Alexa back.

"Promise me." He did not have to add more for her to understand what he wanted.

Alexa cupped his cheek with her hand, staring deeply into his eyes. She let the walls around her mind fall back enough for him to feel her undying love. His arms clutched at her in desperation. Grabbing hold of her, he hauled her into his arms, holding her pressed against him while his heart answered hers. Their beats drummed in unison. Her blood flowed through him, just as his flowed through her. It forever linked them together.

"I promise, Aidan. You have nothing to worry about. Trust me." She spoke.

He pulled away to look into her eyes. She meant every word she said. *I have to trust her*. Realizing he had no other choice, he accepted he must do whatever she wanted. Breathing deeply, he dreaded letting her go, but time was running out. Taking her hand, he led the way out of the room to meet up with their friends.

In the narrow corridor, they found the others waiting. He let Elron and Liam take the lead, choosing to remain by Alexa. Tory fell into step behind them. Aidan held onto Alexa's hand, his sword now at the ready in his other.

The way led directly to the chapel. Stepping inside the circular room, silence surrounded them. Few signs that it had been a prayer room were evident. A few pews were placed in front of a pulpit. The pulpit itself was nothing but a stone pedestal set on the other side of the room. They advanced slowly towards it, where a doorway could be seen behind it. They had barely made it to the middle of the room, when out of nowhere, a shield of energy descended from above.

Their steps faltered as the energy barred their way. Caught off guard, Aidan swore. Any direction he turned, he found their way cut off. Warlocks. Only warlocks could have created the shield. Echoing through the chamber, someone was gleefully laughing at their predicament.

"Did you think it would be so easy? Give me the Kaemorra and I will let you live." Elsam's voice rang out.

The man himself materialized near the pulpit. With Elsam came ten warlocks standing silently next to him. They were the ones who had created the barrier. Aidan felt no fear in Alexa. She stood easily, unafraid before Elsam. Aidan knew her new powers had yet to be fully released.

She kept them at bay. What she was capable of was unknown. *Does she possess enough power to take down the man alone? Is she able to handle the warlocks?* Aidan hoped for all their sakes that Alexa was indeed powerful enough.

Prepared for the worst, Aidan took a step closer to Alexa. He would die protecting her. In front of him, a shimmering alerted him of someone else arriving. The space gave way to someone unexpected. Solas, sword in hand, stood staring with eyes only for his father. His arrival on the scene came as a surprise to Aidan. Alexa, however, appeared to have been anticipating him. Aidan wondered if he should be concerned over whose side he would be on.

"You have come to join me, my son." Elsam grinned.

Solas gave no answer back. He turned slightly to glance at Alexa. Whatever passed between them was over in mere seconds. Turning back, he raised his sword to point it at his father.

"I have come to avenge my mother." His stone cold eyes met Elsam's.

"So be it." Elsam said. He waved his hand absently.

Around them Aidan saw movement. The floor grew littered with slithering shadowy shapes. Shadows rose from the ground taking human shape. Surrounding them, cutting off any means of escape, the only thing keeping them safe was the shield. Aidan pulled Alexa behind him, watching the energy of the shield drop ever so slightly. Watching it continue to dissolve, Aidan worried what would happen once it completely fell away. *Are we already doomed?*

Chapter 33 - Alexa

I watched the scene unfold before me with cold detachment. The decreasing power of the shield surrounding us hissed and snapped as its strength diminished. Its curtain of blue translucent particles gradually dropped below my eye level. Descending further in an uneven wave, I had an unblemished view of Elsam and Solas, who were locked in a deadly staring contest. Each of them was prepared to die that day. For the moment, neither had made a move. The arrival of the shadows, not knowing whose side they would be on, momentarily forestalled Solas's attack.

Breaking eye contact with his father, he half-turned to keep the shapes meandering towards him within his sight. Elsam exhibited signs of uncertainty and mistrust on seeing the outlines on the ground. He took a step backward towards the door to the far side of the pulpit.

Coward, I thought. Would he flee? Solas, seeing his father's intent, matched him step for step. He would not allow his father to escape. Elsam instead placed himself behind his warlocks, relying on them to be his first line of defense. The warlocks showed signs of readying to flee themselves. They pressed closer together, as if their numbers alone could protect them. Nervous and tense, they stared wide-eyed at the threat approaching them. Elron and Tory stepped to my side, their swords out and at the ready. My side had no reservations with engaging the enemy. They were ready, and willing. Sure of their steadfastness, I concentrated on the scene unfolding.

I'll watch your back. Aidan, even with his preoccupation of the shadows' swaying closer to our position, managed to warn me. Backing up to join Elron, Liam and Tory, they protected me within a closed circle. I focused on the approaching slithering shapes on the floor, trying to identify their leader. One of shadows glided past the others, breaking away from the group. Rising up from the floor, taking on a more human shape, I found the one leading the pack.

With the shield now at knee level, Erebus's incensed expression could be seen clearly. His two red orbs flashed, gave a passing glance at me staring at his grossly misshapen form, before turning them on Elsam. Between Solas and Erebus, I could not tell who hated Elsam more. Erebus for the deceit he now perceived, or Solas who held him accountable for Vanya's death. Elsam had promised the shadow lord the Kaemorra. Erebus now understood the emptiness of the promise. Elsam did not mean to give him the powerful crystal.

Time seemed to still. The wait over what orders Erebus would give silenced all sound within the room. I cocked my head to the side, narrowing my eyes, attempting to see into the future. My seer abilities were hazy. Many possible outcomes presented themselves to me. Surrounded by shadows, the floor continuously shifted with their splotchy, inky shapes. Would they turn on Elsam or would they attack us?

Erebus's snarl drew my eyes back to him. His dark shape elongated, as he inched closer to Elsam. The other shadows reacted instantly. Following their leader, they crawled after Erebus. Freed from their threat, I heard Aidan's voice in my head. *Alexa, now would be a good time.* Aidan was right. It was the time for our side to take control of the situation. I took my attention away from the oncoming exchange between Erebus and Elsam, focusing instead on the next part of my plan.

Opening my mind, I reached across the expanse of space to locate our allies. I touched the mind of my mother first, giving her warning. She would let the others know. *It is time. I am bringing you now.* The other mind was one I was unfamiliar with. Ronan, the Sidhe general, had amassed twenty of his best warriors to support us. They were prepared for battle with spelled swords, which could defeat the shadows. I myself had cast the spell. Once the swords touched upon the shadowy shapes, a light would be emitted from the blades. Coming into contact with the illuminating swords, the shadows would be sent back to where they had come from.

Entering Ronan's mind, I felt his momentary surprise. Giving him the same message, I searched for a safe place to transport them all. They needed to be placed somewhere out of reach of the shadows. Seeing the space by the door unoccupied, I pulled the whole legion of warlocks and witches to that location. The Sidhe I placed in front of us, where they stood as a barrier between us and the shadows.

More than twenty-five of my grandfather's supporters materialized by the door. Standing in front of the group, my grandfather caught my eye. Inclining his head, he assured me his forces were prepared for the fight to come. My parents next to him were in full battle readiness. Rider, his own sword in hand, stepped away from the group, meeting up with Ronan and taking position beside him. He belonged with his own kind. My mom stayed by her father, knowing she would be needed there. Our army was ready.

Turning back to Elsam, his surprise at finding them present almost made me smile. His cockiness was gone. In its place, I saw uncertainty take hold. From his left, Erebus was closing in. On his right, Solas waited to exact his own revenge. Seeing himself surrounded, he did the only thing he could. He fled behind the pulpit to the door leading down to the underground. Erebus and Solas, keeping their distance from each other, ran after him.

I let them go, for now, concentrating on the action around me instead. My help would be needed there. Defeating the warlocks would clear the way to corner Elsam. My grandfather wasted no time in launching the first volley. I watched him send a bolt of electricity towards the warlocks by the pulpit.

In disarray over Elsam's abandonment, with no one to issue orders, their defense lacked cohesion. The force of the current my grandfather sent their way drove them back in panic. One warlock showed backbone, calling out to the others to attack. The youngest of them all cast his glance my way. Gathering his powers, he threw a deadly current of energy towards me.

Aidan intercepted the threat by diving to my side. Grabbing me out of the way, the beam of energy blasted past where I had stood. Elron and Liam quickly gathered around me. Encircling me, we were further endangered by shadows moving in our direction. I knew my grandfather's forces could control the danger from the other warlocks. The shadows were my only concern.

As streaks of colored energy blasted around me, I gave orders to Ronan. *Keep them back. I only need a minute or two.* Concentrating to grab onto the power I needed, the battle around me grew fierce. The two opposing sides of warlocks were suddenly in a fight to the death. The Sidhe warriors were slowly gaining the upper hand over the shadows. Shades of green, yellow and red current blasted around the room.

Unworldly screams filled the air from shadows being dispatched back to where they came from. Ducking, as I caught sight of a beam of energy heading my way, I heard Aidan swear. *Alexa, pay attention.* He grabbed me again, pulling me behind him and took my place. Placing himself in danger was a needless act. I knew what to do to ensure our protection.

It was my turn to enact a shield to keep us safe from the battle. I raised my hands, my fingers spreading out as I gathered a current of energy to do my bidding. From the ground, an impenetrable blueish wall rose to encircle us. On the other side of the blue screen, Elsam's warlocks vainly tried to pierce it. While they could not reach us, our side continued to lob volleys their way. The shield afforded an added protection from the shadows, who shrieked as they came in contact with it. They quickly drew back, scanning for a way to bypass the shield.

The Sidhe warriors took advantage of the shadows' distraction. Using their magical swords, they drove them to the floor, wherever they saw a darkened mass. Screeching filled the air. Accepting their inevitable defeat, the shadows retreated to safety by the pulpit steps. One of them rose up enough for a face to form. His red glowing eyes sought me out.

"We leave. Not our fight." He hissed.

Trusting in his words came hard. I penetrated his mind, revulsion filling me at what I found. I gagged at the depth of darkness, evil and despair within the creature. With my stomach heaving, I sank to my knees, all the while hearing his thoughts. *Nowhere to go. Our life over. Our world dying. Last chance to survive. Nothing to return to.* He cleared the way for me to see their world.

The landscape, dark and foreboding, was being consumed by the outside world. The edges of it were allowing light to enter making their living space barely habitable. There were so many of them. They crawled over each other to escape the incoming rays. I could not bear the depth of their desperation.

"If I repair the breach, will you leave and never return?" I managed to get out.

His eyes narrowed into slits. Through our mind link, I promised I could fix the problem, but only if they accepted my terms. The other shadows squirmed, as they too heard my thoughts. I felt Aidan's presence, asking me what I was doing. He had dropped down beside me, his features covered with the same distaste as my own. I barely glanced at him. The shadow I communicated with slid closer to me. *Yes, we agree.*

Giving his agreement, he rejoined his fellow shadows, waiting for me to make good on my promise. I shut my eyes, directing my power to their world. It was easy, took little effort, to heal the cracks permitting light to enter. When the last fissure closed, I opened my eyes.

Sidhe warriors were closing in on the horde of shadows. I called them off before they could strike. *Leave. Your world is now safe.* They gave no response to my ordering them away. One minute the floor was covered with black shapes, the next they were gone. One problem was resolved.

The battle between the warlocks and witches continued to rage on around me. Casting my mind to that problem, I saw Elsam's warlocks were quickly losing the fight. They were no match for the power of my grandfather and his followers. Kesia used her earthly element to create a maelstrom out of the dust and dirt covering the floor. It flew at and blinded the opposing warlocks. Covering their eyes, they stopped attacking in order to protect their faces.

Using the opportunity, Solana gathered the air to create a funnel. It spun around them, encasing them within a current nearing the power of a tornado. Blinded, held powerless, my grandfather struck the enemy without mercy, throwing out all his immeasurable energy.

Awed at his strength, I watched him create a lasso out of a stream of electric current. Blasting it out towards the warlocks who were helpless from Kesia and Solana's unrelenting assault, they were bound by the lasso, their arms pinned by their sides. All fight left them at being held immobile by the tightening ring of power from the current.

I focused my attention on the pulpit, where all but one warlock remained unchecked. My grandfather would be able to handle him alone. I needed to focus on finding Elsam and ending it once and for all. My plans were put on hold by the arrival of an army of Elsam's Sidhe warriors.

Appearing out of nowhere, they caught us all by surprise. In no time, they managed to overpower Ronan and our warriors. *Alexa, you know what must be done. You have no time to waste. The hour of the solstice is upon us.* Eliana's words echoed in my mind. She must have been watching the entire time. There was only one way to combat the new arrivals.

Recalling the words Eliana made me memorize weeks ago, came easily. They were ingrained in my memory. I hesitated to speak them, not knowing if I could trust in what it would unleash. In the past, relying on the world of gods and goddesses came with unexpected results. Would my call be answered that time? There was only one way to find out.

I looked over at Aidan, who waited for me to decide what to do. He would stand by me no matter what. I nodded slightly to let him know I was ready. He moved to stand away from me, closer to Elron, Liam and Tory who had been protecting me since the battle had started. They were also waiting for me.

I took a deep breath and released it slowly. Lifting my arms away from my sides, I held them up to shoulder level. My fingers splayed wide, drawing power from the elements around me, I turned my body around making a circle while closing my eyes. The power in me hummed, building to a level I had never allowed before.

Released from its confinement, I felt the infinite power of the elements around me. I gathered them closely to me, letting them grow within me. My mind settled on the words that would bring Freya's army to my side.

"*Risa eôa hefna minn drengr. Slàtra vàrr andskotti.*" I whispered under my breath. "*Risa eôa hefna minn drengr. Slàtra vàrr andskotti.*" I repeated for good measure.

I opened my eyes, stilling myself, waiting for something to happen. The witches and warlocks ceased their fight, startled at the words that had passed my lips. Their wide-eyed, stunned expressions the only proof they understood the meaning of what I had pronounced. Sidhe from both sides froze in mid-action.

The words I had spoken reverberated throughout the now-hushed chapel. At first nothing happened. It seemed as if I would be let down again. As my echoing words diminished, not a sound could be heard within the room. Aidan stepped closer, worried at the lack of action. We held our breath.

"Is something supposed to happen?" Liam asked.

His voice boomed into the hush of the room. In response, Tory suddenly went rigid. What he sensed, he never got a chance to say. His eyes narrowed when they met mine. The corner of his mouth inched up slightly, as if he might grin. I felt them coming. Rousing from their sleep, breaking through the plain holding them in the afterlife, warriors climbed their way out to respond to my call.

"Yes, they are coming." Tory answered Liam's question.

The ground beneath my feet rumbled. A groaning sound echoed throughout the room. Another wave of shaking moved the stones at my feet. Aidan, wishing to steady me, grabbed onto me even though I kept my balance. His need was more for reassurance than anything else. I had nothing to fear. My call had been answered.

"Keep close to me." Aidan told me.

Before I could reply, the floor near the pulpit, where Elsam's warlocks were still bound, opened up, creating a deep crevice. The warlocks were at a disadvantage. Their closeness to the expanding hole caused them to lose their footing. Slipping, they fell screaming, disappearing down the opening that continued to grow ever wider. The two opposing sides of Sidhe warriors just barely managed to distance themselves from the deepening crater. The depression forced them to break apart, separating them on opposite sides of the hole. My grandfather and his followers were safe where they remained.

Reaching the end of its expansion, the crevice took up almost half the room. A steam of reddish plume escaped from deep within it. Rising up out of it, the goddess herself emerged. Freya, dressed in her armor, ready for battle, just as in the picture I had seen in the library, stared back at me.

Child, you have called for me. Her words were echoing in my mind, though her lips had not moved at all.

What do you say to a goddess? I had only been told the words that would raise her and her army from slumber. Ordering her to do my bidding was another matter altogether. How could I command her to save us? Would she listen to me? But, I did not need to say anything after all. Every thought running through my mind transmitted to her. She glanced around us, saw the threat and actually smiled.

It has been too long since we have enjoyed a good fight, I heard her say. Her gaze took in the room, appraisingly identifying friend from foe. I felt Aidan's fingers tighten around my wrist. I communicated to him what was being said to put him at ease. Whether it did or not I could not say. At that moment, Freya raised her sword in the air, taking my full attention. Standing with her feet apart, her mouth opened to speak.

Rise men. Prepare to defeat the enemy, Freya commanded. I pushed Aidan out of the way, as I watched warrior after warrior rise out of the crevice where Freya stood. Her ghostly army took position to her right, awaiting her further orders. They were corporeal, existing in another plane. Shimmering, they were being projected from beyond our world.

Alexa, you have somewhere to be. We will take care of your enemy. Take your men and go. Her voice entered my head.

I no longer needed the help of my grandfather and his people. Freya would finish the fight. Glancing around the room, I found my mother, seeing her staring at Freya. *Mom, I will have to get you all out. I will see you later.* I tried to sound sure of what I told her. She may have an idea of what I meant to do, but it did not lessen the impact of the worry she felt. She did not need to know the full extent of what I would set in motion or that it might be a long time before I saw her again.

Hearing me, she turned her gaze to me. I could see she did not want to leave me. Before she could voice her displeasure, I moved her and everyone from my grandfather's group back to their home. Only Freya, her army, the Sidhe and us remained.

Aidan's startled eyes met mine, surprised at my removing them. We don't need them anymore, I assured him. Without waiting to see what Freya would unleash on the enemy, I let the shield that still protected us fall. Released from the wall of energy, I took off, racing to where Elsam had escaped.

Aidan yelled at me to stop, while they all raced after me. I did not heed his call. Passing through the doorway leading underground, Freya's words and the responding screams from the Sidhe were the last things I heard behind me. *Attack the enemy*, she ordered.

The narrow corridor I had entered led in one direction. The floor gradually sloped downward. There were no stairs to be seen yet. I continued down, deeper into the cavern dug so long ago. I could hear the others keeping close behind me. Our feet echoed, as we trudged deeper. I unsheathed my sword, expecting trouble any second.

"How much further is it?" Elron said from behind.

I had no idea. Stopping, I turned to face them in the dark. Liam held his hand out, creating a tiny light in his palm so we could see each other.

"Aidan, give me the Kaemorra. It will be safer with me." I told him.

About to refuse, I stared fixedly at him, extending out my hand. Opening my palm, I begged him with my eyes to do as I asked. Everything in him warned against it. Seeing I would not be swayed, he finally acquiesced. Removing it from his pocket, he placed it in my hand. His fingers wrapped around my hand clutching the Kaemorra.

Trying to penetrate my mind, to glimpse what I would do, he failed in his attempt. I knew his nerves were on edge by his increasing pulse. I squeezed his hand just as the crystal vibrated. Its red aura colored the walls of the passage. Removing his hand, Aidan watched me put the crystal away in my pocket. I made to move again, but Aidan stilled me. Keeping my fingers in his, he warned me.

"Do not leave my sight." He ordered me.

I could not meet his eyes. Nodding, I pulled away from his grasp, resuming my way down the corridor.

"We won't let her come to danger." Liam assured his brother.

Whether Aidan responded in any way I could not see. Tory came up behind me, whispering softly so that only I could hear.

"I hope you know what you are doing. I'm not sure if I can pull it off." He said.

Answering, I whispered back. "I will help you. You can do this, Tory. Together we will do it."

He shook his head, not sure of anything. In front of me the corridor split in three directions. Which way do we go? I halted my steps, staring at the fork in front me. I sensed nothing to tell me where to go.

"We will need to split up. I will keep my mind open for your communications. If one of you finds the room let me know." I told them.

"What room? How will we know which one it is?" Liam spoke up.

It was true, they had not seen the vision of where I needed to go. I pulled the image into my mind and transmitted it to them. The sudden intrusion into their thoughts startled them. They concentrated on the room I projected, seeing the items within it. When I was sure they understood, I asked them to split up.

"Elron and Tory, go right. Liam and Aidan take the left. I will go through the middle." My words were met with argument.

"No way are you going anywhere alone." Aidan insisted.

"Have you lost your mind? One of us will go with you." Liam piped in.

Sighing, I could not afford to lose time fighting them. I would be safe. Having foreseen the events, I knew I would at least make it to the room. We had not seen Elsam or Erebus so far. Solas was also absent. Where they were I did not know. Somehow I knew they were not a threat.

"Listen to me. Do not doubt I can handle anything I could possibly face. We will cover more ground if we split up." I insisted.

"I do not doubt we can cover more ground. Why do you need to go alone? What are you up to?" Elron eyed me suspiciously.

Not him too. Coming up with a plausible response, I never got to speak it. Tory, having understood that I would not be facing danger by going alone, stepped between me and the men, interrupting them.

"I can vouch that Alexa will be safe. You should trust her." He told them.

I left them. Taking the middle corridor, I wasted no time in moving down its long dark passage. Aidan was yelling to be let go. I could only assume it was Tory who held him back. I could still hear them arguing behind me.

Following the path that turned left before me, I was soon out of their sight. I hoped they were already moving as well. The silence, broken by my steps and my breathing, kept me moving forward. I needed to find the room from my vision. A steady stream of light in front of me led the way.

I made my way closer to it, stopping once I had reached it. The corridor ended. Stairs leading down were the only way forward. I continued the descent, taking the steps that wound deeper underground. They seemed to go on forever. After what felt like hours, I stepped onto solid ground.

I had arrived in a massive room with solid rock walls. The entire space was devoid of furniture. The floor spanned ahead of me, where my eyes fastened on an unmoving body that I easily identified. Fear clutched my heart at what I beheld. Solas lay on the ground, bloodied and broken. I ran to him, getting down on my knees to check on him.

Even without touching him, I could tell he was dead. His open eyes, stared off unseeing. His sword lay feet away from him. I struggled to come to grips with his death. As a tear fell, I heard a sound from behind me. Knowing who it was, I turned just enough to see the cause of all the mayhem appear. From where I had entered the room, Elsam blocked the only way out of the cavern. Fury covered his face. His sword, held by his side, dripped with what I could only assume was Solas's blood.

Chapter 35 - Aidan

It had been a stupid idea. With each step he took, the urge to run back to find Alexa grew in intensity. He never should have allowed her to go off on her own. *Why did I listen to Tory?* He had been persuaded by Tory to leave Alexa against every instinct that screamed at him to still go after her. The answering footfalls of Liam behind him were the only thing keeping him moving forward.

His brother followed him down the never-ending corridor, not saying a word. Aidan knew that Liam could feel his anxiety increasing. He too would have preferred to keep Alexa near, if for no other reason than ensuring she stayed safe for Aidan's sake. Aidan took two more steps before stopping. He could see no end to the darkened passage. Liam collided with him, unable to see that Aidan had stopped.

"Do you see anything?" Liam's voice broke the silence.

"Nothing. I'm going back. Turn around, Liam. There's nothing here to find." Aidan responded.

"I agree. We need to get back to Alexa. Something is wrong. I can feel it." Liam's answer increased Aidan's foreboding.

He too had sensed something was off. Without further discussion, Liam turned back the way they had come, steadily increasing his pace. Aidan wasted no time in retracing his own steps. The walk back seemed longer than the time it had taken them to traverse the distance. Abruptly, a sense of grief hit him. His steps faltered at the magnitude of the loss he experienced.

Knowing it came from Alexa, Aidan ran past his brother, taking the lead. Sure that someone close had met a dire ending, he hurried to get to her. The fear that gripped her following the pain of loss increased the speed with which he reached her. Liam, attuned to his brother's emotions, kept up as they raced down the corridor.

Aidan grew panicked over Alexa's safety. Someone or something posed an imminent danger to her. One second he sensed her terror, the next their link was cut off. *Is she harmed?* Aidan could not go further than imagining her hurt. *She can't be dead. I would know if she no longer existed.* Swearing at the time it took to reach her, he tried to transport. His attempt yielded no results. Something blocked him. Rounding a corner, his ears picked up sounds echoing towards him.

Noises could be heard from up ahead. The clanging of swords reverberated through the narrow corridor. Finally, in the near distance, he saw light to guide them. Liam pushed past Aidan, making his way carefully towards the opening that returned them to the split in the tunnel.

Unsheathing his sword, Liam approached the exit expecting the worst. Aidan followed suit, grasping his own sword in his hand. That was where they had separated from Alexa. Aidan kept up with Liam, who reached the entrance to their corridor a mere step before him. What they were confronted by delayed Aidan from getting to Alexa.

Seeing the scene before them, they both brought their swords forward, prepared to defend their friends. Elron was being attacked by two Sidhe, while Tory fought off a lone attacker. These must be more of Elsam's men. He had no time to wonder where they had been, why they were only now showing themselves. Their friends were in trouble.

Aidan quickly went to Elron, blocking an upswing of the blade from the Sidhe to his left. The man, surprised by the arrival of Aidan, left Elron's side to engage Aidan. Aidan backed up, keeping alert for any danger from the Sidhe still combating Elron. The one shadowing him kept pace, as Aidan increased the distance from Elron. Facing each other, they circled one another, looking for a weakness.

"You are no match for me, Prince." The Sidhe spat his title at Aidan in disgust.

Aidan would have grinned at the Sidhe, but the opportunity was lost. The Sidhe lifted his sword, swinging it viciously from side to side, driving it towards Aidan. The blade came within inches of Aidan's stomach. He managed to pull away at the last second. The Sidhe growled at his missed chance. Spreading his legs, bracing himself, Aidan gripped his sword, his fingers tightening on the hilt. The Sidhe brought his sword down, going for Aidan's sword arm.

The sound of steel, as Aidan met the attack with his own sword, filled the space. Gripped by the man, Aidan smelled his foul breath, while their swords locked together, each fighting for the upper hand. Locked in close proximity, Aidan could see the hatred that filled the other Sidhe. He managed to push away from the Sidhe, jumping back to put distance between them.

"Is that all you got?" Aidan baited him. He barely registered the sounds of the others fighting near him. Elron and Liam would be able to overcome the Sidhe they were fighting against, of that he had no doubt.

Growling in fury, the Sidhe he was fighting came at him again. The force of his sword resonated down Aidan's arm, as steel met steel. His taunt had caused the response he was hoping for. The Sidhe lost his reason, coming at Aidan with no control. Meeting each swipe from the man, Aidan drove the Sidhe back towards the wall of the passage. Finding himself with his back pressed against the rock face, the Sidhe realized his disadvantage. There was no further room for him to retreat. Aidan stilled the other's action by bringing his sword to the man's throat. They stared at each other.

"Give." Aidan ordered.

A hollow laugh left the Sidhe. "There is no give where Elsam is concerned. It is fight or die."

With those words, the Sidhe made a final stab at Aidan. His sword came up, attempting to drive into Aidan's side. With no choice, Aidan sidestepped the blade, driving his own through the man's extended neck. Blood squirted out of the cut, covering his blade with its crimson stickiness. He watched regrettably as the Sidhe crumbled to the ground, his eyes never leaving Aidan's. A last breath escaped him before he fell limp. It gave Aidan no pleasure killing the man. Dragging his stare from the dead man, he turned away, his attention returning to the ongoing fight that threatened his friends.

Liam had gained control over the Sidhe he fought before Aidan could come to his aid. His brother expertly maneuvered the attacking Sidhe to expose himself. With one fell swoop, his sword found its mark, stabbing his attacker through the heart.

Aidan caught sight of Tory who kept out of the way, huddled on the floor, watching the scene unfold. Elron, who had already defeated the Sidhe who had engaged him, made his way to Aidan. By the time he met up with Aidan, Liam was helping Tory to his feet. Their uneven breathing was the only sound in the corridor.

"Where did these fools come from? Why now?" Elron asked the question Aidan had brushed aside earlier.

"They must have been waiting for Elsam's orders." Liam offered an explanation.

That worried Aidan. *How many more are lurking in these tunnels? Have they found Alexa?* He wanted to take off after her. The corridor she had taken was straight in front of him. Wherever she was, Aidan had lost her signature completely.

"Did you find anything where you were?" Elron wanted to know.

"Nothing but an endless passage. What about you?" Liam answered.

"The same. It seems the middle one was the right one. Should we go after her?" Tory piped in.

"Yes, we go now." Aidan held his sword, prepared for any oncoming threat.

The men started to make their way to the entrance of the corridor Alexa had taken. Before they could reach it, from behind them, the sound of swords unsheathing rang out. Turning, they were faced by five more Sidhe warriors.

Elron roughly shoved Tory into the darkened corridor, ordering him to stay put. His last thought before joining the battle was that he should be using his powers. He kept them at bay, not trusting in them. They still made him uneasy, and he really had no control over them.

Aidan, with Liam by his side, advanced to meet the Sidhe moving to encircle them. Elron hesitated, wondering if now would be the time to attempt to use the powers his mother had given him. His uncertainty over how to get them to do what he needed took too long. Time was not on his side in deciding what to do.

A Sidhe reached him, giving him no choice but to fight. His friends were also locked in battle. Elron made swift work of maiming the Sidhe he faced. With one swipe, his sword cut the man down. Liam also dispatched the one he fought fairly quickly. Aidan on the other hand was in danger. There were two attacking him at the same time.

Elron watched Liam kill the only other Sidhe not pressing Aidan. Now only the two fighting his friend remained. Elron started over to offer his assistance. Helplessly, unable to reach him in time, he watched in horror as one managed to overcome Aidan, driving his sword towards Aidan's chest.

Elron closed his eyes to block the sight of his friend falling. He wished that they were safe from harm. He wished that they were alone, that there were no more Sidhe to fight. A pressure developed in his chest. Sudden silence fell in the corridor. Liam's gasp made him open his eyes, expecting to see Aidan on the ground dead. Instead, what he saw was Aidan standing, grinning back at him.

"Your doing I presume?" Liam said, looking at Elron.

In the cramped area, they were alone. Even the bodies of the Sidhe they had killed were gone. For the first time, he thanked his mother for bestowing her gift on him. Tory stepped out from his hiding place, impressed by his brother. Aidan came over to Elron, touching his arm.

"Thank you. Now, we have somewhere to be. Alexa needs us." He sidestepped around Elron, making for the corridor Alexa had taken.

Chapter 36 - Alexa

There was nothing I could do for Solas. His peaceful features brought tears to my eyes, as I passed my hand over his vacant eyes to shut them. His death at his father's hand, the man who moved stealthily towards me, would need to be grieved at a later time.

Casting one last glance at Solas's prone, broken body, I slowly moved away from him. Careful not to make any sudden movements, I left his side to rise up from the floor. His father's looming presence underscored my need to keep vigilant. Elsam took his time getting to me, certain he held the upper hand. Our eyes locked once I found my footing. His smug grin caused a shiver to trace its way up my back. My eyes never leaving his, I reached behind my back, grabbing the hilt of my sword.

In one fluid motion, I pulled it out, extending it in front of me. All the lessons Elron had put me through would be put to the test in the moments to come. In response to my handling it, the sword vibrated, giving off a brief silvery glow. Along the blade, the words engraved on its side seemed to come alive. They ran back and forth on the sharp edge in eagerness, ready to battle their foe. Catching sight of the sword pointed at him brought Elsam up short.

Upon seeing what I held in my hand, his face registered confusion. The sword that had abandoned him centuries before held him transfixed. I saw the muscles in his jaw work, saw him hesitate in deciding what to do. Recognition of my being in possession of his sword, grew into fury.

The malice I sensed in him, made me take a step back. He continued to stare fixedly at the object I gripped. Waiting for what he would do next, I planted my feet beneath me, bracing for his attack. There was only one possible outcome to the fight. Either he would die or I would.

When he made no move, I took the opportunity to create a diversion. Concentrating all my energy on what I wanted, I pulled at the forces around me. Using all the elements at my disposal, I drew them together to create a wind tunnel. Elsam seemed to rouse from his daze when he realized what my intent was. His eyes left the sword in my hand and found my eyes.

Ignoring his hateful stare, I quickened my actions before he could respond. When enough power was amassed, I let it loose, sending it barreling at the man who had no chance to sidestep the oncoming threat. The force of the wind slammed into him before he could react. I watched him being dragged backward. The violent wind encircled him, wrapping him, imprisoning him within its force. It spiraled around him with endless fury.

I took a step forward, inching my way to him. I would have only one shot at it. While the winds kept him occupied, I had but one chance to best him. Would I be able to kill him? Was I capable of harming someone? All the trials, the training Elron had put me through, I would need to remember. It was more than one of his playacting tests. This involved actually driving my sword through someone. I gathered my courage to do what I must. The hesitation in following through led to my downfall.

Somehow the wind died down. I tried to recapture the energy, but found myself unable to use any of my power. Something or someone had blocked me. Behind Elsam, through the opening to the room, I watched five warlocks step through. They took positions along the wall around the entrance. Their eyes were pure white, their pupils completely immersed in a cloudy film. Together they were too much for me.

With no choice, I backed away from Elsam. There was nowhere to hide in the cavern. I saw him come to his senses, take a deep breath and resume his advance with more purpose. This is it, I thought. I hoped I had learned enough to be able to take him. His size, the sheer power I saw in his arms, frightened me. His strength caused a tremor in my hand. My sword responded instantly by glowing more brightly. I took another step back, and stumbled. My foot ran into Solas, who lay on the ground. Elsam's eyes looked down at my feet, seeing his son's bloodied form. His face took on a fury unlike anything I had ever seen. He tore his seething eyes away from his son, returning them to me.

"Your fault. All of this is your fault!" He screamed. "You are an abomination. A witch and a Sidhe should never have created you. Your parents should never have been allowed to mate. You have taken everything from me. My throne, Agatha and now my son."

Stunned at his pronouncement, I stared at him. How was it my fault? He had started it. The man had gone completely insane. I took a step towards him, suddenly unafraid.

"You have caused this. You and your need for power. Your

throne never existed. It was never yours." I spat at him. "Agatha preferred dying to living with you. And in case you didn't know it, her son still lives. She made sure to keep him safe, away from you."

A snarl broke from his lips upon hearing my condemnation. Jumping the distance that bridged us, he drove his sword at me. I moved with ease to avoid its point. Circling around him, I kept him in sight, all the while trying to find an opening in order to put a stop to him. His fury at my words knew no bounds. He stalked my movements, maneuvering me away from Solas's fallen body to the center of the room.

"Who is my son? Where is he?" He bellowed at me.

"You will never know." I further infuriated him.

He took another run at me. I fell to the floor, rolling away to avoid him. Jumping back to my feet, I saw opportunity in keeping him off balance. Baiting him might give me an advantage. I could already see how out of control he had grown. Screaming in fury, he bridged the space between us, his sword coming dangerously close to my side. In answer, my sword rose of its own volition to block him. The sound of the clanging metal when the two swords met rang out loudly.

Too late, I realized my folly. In anger, adrenaline lent him added strength. He drove me backward, unbalancing me. Falling, I landed on my behind, losing my sword in the process. My panicked eyes followed it as it bounced, clanging its way across the room. Elsam seemed poised to stab me at any moment.

This was not the way I wanted to die. I had a destiny set before me. Where was Meredith when I needed her? Why did the gods not aid me? Were they still hoping I would meet my end? Their infighting would be the end of us all. I backpedaled away from Elsam. Opportunity to stand up was nearly impossible with him almost on top of me. Looking up at him, his glee at seeing me at his mercy almost broke me. I awaited my end.

With nothing to protect myself, I stopped moving away. I had nowhere to go to escape the inevitable. Towering over me, preparing to drive his sword through me, a sudden shift of energy in the room caused my nerve endings to tingle. My fingers snapped with unreleased energy. Elsam stopped, sensing the change as well.

Behind him, the warlocks keeping my power at bay, lay crumpled on the ground. I thought I momentarily glimpsed a woman by the door. The shape of her vanished before I could make out who it could have been. Whoever had come to my rescue, I blessed her for coming.

Before Elsam could return his attention to me, I instantly re-conjured the wind tunnel to drive him back. Blinded by the force of the wind, he brought his hands up to his eyes, covering them from the flying dust rising from the floor. I found my feet, racing to my sword while the currents I had created kept him occupied.

I never made it. His arm reached out from the maelstrom, grabbing me, forcing me to stop. In a rage, he picked me up, ignoring the wind whipping around us in its fury. His intent to strangle me became clear. His hand wrapped around my throat. Lifted off the floor, unable to draw breath, my head swam.

"I will end you now!" His voice could be heard above the

relentless noise the wind created.

My hands automatically lifted to his, which were wrapped around my neck. Uselessly, I attempted to pry his fingers off, to break free of his restraint. His beefy hands applied more pressure while his wrath grew. His cold, lethal stare was all the impetus I needed. With my feet leaving the floor, I knew time was short. Drawing power, I drove a current of electricity through him. Seeing him flinch as it entered his body, I continued to send wave upon wave of feral electric streams into him.

His grip on my throat loosened marginally. Taking advantage of it, I increased the level of power flowing through me. Unable to keep his hold on me, he released me, tossing me clear across the room. My back made hard contact with the floor. I gasped in pain. The break in concentration over the elements had the wind dying down. Elsam wasted no time in coming at me again. Any command over his emotions was lost. He was deranged with his need for vengeance.

My sword lay several feet away from me. It was impossible for me to get to it. Elsam, his massive body blocking my view, stood between me and the sword vibrating on the stone floor. His looming advance effectively put it out of reach. Seeing my disadvantage, he moved towards me leisurely, as if he had no care in the world. Behind him, I could hear the sword's call, its need to find my hand.

Too late, I thought. In no time, Elsam stood over me. With him upon me, the sword became visible to me. I cast a glance at it. The distance to it could have been miles from my precarious position. I raised up on my elbows, with no idea how to defend myself.

Pulling on the elements around me would be ineffectual. There was no time to create the power I needed. He loomed over me ready to strike. His bitter, hate-filled eyes never leaving mine, he raised his sword. In slow motion, I followed its trajectory down towards my body. In seconds it would reach my skin, just above my heart. He bent to apply the pressure needed to inflict his mortal wound. In the back of my mind, I heard a voice, its echo faint but insistent. I opened up my senses to hear it clearer. *Call me, guide me*, it seemed to say.

My sword glowed a bright fiery red in the distance. Out of the corner of my eye, I watched it bounce, clanging loudly in the silence that had fallen. The engraved words on the blade seemed to rise above it, changing shape, creating a plume of purplish vapor. From within it a ghostly face of a woman formed. Floating across the floor, in a shimmering mist, the apparition moved closer to Elsam. Profound sadness covered her features.

Stunned at the appearance, not understanding what my eyes were seeing, I felt time slow. The apparition, once it neared Elsam, circled around him. I struggled to comprehend her materialization. Her being there made no sense to me. How long had the spirit of Agatha resided within the sword?

Slowly, the realization that she had been the one to guide the sword took hold of me. It had been Agatha who had made sure I received it at the well. Leaving Elsam, her melancholy gaze trapped mine. Reaching into my mind, hearing her thoughts, she instructed me on what to do. *Use my sister's powers. The sword is yours to command.* Drawing away from both of us, she hovered above Elsam, waiting for me to put her thoughts into action.

I again sensed the sword calling me. Its signature grew in intensity. Agatha's words held little meaning to me. I mostly relied on the elements to protect myself. Meredith's abilities were an untapped resource of power. Across the distance, the sword had other ideas. It pulled at my subconscious, demanding me to command it. Reaching out with my mind, I made contact with it. Its momentous power yielded to me instantly. Come, I told it.

Time resumed. Elsam's sword was inches from me. With his body off to the side, he did not have time to react to what happened next. My sword sprang across the floor, speeding its way into my hand. Rising up of its own accord, it entered Elsam's abdomen, nearly piercing through his body. The man's shocked eyes never left mine, as he fell, landing on his knees beside me. He groaned, collapsing on his side. My sword glowed brighter at feeling its former master's life ebb.

Frozen, shocked to find his blood dripping onto my hands, I recoiled at what I had done. The sound of his sword falling from his fingers, steel meeting stone, made me jump. I pulled away, drawing my knees to my chest. Shaking, I stared at the man who wore an incredulous expression. He coughed once. Blood splattered from his mouth. Glazed emerald eyes met mine.

"Tell my son I would have liked to have known him." His final words were nothing but a whisper.

Agatha floated above Elsam, grief marking her face. *So much potential. Such a waste.* Her thoughts were pained at his passing. She hovered lower, closer to his slackened face. Waiting, listening to Elsam's unsteady, raspy breaths, she made no further comment.

Hearing his last breath, a single shimmering tear broke from her eye. She had loved him, expected the best from him. His dishonor of all she held dear, seeking power at the expense of their love, had given her no other choice but to see to it that he failed. Levitating away, she spoke two words to me. *Finish it.* With her mission completed, she dissolved into a puff of smoke, finally released by having atoned for her past.

Getting up from the floor, I stared down at the man I had just killed. Elsam's blood covered my shaking hands. Tears flooded my eyes. The sword still gripped in my fingers, dripped droplets of crimson red. I let it fall, as guilt consumed me. I staggered to the furthest corner of the room, where I collapsed. Dry racking sobs broke from me, as I tried to come to terms with what I had done.

Chapter 37 - Aidan

Aidan's heartbeat had accelerated into a crescendo. He heard none of the sounds around him. Pinpointing where he could find Alexa remained his central focus. Aidan's all-consuming need to reach her drove him forward at a remarkable speed. His body tense, every fiber of his being knowing Alexa was in trouble.

Even with her blocking him, the fact that her emotions were readily transmitting themselves to him deeply disturbed him. Only her lack of concentration would allow it to happen. It could only mean something had gone dangerously wrong. Close to panic, Aidan tried to keep his emotions controlled. Giving into the swelling terror over her safety would only slow him down.

His steps faltered as an unimaginable searing pain developed in his lower back. Gasping for breath, he landed hard on his knees. He leaned forward as the sensation of a red hot poker being shoved into his back cascaded down his legs. In front of him, Liam's concerned face came into view. Elron's arms reached out to help him stand. There was no time for him to explain Alexa had been hurt. He needed to get to her as quickly as possible. Pulling away from both of the men, the urgency of locating Alexa became critical.

Leaving them to follow him, Aidan resumed his run with increasing speed down the corridor. He knew Alexa had been harmed and that the pain he felt was hers. Her signature though still remained strong. He wished she would communicate with him, let him know what was going on. Not knowing her condition, his mind refused to allow the possibility of her dying. Behind him, his friends and brother, kept up with him. Liam and Elron were close on his heels, with Tory several steps behind. Up ahead, he saw the end of the corridor looming.

He reached the entrance to an immense cavern, catching sight of Alexa huddled in the far corner crying. Relieved to see her alive, his panic receded slightly. Aidan could see she was unharmed, but emotionally distressed. He approached her carefully, not wanting to startle her. When he stood over her, she gave no indication she was aware of him at all.

Falling to his knees, he gathered her in his arms, all the while running his hands over her body to ascertain if she had any injuries. What he found was she was unhurt, although in extreme shock over what she had gone through. Pulling her onto his lap, he held her, tortuously listening to her uncontrollable sobs.

While he cradled her in his arms, he scanned the room to ascertain what had transpired. His hand gently held her head against his chest, while evidence of her battle with Elsam displayed itself. Although the room was bare, the damage caused from their fight could not be denied. Aidan saw the gray-veined markings of Alexa casting her electric currents to repel Elsam.

The dust from the wind she had created had yet to dissipate. Dust particles still clung in the air, creating a haze over the space. Further examination led to his eyes landing on a body, lying in a heap on the floor. Elsam's dead corpse should have given him a sense of relief. Instead, he felt a profound anger take over him.

The man had caused nothing but havoc in their lives. His attempts to kill his family and friends, and his recent attack on Alexa, made Aidan wish him alive so he could end him himself. Giving a sign to Liam to check on whether Elsam was truly gone, his brother went over to the body to check for a pulse. Shaking his head, Liam confirmed his death.

Elsam's face was devoid of any expression. His eyes were thankfully closed. It would spare Alexa from having to stare into his unseeing eyes. Hearing her sobs were now nothing more than silent tears, he pulled away to see glazed eyes, unfocused and still shell-shocked.

"Are you all right?" He shook her to snap her out of her immobility.

She brought her eyes to his, blinking his presence into awareness. Recognition came slowly. Seeing who held her, she clutched at him. She sunk into his embrace, shivering violently. He held her, while she struggled to regain her composure. Having him near seemed to calm her.

Alexa raised her eyes to his again, as if looking to assure herself he was really there. Dragging in a deep breath, she calmed further, as she released it in a long measured exhale. Separating from him, she then scanned the room. He followed her gaze, catching sight of a possible threat. His eyes narrowed at seeing other fallen bodies on the floor next to the wall of the corridor from where he had entered. He took in the forms of the warlocks, who were either unconscious or dead.

"Elron, check on the warlocks. Make sure they cannot harm us."

He ordered Elron.

His friend, followed by Liam, did as he asked. He caught sight of Tory, who remained by the doorway studying a spot behind Aidan. His pained look could only mean one thing. Someone close to them had perished. Aidan turned to see what caused the reaction.

Seeing Solas's prone, unmoving body, he gently disentangled himself from Alexa. Leaving her side, he crawled over to his brother, knowing what he would find. Solas's waxy complexion, his face drained of any color, could only mean he had been dead for a while.

"I'm sorry, Aidan. I arrived too late to save him." Alexa had made her way to him.

Solas's death was not hers to bear. Alexa had done nothing to trigger the unfortunate event. The man responsible had already paid the ultimate price. Elsam could no longer harm any of them. His mother would feel Solas's loss profoundly. Aidan knew she was consumed with guilt at abandoning his brother. He looked up at Alexa standing over him. Rising to his feet, he took her back in his arms.

"It's not your fault." He whispered next to her ear.

"They're dead." Elron stated from where he checked on the warlocks.

Alexa did not seem surprised at his pronouncement. Aidan wondered what had gone on in the room before they had entered. He pulled away from Alexa, wary about asking her to relive the horror. Sensing what he would ask, she opened her mind, letting him see the events. When she reached the part where Agatha made her appearance, Aidan started, his glance straying to Elron. The other man responded with a questioning look.

Aidan, totally immersed in what Alexa shared, could not spare a moment to clarify. Alexa had arrived at the pivotal moment of her story. Reliving the final moments, when the sword penetrated Elsam, she visibly flinched. She brought herself out of the memory, restoring her walls to cut off their link. Aidan could not be sorry over Elsam's death. He had been just seconds away from doing the same to Alexa.

"What do we do now?" Tory asked.

Aidan waited for Alexa to answer. After all, they were there because of her vision. She, in turn, cast her eyes around the room. Aidan could see uncertainty cloud her face. For some reason, that was not how she had foreseen things. Before he could speak up, she left his side to walk around the space. He gave her a moment to collect her thoughts. The vast area was bare. There were no markings, no indications to guide them. His brief look at Liam, seeing he too followed Alexa's movement around the room, let him know that his brother also had no clue why Alexa had brought them there. Elron awaited Alexa's instructions next to Liam. The only one standing alone, keeping his distance, was Tory. He had not moved from the doorway. Their eyes met briefly before Tory lowered them to the floor.

"Aidan, it's not the same. I don't know where to go." Alexa spoke up, forcing his contemplation away from what he sensed from Tory. He put aside his suspicions over the other man avoiding his glance. Tory knew something, of that Aidan was sure.

"What did you see in your vision?" Liam asked Alexa.

Aidan concentrated on helping Alexa, ignoring the cold shiver that raced up his spine. Alexa gave no immediate response to Liam's question. She spun around slowly, studying the room, stopping once she faced Aidan again. Biting her lower lip, doubt darkened her silver eyes into a deep gray.

Her voice started out low, building in strength as she described the room they were to be in. There should be a table in the center of the room, several bookcases along the wall. On the floor, she remembered there had been a carpet covering the spot where a leather sofa sat.

Maybe we are in the wrong room, Aidan thought. Maybe they needed to explore more of the site. He opened his mouth to suggest they do just that. The words never left his lips. Aidan drew closer to Alexa when he sensed the air shift. Forced to step back from where she stood, Alexa showed surprise at the arrival of Freya, accompanied by two warriors, coalescing before her. The two women stared at each other. Aidan was struck by their resemblance. It was like looking at a mirror image.

"The battle is won. The enemy will no longer pose a threat." Freya addressed Alexa. "We are no longer required and will return to whence we came."

A softness entered Freya's eyes, putting Aidan at ease over any fears he was experiencing. The goddess could have easily reached out and hurt Alexa, but Freya glanced his way, smiling at the direction of his thoughts. She returned her gaze to Alexa, continuing to speak directly to her.

"You are in the right place. We will leave you to finish what was started. Take care, Alexa. I am but a call away if you have need of me again." As quickly as she had arrived, she and her warriors vanished.

With their departure, the room hazily transformed before his eyes. Out of a fog that consumed the room, Aidan marveled at the changes. Alexa came to him, grabbing his hand, and wrapping their fingers together. Their amazement over the room from her vision coming to life kept them rooted. Liam and Elron stood transfixed at the evolving spectacle as well. Tory finally left the doorway to make his way to Alexa. He waited next to her for the room to come fully into creation.

"What now?" Elron asked, once the transformation was completed.

Alexa would have to guide them. After all, this was her show. Now that the time had come, she seemed hesitant to continue. Again he was besieged with suspicions over her reticence to share with him why they were there. She regrettably removed her hand from his, keeping her face downcast.

Preparing to leave his side, Aidan stopped her. Grabbing her elbow, he turned her to face him. Aidan had a sinking feeling about what was going to take place. He could see that Alexa was steeling herself for what she would do. It increased his fears. Holding her chin, he lifted her head to stare into her troubled silver eyes.

"Are you sure?" He asked her.

Her eyes filled with tears, as she stared back at him. A hand of doom wrapped itself around his heart. His heart accelerated at the premonition he was about to lose her. Cupping her cheek with his palm, his own sight grew blurry. A feeling of immense loss enveloped him. He had to stop whatever she had planned. Gazing into her eyes, he saw her resolve would not be swayed. She would not be deterred from her course of action. That it was causing her pain was evident as a tear traveled down her cheek.

"It has to be done, Aidan. Know I love you. It will work out." She tried to reassure him. Lifting up on her toes, she pressed her lips against his, giving him a bittersweet kiss.

Aidan wrapped her in his arms, deepening their kiss. She clutched at him, as if it would be the last time she held him. He knew something monumental was about to happen, something that would tear them apart. He felt it in his bones. He could not, would not lose her.

"I refuse to lose you." He said with his lips still pressed against hers.

"You won't." Was all she offered back. She slowly stepped away from him, her arms dropping to her side.

"Elron, I need you here between us. Liam, you need to stand back. By the bookcases will be fine." She informed them.

Elron and Liam did as she asked. Elron moved to Aidan's side just as Alexa instructed him. Liam made his way to the bookcases, clearly not happy at having nothing to do. Elron shrugged at Aidan, who gave him a questioning look. Elron was just as much in the dark as his friend. They both waited expectantly for Alexa to give them more information.

"What do I do?" Tory asked her.

She looked over to where he waited for instructions. Going to him, they whispered low so no one could hear. Aidan's curiosity got the better of him. Needing to know everything, he joined them to hear what they were discussing. When he neared, Alexa and Tory stopped their conversation. Tory already had his instructions. He left them to go to the table that lay bare. From his backpack he removed an elaborate looking hourglass. The sand within it lay still as he placed the item on the table on its side.

Alexa grabbed Aidan's hand, taking him back to where Elron remained motionless. She resumed her position to Elron's left and guided Aidan to his right. Alexa and Aidan were now facing each other. Elron was to their side waiting for Alexa to tell him what to do.

"Your blade, the one Agatha gave you. When I tell you, drive it into the Kaemorra. It will easily cut into it. Do not remove your hand from it no matter what happens." Alexa told Elron.

Aidan followed Elron's hand to the sheath housing the blade. He watched as Elron grabbed the blade, removing it from its leather holster. Holding it firmly in his hand, he brought it forward so he could follow through on Alexa's order. They all saw the blade give off a bluish glow in response to being held.

"Hold your hands out, palms open, Aidan." Alexa said.

Aidan hesitated. *Do I really want to go through with this? Do I risk losing her?* Repeating what she needed of him, Alexa willed him to do as she asked. Knowing he had little choice, he held his hands open between them, waiting for what came next. Alexa reached in her pocket, bringing the Kaemorra into view. The crystal came alive at her touch. It glowed brilliantly, casting its crimson rays around the room. She placed it in Aidan's hands, where it dimmed from losing contact with her. She took a deep breath in, preparing for the next step. She brought her hands to Aidan's, wrapping them around his. Together they held the Kaemorra, which vibrated, glowing brighter. Alexa looked at Aidan, taking in his features, memorizing everything about him.

"It's time." She said to stop him from speaking. "Tory get ready."

Aidan had Tory in his sight. He saw him reach for the hourglass preparing to move it. At his touch, the housing around the glass morphed from its gold coloring to a breathtaking sky blue. Aidan could not take his eyes off it. It pulled at something deep within him.

Wrenched away from its spell by a buzzing sound that filled the room, he tried to identify where it came from. He was stunned to find it coming from the Kaemorra. The crystal glowed brighter by the second. Alexa, with her eyes closed, drew power from the crystal. Aidan knew it would not be long before the Kaemorra reached its maximum strength.

Chapter 38 - Alexa

The tension coming from Aidan was electrifying. Sheer terror had found him. His thought patterns collided with the other men's equally shaken mental state. Their combined anxious energy was breaking my concentration. Their fear of what was to come drove into me. I needed to block out everything but what required my focus.

Digging deeper inside myself, I intensified my concentration on the current of power I drew from the Kaemorra. The crystal understood my motives, knew what I expected of it. It answered my call by releasing all of its power to me. Humming, buzzing, the energy within it steadily transferred itself to me. There remained one last message I needed to send before I released the energy back into the crystal.

Eliana, I have started. You know what you must do. Remember everything that has occurred.

Her response came instantaneously. She had been waiting for my call. Everything going forward rested with her. She had to make sure it worked out for all of us. Only she would be able to set things on their proper course. She asked no questions of our safety, if anyone had been hurt. In the end, it would make no difference. Her answer bolstered my courage to continue on my path.

It will be as has been foreseen, Alexa. I will do my part. Thank you my dear for giving us hope. I look forward to seeing you again.

Relaying her message to me, she cut our communication from her end. She knew time was running short. Aidan had tensed, his hand gripping mine painfully on hearing his mother's words. I had been unable to block what she had said. All my attention needed to rest on the Kaemorra and the rising power within me. Aidan had heard every word his mother had uttered. I held his hands firmly so he would not let go. He had to maintain contact with me and the crystal. Elron, having heard none of what Eliana said, could see something had upset Aidan. I shook my head at him to keep him focused. He had to act immediately when I asked him to.

"Keep your focus. It won't be long. I almost have all of its power gathered." I told them.

Drawing further power from the crystal, I stared into Aidan's eyes. His grew wide at what he was seeing. I could not imagine the metamorphosis the Kaemorra had triggered. Infused with power beyond belief, my skin had turned almost translucent. The hair I glimpsed on my shoulder appeared almost white. What other changes I was being subjected to, I could not tell. Only Aidan's shocked stare revealed the enormity of them. I gripped his hand firmly, not allowing him to lose contact with me.

I had pushed him away for months, wasting the precious time I could have spent by his side. My stubbornness knew no bounds. Why he never gave up on me, after all I put him through, I could not explain. Did our bond force him into believing that someday I would accept him? No, I knew we were meant to be. I belonged with him. I felt tears gather in my eyes at the feeling of inevitability that bloomed. I loved him so much it was impossible to believe that we would not find our way back. I had to believe, otherwise all would be for nothing.

The buzzing grew louder, the crystal's inner light dimmed further. The time grew near for me to unleash the energy pulsing in me. I glanced at Tory, who waited for the sign to commence. He had little faith he would be able to harness the powers in the hourglass. I would have to help him. Giving him some of my own strength was the only way for him to understand what he could do. He was powerful, beyond anything he could imagine.

"Elron get ready." My voice could hardly be heard above the crystal's humming.

Aidan squeezed my hands to get my attention. My eyes locked on his. Wary, he looked so wary. That might be the last time I had the chance to gaze upon his handsome face. His emerald eyes held tears, as if knowing what passed through my mind. I tried a smile to give him solace. It did not have the desired effect. It only increased his fear. Any response I could have given to ease his disquiet was circumvented by the Kaemorra's last pulse of energy entering me.

I was seized by a current of power so strong it forced my back to arch. The unrelenting energies coursing through me were too much for me. Their strength became impossible to contain. I could not hold all that power within me for long. It was time to return it to its owner. The Kaemorra awaited for the return of its power. I let go. The energy washed out of me, searching for its owner. The first shock slammed back into the crystal in one massive electric strike. Secondary waves upon waves of electricity left me.

"Now." I yelled at Elron.

Elron startled at my yelling for him to act. Recovering quickly, I watched him bring the blade down, driving it into the crystal. Cutting into the Kaemorra, the blade immersed itself fully into the core of it. The two bonded, drawing further energy out from me as they merged together. Electricity continued to flow out of me into the two objects. It was time to get Tory to act. I looked his way, seeing he was waiting for me to tell him what to do.

"Turn in. When the sand starts to flow open the gate." I told him.

He looked unsure what I meant. I nodded at him to do as I asked. His fingers flipped the hourglass to get the sand flowing. He placed it on the table and took a step back. I could tell he was experiencing an increase of his own powers. He stood rod straight, his eyes never leaving the hourglass. A beam of light encased him, tendrils of which reached to the hourglass, causing it to grow in size. Bigger and larger it grew. It soon covered the whole tabletop. Tory was now nothing but light. He lost all cohesion in his human form. He glowed brighter, as he drifted to the hourglass. When they met, the room shook under my feet.

The Kaemorra shook where it lay in our hands. Aidan, transfixed at the changes it was undergoing, had eyes only for the mutating crystal. The usual blood-red color of the crystal was being converted to a steely blue. The new coloring slowly infused the Kaemorra. We both stared as the blade that cut into it was drawn into the depths of the crystal.

When it had completely entered the Kaemorra, the crystal lay pulsing its new blue color. Across the room, Liam, who had not moved since I asked him to stand there, was being pulled by a wind that rose from Tory's position.

Tory was nowhere to be seen. Any trace of him was gone. All that remained was the glowing, pulsating hourglass that faded in and out of view. Gradually it too vanished. In its place, the violent, unfurling winds it created were ripping an opening in time. The growing maelstrom increased in size, slowly engulfing the room. The winds whipped closer to where we stood. I knew that soon it would consume space and time. Liam fought against its pull, grabbing at the bookcases to thwart losing his footing. He was the first to be dragged in, yelling incomprehensibly into the black hole that had developed.

Aidan held on more tightly to me, fearing being drawn away. Elron had no such fear. As the black void neared him, he let it pull him into its core. I watched as he flayed about before disappearing. I had to get Aidan to let go.

"Let go, Aidan. It will be all right." I yelled above the noise.

I saw he would refuse. Any pain I felt at losing him was overshadowed by my need to save him. He had to enter the maelstrom. The wind lashed at us while he gripped my hand more tightly still. I would have to force his hand. I pulled my hands, trying to get him to let go. He would not relinquish me. There was only one way to escape his hold.

With a sad, resigned look on my face, I drove a spark of electricity at him. Shock overtook his features at my action. He had no choice but to back away. The loss of contact had the desired effect. Aidan, pulled by the winds, was drawn closer to the void overtaking us. I saw him try to clutch at me, but I moved away.

The look of betrayal he gave me before he was yanked into the maelstrom had fresh tears running down my face. Still, he tried to grab at anything to stop his momentum. Even as he attempted to fight being consumed by it, the force of it outmatched his strength. He flayed about, trying to grasp at anything to stop his descent. His eyes locked on mine, showing hurt, fear and loss, before I lost sight of him. He was gone.

The winds were relentless as they steadily grew around me. The room was quickly being pulled into the darkness. The bookcases, table and sofa had already been consumed by it. I stood within the bare room allowing it to draw me within it. I let go. I tumbled into the depths of the maelstrom, accepting the inevitable. My time had come to an end.

Chapter 39 - Eliana

Queen Eliana allowed the link between herself and the Kaemorra to grow. Feeling her presence, the Kaemorra brightened, infusing the room with its spreading crimson-colored rays of light. She had arrived moments ago to pronounce Elsam's sentencing. The gateway to the passages between time remained closed. She only needed to speak the ancient words that would open the doorway.

On the other side of the room, Elsam stood ready to hear his sentencing. The two guards holding him in place were prepared for any attempts of escape. With his arms tied behind his back, Elsam stared coldly back at his queen. His contempt of her and all she wished to accomplish by keeping her people safe, had his seething emerald eyes fastened on her face.

The red crimson flooding the room suddenly dimmed, alerting her to a change within the Kaemorra. Eliana felt as though a spirit passed through her. She shivered as the hair rose on her arms. The room shimmered along its edges for a second before it stilled. A coldness fell over her, feeling as if she were split in two.

Coming back to herself, she gave no indication that anything had occurred. The guards, not having experienced the shift, simply waited for her orders. It was as if nothing had happened. Only she could see that the Kaemorra now pulsed a steely blue. Everyone else in the room seemed not to notice. It was as it should be. Only she was aware of the changes.

The time had come to set things on their proper course. She let her link to the Kaemorra reestablish itself. Honed in to its power, she cast her senses to see into the future. What she saw made her smile. Everything would be fine. Alexa had prevailed. Elsam, who had been watching her, narrowed his eyes on seeing her lips curl. His gaze landed on the Kaemorra, fear overtaking him as he studied it.

Eliana knew he did not see the change. Elsam vainly tried to ascertain from her cheerful expression what awaited him. She gave nothing away, effortlessly concealing what she meant to do with him. He would not be allowed to escape her wrath this time. He had done so much harm to everyone she loved. Her future would now be free from his machinations.

Eliana began the process of opening the spaces between time. She spread her arms out, speaking the same words she remembered previously uttering. A feeling of déjà vu hit her, as her past collided with her present. The Kaemorra, on hearing the ancient call to action, responded instantly. It cast its rays out, smothering the room within its new silvery shade. She repeated the words, but with a slight modification. She smiled again on seeing Elsam recognize what she had in store for him.

Struggling at his restraints, trying to free himself from the guards' hold, Elsam furiously attempted to escape. The Kaemorra responded to Eliana's repeated words by capturing Elsam within its tendril of light. Drawing him closer, he fruitlessly fought against its pull.

His strength was no match for the pulsating crystal. He did not have the power to break free of its hold. She watched happily as it pulled him within it, casting him forever into the darkened corridors of empty space. He would forever remain lost in the passages between time. She would not spare one further thought on him or regret what she had done.

Letting the power of the Kaemorra go, she left the room, returning to her private chambers. There Vanya awaited her. She appeared unaware of Eliana's sentencing Elsam to endless captivity. Even with the altered timeline, the woman would need to be kept under watch. Eliana had lost all trust in her. Maybe the fact that Elsam would not be released would keep her loyal.

Eliana would have to wait and see. As she sat on her chair waiting to hear that Vanya had found Sara, her hand went to her belly. Solas was already growing inside of her. Her child would not be abandoned this time. The mistakes of the past would not be repeated. She would love and raise him herself.

Hearing Vanya relate that Sara was waiting for her, she asked the woman to leave her. She had much to do before meeting her friend at the inn. Once Vanya retired from her room, Eliana changed, readying for the meeting. She sat at her desk, writing out everything that had taken place, not leaving out any detail.

The history would have to be maintained, guarded for the future. It was imperative that Meredith's line keep it safe and pass it along to her descendants. It took her over an hour to transcribe everything into words. She was running late.

Gathering the pages together, she placed them in an envelope and sealed it. Sara would have to be apprised of what Meredith would set in motion. They had to dissuade her from her course. The immortal woman could not hide anymore. Eliana knew who she was and what she had done. Grabbing a shawl, she left the room through the mirror, which gave access to the human world.

As before, the stark contrast from her hidden island paradise had her shivering from the harsh cold winds that met her. She approached the inn, quickly making her way to the front door, entering it without delay. Inside, she found Sara exactly where she remembered her. She approached, standing next to her, speaking before the witch could say anything.

"Sara, come. Grab my hand, I know where we must go." Eliana waited for Sara to do as she asked.

Surprised at the command, Sara nonetheless quickly got to her feet. Eliana grabbed her hand, and without warning, transported them both to a forested area. She took off through the trees with Sara following bemusedly. Emerging from the forest, Eliana stopped before a force field. She made quick work of disabling it. Sara stayed frozen, as Eliana took off towards the lone thatched home before them. When Eliana reached the door, she turned to find Sara still at the edge of the tree line.

"Sara, we have no time to waste. Please come. Meredith needs us." Eliana prodded her.

Sara's questions would have to wait. Eliana disappeared inside the house. She was already seated next to Meredith when Sara entered. Meredith gave no sign that she knew they were there.

"You can stop the act. I know what you have done. You must

undo it now." Eliana spoke to the woman lying on the bed.

Meredith's eyes opened, staring at Eliana. Sara came forward, worried for the woman who looked like she had seen better days. Eliana held onto Sara's arm when it looked as if she would come to Meredith's aid. The woman did not need their help. What she needed was a talking to. She had caused so much pain and harm in what she had set in motion.

"Elsam will never be allowed to escape his prison. I have cast him out forever. Your plan is no longer necessary." Eliana told Meredith.

"I have no plans." Meredith eyed the queen warily.

She had lied. Meredith knew exactly what she had set in motion. Eliana could see from her expression that the other woman was aware of how time had been set on a new course. Eliana removed the envelope in her possession from under her shawl. She passed it to Sara, seeing her face become suspicious of its contents. Opening the envelope, Sara pulled the sheets of paper out, casting a nervous glance at Meredith.

"Read it. Both of you. Then we can discuss what needs to be done." Eliana said.

Eliana left them to step outside for some fresh air. They would let her know when they were done. She sat down on the step, looking up at the sky. The stars above filled the darkness with their twinkling lights. A crescent moon sat high in the cloudless sky. Eliana felt a peace she had seldom experienced.

It had been too long since she had appreciated the simple things in life. Taking in a deep breath, her senses picked out the subtle perfumes in the air. Fir was the most predominant. In the mix, she smelled the heavy aroma of wild rose bushes nearby. Other pleasant, earthy scents were diffused by the overpowering roses.

"We are finished." Sara stood at the door. "It is an incredible story."

Eliana rose up, taking a step towards Sara. "I wish it were a story, unfortunately Meredith let all this happen."

Sara let Eliana pass by unable to refute her story. When she crept back into the room, she saw Eliana already seated on the chair next to the bed. Meredith still held the pages in her hand. Sara had nowhere to sit, so she perched herself on the edge of the bed. Meredith's eyes came up to study Eliana.

"When I started this, it seemed appropriate at the time." Meredith tried to explain.

Eliana stared back at the woman. Knowing who she was, Eliana had a hard time understanding how she had not seen it before. It was obvious she was an immortal.

"None of this was necessary. Do you understand what your little tantrum let happen?" Eliana furiously confronted her.

Meredith lowered her eyes. Eliana did not believe for a moment the woman could feel remorse over her actions. All she knew was that whatever she had done to the Kaemorra needed to be undone. The spell cast on it to disappear remained. Everything else would have to be reworked. Her primary goal was to keep her people safe. They needed to keep themselves cloaked.

"I will take the spell away." Meredith finally said.

She closed her eyes for a second. Was that all it took? Eliana marveled at the immense power the being possessed. She emitted auras that were nearly blinding. Alexa would one day be her equal, almost match her in abilities. Eliana knew Meredith to be much more powerful than herself and Sara put together. That being had bequeathed all her powers to Alexa when she realized the harm she had created.

Eliana had not mentioned to Alexa that she had obtained immortality upon receiving Meredith's powers. At the time, it would not have made any difference. Now, it was imperative that something be done to give Alexa the happiness she deserved. *Can I trust that Meredith will really take away the spell on the Kaemorra? Can I expect the woman to acquiesce to what I hoped for?*

"I will do as you say. It seems that not only you were affected, but my line was as well. From what I read, I will have a descendant almost matching my own powers. Alexa, that is her name, no? Yes, I cannot allow her to suffer for my vanity." Meredith promised.

Eliana had two more requests of Meredith. She did not have to put them into words.

"Your son will be reunited with her. I can promise you that they were meant to be. It was not something I had foreseen. Their bond would have happened in any case." She tilted her head to the side. Eliana understood she was in communication with someone. "On her nineteenth birthday, her transformation, as you have requested, will transpire."

Epilogue - Alexa

I closed my book, rose from the sofa and deposited it on the kitchen table. My hand remained on the cover, tracing the picture that adorned it. I struggled to understand the pull the book had on me. Removing my fingers, a longing to reopen the pages almost overpowered me. I let go a breath, stepped away from the table and strode to the door. Searching for my parents, I stepped outside to a blazing sun warming the day.

The sun's rays blinded me after emerging from the dimmed cabin. Hastily putting my sunglasses on, I caught sight of my parents not too far from where I stood. They were strolling through the well-tended gardens surrounding the house. We spent our summers there. When we were absent, an elder gentleman from the nearest town took care of any upkeep to the property.

For three months each year, we arrived for rest, play and remembering. Our family vacations kept us close. At times, during our stays there, my grandparents would join us. Only my warlock grandfather and my Sidhe grandmother were alive. I still sustained hope for those two. Call me a romantic, but everyone deserved love and happiness. They had both been alone for far too long.

Lately, I sensed they were more involved than they let on, but that they were being coy. Near the cliffs of our property, my parents continued on their stroll, blissfully unaware I was watching them. Engrossed in their conversation, my dad had his arm draped across my mom's shoulders. Leaning into him, she smiled back at something he had said. They seemed too content for me to interrupt. I chose instead to return inside. It was as much their time to be alone, as it was for us to be a family.

On entering, I took in the room I was walking back into. The doorway led directly into the small dining room, which still needed work. That section of the house had not been renovated yet. It desperately needed some attention. Its paint had peeled off the wall in large sections long ago. The scant furniture, nothing but an old kitchen table and six chairs, was falling apart. My parents had started remodeling the cabin around the time I reached my third birthday.

As far back as I could remember, we came there every year once school let out. My father added an extension to the house, giving us more space, once I entered my teenage years. We gained another three bedrooms, making it into a total of four beautifully decorated rooms.

My mom, with her flair for color swatches and matching decor, tried to retain the cabin's original feel. Every item of furniture she had purchased was a restored antique. A new roof had been commissioned and installed to the same specifications as the original thatched one. Only the refurbished kitchen held any modern conveniences.

Standing in the doorway, I had barely stepped through when my gaze strayed back, pulled as if by an invisible cord, to the book on the table. Mom used to read me stories from it at bedtime. When I was younger, the tales of a princess meeting her prince, the forces trying to keep them apart, the battles and unnatural powers, were nothing but fairy tales to me.

Not until my eighteenth birthday did they take on a life unto themselves. The dreams started sporadically, but had increased lately. The realism I experienced, the feelings they evoked were strongly affecting me. I kept all of it to myself. In the dreams, I relived the stories, placing myself as the heroine. The prince invoked emotions in me that I struggled to understand. How could I be missing someone I had never met? His absence ate at me, making the loss I felt seep into my waking hours.

I found myself back at the table, staring down at the cover. Involuntarily, my fingers reached out to trace along the edges of the picture depicting two people. The woman looked too much like me to be a coincidence. Could the stories be true? What kept me from asking my parents?

When I asked to be there for my nineteenth birthday, my mother's smile held a hidden meaning. Was she aware of what I was experiencing? What could it possibly mean? All I knew was that I was pulled to this place for a reason. The man on the cover was invading my dreams. His nightly presence made me feel safe, loved and, above all, as if I already knew him.

Impossible, I thought. Just fanciful thinking. They were only stories. I removed my hand from the book and walked back outside. My parents were off by the cliff, staring out across the sea. Nothing could be seen but rolling waves on their way to the shore. The sun blazed down, making me squint.

In the distance, I caught a glimpse of something. An island? When I looked again, nothing was there. My imaginings were out of control. Brushing it aside, I walked towards my parents. My senses picked up the harmony they were surrounded by. I hoped I would find their kind of love for myself. As I neared them, I caught the tail end of my mother speaking.

"A few days until she is ready." She was saying.

I knew what she was referring to. On my birthday, I would come into my powers. I already had increased awareness of the changes I was going through. My senses were heightened. From what my mother told me, I would inherit abilities from both my parents. She was the daughter of the warlock leading the council of witches. My dad was from a race known as the Sidhe. That is to say, a race we knew of. Humans had no idea they existed, or for that matter that witches and other supernatural beings lived among them. It was a well-guarded secret.

My ancestor, Meredith, was an immortal. She still existed somewhere, though no one had seen her for centuries. It was her cabin we were staying in. She had bequeathed the property to me upon my birth.

My parents spotted me approaching and walked over to join me. Mom's eyes twinkled as she smiled at me. She was just as anxious as I was to see what powers I would ultimately inherit. She had warned me of how unpredictable my change would be. When they reached me, she hooked her arm through mine, while my dad took my hand. I loved them so much. They were always there for me.

Smiling back, I let her lead me back to the house. It was time for my grandparents to arrive for supper. Mom would whip up something with her abilities, so there was no need for us to cook anything. Walking indoors, we found they had already arrived. Grandpa was a powerful warlock, in command of all the elements. His aura was multicolored. It was hard to ignore the spectra of lights he was throwing off. My grandmother on the other hand was a full Sidhe. She kept herself veiled, making it impossible to see how strong she was.

The two of them were seated on the sofa. I sensed we had interrupted them. Was that a blush I saw color her cheeks? I hid a smile. They were not fooling anyone. The evening was spent pleasantly. We ate, drank, played some games and then went outside to watch the sunset.

Soon the time had come for bed. My grandparents took their leave, and my parents retired to bed. I was wide awake, enjoying the late hour by myself outside. I moved back and forth on the swing chair on our patio, staring up at the sky. *Soon*, a voice whispered in the still night. I stopped swinging, concentrating my ears on the sounds around me. Hearing the word should have alarmed me. Instead, I felt comforted by the promise.

Two days later, my birthday dawned. By midmorning, I had lost consciousness. I spent five days lost in dreams, cocooned in a sense of peace. The presence of someone I could not see soothed me. Whoever it was, kept their distance, never letting me see their face. Oh, but deep inside me I knew. It was him. I hungered for him to come nearer. My need for him was growing beyond reason.

As if realizing his hiding was unnecessary, a pair of emerald eyes grew larger, black specs dancing as his face appeared. It was the face from my dreams, the one pictured on the book cover that gazed out at me. His strong arms wrapped around me, drawing me closer. He held me all the while, as the waiting to wake became unbearable. I had to find him. He was somewhere close by. His true self was waiting for me.

My eyes snapped open, every bit of me alert. My sitting up woke my mom from where she had fallen asleep on her chair. I looked around the room, searching for him. Sorrow filled me at not seeing him. I launched off the bed, running out of the room, out into the night. My mom ran after me, trying to keep up. I felt panic at not finding him. He had to be there. Why was he not coming?

"Alexa, take your time. Everything is new." My mom reached my side.

I remembered all of it. The past caught up to me, making me relive the final moments of sending Aidan through the maelstrom. Did he hate me? Is that why he was not there? I fell to the ground, anguished, as memory after memory assailed me.

I remembered Elsam, the dangers, Eliana, Liam, but most of all the love I felt for Aidan. His not being there must mean he had forgotten me. Either that, or he did not love me any longer. I broke down completely then. Endless tears flowed out of me. My heart broke. My mom fell next to me not understanding what I was going through. Suddenly my father gathered me in his arms, cradling me, carrying me back to my room. I sobbed at the loss I felt. It took hours before I drifted into a dreamless state.

I woke again to the sound of birds chirping happily outside my window. I felt hollow inside. Rising out of bed, I dressed mechanically. I went in search of my mother, hoping she would have answers. My parents were outside conversing quietly, trying not to wake me. Seeing me, mom patted the seat next to her. I woodenly went to sit.

"I don't have the answers you are seeking. All I know is that the stories are true. What is written in the book happened at one time. How are you feeling? Any increased senses, powers?" She asked me.

I felt no different. From my memories it should be hours before I receive my added abilities. Answering her question, we fell silent. I looked out to where I now knew the island to be. It remained hidden from view. The Kaemorra's power masked its presence. Would I be able to get to it? Could Aidan see me? I had no way of knowing. Wanting to be alone with my memories, I stood and walked to the cliff. I gazed out, calling to him with my mind. There was no response.

A sharp gasp from my mother forced me to turn to see what had caused it. Between the space that separated us, a form was taking shape. Within it a woman was coalescing. The unmistakable form of Meredith had me racing to meet her. I reached her before she fully took shape. Her smile brought tears to my eyes. She would fix things. Why else would she have come?

"Little one, I hope you are well." She spoke.

"Meredith, fix this. Please take me to him." I cried, grabbing onto her.

She simply held me, as I gave way to tears again. She patted my back, patiently letting all the pain wash out of me. When I pulled back, she calmly nodded, leading me back to my parents. She pulled me down to sit beside her.

"Before he can come, there is work to be done." She told me.

My parents allowed her to take over. After all, she was an immortal. There was little they could do to stop her. Meredith explained to my parents what I was going through. She told them my memories of the other timeline had been restored. I was experiencing the effects of the bond with Queen Eliana's son. The distance between us was creating unbearable pain due to his absence. Before I could join him, she needed to add to the changes I was going through.

"What changes? What are you going to do to her?" My father was on guard.

Meredith simply smiled, took my hand and led me to the open field. I hoped it would not be as painful as the last time. I recalled the agonizing pain she put me through. Her bestowing her powers to me had nearly killed me.

"I will not give it all to you this time. There are only one or two that you need. Aidan will live a long life. I want to give you the same. Immortality for as long as Aidan lives. You are bound together. Also, I think you both deserve peace during your lifetime. I will bestow on you the power to foresee future threats and remove them from your path. Now stand over there." She pointed where I was to go.

I saw my parents watching apprehensively from the patio. I did as she asked. I put some distance between us, and waited. The clap of thunder could be heard overhead where no clouds showed. Coming down, a bolt dropped, slamming into me with such force it drove me to the ground. Another hit me, then another. My own energy rose to meet the discharges. Increasing power built up inside of me, searching for a release.

Forced back to my feet by the energy, my back strained, arching, as my arms rose up from my sides. The bolts from above stopped. Held within the consuming energy, feeling it strain to break free, I could not hold in it any longer. Releasing it, streams of electricity exploded from my fingertips. They went on for what seemed like forever, before I landed on my knees, spent. I raised my head to find Meredith.

"That was different from last time." I gasped.

I had my powers back. Every last one of them infused me with their strength. It was just as I remembered. My eyes saw so much more than I thought possible. The nuances in nature were brilliantly displayed for me. Sound was magnified around me. I easily grew re-accustomed to the changes. It was as if I had never lost them.

"I will go now. If you need me, I will come, Alexa. You have only to call for me. I will hear you." Meredith spoke, looking up at the sky. "The gods thank-you. You have performed beyond their hopes."

With that, she took her leave. Fading from sight, she left no trace behind her. I spun around, enjoying the increase in my powers. I was caught, stopped by my mother, who grabbed my arm. She enveloped me in her arms, while my dad wrapped his around both of us.

"Are you all right?" Mom whispered.

She let go of me to stare at my face. I already knew what she was seeing. My eyes were a steely silver, my hair had a streak of white running down the side. This time I did not need to look in a mirror to see the changes. I nodded, seeing movement across the water.

The island had become fully visible to me. I could see the green landscape even from that distance. Floating on the water, waves breaking from the hull, a boat was making its way to us. There were two people on it. I left my parents to go to the cliff. The steepness of it would make it difficult to climb down. Climbing though was not required.

"Mom, dad, I will see you in a few days." I told them.

I pictured the shore below, seeing an outcrop that would be wide enough for me to stand on. Transporting myself down there easily, I waited for the boat to reach me. Above, my parents stared down at me. I had eyes only for the boat that drew closer.

And closer it came. It reached me, stopping, floating before me. He stepped off, coming to me directly. I did not know if he remembered or if impulse drove him. I did not care. My hand came up, my fingers almost afraid to touch him. Slowly, I touched his face, tracing his jawline as we faced each other. He shivered at my touch. Deep inside me, I felt a jolt of a recognizable beat. His drop of blood still flowed through me, beating in unison to his heart.

Those emerald eyes were unforgettable, as they gazed into mine. The black specks danced in merriment. His smile told me everything I needed to know. He remembered. Miraculously, he remembered everything. I jumped into his waiting arms, wrapping my legs around his waist. Our lips met. An explosion of memories of our time together gripped me. Blinded by tears, happy to have him in my arms, I could not stop kissing him.

"Excuse me. Aren't you happy to see me?" Liam teased us.

Climbing down off of Aidan, I looked over at Liam. They both looked exactly the same. The centuries that had passed were nothing. I smiled at him.

"Come, mother would like to see you, and I think Bet would never forgive you if you didn't see her." Aidan took my hand, leading me to the boat.

The ride back to the island was spent with me on Aidan's lap, his arm holding me tightly to his side and Liam regaling us with some of what life had been like for them. I learned that they too remembered everything recently.

Aidan explained that his mother had kept him from coming to me until today. The moments waiting to be reunited with me were endless. She must have had her reasons, I thought. Eliana never did anything without some plan in mind. Our boat floated closer to the island. I left Aidan's lap so I could sit and watch the view unhindered. We arrived at a magnificent port, surrounded by a town whose houses adorned the hills. The weather was warmer than the mainland. The plant life was unlike anything I had ever seen.

Aidan helped me off the boat. In between the two men, I walked up the hill to a castle that lay nestled within luxurious gardens. Aidan guided me inside the enormous hall where his mother, seated on her throne, waited for us. I made it half way there before Bet barreled into me. Grabbing onto me, she hugged me tightly, nearly squeezing the life out of me.

"Let the poor woman go, Bet." Liam laughed.

Bet did let me go, but kept my arm in her hands. Elron appeared behind her, carrying a small girl in his arms. The only sign he was pleased to see me was in his eyes. Always stoic, he kept his emotions in check, but his eyes showed his relief nonetheless. I had barely lifted my finger to the little girl before she grabbed it and put it in her mouth, gnawing on it happily. With my other hand, I pinched her rosy cheek. Elron pulled my finger out of her mouth. Her eyes clouded, her mouth opening, ready to start shrieking. To stop her, he put his own finger in to replace mine, stifling the scream from his daughter. Their little girl was a mix of both of them. She would be a handful if she took after Bet, with her impetuous personality. I felt for poor Elron.

"This is Alexandra." Bet told me. "She was named after you. It was Mom's suggestion…"

Overcome with emotion, I looked across the distance to Eliana. She stayed seated, smiling back at all of us. Asher, alive and well, was seated next to her, grinning happily. Aidan inclined his head for us to go over. We made our way to the queen. Should I bow? Forgetting Aidan could read my thoughts and answer back, I heard him enter my mind. *No bowing. She is to be your mother-in-law after all.* His words thrilled me. I could not wait to be his in every way.

Eliana rose from her seat when we neared. She stepped down from her dais, taking me in her arms. I wrapped my arms around her, ecstatic to see her again. For a while, I was unsure whether to trust her. In the end, she had come through for all of us. She returned to her throne, where I saw Vanya and Solas not far to the left.

It was another sign that everything had worked out. Only Tory and Rina were missing. Aidan quickly assured me that I would be seeing them the next day. I would need to hear all of their stories. For the moment, I wanted nothing more than to be alone with Aidan. I was looking for an excuse to ask, when I saw Mara enter the room. Liam met her, bringing her forward.

"Alexa, our mother was able to save Mara because of you." Liam explained.

Mara grasped my hand in thanks. I was not alone in how well things had worked out. We had all played our parts.

"Alexa must be tired. Aidan see to it that she has a room to rest." Eliana actually winked at me.

Aidan did not have to be told twice. He guided me out of the room, further into the castle. We wound our way around a corridor, taking the spiral staircase up. We came to a set of double doors. Aidan took hold of the knob and turned to me.

"I hope you don't mind that it's my room. I can take you to one of the guest bedrooms if you like." His voice held a note of nervousness, which I found endearing. His room was where I belonged.

"Your room is exactly where I want to be." I told him.

He turned the knob to open the door. Pushing it with his palm to open it wider, he lifted me into his arms, carrying me over the threshold. With his foot he shut the door behind us. Our immortal life together was just beginning.

About the Author

Nia Markos was born in Montreal, Canada and is of Greek heritage. After thirty years working in the financial sector, she has turned her passion of reading into a new career in writing.

Released books:

The Crystal Series Books 1 to 3
Elements
Venture
Harmony

Upcoming release:

Sudden Shock - The Elleanor Stone Collection